Order of Nehor & the Brotherhood

Enjoy

[signature]

This book is dedicated to my son –
who inspires me to be a better writer
…and a better human being.

ORDER OF NEHOR & the BROTHERHOOD

S.J. Kootz

ARCHWAY
PUBLISHING

Archway Publishing books may be ordered through booksellers or by contacting:

Archway Publishing
1663 Liberty Drive
Bloomington, IN 47403
www.archwaypublishing.com
1 (888) 242-5904

Because of the dynamic nature of the Internet, any web addresses or links contained in this book may have changed since publication and may no longer be valid. The views expressed in this work are solely those of the author and do not necessarily reflect the views of the publisher, and the publisher hereby disclaims any responsibility for them.

Any people depicted in stock imagery provided by Thinkstock are models, and such images are being used for illustrative purposes only. Certain stock imagery © Thinkstock.

ISBN: 978-1-4808-4670-8 (sc)
ISBN: 978-1-4808-4671-5 (hc)
ISBN: 978-1-4808-4672-2 (e)

Library of Congress Control Number: 2017919111

Print information available on the last page.

Archway Publishing rev. date: 01/18/2018

To young people and young at heart:
May you embrace the courage and truth
that will make your soul soar.

"…the guilty taketh the truth to be hard,
for it cutteth them to the very center."
1 Nephi 16:2

Introduction to

Order of Nehor & the Brotherhood

In the year 82 B.C., in a thriving Central American society, Raasah, the young Nephite daughter of a powerful pochtecatl, must discover why she alone was spared from the carnage of a vicious attack on her father's caravan. But her quest is frustrated as she returns to her city of Ammonihah to discover a growing evil that is permeating its very fabric. Amid secret combinations of intrigue and tyranny, Raasah must re-evaluate her values and beliefs that had been ingrained in her by the priestcraft teachings of her day and be willing to give up everything to find what she seeks.

Follow the journey of discovery, sorrow, and … well, read on.

Chapter 1

Lamonhah Ridge

Wrapped in a generous soft robe, Raasah looked like a fragile child, her full lips pulled tight in concentration. Sloughed over on a low log, she slowly rolled moist rubber into an awkward oval shape with her small of her palms, as Abul, sitting cross-legged in front of her, expertly fashioned his own into a smooth round ball three times the size. He playfully taunted her to keep up.

"Silence, you insolent cloudman," she mumbled and then giggled, despite her frustration, as she gave Abul a light swift kick. Raasah had always taken such great pleasure in Abul's company but today, despite her enjoyment of their activity, she also had an unexplainable feeling of disquiet that she could not shake off.

Abul smoothed the last imperfection out of the surface of his own rubber sphere. "You may not become a great Morcum ball maker, (Raasah swatted him again with her foot and pretended to pout) "… but, Burshon, maybe your creation will inspire a great sculptor…!"

'Burshon', a pet name given in his own native tongue, meant 'gentle fawn'. Abul, only a couple of years older than her, was a slave from the Cohite runner tribe of the Hunitite Mountains. Though quite young when sold into servitude, he loved to tell her stories he remembered of his country, done so vividly over the many years that Raasah could actually imagine herself in Abul's cloud forest home, walking among the gigantic trees where silence is broken only by wondrous song birds among the draping moss and flowering bromeliads. She could picture the racing water below his village as Abul propelled his water craft like an arrow through the rapids that threatened to smash him against the rocks, his strong young arms straining against the oars as he fought for control.

But an uneasiness growing inside her kept Raasah from these happy thoughts, though nothing seemed out of place – in fact, everything looked perfect. This idyllic spot on Lamonhah Ridge offered travelers water from a leisurely-flowing river, a tall vantage point of rock to oversee their safety, and a large clearing already set up with firepits and seating for the regular caravans that frequented the area. It was here, in the center of camp, where a festive atmosphere was building. The accompanying entertainers were preparing a complimentary performance for their fellow travellers, which was customary to show their gratitude for their protective company. Jostling jugglers were busily donning their outlandish outfits and applying their outrageous make-up. Until yesterday, Raasah could not have imagined a more merry life or one more free of strife. She gave a shudder.

At their last stop, Raasah had happened upon one of the long-limbed jugglers on her way to her sleeping quarters, a smidgeon of makeup still lining his hairline and thin neck. He had nearly knocked her over in his haste to re-enter the clearing. Gruffly he had grabbed her arm, giving her the leverage to keep from falling. Now she was not so sure that assisting her was the intent. As she had righted herself, she saw a figure beyond him amid the trees, but the juggler's frame promptly blocked the view. For a long moment he retained his hold on her arm. Fearfully she had looked into his cold, darting eyes, his tongue slipping back and forth across his thin lips, before he brushed her off like an irritating gnat. So tonight, as she watched the colourful troop set up on this their last night of their journey, she wondered, with trepidation, which of the comical smiles hid that intimidating face.

Gratefully, the trills and fluttering of the fowler's caged birds distracted her. From the surrounding trees, a marvellous orchestra of wild birds added their own songs of shrill twittering and rythmatic base. Howler monkeys hooted and grunted hauntingly off in the distant hills, gloriously completing the spontaneous chorus. Then there was a muffled rustling of wind in the canopy beyond ...*or was it something more ominous?*

Squashing negative thoughts, she allowed the soothing perfume of the forest to envelope her. "Oh, Abul," she said wistfully. "Tomorrow we will be back in Ammonihah and all this will end. I have learned so well to love the sights and sounds of the merchant traveller. One can feel peaceful and alive at the same time. Do you feel this too?"

"My Burshon, what do I know? I am but your lowly servant," he replied with head solemnly bowed.

"Abul, you know you are much more than that," she laughed. Then Raasah soberly gazed around her. "Yea, I can see why my father prefers this life to one languishing in the judgment seat day-after-day." A whiff of roasting meat and spices drifted enticingly under her nose and with her good friend by her side... she should have been so content....

Suddenly, Raasah twirled around as a feeling of anxiety surged through her.

"Are you alright, Burshon?" Abul's brown eyes, looking black in the receding light, gazed intensely at her under knit brows.

Raasah berated herself silently. "I'm just tired. It's been a long journey."

"Yea, we have been on the road well after the second moon. Nothing like your cozy villa back home." Catching Raasah's eye, he made a crooked grin. She tried to exaggerate his ridiculous grin back and they laughed warmly together.

On this night, as on other nights, Raasah had warily chosen to sit close to the bearers, but not among them, near the outskirts of the clearing. If her mother had known whom she was keeping company, she would adamantly have disapproved. Her mother, a priestess elite, strongly believed her creditability would be tarnished if a family member socialized with those of lower station – AND, to be enjoying the company of a slave… *scandalous!!* Even though her mother was not there and rarely had been present as she grew up, just the same, Raasah nervously pulled the hood of her cape further forward concealing the fine fair features of her young face. She still had to keep up some semblance of discretion *if only for my mother's sake!* Because she was now a young lady of high society, expectations and responsibilities lay heavy on her slender shoulders, especially in regard to those she associated with, and she would never wish to disgrace her family, especially her mother.

So it was definitely not because she wanted to defy her mother, nevertheless, since Abul first arrived at the age of eight, he had quickly become an important presence in Raasah's life and he now felt more like family than someone the family owned. They both coveted their secret friendship and the fondness for each other grew. At least, this is what she believed….

The shimmering of the river silhouetted the large forms of the other bearers in the darkening shadows. Standing apart from them was the dark form of one of the company's armed escorts. He was a formidable solemn man with heavy leather armor, fearsome sheathed weapons ever ready at his waist but, despite the implied promise of safety that such hired protectors were supposed to bring, it did not squash the puzzling fearfulness growing inside her.

"Your father comes yonder. You should join him now," Abul said kindly, looking up the gradual bank to shadowy forms gathering. Deep laughter mingled with the growing volume and variation of voices.

"Sometimes I think you are mystic," Raasah mused. "Nothing appears to get by you."

Abul looked thoughtful for a moment and then smiled his heart-warming smile that almost shone from his dark face. "Yea, Abul, the Mystic... And for my next act...." Rising, he withdrew a small ball from his pocket and balanced it upon his nose. Flinging it high in the air with a jerk of his head, he kneed it up once more on its return to catch it with a ceremonious flare. With an exaggerated wave, he extended his other hand toward Raasah.

"Thank you for the many lessons, my good friend," Raasah laughed, as she accepted his assistance. Abul tenderly held her small hand a fraction longer than was necessary.

"You are a good person, Raasah," he said, hauntingly hesitant.

She touched his brawny sun-baked arm, a touch that told him of the strong bond between them, to which he brightened, laughing.

"Go to your father, Burshon," he ordered playful.

"Wa-ie, my friend," she said softly. Running up the rise in smooth lengthened strides, Raasah imaged wings on her feet such as Abul had described so often in his fanciful stories of his people. The resulting tinkling of her bracelets was like a comforting song.

She tried to dismiss her uneasiness as guilt that her mother had evoked from afar for her sin of indiscretion. Abruptly she composed herself to equate the dignity of her stature before her mother could summon up more guilt feelings and straightened out her gown that had revealed itself through the loosened cape. The high downy neck of the overlaying tunic framed Raasah's delicate smooth face, emphasizing the most unique emerald-green eyes ever beheld in a Nephite maid. Her thick dark hair was piled loosely on her head in a manner that would have appalled her maid servant who, thankfully, had stayed behind at their villa. Raasah thrust her shoulders back resuming the posture of nobility that would deter anymore negative vibes from home.

Once giving her soft rubber mass one more squeeze, Raasah slipped it quickly into her purse attached at her waist before she approached the large stooped form under the massive ceiba tree. Her father's dark hair was pulled back at the front by two braided sections that extended into a bun, displaying his jade embedded earplugs and deep creases at the corners of his bemusing brown eyes. Close-cut and neat, his thick beard did not hide his generous smile. The jaguar-skin vest, open in the front, displayed a simple jade pectoral necklace against his hard, bare chest.

Nestled under the cavernous canopy, rested the carriage that Abul and his fellow bearers had carried them in. Other colourful carriages were also dotted close by at the edge of the small clearing, temporarily abandoned by their previous occupants. Each carriage was adorned in the owner's family colours and traditions, many with symbols of their status, so as to distinguish their carriage from their companions. An exaggerated wooden sculpture, customarily over-laid with gold and paint, dominated each roof.

Raasah's father had chosen the image of the iguana to embellish their carriage and, of course, the wooden image of a large dragon iguana was perched on the very top. The latter was not guilded in gold, though, as would have been expected, but tastefully decorated with shiny metal scales and hues of green and red. And it seemed to have a hint of a friendly smile as it looked out at the procession. Upon hearing some ridicule from her father's peers over his choice of mascot, Raasah, then puzzled, had asked her father why he had not chosen a more noble beast. He smiled patiently at her and explained, 'What could be more noble? Our iguana has a calm disposition which is best to make good decisions. It would rather love than fight – a beast of peace. It is very social and knows how to enjoy a sunny day with friends – a valuable trait. And look at him...," he paused. "It always looks so dignified in an ancient manner which denotes wisdom and honour. What better symbol for our family could we possibly have?"

Raasah looked at the image of the iguana, with all the noble traits of her father. She had always admired her father's ability to stand confidently and dignified amid opposition and taunting. Within a very short time and probably because of her father's affable response to it all, the ridicule gradually turned to genial teasing that her father embraced. Before long, far and wide, his reputation as the 'Pochtecatl of the Iguana' preceded him; people respected him for all the traits it now symbolized and the honourable way he dealt with his fellow men. His was a choice of a noble beast most befitting of him. Tattooed on his upper arm under a series of long scars, an additional iguana wound its body of green, its head and dark eyes directed up.

"Wa-ie, Pei-wa-ni." Raasah greeted her father with a light kiss, sitting next to him on the carriage's cushioned seat. She fingered her bracelets, stroking the imbedded fragments of shell with all their wonderful hues of pastels. Her father had surprised her with these trinkets during their time on the coast after spying her admiring the artisan's crafts.

Her father was absorbed in carving the finishing touches into a small wooden toy. Curious round disks were attached to the lower sides of the small square carriage on opposite sides slightly below the lower edge of the hollowed container. Her father was saying something to her as she surfaced out of her own thoughts.

"…so your Aunt Ester would love to have you visit …."

"What do you call that?" Raasah interrupted, pointing to the wooden object as her father buffed the detailed relief on the front of the toy. As he blew over the surface to reveal a smiling monkey face, he turned it slightly left and right to inspect it.

"It is the strangest carriage my eyes have ever beheld," Raasah mused. In a hole under the monkey face, her father had inserted some twine to which he now tied a knot so it couldn't be pulled through. Placing the toy at arm-length, he handed the free end of the twine to Raasah. "Give it a tug."

Raasah gingerly pulled on the string and the toy toddled forward over the rough gravelly ground, the four attached disks turning easily. She laughed. "A carriage that can travel without bearers!"

She had also wanted to say how much Abul would have appreciated such a rig, but she wisely stopped short of it. Though she was sure her father suspected her friendship with Abul, it was unspoken. And Abul, who from doing heavier and heavier menial chores to becoming their chief bearer, had benefitted by acquiring a powerful hard body that she knew turned heads of women he passed.

She glanced over to where she had left Abul but, instead, spied Noalas, the leader of the mercenaries that guarded the small company. His gaze met hers and she trembled. Though Noalas and his men were essential to their safety, his scowling face with the distinct white scar unnerved her and she did her best to keep her distance from him.

Meanwhile, into the interior of the toy vessel, her father, the novice carver, placed a rough round wooden figure with a small swath of red cloth wrapped around it. "Antionah rides in his magic monkey carriage." Raasah watched wide-eyed as her father faked a 'royal sit', mimicking the deep, monotone voice of Antionah announcing his urgent meeting with the royal caterers.

Raasah giggled. "Shush, Pei-wa-ni. Someone might hear you!" Antionah was the well-adorned governor of their illustrious city but the actual power of ruling he left to the priests and judges. Antionah, instead, dedicated himself to inventing celebrations so he could show off his elaborate clothes, his beautifully decorated women, and his sparkly overstated jewelry, …and then to eat to excess.

Looking around nervously, Raasah whispered conspiratorially, "Why do we not call the carriage the Antionage?" Her father laughed his approval. Gripping the string, Raasah walked slowly backward, the toy obediently wobbling after her.

On its way back, her father loaded up the tiny carriage with several small pebbles announcing solemnly, "…the royal pudding, the fragrant pastries, the roasted peacock, and… oh, Your Generously-Enhanced Graceship, the savory deer roast!" With a gracious bow, he plopped the last pebble into the miniature carriage. "Yea, Antionage it is," he concluded as Raasah muffled her amusement at the ruler's expense. "Can you imagine real people riding in such a self-propelled carriage some day?" he added.

Raasah laughed, "Oh, Pei-wa-ni! That is so foolish! Next you would be desirous to invent a magical flying carriage!!"

Her father laughed deep and long with her. Raasah adored her father. She loved her mother as well, of course, but her parents had a strained relationship, causing her to feel pulled between her loyalties. Her father, Botholuem the Pochtecatl, considered himself foremost as a professional long-distance merchant. Pochtecatl were of a small, but important class because they not only facilitated commerce, but also communicated vital information across the empire and beyond its borders. What was most impressive, though, was that Botholuem was also serving as the envied Chief Royal Attendant, which held the highest administrative position of the court coupled with the distinguished duty of personal advisor to Governor Antionah. Botholuem was, indeed, a most influential man, but, nevertheless, he humbly preferred the simple pleasures of life and treasured the friendships he cultivated around him, especially in the merchants' guilds.

This was Raasah's first trip accompanying her father to the trading cities since she was a small child. There was a festival in the city of Amulet where he traded regularly and he believed it to be a perfect time for him to introduce his family to many of his distant friends and associates. It was not a surprise when her mother declined, but the fierceness of her objection was!

The argument that followed was like nothing her parents had had before. Her mother had venom in her voice as she insisted Raasah stay behind. Despite her compelling need to please her mother, Raasah's desire to spend this precious time with her father pulled at her sensibilities. Her brother had regularly accompanied their father on his trips and Raasah longed to see the wonderful sights that Terjah often described. As much as she wanted to hear the substance of her mother's adamant objections, Hannah, her servant, had ushered her out of hearing range.

Although Raasah was deeply saddened that the planned trip had renewed disharmony between her parents, she was delighted now that she had been able to make the trip. She had so many great stories of strange sights to share with her friends and brother when she returned. It had been disappointing that Terjah had not been able to join them as he said he had some business to attend to, but he was to meet them on their final day of travel on the main road to Ammonihah. It would be so good to see her brother after their long trip and she could hardly wait to be the one to rehearse to him her tales of adventure and far-away places. The message runner had been sent on ahead to Ammonihah to inform the family members there of the caravan's location. It would be a joyful reunion.

The bearer's fire appeared to get brighter as the shadows deepened in their clearing. Their own central fire highlighted the slowly turning carcass of a deer that was skewered high over the gathering flames. Bright flames leapt up as the juice and grease dripped from the sizzling carcase. With mouth-watering, Raasah could almost taste the tender succulent meat. She hadn't realized how hungry she was.

Botholuem scooped up the toy and placed it in a duffle bag that also held the tools of his hobby and other small toy items in various stages of development. He settled the bag into the carriage before standing, wrapping his thick arms around Raasah's small shoulders.

Father and daughter joined the rest of their companions around the main campfire. The musicians were warming up and the jugglers were trying out new moves for their routines. Servants offered platters of refreshing snacks while they awaited their welcome venison feast, compliments of the skills of Noalas and his armed band.

Raasah tried to summon up appreciation for their protectors and the skill and proficiency that they had attended them, but it waned as fast as she could conjure it up. She just did not like the overbearing strongman with his rigorous troop. Six members of this armed band stood at strategic locations on the outskirts of the clearing, armed, looking fierce and alert. A seventh member of the band was still watching over the bearers' camp. Despite her personal feeling about them, Raasah should have felt safe....

"Look, Pei-wa-ni, there's Geshem!" Raasah exclaimed to distract herself. The fowler could always brighten her day. Geshem, a jovial wild-bearded man, walked among the assembled travelers with his pet macaw prancing about his shoulders. He was thin with a protruding forehead and a wide nose, but his best feature was his wrinkled eyes that almost disappeared when he laughed, which was often, as he intermingled with those around him. The large red bird mounted Geshem's head.

"Ackoutl, come down from there!" Geshem laughed. As Geshem put the bird through its comical paces in an abbreviated performance, his small audience gaily clapped their appreciation.

Raasah's view, though, was obstructed as Zerin, a promising young guild member, strutted up. "Pochtecatl Botholuem,"

(Botholuem insisted on this title, not Chief Attendant, while on the road) "behold yon son of Mosiahah, the defier of a seafarer's death." He swung an arm in the direction of Moab, who was once more bragging about his miraculous escape from the undertows of the coastal waters.

"Again, how strong was that monstrous current, lad?" Botholuem shouted to the braggart.

"Strong like a… like a python who has wrapped you in its deathly coils… squeezing the very life-stem from your soul!" Moab exclaimed.

"I do fear," Botholuem jested to Mosiahah, "the next time your son tells his story, the strength of the fabled current will have increased enough to suck all of Ammonihah to its watery death!" Laughter erupted around him, oblivious to the groomed young man who continued to retell the enhanced details of his story. Despite her father making light of the incident, though, it still frightened Raasah to think that Moab, a dear friend of her brother's, could have vanished forever in the sea's depths.

The underlying fear that she had been feeling now surged once more inside her – the intenseness of her feelings catching her by surprise. She heard the murmurings of conversations around her, the crackling of the fire, the shuffling of sandals as they passed her, but she knew she was missing something, a serious detail that she should have noticed. Still not understanding why, any trepidation she had felt for this young man shifted suddenly to terror for the entire assembly. Raasah surveyed the happy company. To the left she heard gay conversation; to the right, carefree laughter. *What could possibly be wrong?*

In sudden panic, she whipped her head around. The sounds of

the forest, the voices of the bearers… they were no longer heard; the bearers' fire… abandoned. What she did hear was a whish through the air – then another. Suddenly groans and cries filled the night air. Just in front of her, Zerin exhaled sharply and crumpled to the ground.

Before she could register what was happening, she felt herself yanked from her perch. Pain shot through her head as it thumped to the ground. As her world began to spin, she briefly spied… *Abul? Is that you, Abul?* She heard her father yelling but she could not make out the words. In a fog, she desperately tried to focus. A grotesquely masked man loomed over her, jeering, speaking words she couldn't hear. Another masked man…. Screams from men and women wounded or dying engulfed her. She opened her mouth to scream….

Raasah woke from her nightmare gasping for breath, tears streaming down where wet strands of hair clung to her face. An older woman, with a shawl fluttering behind her, hastened to her side and tenderly brushed aside the tears and dishevelled locks.

"Hush, hush, my granddaughter, you are home now." The woman, Marian, put a gentle arm around the shaken girl. "Another nightmare?"

Raasah nodded, her shoulders shuddering with a sob. Marian drew her to her breast as the girl abandoned herself to her tears.

Chapter 2

The Orphan

The towering ziggurat[1], strategically built upon its mound, overlooked several elevated courtyards still deep in shadows. This was the Palenia Palace, the sacred centre of Ammonihah. Shrines and temples were scattered here and there throughout the city and countryside, but a worship locale of real prestige demanded the presence of an elevated temple structure within a community. Dominating the top of this palace, the highest structure in Ammonihah, sat the magnificent Temple of the Sun.

Palenia's temple was a meticulously decorated structure topped with a grandiose roofcomb[2] depicting the creation. Here, with this sacred temple as backdrop, Raasah had sought solitary prayer in the quiet of the pre-dawn. She knew there could be serious consequences for coming to this sanctioned area unsummoned and unaccompanied but she did not know where else to go to accomplish what she needed. Quietly slipping past the sleepy gate guards, she had entered through a dust covered entrance allotted solely for appointed temple artisans. Large bags of red plaster lay against the walls littered with other construction debris. She stepped carefully past an ornate stucco god mask, one of a dozen or more that will be created for decorating Palenia by order of the Ammonihah governor. Relieved that she had arrived ahead of the artisans, she tip-toed up a less traveled stairway, past the three extensive platforms that surrounded the structure to eventually reach this sacred house at its very top.

A place of wonder and awe, the top of Palenia had always been a divine, even heavenly, place for Raasah even when a mass of activity was in progress below. Even the pesky insects seemed to understand the sacredness of this hallowed place – in fact, in the light of day, the air was dotted only with the fragile beauty of small fluttering butterflies like tiny spirit sentinels guarding and purifying this sanctioned space. And foremost on the Temple platform, set with precious stones, was a magnificent gold altar.

This was her first venture outside the confines of her home since her father's burial. She came to seek solace in a place that in the past had given her great peace. She had not entered the Temple itself, of course. Those who entered were divinely set apart as the sacred Sun Temple elite, and to enter without this sanction would bring down the wrath of the Creator Himself. Raasah revered the religious protocol and ordinances as taught by her teachers and would never dream to defile her Creator's House, but she did long for answers, understanding, and peace.

Upon the cool iron grate of the altar, Raasah had timidly laid her bound dove for the priests when they should arrive. Its pretty blue head peered out innocently and cooed again ever so softly. But now, even after her long heart-felt prayers and pleadings, the comfort she had sought had not embraced her. She had hoped for a miracle of healing but it had not come. The intense sadness still weighed heavily upon her.

Raasah knelt hunched over on the cool stone platform, blankly staring southwest. From this advantageous position atop of Palenia, she could take in much of the city and the farmland beyond. Still further out, amid the canopy of trees, rose the Great Oluffa, the Goddess Guardian of Ammonihah embodied in the ancient vapour-enshrouded volcano. Raasah had sent her prayers out to Oluffa as well but she was only answered with silence. She gazed to the west, where, outlined on the horizon, were the Hunitite Mountains of Abul's clan. Abul – he too was gone from her life. She wondered if he was there with his tribe now and her face grew hot with ire.

A slave revolt – that's what they were saying. The slaves killed and escaped. Her brother and other relatives of those deceased had ridden out with the soldiers to hunt down the runaways. The angry mob had divided into two search parties with one heading toward Oluffa and her brother's heading toward the Hunitite Mountains. Raasah turned from those mountains. The treachery hurt too much. She stared absently down upon the city.

Raasah had slipped out unassisted before the rest of the household awoke. She had chosen a simple silk gown and donned the least of her fashionable cloaks over it that, nevertheless, still made a stylish statement despite the intent. Her thick hair was loosely braided back by Raasah's unexperienced hands. Thus it was that this forlorn young woman, from one of the most prestigious families of Ammonihah, with eyes rimmed with dark circles, sat.

Shadowy figures were just setting up their wares in the Great Plaza below. Despite the height, the murmur of their voices and their bustling noises increasingly invaded her quiet space, accentuated, no doubt, by the superb acoustics of the Grand Plaza's floor itself. She spied a seller of mai[4] and other such ointments laying out his wares. He called to a fellow vendor that was lying out his bolts of cloth.

"Cadoth, you smarmy dung bug, where is that sleazy son of yours?" As if on cue, a curly mop of a head slowly emerged from behind a bulging sack and the young man beneath stumble forward with a small armful of colourful textiles. The mai seller laughed boisterously. "He looks like something a boar dragged through a thicket and then repeatedly wiped the ground with!" he roared.

The other glared at his taunting neighbour just before he snatched the articles from his son in question, cuffing him to send the haggard youth back to retrieve more.

"…caught once again staggering out of Harlot Halboth's," the mai seller hackled, but Raasah's mind absorbed no more words as she raised her face to the eastern horizon to distant herself from such frequent base talk of the market.

As the morning's first light broke, Raasah stood up mechanically directly in front of the temple. It was one day past the time of the zenial[3] passage. This solar phenomena only occurred twice a year equidistant from the solstice. As in years past, she turned and gazed up as the sun's brilliance fingered the stone frieze atop the temple, pouring like golden honey down the roofcomb and onto the wall of the temple itself. Numbly, Raasah gazed through the open cavernous entrance.

The far wall inside the compact temple was painted with colourful scenes of landscapes, animals, heavenly bodies, and other wonderful scenes that had gradually immerged out of the shadows with the growing light. Carefully engineered portals in the structural eastern wall focused and inverted the sun's rays against these scenes as it washed down the outside walls, forming illuminated figures that, as the sun rose ever so slowly, descended down the interior wall. It was as if heavenly beings were travelling through the series of realistic scenes.

'This is symbolic of the continued presence of a deity's steward-ship upon the earth,' her mother had told her and, even though the zenial passage was waning, the images were still impressive. As a young child accompanied by her priestess mother, the miracle of creation had magically come alive for Raasah through this solar display. Raasah watched the breathtaking spectacle silently, long-ingly, but this morning, instead of awe, she felt only more alone and lonely.

As the images blurred and faded away, Raasah turned. Covering her head, she slipped the strap of her satchel upon her shoulder and despondently descended down the steep Palenia steps. Below her, the growing number of fellow citizens drifted among the vendors as if in a slow leisurely dance. The artisans had arrived and their pounding and chiselling were adding to the increasing din from the Plaza. She slipped unnoticed past four loin-clothed labourers straining to lift a mask almost double their height. With a numb-ness of mind, she found herself drifting between the scenes around her and the horrifying day of carnage. It had been ten long days since the death of her father and their traveling companions – ten long nights afraid to close her eyes for fear of reliving that devas-tating evening on the ridge.

Raasah paused and found herself staring as a prominent fem-inine figure came into view donned in layers of sheer graceful crimson and adorned delicately in sparkling jewels. When this stately woman approached a vendor, voices hushed. This was Zillah, priestess of the market, strict enforcer of market rules and regula-tions. She was surrounded by her entourage of young fashionable attendees fanning her, conversing with her, assisting her, and adding their own soft flowing hues of colours amid the market's crowds.

Zillah was highly respected by all the citizens of Ammonihah – that is except among a growing number of elite. Only months earlier, when Raasah had questioned her brother about the disquieting murmurings regarding the priestess, he had dismissed her like a small child. Insulted, Raasah had pursued the inquiry with her mother who had responded with unexpected anger. Raasah had not brought it up since.

Zillah gazed up, her penetrating eyes fixing on Raasah. Feeling suddenly vulnerable, Raasah froze but the stately priestess gave an unpretentious smile, then a nod and resumed her attention to those around her. Confused, Raasah quickly restarted her descend to the Palenia's formidable courtyard. She made a mental note to inquire more about the Priestess of the Market.

Within 15 steps of the walled courtyard, Raasah had to make a slight detour around the tools and supplies of the engravers. The only official business that Governor Antionah felt impressed enough to officiate over these days – *besides feasts & celebrations* – were of superficial facelifts on all the major civil and religious buildings of Ammonihah. Six-days-a-week, dawn to dusk, the sounds of thumping, clanging, and scraping rang out over the plazas and courtyards. In contrast, *thank goodness*, the silence of the seventh day seemed all the more hallowed to the ears, but, sadly, not to the eyes. Once on ground level, the evidence of the city's 'improvements' lay blatantly in unfinished carved blocks, half-finished stelae[5], partial walls, and dust-covered building materials littered by each major edifice. Lately the view of central Ammonihah from above was far more impressive than from below.

The lesser priests were already busy just inside the courtyard, dressed in their official gowns and headdresses of lush feathers and fur. The solemn public, scrubbed and neatly attired, were continually arriving to partake of the religious rites, clutching, among other things, offerings of sweet incense, fruit and grains. Twelve steps from the courtyard Raasah quickened her pace once more, anxious to vacate the stairs that could implicate her in transgression.

Only eight steps from the courtyard her heart sank. Only eight more steps would have brought her back on public ground where she could assimilate undiscovered. But this was not to be.

A foreboding guard was striding toward Raasah, gruffly waving her down the remaining stairs. As he approached, she heard his voice like gravel, "What is this? Impudent girl, this area is forbidden...."

Raasah side-stepped and then again, her heart thumping in her ears. She looked longingly at the courtyard so close but she knew he could easily block her path to the gate in a few long strides. She pulled her hood closer to her face as she pictured her mother's indignation when she was informed where her daughter had been and the scandal that could be made of it. The guard was closing in fast, threatening and cursing.

"Ya daft little hussy, ya need me get ya a good whipping, ya do." He was three long strides from reaching her. Shamefully, she continued to shuffle sideways, eyes darting and searching hopelessly for an escape. Two strides from reaching her, the uniformed ruffian suddenly paused as he evaluated his subject.

"Oh, my succulent sorceress," he sneered, leeringly drawing his fat splattering tongue over blackened teeth. His hooded eyes were wide with delight at the treasure he had discovered. In contrast,

Raasah's stomach lurched in disgust as she back up a step, clutching her satchel to her chest as if it could shield her from him. One stride from her, his swarthy hand reached out to her. Pasty sick bile swelled in the back of her throat, threatening to gag her.

"Armus, ya wartwit…."

The brutish guard whipped his head in the direction of the insult. Raasah sprinted recklessly under the outstretched arm, two stairs at a time. Mercifully, a scuffle of a patron and guard below them had drawn the attention of the lewd guard. Behind her, she heard the foul-minded guard cursing the very the gods whose sanctity he was supposed to be upholding as she flew down the remaining stairs in neck-breaking speed. Her head pounded. Four steps, two steps… just as she thought she would miraculously make it safely through the gate, she slipped, landing indignantly on her backside. Recovering quickly, she scooted past the muralled wall of the courtyard, melting awkwardly into the growing throng, her heart thumping so hard she thought her ribs would break.

Resisting the urge to look back, Raasah replaced her hood with her scarf and, hunching her shoulders, she attempted to make herself less visible. Tense with fear that her pathetic masquerade would be uncovered and a swarthy hand would seize her at any moment, she joined herself to an unsuspecting cluster of peasant women. Long moments passed and, once making some distance between her and the gate she had entered by, her tautened chest finally began to relax. Raasah smiled awkwardly at the small group of women now whispering amongst themselves, stealing sideways glances her way as they edged slowly away. Surveying the immediate area for unfriendly brutish guards and, seeing none, Raasah addressed her puzzled companions.

"Thank you, good women," she said as confidently and refined as her shaken disposition would allow. "...for your gracious company. I wish you all a very good day."

With a nod and before they could respond, Raasah slipped away, ascending a short set of steps to a humble shrine in the furthest corner of the courtyard. Still shuddering at the thought of that foul guard, she wrapped her cloak tightly around her and settled on a pony wall next to the stairs.

At first Raasah felt subconscious sitting among the citizens she had been isolating herself from but the persistent memories of the attack, like ghosts haunting the crevices of her mind, soon took precedence. Other haphazard thoughts of unpleasant events distant, present, and conjectured materialized and faded as she strained to blank it all out. As her inward battle waged on, she was unaware of the increasing commotion, echoing footsteps, and growing mass around her until the billowing folds of a priest's fur cape slapped the satchel from her shoulder.

A small ragged boy, amid the swirling clothes and shuffling sandals, daftly grabbed the bag as it started slumping down the stairs. He brought it shyly back to her. Nodding a pleasant 'thank-you', Raasah accepted the bag from his outstretched hand. Then rising, she turned her back to the boy to dismiss him, as her station would demand. She descended toward a busy minor temple near the east gate.

Raasah couldn't help glancing back at the boy who now appeared to be following her. She should have been annoyed but, instead, she felt drawn somehow. There was something powerful and sad in his eyes that tugged at her heart and a slight sob erupted from her throat. She fingered the small tender cut at the base of her skull, tangible evidence that the terrible events on Lamonhah Ridge were not just persistent nightmares. It was true – her father's sparkling laughter would never brighten a room again. He was gone.…

She sat upon a stone bench and pulled out a parchment. The boy came closer as she began to sketch. She was aware of him and, surprisingly, it felt very comfortable. Her grandmother had often told her to trust her feelings so she just kept sketching. *Why hadn't I trusted my feelings the night of the carnage?* she questioned for the umpteenth time. *But what could a young girl had done to stop it...?* She kept sketching – she wasn't good but she got some comfort from it.

At first the boy sat cross-legged on the ground by the other end of the bench. Slowly, though, the shaggy-haired boy edged along the pavestones and then eased himself up upon the bench close enough to Raasah to observe the details on her parchment as she penned them down. Without speaking, he sat with her just outside of the yawning doorway of the lower temple. Time passed and they become a centre of tranquility in a swirling pool of hundreds. Though she tried to ignore him, his presence seemed to ease the grieving in her heart as she attempted to concentrate on the new scene in front of her. The roof comb she was sketching was decorated with painted stucco reliefs as was the temple walls. The roof was latticed with stonework that added to the height.

"The architects do their best to make the buildings grand but it is the artists that truly accomplish it," she said softly.

From the corner of her eye she saw the thin innocent face nodding as if he was involved a deep intellectual discussion. It was a sudden reminder of her father who had pursued such discussions with the learned men of Ammonihah. A renewed wash of emotion enveloped her at the thought. Sluggishly, she rolled up her parchment, and stood, the boy standing beside her, prepared to enter the temple.

The unlikely pair of poor ragged boy and refined young lady stepped between the ornately carved door posts. Shafts of light cut through smoke from the burning candles and sweet grass. Inside, the soothing sounds of the reverent populace melded with the scent and light. Individuals and segments of families cluster around square rock alters, swaying back and forth as they chanted melodiously in front of their offerings and flickering candles. From her waist pouch, Raasah dropped 2 coins into the money box just inside the entrance and gave a third coin to the boy.

Eagerly he scampered off and returned with candles and change. Together they lit the candles and placed them on an altar. Kneeling side-by-side, they each silently offered their prayers. Flashes of her father, of all their fellow travellers, of handsome Abul and jovial Geshem – even Ackoutl the brazen macaw – interjected her pleadings and woeful prayer. Raasah blinked her eyes open, stealing a look at her small companion, and couldn't help but appreciate the angelic face of her new little friend bowed intently next to her. With renewed concentration and calm, Raasah concluded her prayer with gratitude for the loan of a loving wise father and a plea for his worthiness to partake in the heavenly rewards. Then she rose to face the reality around her.

A young woman with a baby cradled in her arms was weeping before her own wax-strewn altar. Disheartened, Raasah realized that this was the wife of Zerin – Zerin who had perished with her father. Once more, those dreaded memories washed over her, causing a wave of dizziness to rock her on her feet. A gallant part of her wanted to go over and comfort the young mother, but anxiety gripped at her chest at the thought. *What do I know about easing someone's pain? I can't even deal with my own grief?* Ashamed and embarrassed, she backed towards the entrance.

As her eyes adjusted to the brightness emitting from without, Raasah recognized yet another worshipper – a young man next to the entrance with braided ebony hair. He was kneeling, back straight, facing an altar with a single lit candle. Though his clothing was dark, he seemed to glow as he soaked up a shaft of sunlight that had come to rest upon him. He was deep in prayer.

This was Chemish. He was from a long line of exceptional carpenters whom her father had purchased furniture and carvings from to trade. Their shop was on the causeway leading to the Acropolis of the Moon where she attended her priestess instruction. He and his family had come to her father's burial and said kind words to her but most of that day was just a muddle of foggy memories. She had been so distraught that she barely recalled the smells of the poignant spices offered by the priests, the eulogies offered by friends and associates, or the mournful sound of the hired minstrels and singers that attended the parade to the burial site. There were sounds of many mournful parades that day. Even so, she did clearly remember Chemish, with his kind face and gentle manner and his large warm hands briefly enclosing hers as he gave his condolences.

Chemish had always had a smile for her when she had passed on her way to the Acropolis. Each time, though, she had ignored his civility, ignoring as well her perplexing attraction to this young labourer. It was unthinkable that she should entertain the attentions of a common carpenter. But, in spite of herself, she studied the soundless man before her in meek prayer. Today, as during that sorrowful occasion on the day of her father's dedication, he was not covered in the sweat and dirt typical of his trade. He was groomed and donned in an unpretentious trim tunic. His handsome tan face was bowed; his thick muscular arms folded in front of him.

Just then a bulky bearded guard gruffly laid his hand on Chemish, brandishing a polished club in the other. He was dressed in leather armour and his sandals were embossed with the crest of the governor. Raasah saw three other men in similar garb with clubs just outside the entrance.

"Grovelling cockroach! You dare insult our sacred ground and dishonour decent citizens with your travesty of worship!" All eyes turned upon them. "Miserable heathen, you must tithe double at our sacred temples."

Chemish slowly rose to exceed the height of the guard as the other apprehensive club-clutching men tensed menacingly. Chemish held up his palms submissively.

"I mean no disrespect," Chemish explained softly. "I have come only to honour our Creator and I have given a generous tithe."

Raasah witnessed the guard's thin chapped mouth curl into a smile at this submission and he raised his club threateningly. "You will pay a senon of gold for your insolence." he said, pointing to the money box.

Chemish, with a steady quiet voice, explained to him that he already put in more than that but the guard became angrier. The money box was closely guarded and Raasah wondered how the guard could not have possibly seen Chemish put in his offering, but her heart told her that he had.

"Will you cheat your priests, cheat your Creator?"

"I do not desire to disturb the sanctity of our Lord's house," Chemish said, his gaze encompassing the congregation around him. "I beg the forgiveness of yon good people for the contentious spirit that has descended upon it on my account." Fumbling in his purse, he presented three coins, "...but I cannot impart to you an amount to which I do not possess," Chemish said softly, looking the guard unflinchingly in the eye. "Yea, we are in a sacred house. We should not contend one with another in this place. Contention is a subtlety of the devil." Chemish extended his coins to the guard.

The scowling guard grabbed the coins. His grimace transformed into a hideous smirk as he stormed out past the money box with his jeering comrades directly behind. Raasah's growing trepidation for Chemish changed to sympathy. She knew that the coins were conferred by him at great sacrifice, for his family was not well off despite their expert craftsmanship. The local elite tended to shun the family, though Chemish and his father did get the odd orders covertly obtained from the hypocritical citizens which the family reluctantly charged much under their worth. Her father, nevertheless, still dealt outwardly and honestly with them – or had (she swallowed hard) – and could always get a substantially better price for the family when he took their crafts to other locales where they were always valued and admired. Raasah did not understand the politics of it all and, until now, it had not been her concern. Now she was both curious and concerned.

In spite the confrontation of the guards, Chemish stepped with head high out into the glorious morning light. He descended to the main platform to exit the walled enclosure. Outside the Temple Square, he paused to observe another spacious platform shared with the impressive civil building where judgement was dealt out on the affairs of the populace. The ominously attired judges leaned on their ceremonial staffs as they discussed a matter of law among themselves. Before them, an extremely nervous peasant fluttered his hands like angry birds as he continued to explain his case and a grizzled vagrant stood detained between two guards, hanging his head submissively. As one heavy-set guard yanked this frightened prisoner forward by the arm, Raasah was startled to see that the guard was the dreaded blasphemer she had encountered on the steps of Palenia. Her throat went dry. She did not want to imagine what could have become of her if he had gotten hold of her.

She quickly returned her attention to Chemish. *What was insinuated when he was accused of 'travesty of worship'?* The small boy, momentarily forgotten, tugged on her sleeve. Raasah looked inquisitively down at the face of the child with the dark pleading eyes but then again returned her gaze toward the gate. Regretfully, her view of Chemish was now blocked by the fanned headdresses of the more elite priests.

The boy tugged once more on her sleeve. Reluctantly, she followed after the beckoning child down the steep stone stairs, still scanning vainly for one more glimpse of Chemish. Once they had descended to the Grand Plaza, they wound their way across the marketplace now filled with citizens bantering and bartering, instruments tinkling and drumming, and tools clanging and banging. The smells from the preparers of atole[6] and tamales were already permeating the air and tantalizing patrons.

Leaving the latter behind, they entered a narrow crowded alley, Raasah following silently. Shouldering her way against the human flow, Raasah strained to keep in her sight her mysterious short guide who dodged effortless around swinging arms and bulky packages. Oncoming bodies crowded and jostled her repeatedly; the reek of perfume and sweat was strong; and wafting through it all was the sweet smell of hemp tied bundles and pungent smell of freshly sewn furs. Suddenly an olfactory memory overpowered her – the smell of her attackers – sour-sweet perfume and pongy sweat. It constricted her throat – the taste was bitter. With her head spinning, Raasah pushed blindly through the crowd unaware now where the boy had gone – only conscience that she needed to escape the bodies pressing in upon her.

As if God-sent, a small gentle hand enclosed her wrist. To her relief, she looked into the warm brown eyes of the boy. The eyes spoke to her, though she couldn't say what the words were but the message was clear: *"You will be alright. You can trust me."* Raasah wiped away a tear that had snuck down her cheek. *"I know that now,"* her eyes told him back. She ran her tongue across the top of her dry mouth. *"I did not know panic had a taste,"* she reflected. Thankfully, the sensation slowly subsided.

Raasah was lead out of the mass of people to a wide bricked avenue lined by spacious stucco residences. It was not an elite neighbourhood but definitely of successful businessmen who were socially establishing themselves. She breathed in deep. Absent of the bustling crowd, the air here was fresh and fragrant with herbs, flowers, freshly turned earth – and peace. *"I didn't know peace had a smell,"* she mused.

Allowing herself to be lead on, the boy now only a few steps ahead, she began to wonder where the boy was leading her and, in retrospect, wondered why she hadn't wondered before. They were entering the main causeway leading to Ammonihah's east gate, passing a slow procession of people who would join throngs heading to the many markets. Some of the merchants and other adults bowed questioningly to her before stepping aside to give her clear passage.

Bowing was customary for the lower class when they met the society's elite but to see an elite young woman unaccompanied in this part of the city caught many by surprise. Raasah nodded respectfully back each time, but, also each time, it delayed her from her pursuit of the boy who was gaining more distance between them. She hoped he had not forgotten about her. She skirted by a gay group of middle class women in their draping shawls and embroidered huipiles[7], adeptly balancing large earthen jars atop their heads. Raasah was glad they were so enveloped in their visiting that they hadn't noticed her.

Vendors of all sizes and shapes, chatting lazily, lugged their oversized bundle of wares toward the markets. Two thin, wiry men in simple bright pati[8] were deeply engaged in conversation also unaware of the out-of-place young lady. Both had skin like burnt sienna[9]; and straight black hair that fell across their eyes. Drawing her robe tightly around her, she made a wide berth around them before they noticed her.

Without a break in his pace, the boy led her past the sentry guards and out the gate. Here beyond the walls, the scenery changed dramatically with flat paved streets giving way to thrown-up roads and colourful fields stretching beyond. The small homes were of sun-baked adobe surrounded by simple family gardens. Giggling, two little girls with curly dark locks popped up from behind a large philodendron in front of her boy companion. They posed playfully in a royal gesture of greeting, then, putting their wee hands to their mouths, they ineffectively concealed more giggling. The boy, straightening up tall to imitate the elite, nodded his tousled head ever so slightly to acknowledge them. Delighted, the girls scampered off to resume their game of tag between the unassuming adobe structures.

Raasah stood astounded at herself. She should have felt anger at the mischievous mimicking of the elite by these common children but, instead, she found herself smiling at what she had now interpreted as a harmless, refreshing scene. *Besides, their deportment is convincingly of noble status, even more so than I could have carried off at that age!* The boy smiled broadly back at Raasah as if in agreement.

She continued following the boy from the city down a path lined with low cobble-stone walls. The gray bodies of lizards sunning themselves were barely visible against the stone. Behind the walls were acre-after-acre of the sword-leafed henequen[10] ripe for the rope maker to gather. They meandered down one hill and up another. Raasah had never been to this part of the countryside before. Her legs were tiring rapidly, no doubt, because of her extensive lethargic period of mourning, but the soft breeze was revitalizing.

The road had been reduced to a well-travelled trail that led them to a field of withering maize. Before them was a mud-walled home with a sod roof; other smaller dwellings and holding bins formed an orderly cluster around it that seemed to welcome one in. Despite this, Raasah held back next to the crop's tall stalks, thankful for the rest, as the boy continued past a large firepit and a multi-layered oven to approach the open entrance.

A slender comely woman in a plain beige shift appeared at the doorway wiping her hands, her straight dark hair knotted in a sleek bun. She smiled at the boy. After a few brief words, she left him at the door, returning to hand him a cloth wrapped package. As he turned to go, the woman looked toward Raasah. Feeling exposed, Raasah stumbled back behind a stiff brittle stalk and, when she had composed herself to return the look, the woman was gone.

"This is ridiculous!" she muttered. "Cowering like a frightened child!" But, she was a frightened child – reliving the fear, the sights, and smells of that terrible night, but mostly the fear.

And what am I doing here – following a vagrant boy all over the countryside?

The small hand once more gently pressed against her wrist. She wasn't sure if she had spoken aloud or in her troubled mind. The round angelic face looked up at her. Through those eyes, he talked to her once more and she answered with her smile, *I'll come.* What else could she do? She was compelled to go on, not by the boy, but by a need to know. Know what, she wasn't sure but, importantly, she was no longer afraid.

The pair resumed their hike between rows of peppers and onions into the shadowy forest on a less traveled path of low boughs and tangled vines. Small brilliant birds fluttered into the trees; the smell of rotting earth and fragrant herbs filled her senses. The boy never strayed more than a few steps from Raasah until she saw the sunlight just ahead. Her relief, though, was short-lived when she saw a sharp rise of a rocky cliff before her.

"Nah, not up there, please, young boy!"

The boy only gestured with a raised hand, giving her a warm smile.

"Alright!" Raasah heaved a sigh. "Lead the way."

The path became arduous and the sun was wearing. Raasah slipped off her robe and placed it neatly on a low bush. A light breeze tickled and cooled her moist neckline. Small rocks clattered down the path to lay to rest at her feet.

"Boy, wait, please!" she pleaded as he disappeared over a ridge.

"Come on, Raasah," she chided herself, "You are not going to let a mere boy out do you, are you?"

Summoning what was left of her strength, she climbed the last few steps and then, hiking up her skirts, she scrambled unceremoniously over the top. From her undignified position upon the ground, Raasah looked up at the boy beaming before her. Raasah gripped his small hand and rose to stand beside him, following his gaze.

"Incredible!" she exclaimed. She stood upon the plateau overlooking a half-harvested field between her and Ammonihah. Visible, unobstructed and dominate above her stately city, was the grandiose creation wall atop the Temple of the Sun. Distinct, even from this distance, was the sun and moon depictions carved therein, a magnificent example of the skills and foresight of the architects of her day. In addition, she could make out the top red platforms of three other dominant civil structures and many of the decorative buildings of the elite. The more common white-bleach homes of the common class appeared to compliment the latter like the final trim or frame to a beautiful painting. It was an impressive sight.

With a blur of wings, a brilliant hummingbird darted around them several times and then paused in mid-air like a sentinel awaiting instruction. Then, as if in receipt of its orders, it darted past them through an opening amid a mini forest of Guarumo trees – returning briefly, as if to summon them, only to disappear once again. Raasah followed obediently with the boy, stepping in the refreshing shade. The child took the lead down nature's esplanade until it opened up to a clearing dominated by a cairn of stones. A large flat-faced boulder with a primitive carved face protruded about a cubit[11] above the rest. And in front of the cairn lay ashes and traces of candle wax upon the ground. Raasah stood to the side, the boy beside her – tranquil, thoughtful, waiting.

The trees moaned as a gust of air pushed its way through the small canopy. Raasah shivered and then the breeze whipped around her like a hug – a heavenly, assuring hug. She felt the tiny squeeze of the boy's hand as if to say he felt it too. The air continued to press consolingly around her, warming her heart and calming her spirit. Raasah closed her eyes and imagined her father holding her, promising to watch over her. For several long moments it stayed – oh, how she longed for it to stay! – but, as quickly as it had come, the miraculous embrace was gone. Despite its absence, though, its comfort and peace lingered in her bosom. She stood a moment longer clinging to the loving image of her father behind closed eyes, reluctant to let it fade.

As the twittering of birds filled the fragrant air, the boy unwrapped the still warm flat bread and assortment of fruit from the friendly country woman. The glorious hummingbird checked on them once more before swooping over their heads and into the glorious sky. Truly alone now, they enjoyed the simple but satisfying picnic together overlooking the panoramic wilderness beyond.

Feeling an unexplainable bond with this boy, Raasah finally felt free to talk of things dear to her heart, of her Pei-wa-ni, of Geshem and his birds, and of the wonders she had shared with them on their last trip together. She talked of Abul and his stories and their games when they were little, much younger than this attentive boy before her. She intuitively knew the boy was incapable of speech, but this did not deter her from expressing herself, possibly even encouraged her. There were no tears, only a release of tension and need. She only felt choked up once when she acknowledged to the silent boy how much she missed her father – but she did not cry. Her new friend slipped his small hand into hers and his eyes told her he understood.

In a surprisingly short time, they had returned to the Grand Plaza energized by the staccato sounds of the marketplace. A mountain of red tomatoes, a hill of golden mangoes, and a shimmer of green melons blinked through the enshrouded bodies of the gathering mass of humanity. Regretfully, Raasah watched as the boy nimbly dodged flapping robes, skipping children, and swinging baskets through various congregated groups before he melted into the crowd.

Instinctively, Raasah gravitated toward a booth filled with en-graved items and embroidered textiles. She had seen this booth before but this time she noticed the sign carved into the post beside it. The glyphs[12] read: 'Orphans and Widows'. Another memory surfaced – a tame one this time – of a humble group of adobe structures that housed those orphaned and widowed outside the walled perimeters of the city. She had visited them once when she was accompanying her grandmother on one of her charity runs.

"I remember, but they were of no concern to me," Raasah thought

guiltily. She remembered how she had been anxious to be somewhere else. She looked shyly into the booth.

She made out many small faces beyond the merchandize for sale and then she spied the young boy now sitting in a far corner. He was quietly working on a carving of stone. Her heart had been touched by this lone mute boy. Gazing upon his small form hunched over his work, Raasah was now painfully aware of the reason for the sadness in his eyes. He, no doubt, had experienced similar sorrow as hers. But there was something special about this little man. He had given her something wonderful and valuable. And he had given her needed empathy and hope.

He greeted her with his eyes.

Just then, anxious voices called out her name. Twirling around, she saw her exasperated brother pressing through a group of farmers with two of their trusted servants in tow. Time had disappeared. She had not meant to be so long. The sun had long ago passed the mid-day mark. Once more, returning her gaze to the boy, her heart swelled with warmth as their eyes met once more. The Creator had answered her prayers for solace after all. It wasn't in a temple light display manufactured by urban planners or by a miraculous voice with words of wisdom from above. It was on a humble hilltop with this simple boy who used the wind to touch her soul.

---

1   *Ziggurat: among the Assyrians and Babylonians, a terraced tower pyramidal in form, each successive story being smaller than the one below, leaving a platform around each of the floors. In this story they are much shorter, only two to five stories high built on small mounds to give them the look of much more height. Extended courtyards were often built on one side of a platform*

of an official building or one of prestige where people could gather. Examples of these are now known as the Mayan Ruins.

2   Roofcomb: These were often built atop a temple or other important building and used as a grand billboard for the display of religious and political imagery.

3   Zenial: The passing of the sun directly overhead such that no shadows are cast by a pole sticking straight up from the ground. These conditions only occur in locations between the Tropic of Cancer and the Tropic of Capricorn.

4   Mai: tobacco prepared as an ointment.

5   Stelae: Hundreds of stelae have been recorded in the Maya region, displaying a wide stylistic variation. Many are upright slabs of limestone sculpted on one or more faces with figures and hieroglyphic text carved in relief. Stelae are believed to be stone banners raised to glorify the rulers or even gods, and they would record their deeds and scenes. The singular for stelae is stela.

6   Atole: a hot drink that typically includes mesa (corn meal), water, dark brown sugar, cinnamon, vanilla and optional chocolate or fruit.

7   Huipiles: rectangular cloth with a hole in the middle for one's head; colourful blouses or shift like dresses worn by the ancient South American women.

8   Pati: a square of cotton around one's shoulders.

9   Sienna: a form of limonite clay used in the production of oil paint pigments. "Burnt sienna", which is a more common pigment than the raw form, has been heated to remove the water from the clay and to redden its brownish colour.

10 Henequen: a reddish fiber obtained from the leaves of a tropical American plant. Uses: rope, twine, coarse fabric.

11 Cubit: an ancient unit of length equal to the distance from the elbow to the tip of the middle finger, approximately 43-56 cm/17-22 in.

12 Glyphs: In the last 50 years, anthropologists and other experts researching ancient Central American history have slowly been piecing together the beliefs, daily life, and culture of the people of this pre-classic period. It is now believed that these people had formed an advanced civilization which surpassed or equalled the skill and knowledge of the Egyptians during the time of the Pharaohs. In fact, because of the many similarities between the two cultures, including the pyramidal structures and their hieroglyphs, the evidence is there that these two groups of peoples could have co-existed in Egypt prior to the aforementioned people arriving on the American continents.

Chapter 3

The Prisoners

Raasah awoke, heart racing. She had been having the nightmare again but, though her eyes were open, she was still reliving the aural chaos that ensued that awful night of the attack. Sitting upright, she realized it was the angry voices and cries just outside their villa that had melded with her nightmare. She pushed aside her dreaded dream. "Hannah, what's happening?"

Hannah rushed into the room. "Dems second party of soldiers returned, my chil'. Deys captured five of dose murderin' slaves!"

Raasah jumped out of bed. "You must help me get ready. I need to see them…."

"I's beginnin' ta worry dos scoundrels woulds get away wid dare murderous deeds whens Terjah returned withouts a sign of 'em. By da livin' gods, dey'd got ta feel da scorn of justice upons dare heads…."

"Hannah, please hurry," Raasah pleaded as she tangled her hair in her comb.

"Here, chil', lets me. Oh, da low-lifes! Takin' da life of such an hones' man. Dey'd got ta pay an' dey wills, ya'll see…."

"Hush, Hannah, please, no more such talk." The old matron of the villa leaned heavily against the door opening.

"Apologies, Miz Marian." Hannah bowed respectfully.

The din outside sounded like an angry mob now and was getting louder by the minute.

"Mei-wa-na, did you hear? They caught some of the revolting slaves. They must be taking them to the justice building. I...."

"Granddaughter," Marian's voice was weary. Raasah paused and looked slowly up into the kind, tired face. "This will not bring your father back," Marian continued in a far off voice. She looked so fragile this morning.

"But I must see my father's murderers, I must see their faces...." Raasah looked pleadingly at her grandmother.

"Revenge has an ugly face," Marian said simply. Then she turned and was gone. Raasah looked at where her grandmother had been. She had to remind herself that, though she had lost a father, her grandmother had lost a son....

"Raasah, chil'?" Hannah waited. Raasah stared a moment longer at the empty doorway.

"Help me get ready," Raasah said decisively.

As Hannah straightened the veil over Raasah's shoulders, Raasah looked over to the side table where the lopsided ball of rubber sat – the one she had fashioned with Abul. Hannah had wanted to throw it out when she discovered it in her purse, but Raasah had snatched it up, clinging to it like it would erase all the terrible memories from that night. Raasah pulled her eyes away from it. Her resolve to confront her attackers swelled inside her, even if it included Abul.

"Oh, Hannah, no more fussing. You must fetch Terjah. He tried so hard to find them." Terjah's discouraged party of searchers had returned after a long 7-day fruitless search. "He needs to see we have them in custody."

"Terjah was called for befores ya woke, chil'. He's dare now for sure."

Raasah raised her head to search Hannah's face. She suddenly felt very alone and fearful in the growing whirlwind of hostility. "Please, Hannah, will you come with me?"

Hannah gently caressed Raasah's face in her pale knobby hands and nodded.

Raasah ran through the streets with Hannah's fingers tightly gripped in her own polished hand. Hannah was cursing something under her breath and breathing laboriously as they entered the plaza. Pushing their way through the thick assembly, they found themselves in the front of the crowd abut of the judges platform. The closeness of the frenzied crowd had ripped her veil from her head; hair had come loose from its plaits and now hung on her shoulders. Hannah fussed and muttered as she recouped the plaits and tried to rescue the tattered veil.

There were actually six prisoners, five men and one woman. They had been herded here with their hands shackled to their waists. Their feet were dirty and bleeding and they wore multiple abrasions on their bodies. Raasah was sure a small grey-bearded slave had a broken nose by its slight angle amid swollen bloodied cheeks; his arm was sliced red, flesh dangling. Nevertheless, despite all the damage done on him, Raasah was stunned to recognize him as Abram, slave of Mosiahah, the jewelry merchant. She knew him as a gentle, assiduous man. He was just working off his debt from a crop that failed. Raasah's grandmother often stopped by the little farm with warm loaves of bread and squares of cheese to check on the welfare of his frail wife. Abram and his wife were 'decent people', she remembered Marian saying one day as she packed food carefully in a small basket. 'They had just fallen on bad times....'

Neither did Raasah feel gladness and recompense as she explored the faces of the other five prisoners. They didn't look like murderers. They humbly stooped with the weight of the shackles. The thin ragged dark-skinned woman babbled silently as she leaned heavily on the thick tattooed arm of the tanned man to her right, her robe ripped immodestly displaying a bruised and torn knee. She slowly lifted her face. She also had been brutally beaten – both eyes swollen shut, her lips split but still forming unknown words. The four remaining men were Lamonite carriage bearers, muscular and lean. They were gagged but that didn't hide the bruising and abuse they had endured by their captors.

Raasah felt a surge of pity for these prisoners. She was suddenly relieved Abul was not among them. Hannah was saying over and over, "Oh, ma dear, dear. Oh, dear chil'," as she embraced Raasah's trembling shoulders. Raasah searched the masses for her brother. She did not know what she was supposed to do.

Someone in the crowd threw a rock at Abram, knocking him to the ground. Many other rocks and stones followed and the prisoners bent over so as to use their shackled arms to try to fend them off. A large youthful slave broke rank and somehow tore the gag from his mouth as he lunged towards Raasah. Her heart raced as she pressed herself into Hannah who wrapped her in a hug and drew her back against the crowd. The deep black gash over this man's eyes did not hide the fear – she knew that look well.

"We're innocent, innocent, girl!" he cried. He was on his knees so close Raasah could smell the dust, sweat, and blood upon his dirt-smeared skin. The crowd had hushed. "You've been deceived," he said bluntly, "living among murderersssss…."

A sharp hiss of air left his lips as his bloodied hands gripped the point of a spear that had penetrated out his bare chest. He crumpled forward onto the paved court. Zoric strode forward and stood victoriously over his prisoner's prostrated body. With a re-fined sandaled foot placed firmly on the lifeless form, he ruthlessly yanked the spear from its victim. The body twitched grotesquely and then was still.

"I will remove this scum from your tender presence, my love." Zoric had been the leader of this search party but, though they had been on the hunt for almost two weeks, he was surprisingly fresh and clean, his voice cheerful and spry. "No harm will come to you while I am here, sweet Raasah."

Raasah shuddered. She couldn't take her eyes off the sprawled limp body that would never speak again. She bit her lip, tasting her own blood. Her mind was replaying the hapless prisoner's last words, his final expression, and his last breath of air leaving his lungs while he clung to the bloody barb.

Hannah hugged her tighter. "Begone, youn' sir." She sidestepped into the crowd with Raasah pinned firmly to her side until they were just out of view of the dead prisoner. Raasah turned slowly and stared at Zoric standing proudly with spear in hand. His handsome young face was surpassed by his arrogance and self-importance. His normally extravagant robes and headgear were absent but his grooming had been well attended and his large gold earplugs shone out his vanity. Raasah deeply resented his insistent requests for betrothal and, as of this moment, she felt sickened at the very sight of him.

Terjah suddenly emerged and, gripping Zoric by the shoulder, spun him around to face him. "You didn't have to kill him! We need to question the prisoners."

"Question them…?" Zoric thrust his palm against Terjah's chest, pushing him away as if to dismiss him. He gestured to the crowd. "We want revenge! We want justice!"

Murmuring in the crowd increased and a few shouts repeated Zoric's call. A leather-clad escort was tying a limp Abram to a scourging pole. It was Tola, Zoric's friend and constant companion. "You want to ask questions, let's do it with the ends of a whip!" he bellowed. "Their blood must spill like that of our innocent massacred kin! They must feel our rage and hurt." He defiantly held the leather weapon high in his hand.

A shout mounted from the crowd. "Flog him! Flog him!"

"My son…! You barbaric…!" sobbed a middle-aged man, who then threw his portentous headgear to the ground and flung off his robe. Striding over and snatching the whip from Tola's hands, he cried in a wretched voice, "Your kind killed my son…." With his face tense with hatred and grief, he swung the whip at old Abram's back. Abram screamed as skin tore. The seized whip was a scourge with razor-sharp metal embedded in the leather ends. The blood and screams from Abram seemed to magnify the frenzy of the crowd as the nobleman whipped Abram over and over, faster and faster.

The shackled female fell to her knees, her puffy, grimy face chanting to the heavens.

"Heathen!" The soldier that spoke kicked her. "To your feet!"

Her pulsating chant became louder and louder. The armored lad punched her in the face with the hilt of his sword. Blood splattering from her nose and he kicked her in the stomach. Another citizen grabbed a pleading prisoner by his thick hair and dragged him into the mob. Others set upon him, punching and kicking the hapless prisoner.

Terjah was yelling, "Stop this madness. This is not justice! Stop!" but no one was listening. The crowd descended on the rest of the prisoners and enveloped them with screams and cursings and heartfelt sobs.

Hannah pulled Raasah back through the crowd away from the insanity. Raasah was numbed by the anger and hatred in the air. Though Terjah attempted to pull people back, there were too many of them. He was jostled and knocked aside.

Raasah looked back over toward Abram but, instead, spotted Tola on the steps of the justice building, a wide satisfied grin on his youthful face. He had not lost anyone in the massacre. He was not grieving. He was just... *just enjoying the spectacle of the senseless frenzy.* Zoric joined him. They looked very official, each clad in a similar kilt and light leather armor. Zoric gave his friend a firm pat on the back. He, too, had a wide grin on his face. They were two of a kind – *a contemptuous kind.* Turning, Zoric looked over his shoulder at the darkened arch of the civil building behind him. Raasah thought she saw a figure in the shadows but then it was gone.

Horrified, she searched the cursing, screaming swarm. *What is becoming of my people? How could this be happening in the safe confines of our city?* Her grandmother had been right. Revenge had an ugly face. What's more – it had an aura of evil about it!

Chapter 4

The Citizens of Ammonihah

The blood-stained pavers refused to be scrubbed clean. In the days that followed, the Grand Plaza was eerily vacant and those that did venture on it or were brazen enough to set up their wares, spoke most solemnly. Children were absent; laughter, if heard, sounded forced. There was an air of shame among the citizens – that is, among the decent citizens.

Zoric and his distasteful comrades were not among the solemn ones. Three days after witnessing this cruel scene, Raasah had seen Zoric snickering and joking with his comrades in Lahotite Lane as the reputable artisans abandoned their stalls. With the orphan boy as company, she was just returning with her purchase of spices when she had recognized Zoric's voice. Inquisitively, she peered around the corner at those lurking in the growing shadows. She had planned to turn and walk quickly away before she was discovered, but the boy (whom Raasah had come to call Little Brother) had stealthily slipped closer along the walls remaining unseen by the men in question. When Little Brother looked back at her, Raasah motioned to him to stay hidden. Now curiousity caught hold of her as she strained to see all who were there.

Though the shadows were deepening, Raasah recognized Tola, as well as, to her great surprise, the soldier that had killed the female prisoner. The latter was not in his military gear but she remembered the tight cropped beard and large nose adornments that had glittered in the morning light. His feet were clad with the pointed-toed sandals similar to his comrades. She was puzzled why she was drawn to his footwear. She noted the ornate beading that extended up his calf.

Raasah leaned against the wall just out-of-sight. Closing her eyes, she pictured the scene with the prisoners once more with a sudden quiver. She remembered this soldier kicking the defenseless woman, his foot hitting her in the stomach, his full armor.... *No, full armor included military footwear! This 'soldier' wore the footwear of a nobleman's son just as he was now.* Spying intently around the corner once again at the chunky young man, she realized that she had seen him with Zoric before. He was a son of the quarry owner. He was not a soldier at all. She strained to hear as the quarry son spoke.

"He is asking too many questions."

"All will be taken care of, Zeniff," Zoric said flippantly. "Now, tell me: how is your new fierce stone cutter? You're lucky he did not take your ear off."

"That bloody barbarian! The stalks and whip took a chunk of insolence out of him today. He says, 'I am Abul'," – Raasah's ears burned at the Cohite name – "and I say, 'You are Rat Poop'. He will answer to his new name. He will be tamed."

"Have they found any others?" another asked.

"If they haven't been killed, they will be far into the mountains or maimed and devoured by beasts."

"And thanks to Zeniff's babbling barbarian, you, Zoric, got your pretty prize home safe." Tola slapped Zoric on the back with a low laugh.

"And she will soon be the daughter of the most powerful woman in Ammonihah," Zoric added smugly.

"And you can give Zeniff lessons once you tame this arrogant daughter of Sablon," Tola snickered. Boisterous laughter erupted.

Raasah's finger nails dug into her palm as she realized she was now their subject. She spied around the corner for the boy and was glad to discover he was gone. She did not feel he should be hearing such talk.

"She's not your usual eager strumpet, is she?" another companion laughed. "Guess she is just too prudish for your excruciatingly unfunny luridness." There was a scuffle and then more laughter.

"Let us know if you need any assistance with your prize," Zeniff scoffed. "Your irresistible warped charm does not seem to be working on her. We would be pleased to each give her a turn and wear her down for you...." There was deep cackling and grunting in agreement.

"Don't concern yourselves, my pitiful pals," Zoric guffawed. "She will be my gracious courtesan begging to give me pleasure by the time I'm finished with her...!"

Anger coursed hot through her veins. Aware suddenly of footsteps plodding toward her, she gruffly gripped her pouch to her chest, hankered her shawl down on her head, and stormed toward her home.

"How dare they talk of me as a prize!" she muttered irately, ".....something to be tamed!" She stormed through a small group of boys coming out of the scribe's office, oblivious to causing one young fellow to stagger back out of her way.

"... his gracious courtesan – NEVER!!" she added indignant, almost shouting it and turning heads her way. Increasing her pace still more, her trembling hands held tight to her shawl under her chin.

By the time she arrived at the villa, her face was flushed with emotion and her heart pounding with exasperation. She was so hurt and embarrassed that she could not bring herself to tell anyone of the conversation she overheard. Hannah expressed her concern over Raasah's appearance but Raasah had dismissed it as over-exertion as she handed over the spices.

That night, as Raasah drifted off into fretful sleep, thoughts of Abul entered her mind. She wondered what he had to do with getting her 'home safe'. She relived the attack in her dreams again. This time, she saw Abul clearly above her as she blinked the fogginess from her vision. "Burshon, Burshon…." he whispered anxiously. His strong arms reassuringly supported her as she lay against him. Then suddenly she felt him wrenched away. Abul's face disappeared, being replaced by the dreaded masks. The latter were laughing at her. She struck at the concealed faces, waving her hands frantically.

In her frenzy, she woke with a start, her breath coming in gasps, but she was relieved that she had not awaken anyone else in the household. Bathed in the eerie light of the moon's orb, Raasah lay a trembling hand over her pounding heart, its beat echoing in her ears as she struggled to recall more details, more elements, leading up to the attack. She questioned it again: *How did Abul keep me from harm? Had he really whispered my pet name? …or am I just wanting to believe it was true? After all, Zeniff could have been speaking about another Abul.*

'Burshon' – oh, how she missed hearing Abul say it! She rose from her bed and, approaching the side table, retrieved her pathetic attempt at making a rubber ball, a.k.a. blob. For a reason she didn't understand yet, she still could not throw it away. She lay back in her bed; the rubber held tight against her chest. A tear eased itself out of the corner of her eye and moistened the thick locks that framed her face. She did not know if it was for Abul, for herself, or just out of frustration.

It was a relief to return the next week to the noise and bustle of classes where she would be forced to think of other things. Raasah thought Hannah had fussed way too much over her that morning but it, too, was a good distraction from the infuriating memories of that intercepted conversation in the lane. Hannah carefully adjusted a decorative comb in Raasah's hair and rummaged through a collection of other accessories, mumbling about colours and styles of "youn' peoples dese days".

Hannah had not always been this attentive. She had been the nanny when Raasah was younger who had been preoccupied with her pursuit of a male interest she hoped would cultivate into something comfortable and warm. The day came, though, when he no longer darkened Hannah's doorway. Her sadness converted to zealous devotion to Raasah and her upbringing, ardently trying to amend for any former neglect. The frustrating result of this extra attention was Raasah's difficulty in pursuing the frowned-upon unlady-like afternoons with Abul in the garden playing stick games and hop scotch or indulging in the art of imagination inspired by his stories – all of which she had dearly treasured.

Consequently, Raasah had long resented all this sudden

attention. The abrupt death of her father and the others, though, had changed her world as she had known it. With the additional loss of Abul, Raasah realized that Hannah's annoying fussing and nagging had actually become a comfort to her. Through the looking glass, Raasah observed this crusty, sometimes foul-mouthed woman. She was about the same age as her mother but 'with old skin', or so Raasah remembered thinking as a much younger child.

Raasah also realized how much she now relied on this fervent servant and felt terrible about giving her the fright she did on the day she met Little Brother. Hannah, with her red puffy eyes, had hugged her ever so tight when they had found her in the market. Raasah knew Hannah checked on her frequently in the darkness of the night, tenderly straightening her sheets around her face. Some mornings, before Raasah's grandmother could be disturbed, Hannah would be the one stroking her hand and reassuring her as Raasah awoke from her nightmare. She'd be saying, "Poor chil', restless and frettin' in you' sleep, you's is. I'ms here for ya."

So Raasah put up with the (wo)man-handling and primping each morning and it pleased her to know what great satisfaction Hannah got out of it. Hannah had become very significant in Raasah's life.

This morning, after (almost) inaudible cursing and the skillful twirls of the servant's long fingers, much of Raasah's dark hair was weaved with decorative combs and beads with ringlets crusading down her temples. Her silky gold gown and matching cloak flattered her young figure. To Hannah's frustration, though, Raasah insisted on wearing the same shell-inset jewelry everyday that her father had given her on that fated trip. The bracelets did emphasize her delicate wrists and ankles so Hannah indulged her and coordinated Raasah's clothes so as the latter would complement (or camouflage) them, as she did every morning now.

Before permitting Raasah to take her leave for her first official day back to classes, Hannah stepped back for an inspection of her charge, exclaiming, "Da suitors wills be fightin' dare's ways to you' feets!" Hannah's serious rosy face tipped to one side as she liberally smiled that crooked thin-lipped smile that endearingly dimpled her right cheek. Raasah smiled pleasantly back and bowed a gracious royal bow. Though she did not feel the least bit pretty or joyful, she did not want to offend Hannah who was trying so hard to cheer her up.

It had been four long weeks since 'Lamonhah Ridge' (as Raasah preferred to think of it in the far reaches of her mind) and, with all the life-changing events that had taken place and the transformations that had occurred inside herself, it seemed like another life-time since she had attended her classes of priestess instruction.

Her grandmother had insisted that Raasah be accompanied now when she went any distance from their villa. It was the protocol for any young lady of good status, and, being of marrying age, she had to look after her reputation. At least that was what Marian had said, but Raasah felt there was a lot left unsaid. In any event, Raasah did not want to give her grandmother any reason to worry, so she had convinced Hannah to let Little Brother be her escort to the Hall of Instruction. They hadn't gone far when it became obvious that Little Brother was anxious to be somewhere else, so, when she was out-of-sight of the villa, she had no problem persuading him that she would be alright and off he skipped. Slackening her pace, Raasah scrutinized the passing scenes as thoughts of the suggestive boorish talk of Zoric and his thugs tried to intrude in her mind.

The smells of the morning meals lingered in the cool of the morning, the excited voices of children seeped through the walls, and people from all walks of life were slowly materializing on the streets. Drawn by the delicious smell of freshly baked goods, she politely greeted the baker as he opened up his shop.

"Wa-ie, good sir."

The startled baker bowed low as he recognized her status. "Wa-ie, gracious lady," he stammered, then backed solidly into the door frame before bolting into the safety of his shop.

Raasah had not meant to cause him alarm but she smiled in spite of herself.

Soon, leaving the inviting smells behind her, Raasah froze as she heard a disturbance in the otherwise deserted Lahotite Lane, noted for its picturesque market of artisans during the day and its infamous lair for undesirables – *like Zoric* – at night. A single bedraggled socialite stumbled against a wall next to a now silent tavern. The blotchy, pouched face was vaguely familiar as she sought to see past the sunken, fleeting eyes.

It's the nobleman – the one that laid the deathly stripes across Abram's back! His head was bare as it had become that brutal day but the same hand that had held the whip now clutched a bottle of wine as he tried unsuccessfully to steady himself before slumping in a heap to the ground. All his finery were soiled and in disarray. Glassy-eyed, he looked up; a single tear streaked white down a smudged cheek. The misery Raasah beheld in those red-laced eyes was haunting and dark. A new tear formed and followed the same path down his cheek as he turned back to his bottle.

Marian had understood the road of heartache of a revengeful crowd. A great sadness filled Raasah's heart for this man who had lost more than a son now; sadness filled her for Abram and the other prisoners that had been shackled with him; sadness spilled over for all those who had lost someone they loved.... So much sadness – she walked numbly on, neither looking left or right.

Raasah circumvented the large plaza so as to avoid the site of vengeance. Eventually she stood in front of the Hall of Instruction. Fumbling with her bracelets, she reluctantly started her ascend up the stairs toward the massive arch that would give her entry to her morning class. A few paces from this entrance sitting erect against a pillar, was an unassuming man she recognized as one of the many beggars of Ammonihah. She paused and stared. The man, possibly sensing her presence, tilted his face up toward her, but she did not feel subconscious or hesitate from studying his face – for his useless eyes could not see her. Unlike most beggars of Ammonihah, his beard was neatly trimmed, his thick brown hair was crisply tied back from his weather-worn face, and he wore a clean tidy tunic. Again, unlike most beggars, there was a nobleness about him as he held his head high, as well as something appealing that she had not seen before.

Two elite socialites glanced in the disabled man's direction as they took a wide berth around him. Raasah was abruptly aware of how unfeeling, even cruel, the 'esteemed' people of Ammonihah could be and the plain disregard on their part of those in trying circumstances – so many people going out of their way to pretend they don't see them.

She, herself, had been more blind than this poor man before her. Raasah remembered how embarrassed she felt when her father took the time to visit with him. Even though this man could not be even as old as her father, Botholuem had referred to him as the

'Great Soldier'. He had explained that fate could have a way of altering one's course in life and the war had left this courageous skilled soldier blind and lame. Raasah remembered how her father would talk with him and listen to his stories and then casually wrap his hands around his to discretely deposit some money or other item in his palm before he rose to leave.

Raasah remembered being impatient with her father, not wanting to be near this 'pathetic'-looking man with the twisted leg and scarred eyes. Today, though, she looked at him more like her father had – as the heroic fighter that selflessly sought to protect her people. She saw the injustice of the retched way the citizens treated him after all his dedicated service. Shamefully she remembered the retched way she had regarded him.

Suddenly, the sight-less man raised his hand defensively. Two well-dressed youths pointed and jeered in his direction and then one of them shimmied quickly over to him. After waving one hand playful in front of the man's face, the boy gave the ex-soldier a swift kick, knocking his victim's donation cup over as he withdrew, spilling the precious few coins. Raasah bolted up the stairs.

"Young rogues!" she cried indignantly. "You are a disgrace to your family names!"

The 'rogues' both ran off as she knelt tentatively to right the cup and gathered the coins scattered about the steps. The beggar also swept his fingers in search along the stones. She noticed a fresh trickle of blood from a cut on his cheek, realizing now that the boys' hooliganism must have been preceded by a chucked stone or two.

"I'm so sorry," she said softly as she fumbled for the last coin. The beggar sat up tall again as if he was studying her.

"This is so kind of you, good miss," he replied graciously.

Humbled by the undeserved respect he extended her, Raasah quickly dropped the remaining coin in his cup and hastened away.

Waiting just inside the massive arch were two fellow students from Raasah's classes. They were also her long-time friends. Isobel, tall, shapely, and stern-faced, had all the airs and grace of a young woman of nobility. She looked older than her 15 years and was equally opinionated beyond her years. No matter how good friends they had been since their childhood, Raasah loathed the way Isobel looked down her nose at her whenever Raasah voiced an opinion that differed from hers. She saw that look now, though they had not spoken one word to each other for weeks….

Jaona stepped up next to Isobel. Jaona was petite, very pretty in a childish way, and she knew how to use her big brown eyes and generous pouty lips to get what she wanted, especially from her father. Her father spoiled her with exotic dresses made by the most expert seamstresses and custom jewelry of the most wondrous colours that she loved to show off. Jaona was bubbly and flirty, the complete opposite to Isobel, but, nevertheless, she hung on every dogmatic word Isobel uttered, trying hard to look as serious as she could when occasion required it… and today seemed to one of those occasions as they both stood staring at Raasah like she had commit some horrific deed.

"Raasah, what were you doing with that revolting beggar?" Isobel's sharp tone stung her.

"Those boys, they…."

"Raasah, what's the matter with you?" Isobel exclaimed. "You were having a conversation with him!"

Gaining courage and conviction, Raasah straightened and looked directly at the girls. "He used to be a great soldier, you know," she said in her most assertive voice but her eyes gave away her hesitancy. She continued with more fervency. "He was willing to give his life to defeat the Lamonites who were attacking our city!"

"But look at him, Raasah," Isobel gestured past her, sternly shaking her head. "He is useless now and filthy. It would have been better if he had died!"

"Isobel, that's so callous!" Raasah gasped in a hushed voice as she glanced back at the beggar. He didn't appear to have heard the comment.

Jaona put a gentle arm on Raasah. "Well, the gods certainly have not been compassionate to the 'Great Soldier'. Maybe death would have been much kinder for him." Jaona said it with such sincerity and gentleness that Raasah was pacified despite herself. Jaona did have the gift to smooth over hard words that Isobel would let drip from her perfectly painted lips.

"You heard about that old fowler from your father's caravan," Jaona continued softly; it was not a question. Raasah looked sharply at both girls.

"Yea, yea. A stubborn old man – refuses to die. What does he think he will gain staying alive in his broken-down body?" Isobel's tone is decisive and unfeeling. "I don't understand what all the fuss is about healing a pathetic old man."

Raasah, stunned, was momentarily not cognizant of Isobel's disregard for his life. "There were others … that survived like me?" she stammered.

"Oh, yea," said Jaona, gently squeezing her arm, "but the fowler was not as lucky as you. He sustained very serious injuries and there is little chance he will survive. The baby was untouched, though, and relatives have already taken him home with them to the city of Melek."

"We must hurry or we will be late for class." Isobel said impatiently. "Daunting Deborah will have our heads."

"Yea, our heads," Jaona agreed, smiling and linking her arm into Raasah's to prod her after the retreating Isobel.

Raasah let herself be lugged along, past the rigid guards and through the gate that admitted the girls into the extensive fragrant courtyard. Surrounding the luscious gardens, the many substantial entrances, hallways, and stairways summoned the girls into the depths of the towering ziggurat.

Raasah's mind was in a whirl as she passed the many fine sculptures and impeccably carved obelisks among the carefully attended plants. Just when she had decided to accept she would never really know what happened on that dreadful night, just when her nightmares had quieted and she had some peaceful sleeps, she now learned that there were other survivors and one of which may have the answers she yearned for. And now she had more questions. *Why hadn't anyone told me that there were others that survived? Would the old fowler recover? Did he know who was responsible for the death of her father and others on Lamonhah Ridge?* She barely registered the droning voice of Jaona gossiping about an 'odd' new student as they passed through the decorative limestone hall toward her first class of the day: Altar Duties and Rituals.

Chapter 5

A Survivor

Raasah and her friends were all in their fourth year of studies at this elite Hall of Instruction and, this year, all three of them had been admitted to the advanced priestess training and all the classes that it entailed. Because Raasah had missed a good portion of the studies, Jaona had come by many times with some of her deficient notes, but not much information that was academically useful. What Jaona was not deficient on was chatty news about their classmates that Raasah tolerated to be polite while her mind was flittering around disturbing memories and past events.

"Now this note here explains the ritual of the harvest.... Did you know that Isobel's mother is preparing herself for advancement to high priesthood and the royal court...? Can you read my notes? She was talking so fast." and so Jaona's befuddled dialogue had droned in and out of Raasah's consciousness. "Oh, and that note – well, I was running out of space, so the rest of it is... somewhere.... Did I tell you about this odd new girl...?"

When she did indeed listen to her friend's disconnected interpretation of the lessons, Raasah actually wonder how Jaona could possibly pass her classes. Thankfully, Raasah's mother had sent study matter over by palace courier in the last week that had been much more helpful. It would have been even more helpful if her mother had accompanied the parchments and codices but the delivery method had not surprised her. In fact, she even found herself grateful that her mother had taken the time to consider Raasah's studies at all with all the duties she was responsible for at the temple.

Now, in this, Raasah's first class since her long absenteeism, Teacher Deborah was explaining protocol of sacrifice offering, emphasizing the importance of only the elite attending the alter of the Sun Temple. Raasah's thoughts once more were straying. She was thinking of the orphans and other unfortunate people that her father and her grandmother took time for, wondering what their stories were, coupled with the overwhelming realization that they were also worthwhile and important in the omnipotent plan of life – her friends were wrong about the soldier! She had had many days and sleepless nights to reflect on what she believed and where her values were since her father died and she was ashamed to think how wrong she had been about so many things.

"Why?" Raasah asked suddenly. The entire class turned to gape at her. Silence enveloped the room as the teacher composed herself and then glared.

"Why what?" Teacher Deborah asked stridently through clutched teeth.

Raasah was now aware that all the students were staring, some nervously fidgeting and others just gazing open-mouthed. She hesitated, caught her breath and then, steeling herself, she expounded, "Why can't ALL our deserving citizens attend this altar and worship?" Raasah's voice was surprisingly forthright even to her!

"Are you questioning the priesthood authority, the Holy Temple sacred instructions...?" Teacher Deborah snapped.

"I just don't understand…" Raasah pleaded tenaciously but the teacher continued darkly with gnashing of teeth.

"Young lady, you have been absent for a long time and been through a horrific tragedy. So, for your mother's sake, I will disregard this impertinent behavior."

"But, with all respect, my teacher, there are many stories of poor obscure youth that became great prophets and…."

Colour rose to Deborah's cheeks and her left eye twitched in a most comical manner, but no one dare even snicker. "I never… if ever… this is blasphemy!" the flustered teacher bellowed. "No one has ever questioned the practices of the temple in MY class…."

"But, Good teacher, I meant…."

"Raasah, daughter of Sablon, you will not speak another word but you will see me after class. I never…!!" Deborah cupped her shaking hands in front of her and, with long strides, approached the front of the class, eye still twitching and teeth grinding as she swung around. The students shuffled awkwardly in their seats, except for Jaona. She caught Raasah's eye briefly, trying hard to squash a grin, making a sour face in the effort. Teacher Deborah slapped a rod heavily on her desk, startling rigid compliance focused toward the front. "The class will get out their potshards[13] and pens to take notes."

A few low moans were heard as the girls readied themselves for the tedious work of transcribing. Soon all that was heard was the scratch of 17 pens as the teacher, in a flat monotone voice, listed dress codes and protocol as the girls wrote.

ᛞ

History class was held in the adjacent Palace of Greater Learning
on the third level from which the girls had an impressive view of
the Acropolis of the Moon. Scrolls secured in tubes were slotted
on shelves around the room. A detailed motif of the journey from
the old country to this Land-of-Plenty trimmed the walls along the
ceiling. Intricate tapestries of historical figures hung from these
same stone walls. There were colourful images of their first earthly
parents walking in a garden paradise, an ancient prophet with the
serpent staff healing the people, and, of course, Nephi, their people's namesake, holding his sword up triumphantly overlooking a
field of battle. The teacher paced among the students as she talked,
involving and encouraging class participation as she weaved details
of a harsh ruler from a sparse distant land that had enslaved their
ancestors.

Teacher Martha, a handsome woman in her own fashion, was
foremost an engaging instructor, who spoke with such clarity that
her recount of past events would play vividly across Raasah's mind.
Unpretentious but unmistakably principled, she treated all her students fairly but, nevertheless, sternly when needed. She loved to
give her students a challenge and enthusiastically encouraged de-
bates and discussions on the day's topics. She was, without a doubt,
Raasah's favourite teacher but, even so, as Martha elaborated about
the harsh treatment of their people many centuries ago, Raasah's
thoughts were, as was typical these days, somewhere else.

Raasah had been late for class having had to stay behind after
the Altar Duties & Rituals class. More composed, Teacher Deborah
had lectured Raasah about respect and the folly of sedition. 'If
it wasn't for the high respect I hold for your mother....' she had

emphasized, 'I would have to consider your remarks to be of a reviler, one needing purging with the scourge.'

She had gone on to say that maybe Raasah was not ready to go back to her studies and that this may have to be discussed further. Finally she had cautioned, 'Raasah, if I hear anymore antagonizing remarks from you in MY class... I will not be responsible for the outcome.'

Raasah had shrunk back as if she was slapped. Any further debate on the matter that she may have wanted to pursue dissipated about mid lecture with the mention of the merciless scourge. Raasah had shivered and said nothing.

Now, seated in her second class of the day, Raasah's gaze kept returning to the sacred roofcomb atop of the Acropolis growing brighter as the sun reached its midday high. The light illuminated the wondrous stucco reliefs depicting the Goddess Mother renewing life through new growth and birth. The complexities and disappointments of life were absent from this portrayal – *portrayal, betrayal....*

"What did our slaves have to do with the attack?" she mouthed silently. *"How had Abul helped Zoric bring me home safe?"*

The teacher dismissed the class with a clap of her hands, snapping Raasah back to the present. Jaona practically dragged Raasah from the class to the gardens where servants had set up a wide selection of both fresh fruit and streaming hot food for the students' midday meal. Once under a darkened arch furthest from the tables and after a quick glance about to ensure their privacy, Jaona couldn't contain her curiosity any longer.

"What did Daunting Deborah have to say?"

"Obviously nothing very terrible," Isobel had come up quietly from behind – she had that 'down-her-nose' look again.

"I would have loved to be a bug on HER wall!" Jaona chatted. "The look on Daunting Deborah's face, the twitching eye, she looked like a puppet ready to fly apart…. I have never seen her so speechless. Oh, I would have died if I had to face HER… alone! What did she say?"

"Actually she…," Raasah swallowed remembering vividly the threatened skin-slicing scourge. She did not believe there was a more debilitating or painful torture and a second shiver crusaded down her spine. She could have closed her eyes and seen clearly Abram's torn back.

"What were you thinking to question such a thing?" Jaona was having a rare serious moment as brief as it was, for a mischievous grin formed across her face. "Did you have to plead for your life?"

"Raasah has the right parent," Isobel said sardonically. "The reputable Deborah wouldn't dare implicate the daughter of the soon-to-be High Priestess of the Royal Court."

Raasah gaped at Isobel's up-turned face. Her mother, Sablon, appointed to the royal court? Her head spun with even more questions. She opened her mouth but she didn't know where to start. *Why hadn't Mother said anything to me?*

"I … I….." Before Raasah could finish her thought, Isobel made a theatrical flair of her robes and, with a sigh a mother would give to a disobedient child, she melted into the crowd of students milling about the colourful tables of food.

"Oh, never mind her," Jaona said. "She's just miffed that HER mother wasn't chosen. And her mother, well, Priestess Nora, she did have sonority over YOUR mother, and, well, Nora is NOT happy – GOOD GRACIOUS! – she is fit to dismember anyone who crosses her path right now!! She tossed poor little Mark down the stairs when she marched by him."

Mark was the young timid lad that cleaned and emptied the ash from the Palenia altars each evening. Jaona lowered her voice:

"Nora was shrilling with seething remarks as she approached Darius as if he was a… a loathsome dung-covered swine feeder! Darius, Supreme High Priest of the Palenia Temple. What was she thinking...?" Jaona shook her head slowly and thoughtfully, another brief serious moment.

"Nora had always been resentful of that boy getting this apprenticeship at the temple, so seeing him just then did not help her disposition." Raasah realized that Jaona was now talking about Mark. "These days it is who you know or whose blood runs in your veins that get you good positions. It's certainly not Mark's blood line that secured this temple job. I'm not sure who the family knows..... I mean, the father is just an animal keeper. How could such a man of low position be....? Anyway, the pathetic lad just coward against the stairs where he fell while Nora cursed Darius and said things.... She just screamed things, about promises and oaths broken. Oh, she said some disturbing things, terrible things. Well, everyone's talking about it. She ranted and raved so loud that I wouldn't have been surprised if she had risen the dead!"

"When did this happen? My mother never told me."

"The counsel only decided yesterday. It will be announced on the Sabbath at the temple. We weren't supposed to know till then.

I'm sure your mother was going to tell you before the announce-ment," Jaona patted Raasah on the arm, "but Nora did her own announcing! It WAS understood that Nora was next in line for the position but …. Oh," Jaona grimaced, "she was in such a rage! She cleared the preparation table. Incense and candles were scattered everywhere. I was there. I helped Mark up. He was trembling so hard he could barely stand. Nora demanded to see the prophet, Esrom. She accused Sablon of sedu…." Jaona stopped mid word and looked hesitantly at Raasah. More quietly, she finished, "well, terrible things, just terrible things…."

Raasah felt light-headed. "I'm sorry, Jaona. Please tell Teacher Prisca I'm not well and won't be attending dance class this afternoon."

"Raasah, I didn't mean to upset you," Jaona reached for Raasah's hand.

Raasah took Jaona's hand in both of hers. "I know you would never mean to hurt me." She released Jaona's hand. "I have to go." Before Jaona could respond, Raasah walked briskly across the courtyard.

About midway, a brazen surly-faced girl marched directly in her path. Three other girls blocked all attempts to go around. Raasah focused on the instigator. The intense dark-eyed troublemaker was Zoric's sister, Ruth. She had been a thorn in Raasah's side since Zoric started taking the unwanted interest in her three years earlier.

"I am not in the mood, Ruth." Raasah gritted her teeth.

Ruth leaned toward her, hand on her hip, a sneer on her face. "So, you can't get enough attention from my brother, so you make a spectacle of yourself in Miss Deborah's class! You think you are better than the rest of us?"

"Ruth, I don't have time for this!"

"It's not enough to be the daughter of the most powerful woman in all of Ammonihah…"

Raasah froze abruptly. "What did you say?"

"Oh, you think we should bow to you now?" she sneered. "Oh, shunned embarrassing daughter of the most powerful high priestess…"

The most powerful woman in Ammonihah – that's what he had said…. Raasah recalled Zoric's words in the lane: 'She – I! – will be the daughter of the most powerful woman in Ammonihah.' So this is what he had meant! But he had said this almost two weeks ago. How had he known so far in advance?

Ruth persisted her taunting. "Yea, your mother may be powerful but you are a desperate, sniffling…."

With no pre-thought, with unbelievable force, Raasah open-handedly knocked Ruth off her feet, depositing her into a small pond among the flowers. Ruth's books and shards flew from her arms, water- and plant-bound. Her mousy-brown braids were no longer wrapped gracefully around her head but now hung dripping and plastered about her horrified face. With a squeal, she flung a tiny water snake that had slithered upon her arm while her useless gaping cohorts stood as if suddenly they had grown roots.

Raasah, both surprised and pleased with herself, peered down at her drenched mocker. "You are a sucking leech! The pond is befitting for you…. I have to go." Raasah breezed past the gathering spectators toward the Priestess Preparation Rooms.

Though shaded from the midday sun, the oiled honey-brown of Sablon's skin glistened as she lay naked on the raised fur-lined platform nestled in the flowering enclosure of Porahah. Light shimmered off the east stucco walls reflecting comforting heat as the skillful hands of the slim masseuse worked the muscles of her lower back.

Though it would not happen today, her strict routine that would have followed would have had her go down to soak her sculptured body in the bubbling mud pool, followed by a long relaxing rinse in the warm sulfur spring, both considered sacred gifts from the Goddess Oluffa to the temple priestesses. There were a dozen personal rituals Sablon carefully performed each day and those around her learn quickly not to disturb her during them or face her wrath.

As a child, Raasah had admired her mother and enjoyed the precious time she had with her as she learned simple sacred rituals and knowledge of the priestess craft. Always awed by her mother's grace and beauty, Raasah feared she would never aspire to her mother's standards. Feeling insignificant in her shadow, Raasah soaked in Sablon's every word when in her attendance.

By age eleven, Raasah had become a student of priestess craft, as her mother before her, and her mother before her…. Raasah always studied hard and was an inquisitive student. In fact, so much so, that she had previously been cautioned about asking too many questions and taking up class time, but her two close friends mostly teased her good-naturedly about it – until today.

The masseuse reached for a soft thin robe and laid it upon the smooth shoulders of her mother. Gracefully adjusting herself to a sitting position, Sablon accepted a golden goblet from the masseuse, which she drew delicately to her full lips. Even without makeup, she was a beautiful woman.

Raasah anxiously waited for her escort to announce her presence. The blue-robed doorkeeper parted the hanging beads, bowing low, her many strands of chains and bracelets tingling softly in the stillness.

"Gracious Priestess, your daughter respectfully requests an audience."

"Wa-ie, Mei-wa-ni." Raasah timorously greeted her mother as she stepped into view.

"Du-ba-ni!" Sablon declared pleasantly. She had endowed this heartfelt name upon Raasah when she was tiny, an endearing phrase that meant 'my precious one', but it had been a long time since Raasah had heard it and was comforted by it. "Come closer," Sablon bade. Her voice was smooth, deep, and soft, a sexy voice that made men take notice, which had often bothered Raasah for her father's sake, but she had never blamed her mother for all the attention men regularly bestowed on her. 'Sometimes gifts from the Creator can also be a challenge on earth' her grandmother had explained to her.

Sablon's long firm legs revealed themselves briefly as she stood tall and shapely in contrast to the slim plain figure of Maachah, the masseuse. *Her mother seemed to handle her challenge very well,* Raasah mused absently. Sablon smoothed her dark mane off her shoulders and, with a wave of her hand, dismissed the young women.

Raasah gazed upon this distinguished priestess, her mother, who would soon hold the most powerful position a woman could acquire in the great land. Raasah had not seen much of her mother since the fated trip. Raasah had found her main solace with her grandmother. In fact, Raasah believed she had always venerated Grandmother Marian in a much warmer way than her mother, as much as she had wanted it different. Raasah did love her mother, but, especially of late and with this sudden announcement of royal appointment, she was perplexed about her relationship with her mother and really needed some clarification.

Sablon led her daughter leisurely over to a cushioned set of seats surrounded by luscious orchids – the aroma sweet and delicate. The scene was perfect for having an intimate mother-daughter moment. To make the moment perfect, Raasah longed for her mother to lovingly envelope her hands into her own to distill her apprehension, but, instead, Sablon was aloof, inquiring her about her health.

"Marian spoke to me of the fright you gave her when you took that early morning stroll," Sablon said. "One with station should take more care."

Sleep-deprived and grief-stricken, it had not occurred to her the alarm it would cause anyone then to find her room empty and Raasah had deep remorse for this – though she did not regret meeting Little Brother. "I am sorry, Mei-wa-ni, but I have endeavored to make it right with Mei-wa-na."

"Look at you," Sablon chastened. "You must take better care of yourself. Ashen skin, unkempt nails. A personal masseuse, yea, to tone your body. I should talk to your groomer...."

"Hannah does try her best."

"Hannah, yea, yea," she said absently, "and your hair..." Sablon fingered the rich dark locks at Raasah's forehead, lifting a stray curl slowly and twisting it in between her polished fingers. How Raasah had longed to have those fine fair fingers gently dry her tears since the dreaded day or to have her smooth arms hold her tight as she cried! Raasah fought to stay composed. Besides, she had important things to discuss with her.

"My daughter, aren't you supposed to be in classes now?"

"Honourable mother, I hear of a fowler that survived that night….." Raasah began.

Sablon stiffened, slowly releasing the lock of hair in her hand.

"He may be able to tell us who is responsible for the attack," Raasah continued. "I don't think it was the slaves…."

A shuffle of footsteps drew their attention to where Raasah had entered. Frustrated, Raasah watched as a temple attendee parted the beads and, upon approaching, bowed respectably to the seated pair.

"Hadad," Sablon said sternly, "do you bring me some news?" It appeared her mother was expecting a message.

"Priestess Sablon, I beseech you. Thy presence is requested by the Supreme Darius at mid-afternoon dial." This was no doubt the Darius that Nora had confronted last night in her fury. In addition to his position of Supreme High Priest, he was also Chief Judge. Next to Governor Antionah and the Prophet Esrom, Darius was a most powerful individual and most probably the one responsible for Sablon's advancement in the priesthood. He often summoned her to officiate at important ceremonies. Also, often with little no-tice, Sablon had always complied, though she resented to be rushed for anyone.

"What reply shall I bring Most High Priest?" the girl asked.

Raasah looked to her mother. Sablon grimaced ever so slightly, but recovered almost instantaneously, pasting on a smile.

"Tell Priest Darius that I will graciously attend promptly as requested," she replied genially. Once the temple worker had withdrawn, though, her temperament took a complete turn-about. Sablon stood abruptly.

"Maachah, my robes!" Sablon commanded. As if her masseuse had read her mind, she was already rushing forward with an elegant feather embroiled gown and purple robes. Raasah looked over to the sundial, which was in its place of honour where the movement of the sun left the story of its sky travel each day. There was still generous time till mid-afternoon.

"Please, mother, may I have just a few moments with you?" Raasah said softly but Sablon was snapping orders to Maachah and gave no response to Raasah's appeal. Raasah realized that it would be futile to pursue any discussion with her now and feared her mother's disapproval as much as she wanted some answers. Raasah rose to her feet, drawing attention to her mother momentarily.

"Daughter (*not 'Du-ba-ni'*), we shall continue our visit on a quiet evening in a few days hence." With a whisk of gowns, Sablon turned and flowed into the robing room with Maachah scurrying behind her.

Despite herself, for the first time in days, a tear slid down Raasah's cheek. She had wanted to confirm with her mother about the royal appointment, she wanted to ask about the surviving fowler, she wanted to discuss orphans and the needy, she wanted to understand her mother and who she was….. AND she wanted her mother to tell her everything would be alright!

Raasah retreated to the upper garden terrace where the mystic cloud-ringed peak of Oluffa displayed itself over the cityscape, the sun reflecting a brilliant glow on its misty top. Only four years earlier, an angry Oluffa had lit the night sky with a fiery glow, spilling like blood down its sides – its sentinel mist filled with hot ash had descended on the city, threatening to choke the very life out of the people. In fear, the good citizens of Ammonihah had returned to their neglected temples, entreating the priestess elite to supplement to the gods, to Oluffa, on their behalf. It had been a religious revival and her mother had blossomed with the resurgence of honour and respect extended the female priesthood.

To this day, Oluffa still occasionally rumbled and coughed dark mists into the sky, as if to remind the people what an angry god can do. *Had Oluffa been the one to tear my mother from me? Had I the right to resent my mother's service to our gods?*

Ashamed at these thoughts, Raasah let a second tear slowly escape and she turned away from the sacred mountain, now tranquil and eerily beautiful against the afternoon sun. Numbly, she exited Porahah and wandered silently out to the street.

That night, she slept to dream that terrible dream again.

---

13 *Potshards: large broken pieces of pottery used to practice writing on or taking notes – a common practice before the first century as there was rarely a shortage of pottery that had broken or become cracked and needed to be replaced. Parchment paper was expensive and reserved for good final copies that would be stored. Harder substances, such as metal or clay, were time-consuming, expensive, and saved for historical or other important writings that needed preserving for future reference.*

Chapter 6

The Fowler

Though she still had brief interludes of her nightmare, Raasah could usually awaken herself without screaming or crying. She had returned to a semblance of her everyday activities and responsibilities. The rainy season was upon them. Raasah listened to the last drops of the downpour patter to the pavement outside the Hall of Instruction as she tried to ignore the dagger looks coming from Ruth across the classroom.

Raasah did not question anything in her classes now. Whenever she got the urge to voice any concerns or inquiries regarding practices in the temple or about any other lesson material, she would just picture the scourge with its leather thongs – then think of poor Abram. Raasah wondered what evil minds could have thought up cruel deterrents such as this.

Standing with the other students as they practiced the sacrificial hymn, Raasah did her unenthusiastic imitation of active participation each time the teacher bore down a glare in her direction. Raasah could not concentrate on the words. Anxious for the class to end, she kept sneaking fleeting looks at the doorway to the shadows of the sun's passing in an effort to will its movements faster. As the students concluded their song and settled noisily back into their seats, Raasah mechanically followed suit.

"That will do, girls," Teacher Deborah said briskly. "Pack up your materials and we will see you next week. Know your verse recitals for the sin offering." There was a low moan from the class. Slowly, as the girls deposited their writing materials in their satchels, they began to discussing weekend plans and the mood changed.

Riphlia, a popular student, separated herself from a group of giggly girls and stepped in front of Ruth. "Hey, Leech-lips," she said, "sucking dinner at your favourite pond tonight?" Her friends burst out in laughter. Ruth swung a hateful glare first at her taunter and then at Raasah. This was so untypical of Riphlia to be confrontational. As a direct descendent of Ammonihah, their city's founder, her family was highly esteemed among the elite and she, herself, was self-assured and well-spoken. Riphlia had no reason to go out of her way to insult anyone, though she had never made any pretense of her dislike of Ruth. The opportunity that presented itself must have been too much for Riphlia to resist.

Raasah cringed. The last thing she had wanted was to encourage animosity and she especially did not want to draw more attention to herself from Zoric's family. Ruth shot Raasah the death-glare before she linked arms with one of her loyal cohorts and hurriedly brushed by.

"Come on, Raasah. Let's get out of here while the rain has stopped!" Jaona prompted as she turned with Isobel toward the door. Glancing back to the front of the class, Raasah saw Deborah peering stone-faced over her desk at her. Flustered, Raasah fumbled under her chair for her satchel, coming up empty-handed.

"It's here," a timid voice indicated. This was the girl who silently occupied a desk in the back of the room. There was nothing noteworthy about her. She was thin, not overly pretty, with little makeup – anomalous of her station. Her clothing was not pretentious either. As usual, she was not wearing any adornments except for a modest gold medallion. Giving Raasah a weak smile, she extended the satchel towards her. "It must have gotten kicked back," she said.

"Thank you," Raasah returned the smile as she reached for the bag.

The girl's smile gave her heart-shaped face an attractive glow, a frame of brown curly hair defining her soft features. There was a hint of freckles on her nose and her deep brown eyes laughed with her smile.

"You are new here, aren't you?" Raasah asked politely.

"Yea, I moved here from Zarahemla when my mother remarried. We've been here about five weeks now." The girl looked down at her hands. "My name is Ada."

"Welcome to Ammonihah, Ada. My name is Raasah." She started placing her potshards into her bag.

"I know..... I am so sorry about your father."

A warmth filled Raasah's face.

"That other day..." Ada continued quickly, no doubt to dispel the awkwardness of the moment. She glanced up to where Teacher Deborah had exited the room and lowered her soft voice even more. "...I mean, I, too, have wondered why.... You know... only certain people are allowed to worship at the main temple. I wanted to say something but I am not as brave as you. My teachers in Zarahemla taught...."

"Raasah, are you coming?" It was Jaona with Isobel at the door. Ada resumed her customary downcast face. "It was good to meet you," Ada said weakly and she hurried off.

The three friends walked together, followed closely by two male attendants. Suddenly, Isobel spoke. "Raasah, the company you keep these days…. Why would you talk to HER?"

Jaona expanded, "Don't you realize WHO she is?"

"Her name is Ada," Raasah stated, puzzled.

"She is the daughter of Darius' wife, who was the wife of his deceased brother." Taking much pleasure in gossiping, Jaona continued. "I told you about her. This girl is so different. Don't know much of anything about her father. Darius is trying to make something of her but she has become an embarrassment to the family."

"I don't remember you…."

"That girl is not someone to be seen with," Isobel stated bluntly.

"THAT GIRL has a name," Raasah replied irritatingly.

"Yea, … Ada, isn't it? Even that is not a proper Nephite name. My mother said she will be the downfall to anyone who associates with her. I am surprised Darius doesn't put her away. He can't let her tarnish his esteemed position in the temple."

"What could she possibly have to say to you, Raasah?" Jaona asked sincerely.

"She mentioned the day I questioned Teacher Deborah about the alter worship…."

"She's a trouble-maker, Raasah," Jaona warned. "One of these days, she will get Old Deborah's eye a twitching so bad it'll pop out on the floor."

"And roll right across your path," Isobel added hauntingly.

"Oh, that could not be good…." Jaona tried to look serious but she couldn't keep a straight face and she broke down in laughter with Isobel following right after.

It was good to see her two friends laugh. Raasah had to smile as well at the mental image of this evil-glaring eyeball rolling about but then she had to ask, "Haven't you ever wondered why all of Ammonihah's citizens cannot worship together?"

The laughter stopped abruptly. Isobel went ridged. "What is WRONG with you, Raasah? You must have bumped your head harder than they thought."

"Dear friend," Jaona said soothingly, "How can you ask?"

"Poor station doesn't deserve the same," Isobel spoke slowly, like she was speaking to a toddler.

Jaona looked from an expressionless Isobel to the questioning Raasah. "They are just not valued as much, of course. I mean, Raasah, ….the Lord did make them poor," Jaona expounded.

"And possibly some that marry into the elite, like THAT GIRL, shouldn't be allowed either." Isobel was angry. She turned in a flap and strode off. Her attendant meandered slowly in the direction of his charge, determined to keep her in his sight but not anxious to attend too closely.

"Oh, Raasah. You've gone and done it again," Jaona reprimanded. "You've got to watch yourself. These days one must be mindful of who you are seen with and what you say. Remember!" With that, Jaona rushed off after Isobel, her own attendant close behind.

Raasah stood in the middle of the lane, everyday citizens walking around her. Since she had come back, nothing seemed the same. She didn't know where she belonged or what she should believe. She felt isolated and alone in the midst of a throng of people.

Looking around at Ammonihah and its people, it was like she had never been there before. She heard harmonized singing of two rather round women in a pottery shop and heard an elderly lady expanding her wisdom of weaving to an attentive young woman. She saw a waif of a boy begging for a loaf of bread from a cross double-chinned baker and she saw.... Chemish, in his dusty sweaty work clothes step out of a busy lane as he tied his money pooch onto his belt. Raasah's heart did a skip seeing the young man again and, in her preoccupation, a group of giddy, playful girls accidently knocked her satchel from her shoulder as they skipped by. In dismay, she realized that, in her hurry to leave with her friends, she had not secured its clasp. Its contents spilled out onto the ground.

Crouching, Raasah was anxious to snatch up the scattered shards before they got kicked aside by the foot traffic. She did not want to feel the wrath of Deborah for not having her study material next week. One of the shards had come to rest a couple of steps away in a miniature puddle. She shifted towards the shard, but a large calloused hand retrieved it first and extended it out to her. Raasah looked up slowly.

"This must be yours," Chemish said with a warm smile. Speech seemed to have left her. As Raasah wrestled to regain her poise, to her disbelief, Zoric appeared. Now, instead of feeling alone, she felt overwhelmed!

Zoric grabbed the shard from Chemish and, with a manicured hand to Chemish's worn soiled tunic, he pushed Chemish back. Zoric was donned in extravagant jewelry and his hair was plaited back under his pompous hat that matched his robe. Zoric was the complete opposite of Chemish in all ways imaginable.

"This fine lady does not need the help of a common labourer

and trouble-maker," Zoric said importantly and shoved Chemish a second time, but Chemish held his ground this time.

Tola was right beside Zoric, an evil smile on his face and polished ringed hands on his hips. He was dressed similar to Zoric, which seemed to be a pattern of these two. Despite the costly attired and facial paint, though, Chemish looked far more handsome than either one of them. Tola slugged Chemish on the shoulder which turned him slightly toward his abuser as Zoric possessively slipped his arm around Raasah. Raasah shrunk from his heavily perfumed body.

"Stop it! Just stop it!" Raasah shouted, slightly louder than she intended. She shrugged off his embrace and snatched the shard back from Zoric. "You're a brute! Get your hands off my things!" As she turned, she glanced at Chemish who gave her a weak smile. Then she saw Jaona. Her friend touched her arm tenderly as Raasah hastened away from the middle of the causeway.

Expecting Jaona to follow, Raasah was shocked to hear her friend apologizing to Zoric for her. Angrily, Raasah swung around in time to see Tola wink at Jaona who, in turn, giggled, fluttering her big brown eyes, before skipping over to join Raasah. Chemish, now several paces down the causeway, slowly turned, smiling his wonderful smile and then disappearing through the sea of bodies.

"There is no doubt something is seriously wrong with you!" Jaona gasped quietly. "Zoric is an exceptional suitor. What are you thinking? One might almost believe you had some feelings for that carpenter's son."

Raasah, finding herself still looking in the direction Chemish had taken, whipped around to face her friend.

"I don't know what you mean," she said as nonchalantly as possible.

"You do! You do have feelings for him! Oh, Raasah," the motherly side of Jaona was coming out.

"I didn't say…." It seemed Raasah was not meant to finish a lot of sentences these days when it came to Jaona.

"He is very bad news," Jaona continues. "What is going on with you? Haven't you heard? The carpenter's family has befriended a controversial stranger in the city whom his kin has taken in." Jaona lowered her voice to whisper. "I warned you how important it is to keep the right company. The wrong company will cause all kinds of problems. This would not be good for you or your family. You must be careful."

Jaona looked where Zoric and Tola had been. "Now, Zoric, well, he is the right kind of company. He and his friends have the right families and associations to make life easy and grand – not like that carpenter. You know, I hear that carpenter family has stupid thoughts, probably doing spells in the back of their wood shop. Eerie lights sometimes have been spied from their dirty little abode." Jaona lowered her voice again. "Isobel said the family spoke against the priests. Oh, Raasah, he is not someone you should be seen with."

"Jaona…," Raasah protested gently, for she knew Jaona's concern was heartfelt – possibly misguided, but sincere.

Jaona gripped both of Raasah's hands in hers as she continued. "The priest quorum wonders if there are demons in his family….. You must be careful," she repeated. "Please, be careful."

Raasah only smiled reassuringly to appease her friend.

ю̨

Jaona left to meet her mother at the market. Raasah took this as a good opportunity to find out more about the ailing old fowler. If her grandmother found out she was wandering the city again without an escort, she would be most upset but Raasah could see no other way to accomplish this. She had not been able to acquire any information about him from inquiries of those around her and decided the only way to know was to see the fowler for herself.

Behind the administration building housing the Governor's scribes, tax advisors, and other royal appointees were the healing rooms branching off in its own wide courtyard on the same platform. Health and medicine among Raasah's people were a complex blend of mind, body, religion, and science. Highly esteemed, healers were but a select few, who usually inherited their positions and received their instructions firsthand. The master healer who oversaw all the patients was Esau. He was assisted by Cyrus and Shaquah, both having practiced healing for over 15 years, Cyrus for over 20, and both knew their craft as well as the best of them.

There were doorkeepers posted at the gate that opened up to the healer's courtyard as was the custom with all civil, temple, and royal establishments. Today, though, these doorkeepers were from the soldiers' ranks and were dressed for military readiness. Raasah noted that these two guards, looking staid and official, did indeed have the standard military footwear.

Raasah was puzzled why authorities saw it expedient to enlist such extreme precautions for the healing rooms, precautions which were usually reserved for protecting government officials and visiting royalties. *Who or what were the soldiers guarding?* It did not seem plausible that the rebelling slaves would return to Ammonihah to finish off an old fowler. Just the same, it was comforting to know no more harm could come to him.

Raasah sat uncertainly at the far edge of the platform next to a pillar. *What did she want to say to the fowler? Was she ready for what she might hear or see when she saw him?*

The return of the warm sun left little evidence that the rain had been there at all, except for the refreshing whiff of the weather-changing breeze. Against the outside of the healers' rooms were long benches for those waiting to see a healer. A young veiled mother sat rocking and humming with a wee infant bundled in her arms. Next to her, a middle-aged man leaned on a crutch by the wall. Even if she hadn't notice their modest clothing, Raasah would have known they were commoners. It was not customary for the elite to lower themselves to go to the healer – it was expected the healer go to the elite. That was just the way it was.

A tall clean-faced man with limp hair was pacing at the far side of the platform as if he was waiting for someone, but did not seem to need a healer. Ringing his hands, the young man glanced constantly at the rear of the first building. After six or more full sets of pacing, he hesitantly approached the building and, as he did so, Raasah was sure he looked directly at her. The harried man stopped abruptly, rung his hands once more, then turned quickly toward the rear stairs.

At the top of the stairs, he took a second look at Raasah. In doing so, he neglected to notice an older rather plump man ascending the same stairs. Raasah thought they were going to collide and cringed as she imagined the fatter man rolling down the stairs in a most damaging way. Surprisingly, though, it was the latter that shouldered the younger one sharply against the edge of the stair. Cursing at him, the older man adeptly swatted him across the head for good measure before sending him on his way.

The young man, gripping his left arm, continued his descent down the steep stairs. He looked a third time at Raasah. She saw he was sporting a bloody cut across his cheek. Feeling conspicuous, she pulled her veil further over her face and looked away as he hurried off. Raasah thought he looked familiar but she could not remember where she had seen him before.

Returning her attention back to the entrance of the healers' room, she saw that Terjah had arrived. He had been away for some time and she was delighted to see him. She noted proudly how handsome he looked in his deep purple robe and hat. His slightly wavy brown hair came to his shoulders with the scapular iridescent feathers of the Frigatebirds[14] decorating his back locks. A young woman in a plain white shift and a pale blue robe exited through the door to greet him. She touched his arm as she began to speak to him. She was a head shorter than Terjah and her face was plain and colourless like her shift. Noting the thick, unruly hair tied loosely back from her face, Raasah recognized her as Tara, niece of Gormonaluk, a ruling elder and high priest. Terjah was presently in Gormonaluk's employ transcribing documents and recently had been sent to retrieve some records of his employer's family history from a seaside village.

Tara was apprenticing with Shaquah, who had taken her under her wing. It was unusual for an elite member of society to learn the healing art but Tara was so unlike her adopted family and did tend to go on her own path. This had often caused her aunt Zipporah more than enough displeasure and sharp words from what Raasah had heard. In addition, Tara often wore the clothes of the common people and, as far as Raasah knew, owned very little jewelry of note. But, even though Tara did not embrace the elite ways, Raasah did like her. In some ways, she even envied her. Tara was interesting and fun and, above all, seemed very sincere. The latter was a rare quality these days.

Raasah noted the extra few moments that Tara's hand lay upon Terjah's arm and the hesitant way she looked into his eyes. Her brother spoke to her briefly before Shaquah appeared, a woman of similar stature as Tara but slightly fairer. The healer and Tara exchanged words and, with a second touch on Terjah's arm, Tara joined Shaquah back inside.

Raasah had stood by unnoticed. Terjah no doubt knew about the fowler already and she was bursting to discuss the possible survival of Abul with him. Before she could reveal herself, though, Terjah was turning to descend down the back of the ziggurat passing Cyrus as he proceeded to cross the healer's courtyard.

Cyrus was a man of small build and, despite his thin countenance, he had a double chin and jowls that wobbled as he strode forward. His garb was uncharacteristically flamboyant for those attending the sick and he appeared distracted. Clutching at his garments, he approached the far side of the platform where the pacing man had been. Raasah stepped back outside of his view, then hurried off in the direction of Terjah. If these were the troubled times she had been warned of graciously by her friend, she thought it best to gain the company of her brother quickly.

On the landing, Raasah searched the mass of people and thought she saw the purple cloth wraps of his hat and his robe weaving in and out of the bobbing heads. She descended into the crowded lane and rushed through the gathering citizens so as to reach Terjah before he was hopelessly lost to her in the numbers. Though Terjah often only humoured her when she spoke of serious things, she needed to make him understand that she could comprehend important matters if given a chance – and she needed someone she could trust to listen to her concerns.

Raasah came to a corner that offered three choices of paths. She jumped up several times to view over the many heads, most of which towered over her in their pretentious headgear. There was no sign of him.

She was near the commercial quarter, close to the smith guild plaza now. The poignant smell of molten metal and its sweaty workers lingered on the air like rotten eggs. Raasah could hear the hiss of a red hot blade being plunged into a cold bath and the puffing of the bellows used to keep the fire's extreme temperature.

She turned slowly in a circle, repelled by the smell, surveying the squalid appearance of many of the citizens frequenting the place. Feeling very conspicuous and frustrated, she made the decision to head home. If she was much longer, she reasoned, she would worry her grandmother again. It had taken a lot of convincing before Raasah could assure her that she would be safe to walk home only partway in the company of her friends and she did not want to renew concern and lose the privilege of coming and going as she felt she needed.

Raasah was skirting the small busy marketplace when she was alerted to her brother's voice. Though he had exchanged his fine-looking hat for a plain draped serape, she recognized her opinionated brother intensely debating with men many years his senior. He was next to the shop of Abinahah, a forger of steel whom her father often commissioned to design fine decorative shields for the elite. Surprisingly, Abinahah did not seem to be around though his furnace breathed fingers of flames recently bellowed and, as she approached, the sickeningly warm air hung thick about her.

Raasah paused beside a thick column silently watching as Terjah waved his arms in animated gestures, boldly expounding his comments to a small intense group of six in this unlikely out-of-the-way locale. One of the men she could clearly make out was Normad, their great-uncle, a devote worker of a small temple in a quarter not far from there. As she approached the stela closest to them, she caught a few words spoken and felt the tension in the cluster of men.

"He is not in control of our affairs, nor either of his own," Terjah was saying. "The lawyers use their wiles on him, the priests seduce him with praise and flattering…."

"You are young and idealistic, …which are admirable qualities," grey-haired Normad said, speaking slowly and scanning past Terjah at sellers and consumers busily moving about, "…nevertheless, even the stones can have ears. One must be careful what one says…." (*Hadn't I just heard something similar?*)

"My father would have…."

"Your father was honourable and forthright and I am surprised it was not his undoing sooner!" Raasah realized with a start that this was Adam, Chemish's father, dressed in a simple trim brown robe and sporting a decorative medallion. He spoke sternly but, what surprised her most was that he, a carpenter, was speaking as an equal with others of much more learned and higher status. He continued more gently, "We don't want the same end to come to you, son."

"Yea, young Terjah," Normad consoled, laying a fatherly grip on Terjah's shoulder.

A deep-voiced hooded man, with his back to Raasah, spoke: "You have yet to understand the complexities of …."

At that moment, a young family, laughing and joking, literally bounced right in front of Raasah. Their toddler squealed joyously as his father scooped him up in the air, twirling him round and round as his mother clapped her hands. The delightful scene, alas, completely obstructed Raasah's visual and audible access to her brother and associates. Raasah bent and twisted to peer through and around the little family.

Once she had finally side-stepped around the lighthearted family, her brother's assembly was preparing to disband. Disappointed, she watched as they casually fanned off into the crowd. She could now see the powerfully built Abinahah. He was lowering a thick grey cape from his shoulders and she realized that he had been the hooded member of the small assembly. *What a curious group they were!*

Abinahah had a fierce and dark face, pouched with small scars from flying cinders and, as a child, she remembered hiding from him in fear behind her father's kilt. Though older now, Raasah still did not relish to be in his company. Abinahah went directly back to his bellows and fed the flames.

Once more, Raasah found she had lost sight of Terjah. In resignation, she leaned against the pillar and reflected on what she had heard.

Who had Terjah been speaking of so adamantly? Did this person have something to do with our father? Raasah slowly shook her head. More questions surfaced. *What commonality does our great uncle and Terjah have with meagre tradesmen such as Adam and Abinahah that they would speak as equals? AND who were the other two men?*

Raasah was now apprehensive, almost afraid, of what she might find out. But, find out she must. Terjah and Raasah must put their heads together to come to understand what happened. She resolved that they would talk at the first opportunity.

Terjah did not come home till much after dark and they did not get a chance to talk.

---

14   *The Frigatebird: is a sea bird also known as Man O'War. Although the bird's back is all black, the scapular feathers produce a purple iridescence when they reflect sunlight.*

Chapter 7

A Quest for Answers

Raasah wandered leisurely up the lane toward the city centre. There were no classes today – It was Preparation Day, for tomorrow was the Sabbath. This was also the day Marian spent a great deal of time visiting friends and checking on those who were ill or just needed a friendly face. Terjah and Little Brother had left before Raasah was dressed.

Resigned that her conversation with her brother would have to wait, she volunteered to deliver some packages for her grandmother, who was looking rather wearied this morning. After a previous day of intermittent rain, today's sun was welcoming and she was determine to think of nothing but its warmth on her skin as she browsed the stalls of the many gifted craftsmen. Raasah was very grateful that Marian had agreed to let her set out alone to meet up with Jaona. As she passed the stone sculpturer and the shoe maker, Raasah swung a large basket on her arm destined for the pottery stall that Ela manned for her husband who made meticulously detailed wares for sale to the discerning patrons.

Over the din of the market she soon heard Jaona's voice calling her name and spotted the red plumed hat before she recognized the beaming face beneath. Walking aloofly beside her was Isobel in her many layers of sheer beaded crimson that clung seductively to her maturing curvaceous figure. Their servants accompanied them dutifully shading them from the sun with large leaf-bound fans above their heads. As was her nature, Jaona was chattering away happily more to herself than to anyone in particular.

"Did you see Priestess Zillah cuff that stuttering Radok?" Jaona laughed as they caught up to Raasah. "..... caught him red-handed cheating with a phony weight. She hauled him off by the ear with him crying and carrying on like the miserable waif he is, all the way to the judge assembly. Look!" She pointed to the civil platform.

Zillah stood poised and elegant next to a potbellied ruffian in rumpled clothing even the poorest of farmers would be embarrassed to wear. His unkempt head was bare. As Zillah spoke with graceful sweeps of her arms, she suddenly swatted the back of Radok's head to bring him to attention. "Such a pathetic man!" Jaona mused merrily. "Even the corn he sells is pathetic!" She "tsk, tsk"ed, shaking her head for emphasis, trying unsuccessfully to look serious.

"Yea, well, the only way he could make money on that wretched crop is to cheat unsuspecting souls!" Isobel added gravely, also shaking her head.

"Not much gets by Zillah," Raasah grinned.

"Zealous Zillah," Isobel said grandly. "She can be good for market entertainment."

Raasah caught the hint of disdain in the aforementioned remark but she let it go. She did not want to break the light mood.

"You should have seen the look on his face as she dragged him across the square by his ear!" Jaona said between snickers. As they watched, Zillah swatted him again across the head and the girls burst into laughter.

છ

As they strolled along, Jaona was describing her most recent fashion garment that her father had indulged her with, oblivious to the slight bows of the common people acknowledging their higher status. They approached the pottery stall next to the lane that ran between Palenia and the city's main civil building. The healing rooms were just beyond. As Ela awaited customers, she sat contently embroidering a delicate bird with precious stones onto a huipil behind the displays. She had made quite the name for herself as a weaver and designer of custom clothing. Raasah even had clothing made personally by Ela and she believed many of Jaona's coveted outfits were also commissioned of her.

Ela looked up from her work as the child next to her pulled on her sleeve. The little girl had spied Raasah coming through the parade of people. Ela was a kind soft spoken lady with a pleasant face and bright eyes accented by long black lashes. Her six-year-old daughter sported the same striking eyes.

"I have to deliver a parcel to the potter's wife for my grandmother," Raasah explained to her friends.

Jaona looked at a stone-faced Isobel and back to Raasah. "You go ahead. We will just check out the…" Jaona glanced quickly around and noticed Isobel eying a stand across the road. "…the masks next to the Mosiah stela."

Raasah smiled her reply and, relieved to be able to speak freely to the potter's family, she dismissed herself from her friends.

"How's your grandmother?" Ela inquired as she gripped a beaded veil that was fluttering in the breeze against her face. She did not usually wear a veil as she sat in the shade of her stall but it did look striking against her dark hair, displaying the minute detail that Ela had woven into the delicate material. *Possibly admiring patrons will take note and inquire about purchasing similar textile items.*

"Grandmother was a little tired today." Raasah answered.

Ela's daughter jumped eagerly to her feet, her small hands reaching toward the basket. "Now, Lydia, manners," her mother chided tenderly. To Raasah, she added, "Lydia has been waiting anxiously for you."

"This," Raasah said playfully to the child, "is what you have been really waiting for, isn't it?" She reached into the basket for one of the freshly cooked treats.

Lydia gazed innocently at Raasah. "Grandmother Marian does make good tamales." She looked up at her mother who nodded before Lydia accepted the warm role from Raasah.

Between bites, Lydia added, "I wanted... to see you... too, Raasah.... Really!"

"Sure, sure, little one," Raasah teased as she gently moved a long curl away from the child's face.

Ela reached under the table awkwardly. As she stood, one hand protectively caressed her extended belly and the other hand presented Raasah with a small plant with rich blue flowers, its roots wrapped in wet swaddling cloths. "I know your grandmother loves her flowers. This is from my garden." Ela offered Raasah a coarse weaved shoulder bag to put it in. As she did so, the veil was blown to her shoulders. As she frantically repositioned the veil, her fingertips brushed a dark bruise on her cheek. Raasah smiled and pretended not to notice.

"How are you doing?" Raasah asked politely. Ela pulled the veil tighter around her face and Raasah added quickly, "The baby. Does everything feel well?"

"Oh,.... Yea." She replied. "The last month needs so much patience but it is so very worth it." She lovingly drew one hand over the full round of her bulge. "It won't be long now. Lydia wants a little brother. We'll see what the Lord has for us soon."

Raasah backed away from the stall to slip the plant carefully into the bag. Then, startled, a man spoke over her shoulder. "A lovely flower for a lovely young lady."

Raasah twirled around to face the familiar voice and, in doing so, knocked a bowl of arrowheads from the adjoining vendor's table. She was facing a tunic of worn leather as its owner reached behind her to steady the table – she breathed in a musky smell not at all unpleasant. Shyly her eyes wandered up to the thick muscular neck, distinct strong chin and cheery face of Chemish, son of Adam.

"My arrowheads!" the metal worker snapped behind her in, what seemed to Raasah, a detached, surreal way. Flustered, she reached down abruptly to retrieve the bowl just as Chemish also sought to retrieve it. As their hands touched, an electrifying tingle crept up her arm and Raasah pulled her hand away with such force as to knock the same table again, causing several detailed buckles to join the arrowheads on the ground. The craftsman's cursing increased her unease.

Raising, she tried to address Chemish, but only a whispered "I" came out, that sounded more like a sigh, flustering her all the more. She wanted to say, "I appreciate that you want to help but I can do this myself" but only silence passed her moist parted lips. Her resolve evaporated.

Why was I behaving this way? Has he put a curse on me? Could it have been transmitted through that touch? She turned her eyes away, then lowered her head as her trembling hand reached down once more to retrieve the fallen items. When her head turned it struck the side of the youth's own head who had stooped at the same time. He caught her arms as she tried to steady herself from the awkward stance of not-quite standing and almost crouching. His arms and hands, solid and strong from the maneuvering and shaping of wood, assisted her effortlessly to her feet. She found her face almost brushing the young man's chest. She could smell him, of sweet sweat and fragrant wood.

She was feeling light-headed and short of breath, a feeling that was pleasurable and troubling at the same time. Summoning all her courage to compose herself, Raasah gazed up to confront the personage before her. She found herself gazing into the most tender, hospitable face that, at the same time, seemed to glitter with amusement. Again, she opened her mouth to speak, but words got stuck in her throat. Against all good judgment she wanted to say, "What a beautiful face you have!", but was very thankful later those words would not come. She closed her eyes tight. *Why am I acting like a giddy girl trying to encourage the attentions of a man? Certainly not this man -- from a family denounced by the priests – said to prey on the weak!*

But she was feeling most weak right now herself and very confused. *What power was this that he has over me? Was he indeed of the devil?* But, surprisingly, she was not afraid. When he spoke, his voice was gentle.

"Little flower girl. I didn't mean to startle you."

Raasah was transfixed. Her eyes stared, tracing his long, straight nose and high cheek bones. He smiled a generous smile that made her want to melt. She heard voices but she couldn't decipher what they were saying and part of her did not care. She did not know how long she foolishly stood there, transfixed in his eyes, till she felt a firm grip on her upper arm.

The hand gave a quick shake and, hearing Jaona's voice, the spell that bound her to Chemish broke. With apprehension and a tinge of fear, she became aware that she had been balancing herself with her hands resting upon Chemish's arm. She stepped back from his magnetic body and pulled away from him.

Realizing that her mouth was still ajar, she closed her lips tight as her friend linked her arm and lead her away. Jaona was scolding her once again, this time for conversing with a carpenter. "But I didn't" Raasah protested, and she hadn't, though she now realized that she had wanted to....

Jaona was wagging her head. "Oh, if only I could be betrothed to someone as gorgeous and rich as Zoric," she sighed. "And what about Bathurst? A nobleman, no less, and you turned him down last year. You could have been on the royal grounds now with the best servants and clothes. I don't understand you, Raasah, daughter of the High Priestess. You could have anyone but you wait for someone that does not exist to be your husband and flirt with....with...."

"...with dirty scoundrels." Isobel finished with quiet contempt and her down-the-nose look.

"Jaona, Isobel, I didn't flirt. I ... he...." As she wasn't sure how she was going to end her sentence, Raasah was glad Jaona cut her off. Isobel was exiting in her accustomed flare with her fanning servant scurrying behind.

"You are so lucky Zoric is still caring to make you his wife,"

Jaona said quietly, watching Isobel's departure. "If you know what is good for you, you should entertain his attentions."

"You are starting to sound like my mother."

"Oh, Raasah. He lives in a palace, dear girl, with a magnificent court and walls with the most delicious frescos. My parents took me there once. Countless servants scurrying about ready to grant your every whim. Raasah, if you don't come to your senses, you may wind up with no one worthy." Jaona continued in a whisper, "You know Isobel has her eye on him......" Raasah followed Jaona's gaze. Isobel was watching from a distance but, seeing their eyes turn her way, she scowled and strode off.

Raasah had enjoyed being part of this sisterhood but lately Raasah was feeling a little ill at ease with them. She did not see these suitors the same way they did. She saw self-important, insincere, cold young men who flaunted their riches for vain attention and prestigious position. She did not want to be an award to be presented by her prominent family to enhance their image. She wanted someone who made her feel good about herself, who was interested in who she was and proud of what she had to offer. She wanted someone whom she could feel proud of.

Raasah felt she was drifting down a different path then her friends. They both seemed focused on material gratification and not interested in her new found enlightenment of people and social injustice. As a matter of fact, lately Raasah was having trouble finding common interests to enjoy with them at all. Even in their studies, she found herself in conflict in what they were embracing in the classes.

"Isobel," Jaona called and then turned back to Raasah, "A mercantile caravan from the east coast is setting up their wares. It will be so much fun to see what they have brought and hear the stories about the sea. Come with us."

"I'm sorry, Jaona. I have to do some errands for my grand-mother." Raasah lied.

"That's what servants are for," Jaona scolded. She looked Raasah over for a response and glanced to where Isobel was disappearing into a lane. "It's your loss," she beamed and skipped off after Isobel.

Raasah felt relief with a mixture of loneliness as Jaona melted into the crowd. Raasah rubbed her hand remembering the sensual tingle it had felt, then forced herself to focus. Though she had char-itably offered to deliver the basket to Ela, when she realized how close she would be to the healing room, her secondary quest had immerged: she must try to see the old fowler again. She turned back but was careful not to run into Chemish again.

As she turned into the narrow alley, she heard heated arguing. Between her and her destination, were two large bearded men. Their skin were browned and weathered by the sun and their cloth-ing suggested that they were reserve soldiers on leave or merce-naries hired by the visiting pochtecatl, most likely unwinding in their drunken way from their long trip. Their muscular arms were covered in tattoos and, though Raasah was many strides from the volatile men, she could smell cheap liquor reeking from them.

"You have cheated me for the last time," exclaimed the shorter cruel lipped man with spittle dripped down the matted hair of his chin. He wiped limp straggly hair from his face and Raasah caught sight of a long white scar reaching from the bottom of his ear to disappear into the neck of his tunic. It was obvious that fighting was not a stranger to him. He reached for his sheathed knife, fumbling at its clasp.

"You pathetic moron...... You think you can take ME!" With his ring-shod hand, the darker man forcibly shoved his spluttering accuser who retaliated sinking his calloused fist to his opponent's ample belly. Instantly, there was mad scuffle of battering fists as they tumbled onto the ground.

Raasah retreated a few steps, then scuttled to the far side of the lane before she made a quick dash past them. The sound of cursing and fists hitting their targets was frighteningly close. She shrunk against the wall as three other similarly clad peers stumbled, laughing, toward the fight, echoing a fight chant, swearing, and intensifying the harried scene.

Breathing laboriously, she sprinted up the back stairs to the healing rooms, the same stairs that she had seen the nervous pacing man nearly fall down the day before. She did not look back. Reaching the top stair, she was relieved to put as much distance as possible between her and the hostility below her.

Potential patients were loitering by the healing rooms – a mother cuddling a coughing child; a sick old man and his aging wife; a young man with a head injury; and two young boys, knees tucked under their chins, leaning against the building. Despite feeling ill at ease in her elite attire among these simple folk, she decided quickly that she preferred 'uneasiness' to the fear she felt when she was down with the ruckus below.

Raasah approached the building she had seen Tara disappear in yesterday. At the expansive opening, she was taken aback at the strong scent of bitter herbs and ointments mixed with the putrid stench of sickness and sweet brews.

Lingering by the door, she listened. She heard Esau barking commands and could hear scurrying feet, the clank of metal instruments, and the odd low moan. As her eyes adjusted to the darkened interior, she spied Tara kneeling over a prostrated form on a mat. Suddenly Esau's dark form blocked her view.

"This is not a place for a child of your status." Esau straightened his shoulders, appearing more substantial and intimidating.

"I heard of another survivor of the ….. you know…"

"Yea, yea. The fowler. Very sick. We are doing all we can…. You must hurry along, my dear. If there is anything you must know we will pass it on to your brother."

"Could I just see him?" Raasah asked timidly as she tried to look around him.

Esau blocked her view again. "What use will that do? He sleeps. That is the best thing for him now." When Raasah didn't respond, he added, "You do want him to get better don't you, my dear?"

"Of course!" Raasah did not like it when he called her 'my dear'. Esau steadily held her eyes like he was trying to see into her soul.

She turned her face from him, hugging her shoulder bag to calm her thumping chest. The blossoms peeked over the top of the clutched bag, nodding in beat with her heart. She looked back up defiantly, then, with her courage seeping away, she turned and strode away as bravely as she could muster, fighting tears of frustration, berating herself for letting the healer dismiss her like an ignorant child. Sadly she was aware of her inadequacy to do this on her own. She needed someone she could depend on, voice her concerns with, and brainstorm with. She needed reassurance, she needed information, she needed a good friend she wasn't afraid to express what she was thinking to. But right now she just wanted to be home.

Dejected, Raasah entered the villa compound, absently nodding to Mosia dutifully guarding their gate. Tamar, their household domestic, entered right behind her, startling her when she spoke.

"No escort?" Tamar said with a long face, punctuating her point with a tight-lipped smile.

Raasah grimaced. "Please don't say anything to Grandmother."

Her husband, Elihu, rounded the corner with two young servants laden down with slabs of meat slung over their backs. Elihu, himself, had his arms full of jugs of oils and spices. He stopped abruptly as he spied his wife and mistress staring each other down.

"Ladies?" he inquired nervously.

Neither 'lady' took note of him but continued to face off with each other.

"Please," Raasah repeated softly.

Tamar relaxed and produced the tender smile more typical of the loving woman she was. She gave Raasah a warm hug.

"We worry about you. You know that, don't you?"

"I know. I'm sorry. Please don't say anything...," Raasah repeated. "I was with Jaona and Isobel, but they...," she trailed off.

Tamar hugged her again. "We could use your help preparing dinner."

"I'll be in shortly," Raasah replied, shuffling her feet, "and thank you."

Elihu smiled broadly in relief and immediately ushered his troop into the villa, followed promptly by Tamar barking out lists of assignments to be divvied-up.

Raasah sighed. Kicking a small stone by her foot, she turned to wander into the garden. Coming upon a small pot, she knelt in the soft earth and, carefully lifting the fragile plant from her shoulder bag and its moist cloths, she slipped it into the pot. The well-being of this little plant was paramount to her right now as the ability to look after this plant was within her power, unlike so many other tasks she had tried to accomplish lately only to discover how very inept she really was.

Terjah and Little Brother would not make it for their mid-day meal. Neither of them turned up for the evening meal either. Terjah sent word that he would meet his family at the temple the next day.

Chapter 8

Changes

The Botholuem household joined the clusters of citizens heading for Palenia's temple grounds. As was their Sabbath custom, the Botholuem household bore fresh produce and other essential items destined for the less fortunate. Raasah had proudly taken up this custom as well as she adjusted a basket of buns and dried meats on her arm. Neither she nor her family, though, were prepared for what awaited them at the Temple Square.

Traditionally, on the Sabbath, the Grand Plaza and temple grounds were transformed into the ceremonial center for worship. The citizens would gather around the Palenia Palace: the city's elite in the extensive Temple Square and the rest of its citizens on the outskirts and filling the Grand Plaza below. Lastly, those in need congregated near the temple square gates. It was an uplifting sight with all of Ammonihah dressed in their finest white garments and head coverings, rich and poor basically the same, though the wealthy were still distinct from the rest with their fancy gold stitching, silky gowns, and elaborate adornments. The Botholuem family were less elegant in their finery but their clothing was still well tailored with fine stitching and simple beading that professed their well-to-do status.

The priests wore the colourful ceremonial robes gilded in gold and the lofty ceremonial headdresses depicting their authority and distinction in the sanctioned rites. Communal worship centered around the sacrificial offering. As a young girl, Raasah had been mesmerized by the spectacle of the Prophet Esrom in the shimmering headdress of precious stones. A large serpent was embellished high upon it that was symbolic of faith and healing. Raasah had loved gazing upon the enchanting gold serpent in all its concise details, its jeweled eyes staring back amazingly life-like in the light.

That was the way it had been.... As they approached the main entrance to the Temple Square, their light-hearted chatter died away as they joined others in varies states of awe, delight, and disquiet. There was a festive atmosphere about the walls and gates of the temple square. Bright colored flowers abounded and red banners boasting the governor's crest hung from the walls. Instead of the traditional two temple guards at each gate, Raasah counted at least six all in the royal colors of the Royal Palace.

Taken aback by the colourful sight before her, Raasah did not notice at first what was missing and then she cried, "Mei-wa-na, where is Widow Mary and Old Ama... and... and the orphan children...?"

Indeed, the usual group of needy people, including widows, and orphans, were replaced by ornamental trappings and stalwart guards. As they looked on, a young timid mother and child were ordered gruffly away by one of the dour guards. Hugging her frightened child to her breast, the mother hastened back into the growing crowd. Little Brother, who had been turning in a slow 360-degree, suddenly bolted off through flowing robes and past laden servants. Raasah looked indecisively after him.

Marian did not answer her granddaughter's inquiry. Instead she ushered her family past the fragrant flowers into the Temple

Square before she excused herself and approached one of the cheer-less guards. Though out of hearing-range, Raasah watched as her grandmother spoke and gestured to him and he passively stared down on her short frame. With no expression, he uttered a few words to her that just seemed to upset her more. Marian gestured once more to the guard in a grand sweep of her arm and then briskly disappeared outside the gate.

As Marian disappeared, the lofty sound of the trumpet[15] sounded to signal the appearance of the royal family. The Ammonihah citi-zens all bowed as Governor Antionah strode boldly at the front of the procession looking very short and wide in his flamboyant robe next to the slender graceful woman at his side. The latter was his first coveted bride that, after only 5 years of adorning his bed, had been replaced by a new younger bride that now trailed a few steps behind. Following the first three royals, in no particular order, re-gally walked the children and their nurses, then the royal relatives and various court attendants and advisors.

Although their clothing emphasized the white of the day, trim and exquisite details bore colours and hues that in the past would not have been tolerated or even attempted on the hallowed day of the Most High God. In the brilliant morning light, not only did these brilliant colours irreverently shout their presence, but the assembling members merely shone with the reflections of their extensive jewels and gold about their person. As they settled on an extravagantly furnished platform that loomed above Palenia's grounds, their assistants and attendants rallied into position with fans and shades and other creature comforts for the long morning that lay ahead of them. Raasah looked away from the glare.

A slightly lower tone of a second trumpet sounded to signal

the approach of the staunch religious leaders. The attending crowd settled quietly, eyes averted to Palenia's cavernous opening.

The congregation began their soothing monotone chant prompted by the attending apprentice priests and priestess on a lower terrace. These young people always looked so heavenly in their ceremonial robes and their gold-plated helmets adorned with quetzal plumelet. Raasah, though, only joined the chant distractedly as she scanned the assemblage by the gate until she spied her grandmother once more, now absent of her satchel.

"Mei-wa-na, what is happening?"

"He said they were a threat to the security of the Temple…. a threat to the city's leaders… a threat! Women and children… sick old man….!" She trailed off, wringing her hands.

Raasah had never known her grandmother to be so exasperated before and didn't know how to respond as Marian muttered something indistinguishable under her breath. Raasah laid her hand on the old woman's arm. Marian's face softened and she gently rubbed the comforting hand. Smiling weakly at her granddaughter, she whispered, "But they cannot take away our Sabbath."

Raasah wondered who "they" were. Absently, her eyes scanned the terraces of the young chanting priest-clothed assemblage. She paused. *Isn't that Isobel?* Raasah stared at the blue-robed figure looking so beautiful, noble, and grown-up. *It is Isobel! Why had she not mentioned she had been chosen to join this choice group?* Raasah stared – a feeling of emptiness swelled inside her. Raasah could not summon up a sense of pride for her friend. It was like she was staring at another beautiful object in amidst of pompous fanfare. With a sinking sense of loss, Raasah snuggled in closer to her grandmother.

Life was full of changes – this Raasah knew – witnessing her friend taking her own path in addition to all the gradual changes to their Sabbath – the engaging warmth she had always cherished from the service was rapidly being eroded to only a simulate of what it was. Even their beloved Prophet no longer officiated at the service. For the last few months he was only seen briefly seated at the beginning of official gatherings at which he barely spoke, often only mumbling repetitive phrases, and was attended heavily with over-zealous priests and guards. His authoritive spiritual messages and directions were sorely missed. In addition, the plaza below the temple square was being invaded by increasing numbers of irreverent vendors and rowdy patrons who too often disturbed the peaceful atmosphere of the worship. In small, almost undetectable increments, the worship itself had seemed to become more "theatrical than reverent", as she had heard her grandmother say not so long ago. *Now the eviction of the less fortunate from the presence of the temple….* Raasah did not know what to think!

Today, as well, Raasah noted an unmistakable disparity in the religious procession. Gasps of disbelief murmured around them as Darius, the presiding High Priest, stood in place of the Prophet Esrom of Ammonihah at the altar. Their prophet's presence was nowhere to be seen. Darius was presumptuously clothed in the Beloved Prophet's Sabbath robes and headdress. Upon his head, the symbolic serpent seemed to take on a more malevolence nature – its jade eyes piercing and its ruby tongue seeming to lick the air threateningly in front of it. Raasah shrunk from the sight.

Without explanation, Darius commenced the morning service in the flawless elegance he had done in his other duties in the past months. The hush objections died quickly away.

Following the final blood-letting ritual and supplication, Marian shuffled to her feet before Darius could begin the speech of instruction and backed toward the exit. As Raasah shuffled her own feet under her to follow suit, Hannah slid in next to her and maternally patted her hand. Raasah stared after her grandmother who had just rounded the gate lintels. Reluctantly, she gazed back at Darius.

"Esrom, Most Holy Prophet of Ammonihah, sends his love and prayers to the noble citizens of our great city of Ammonihah." Darius spoke distinctly and slowly, his feather-banded arms sweeping the air in wide arches.

"At least Darius still acknowledges that Esrom is still our prophet," Raasah mumbled irritantly.

"I humbly stand…," Darius began.

"Humbly???" Raasah gasped through gritted teeth.

"… .before you in his absence to announce to you his heartfelt words and desires for this people. Our esteemed prophet has reached the final curtain of his earthly time." There was a stir among the populace with sudden cries of sadness, but nevertheless, as if oblivious to the distressed response, Darius continued unmoved with his measured words. Hannah soothingly stroked Raasah's clutched fist.

"Esrom is now in deliberation with our glorious Omnipotent Creator regarding his successor. We believe in a cyclical nature of time. Our rituals and ceremonies coincide with celestial and terrestrial cycles which we observe and inscribe. It is our priesthood duty to interpret these cycles and provide the prophetic outlook on the future – our future. Our prophet has determined that the celestial bodies are now aligned for the appropriate performing of certain religious ceremonies, most importantly of which is our needed priesthood appointments that Kukulkan[16], our glorious Creator, has directed that we must fulfill.

"We await the decision of the chosen one who will succeed our beloved Esrom in his sacred duty as prophet and seer to our great city but, as we wait, it will be a comfort to you to know your newly appointed Priestess will be assuming her duties...."

Turning toward the blackened opening to the Holy Chambers, Darius had raised his voice grandly, now emphasizing each syllable, "...as your new Most High Priestess of Palenia's Temple."

As he gestured grandly to his right, out of the dark belly of the zaggarat surfaced the beautiful form of what could have been mistaken for a goddess on earth. Though ceremoniously robed as her officiating peer, Sablon's enchanting splendor was enough to stun the whole congregation to silence. She floated to Darius' side.

"I present to you the Supreme High Priestess Sablon of Ammonihah!" Darius shouted with such authority that even the little children were stilled. He smiled broadly as he extended his hand to the grandiose Priestess. Laying her hand gracefully in his, Sablon posed before the crowd. Sablon outshone Darius like the sun to the stars. Her generous red lips parted slightly but did not smile. She held her head high and her dark lined eyes slowly scanned the crowd below her with a slow steady sweep of her head. If she saw her daughter, nothing about her indicated it.

Raasah was just as astounded at the image of her mother as were all those around her. It was like she was seeing her mother for the first time – and the last. In the absence of Esrom, in that moment, her mother and the formidable Darius were in charge of the spiritual well-being of all men, women, and children of their fine city and politically the most influential members of society. The emptiness inside Raasah swelled even more as she felt the loss of a mother that she was beginning to realize she never really had in the first place. Even more devastating, as she gazed at the mesmerizing priestess, she realized that she had lost any chance to ever have her for her mother. Many more despairing thoughts riveted and rebounded inside her head until she couldn't think at all. She just limply stared.

As Raasah hugged in close to Hannah, she felt another hand slip around her free arm. She glanced up into the deep brown eyes of her elusive brother. Instinctively she swung around and wrapped her arms around his middle, sinking her face with leaky eyes into his tunic. Hesitating just a little, Terjah tenderly embraced his sister, confusion written across his face. Then his eyes registered the figure before them just as she began to address the congregation.

"My honorable citizens of Ammonihah!" Sablon's voice was clear and soothing.

Raasah also turned her face toward the familiar voice.

"It is with great respect and admiration for you, my people, that I stand before you. You are a special elect people of Kukulkan, a people blessed and envied by our neighbors and our enemies. Outsiders ingratiate themselves and continuously move among us trying to divide and weaken our resolve. They try to suck us into their false teachings and persuasions.

"But you must remember that YOU are the chosen people. They would take your precious things, your titles, and your reputations as their own, tell you they are for not, have you forsake your pleasures and comforts so as to bring you down. They would tell you that YOUR GREAT CITY WILL BE DESTROYED if we don't do as they say. YOUR GREAT CITY, AMMONIHAH, the city our Omnipotent Creator helped us build.

"The boldness of this new breed of wicked men is apprehensible, criminal, and dangerous. As your spiritual leaders, it is our duty, our responsibility, to guide you and counsel you, and keep you from the wicked, lying wolves of the world! The gods of our fathers have blessed us with prosperity, made our city grand, protected us from our enemies, but we must not doubt our God-given state or we will lose it. We must zealously defend what Kukulkan has given us. We are better than those around us. We must stand tall and REMEMBER WHO WE ARE!!" The silence in the plaza was eerie as her audience sat spellbound below her.

Darius broke the silence with his bellowing voice. "Good Citizens of Ammonihah. The gods of our Fathers have surely graced us with our wise and beautiful new High Priestess. Through Priestess Sablon's inspirations and gifted foresight, the gods will truly bless us and keep us from all harm. In addition, with her special appointment to the Royal Courts, along with our illustrious ruler, our grand city will prosper beyond our comprehension. Surely the Deity, in their wisdom, have answered our prayers for guidance and sanction from those unworthy and seeking our destruction. Let us bow our heads and give thanks...."

There was a stir in the crowd. The poignant smell of incense and burnt offerings wavered thick in the air. Raasah did not close her eyes or lower her head. Defiantly she gazed up at her mother. High Priestess Sablon was smiling over the assembly – a cold smile – and the sun was darkened by a blackened cloud. Raasah trembled against her brother's chest.

---

15   Trumpets: Among the oldest musical instruments, they have been dated back
     to at least 1500 B.C. A ceramic trumpet, dated back to 300 CE was found
     in Lima, Peru. Bronze and silver trumpets from Tutankhamun's grave in
     Egypt date back past 1300 B.C. These early trumpets did not have any valves
     and the mouthpiece was shallow. The player changed the sounds he played
     by changing the position of his lips on the mouthpiece. The notes were very
     limited and usually one trumpet was dedicated for only one or two notes
     and were believed to be used more as signalling instruments for military or
     religious purposes, rather than music in the modern sense.

16   Kukulkan: is a name used by the Mayans for the Creator as indicated by the
     manuscript of the Popol Vuh and, for the purpose of this book, is not meant
     to represent any other pagan god, but only the God of the Patriarch Joseph of
     Egypt. Different isolated cultures tended to adopt their own names for their
     omnipotent Godhead, even though their beliefs may have originated from
     the same ancient records. Whether the name of Kukulkan was actually used
     to refer to their God at the time of this story is just speculative of the author.

Chapter 9

The Council

Her planned meeting with Terjah after class was making her ridiculously jumpy after his parting comment of 'Be careful!' As Raasah laid a coin in the cup of the 'Great Soldier', she greeted him as cheerily as she could muster. As always, he 'looked' up at her with his kind weathered face, thanking her graciously. This gesture was especially comforting today. *Who were 'they' to tell me that this lame soldier, or timid Ada, or, for that matter, Chemish, were the 'wrong' company. I much preferred these to the likes of Zoric and his company!* She straightened her shoulders and continued on her course.

Every morning now, Raasah started out with a young attendee from her household. To Raasah's relief, her grandmother had accepted Raasah's choice of Amos, son of Ahah. He was a lazy lad with skinny white legs disproportionately long for his plump trunk and with a disproportionately long nose to match. His best asset, as far as Raasah was concerned, was his tendency for inattentiveness and distractibility. Such assets suited Raasah just fine as she resented having her freedom monitored as she went about the city. She walked briskly around a puddle to distance herself more from him.

Her regular route to school had a detour that allowed her to extend offerings of assistance to several widows and disabled people along the way. Marian was more than pleased to encourage Raasah and supplied breads and dried fruit in small wraps for Raasah to give away. There was an older widow with her two young grandsons whom Raasah was especially generous to each morning on this lengthened route. Sometimes Little Brother accompanied her for part of the route as well. His playful innocence and eagerness to help always brought a smile to her soft lips. And the good deeds themselves, though done quietly and out-of-the-way so her friends would not find out, brought her joy that energized and warmed her throughout the day. Even today, she felt her anxiety thawing as she started believing her own greeting of "good day". She was beginning to understand the source of her grandmother's peacefulness in spite of the recent grief life had brought her.

A special bonus to this new route was the fact that it conveniently delivered her precisely in front of Chemish's carpentry shop. Chemish always had a warm smile for her or a thoughtful compliment…. And she was always surprised how her heart would thump as she returned a greeting. At first her response was just a shy smile or nod but, as the days then weeks had proceeded, she felt more comfortable adding a pleasant word or expressing admiration of a project he was working on. Because they were so close to the Hall of Instruction from here, Raasah soon was able to assure Amos, without any objection, to take his leave as they neared the shop – appearing more than content within himself that he had done his duty for his mistress.

Her former curious apprehension of her brief meetings with Chemish was soon replaced with anticipation. He made it so easy for her to just be herself and conversation came so naturally. They spoke of places they had been; they spoke of injustices; they spoke of families; they spoke of changes and disappointments. Though their conversations were discrete and brief, they were cherished and surprisingly enlightening. Most importantly, though, Raasah felt safe and liberated as their views were exchanged.

Occasionally, they spoke about the stranger that was causing much contention and discussion in the city. Well, actually Chemish spoke of him and Raasah mostly listened and asked the occasional questions. She had not had the opportunity to hear or see this Alma for herself. Opinions she had heard of him ranged from him being a glorious saint to being a despicable rebel. In either case, Alma was supposed to be a captivating speaker and Chemish's view of him sided more toward the saint concept.

"Alma speaks of a better way to live – one of hope and charity" Chemish said one day. "He speaks of the hallowed worth of humility and good works." His face shone as he spoke of Alma and Raasah's heart was pricked with the words. She was overcome by the passion and warmth in which Chemish spoke.

Then, today, Chemish spoke of his father's Uncle Amulek, a man of no small reputation in Ammonihah, who not only had taken in this fascinating stranger but was endorsing all the words that Alma spoke. Raasah's thoughts swirled like a frenzied turtle struggling to grasp a secure hold of a branch in a strong river eddy. *Does Chemish speak the true knowledge, for the peace that overwhelms me speaks of the truth of the words...? Is this the branch that my frenzied mind is trying to grab hold of? If this Alma is truly sent by the Most High God, that he has come to clarify the truth and redeem our people....* Her eyes moistened suddenly, blurring her vision. Chemish silently reached deep in his apron, producing a clean cloth to dab at a tear slowly tickling down her face. No explanation was needed. In such a short time, what a sweet wonderment it was how close she felt to this stalwart young man! How could these feelings that she was feeling be wrong?

Composing herself, she reluctantly hurried toward the Hall of Instruction, nurturing the warmth stirring in her heart. Reluctantly, though, as she neared the Grand Plaza, familiar voices seeped into her thoughts. They were coming from Lahotite Lane, a most unlikely place to hear the latter for she was sure they were those of several elite members of the city council. It was the commanding voice of Jashorum, Zoric's father, that first perked her ears. Gormonaluk, Tara's uncle, was also foremost of those speaking. The influential group was discussing Alma. Her curiosity of this newcomer was already peaked and she couldn't resist hearing more. Raasah stepped back behind the stone wall within a half-dozen paces from them. In their arrogance, there was little effort to hush their interaction nor did they diligently ensure their conversation was in private, much to Raasah's relief.

"This foreign priest is constantly speaking ill of our priests and our practices of law." Raasah did not know this voice.

"He is gaining quite a following," Gormonaluk spoke in his guttural speech. "If we don't act, he will destroy all we have worked for."

"With our new appointment pending to replace the Prophet Esrom, the appearance of this preacher-prophet of Zarahemla could make our announcement complicated." That was the voice she couldn't place again. Raasah puzzled over the words the latter chose. *The appointment of a prophet is not by a decision of city council. It is made by the senior priests by revelation!*

"Alma must be silenced but he is good with his words." Raasah glanced around the corner and realized the voice came from the large form of Absalom, the quarry owner. There was another wide but shorter man with his back to Raasah. Absalom continued, "Yesterday, we sent lawyers to debate that Alma but he confounded them…. had them babbling like idiots and won even more people to his teachings."

"Yea," Gormonaluk concurred, "and that nephew of Antionah was amongst those who was intrigued by this outsider."

"Reuben has been seen talking with this Alma earlier this week and recently was heard calling him a great teacher," said the man with his back to Raasah. He wore head gear that covered the back of his neck and a full robe typical of the business elite, but she could not make out any personal features. "The people adore Reuben," he continued in a dark nasally voice. "He alone could now cause our downfall if we can't turn him from this path." Raasah tried to place the voice.

"Reuben has been nothing but trouble since he joined our council." Malice darkened Jashorum's voice.

"This royal brat has reduced us to meeting in the streets!" Raasah could not place that voice either. Raasah snuck a second look at the council members. This speaker also had his back to her but she could see he was of small stature. His thick brown hair was pulled back in braids topped with a tall crown-like hat that appeared to glitter in the morning light; his ears stood generously out to the side as if supporting his pompous headgear.

"You know it was necessary to accept Reuben to the council," Absalom stated. "It would have caused Antionah's suspicion if we had denied his own nephew."

"We will deal with him later. First we must contend with this

Alma," Jashorum said, echoed by the sounds of agreement from his peers.

"If we must catch him in his words.... we need our best...." Absalom said.

"Yea, ...we need Zeezrom." Gormonaluk said decisively.

"Yea, he is travelling now but he is the most expert of all the lawyers." Absalom said.

"Yea, yea! He bellows like a bull about his deftness in the court–claims he loves a good challenge," said Jashorum antagonistically. "He is gifted at twisting the law to suit his whims." *Jashorum – he's one of the biggest braggarts himself!*

"Crowing your own song – something that you are quite gifted at yourself, Friend," the wide man echoed Raasah's thoughts with a deep laugh.

Raasah grimaced, pulling her lips into a flat line. *...and, not only a corrupt lawyer, Jashorum is also a very questionable judge of the court. The enmity between these two lawyers over the years has been no secret.*

"We are very aware of your talents, Jashorum," Gormonaluk said in a calming voice, "but I still put my money on Zeezrom for the job. Zeezrom is most devious and will not be silenced by this cunning outsider." There were murmurs of agreement. "If anyone can, Zeezrom will trap Alma in his words."

Resigned, Jashorum added, "We also have the problem of Amulek, one of our own....."

Amulek – the same uncle Chemish had just spoken of. Raasah cupped her mouth, grateful that a flutist had struck up a tune nearby that drowned out her gasp. Raasah was no longer conscious of who was speaking as she strained to make out the words through the twittering of the flute.

"He accompanies this Alma everywhere. This makes it complicated as Amulek is well respected and has very influential friends. He will have to be dealt with discretely."

"We will, of course, tread carefully with Amulek. Listen…. we will talk more at the meeting later tonight."

Raasah heard her name called by a feminine voice. She glanced around for the source as she strained harder to hear more from the council members.

"We must make sure Reuben does not know…."

Raasah spied Jaona skipping towards her. Fumbling with her bag, feigning to adjust the weight of it on her shoulder, Raasah strode quickly toward her friend and away from the councilmen. Other words of the privileged conversation were absorbed by the populace who had now joined the frenzy of entertainers. Stern-faced Isobel stared from across the lane. Raasah's face flushed at the thought that Isobel may have caught her eavesdropping.

"Raasah, we wondered where you were," Jaona said merrily. "What are you doing over here?"

"I…. I had errands to run."

"Oh, Raasah. You are a conundrum these days." Jaona tsk-tsked then twirled to show off her newest body-hugging gown adorned in jewels. "What do you think?"

Raasah pulled on a mask of approval but her mind was on Chemish and his father's uncle, mulling over what recourse the council could be planning. *I need to warn Chemish before that evening meeting should happen.*

"We are going to the Morcum[17] ballcourt after our classes today.

Come with us. We are going to watch the visiting team practice. They are from David...." Jaona had that sweet dreamy look she saved for enthralling prospects. "Josian, of course, will be there." She sighed. "Did you hear? In his last game with the Gideon team, he practically won the game on his own – jumping nearly six feet in the air with the winning shot. It is all the talk about him.... Do come with us," she repeated.

Morcum was a fiercely competitive ball game played between neighbouring cities. When a formal game is played, the city had the festive atmosphere of a civil holiday. Everyday activities practically halted so hyped-up citizens could all attend the sport. Raasah had been so preoccupied the last couple of days, she had totally forgotten that the upcoming game was at the end of the week.

"I don't know if I will be able to today. I will look for you there if I can," Raasah replied, feeling guilty that she couldn't confide in her friend.

The girls neared the Hall of Instruction. Raasah was half-listening to Jaona's chatter about a party her parents were planning and all the possible suitors that could be there. Slowly she built up her courage to inquiry more about Alma. As Jaona finally paused from speaking, Raasah almost spit out the words.

"I heard something about a foreign priest in Ammonihah. I think his name is Alma...."

Jaona stopped short and shot her a look. Isobel, surprisingly, was the one who spoke.

"I heard he was a prince, related to the late King Mosiah, and others say he was the chief judge of the highest court in the realm.... but he gave up his high position to wander the lands like a commoner - spreading stories of doom and turning their citizens to insurgence against their leaders." Isobel tipped her pretty head toward Raasah. "I think he is just a mad man. What fool would give up a prominent position to decide the fate of man and then go around making enemies for himself? Can you imagine?"

Jaona tsk-tsked in agreement.

"If he wanted to change the way leaders think," Isobel continued, "what better way than from a judgment seat! ….. Give up station and power –it is all absurd!" Her nose was in the air. Raasah was relieved that she hadn't shot HER the down-the-nose look.

"Some say he is a prophet," Jaona added as she threw Isobel a sideways glance. Seeing no objection, she continued, "or a son of a prophet, but he is nothing like Esrom…. He is just a trouble-maker." She nervously sought Isobel's approval and looked relieved when she wasn't rebuffed.

"He bewitches people, I say," said Isobel aloof. "That soothsayer has affected Amulek somehow, a prominent member of the council, and turned him against them. I heard my father speaking about it with a man from the palace just last night. They were afraid this will cause much turmoil with the people….. But such troublemakers are always silenced," she concluded confidently. With a satisfied smile, she strutted past the guards in front of the Palace of Greater Learning.

Abruptly Raasah halted. She watched as her haughty friend disappeared under the archway. *Of course, the second unknown speaker – the one with the councilmen – it was Issachar, Isobel's father. The dominant ears and pompous headgear should have given him away!*

Absently, she gazed about her to the reliefs on the walls and then to the normally unwavering guards at the entrance. Until today, she had never given the guards any thought. In this time of peace, they were like the statues and masks that decorate the very walls of the building they were protecting – just there. Raasah looked intently at the nearest guard to her left as he shifted his weight from foot to foot. She was sure she saw his eyes divert away from her as she looked up, his helmet seeming to give a reddish glow to his cheek. *It must be the way the sun was reflecting off the metal brim*, she thought. She turned to the guard on her right and then back to the first. The latter's hand twitched at his side as Raasah scrutinized his face and the reddened cheek. *Was it a reflection or...?"*

"Come along, Raasah," Jaona beckoned.

Shaking her head, Raasah reprimanded herself for her ungrounded paranoia. Once inside the cavernous building, she sat at her assigned table in her History class without another word.

ꙮ

"In all things there must be opposition. This is part of the plan of our Mighty Creator." Teacher Martha lowered her voice, scanning the class to include each student. "Because He loves us, He needs to give us challenges to grow. History is full of examples of such challenges, and sadly, of failures of some of our greatest leaders...."

A rustling of robes and delicate chains distracted teacher and students alike as they turned to determine the source that now blocked the natural light into the room. With a sober face, Martha handed a codice to a senior student and, after whispering brief instructions to her, walked briskly through the archway. The classroom hummed with questions.

"Quiet! Get out your shards for dictation," the senior turned-teacher instructed.

With a chorus of groans, the girls shuffled through their satchels in search of shards, ink, and pens.

Jaona leaned toward Raasah, speaking in a hushed voice. "I wonder what Noami wanted with Teacher Martha."

Raasah turned to face Jaona. "Noami, the head priestess?"

"Yea."

"Noami, Zoric's mother...?" Raasah muttered. "Ruth's mother...?"

Ruth beamed importantly from across the room, answering Raasah's question, as she chatted away with her freckle-faced companion.

"That was her assistant at the door. My mother has had many dealings with her." Jaona explained quietly.

"We will start," the young substitute teacher began loudly.

As Raasah turned back to retrieve her pen, her elbow struck the ink jar on her desk, spilling the black contents. Instantly standing, she saved her skirt from its damaging dye but, as she tried to right the jar, to her dismay, the sleeve of her robe was not spared. Stunned and embarrassed, Raasah just stared, holding her sleeve out from her body to prevent more damage. Voices and snickers rippled through the room.

"Let's get that robe off," Ada said soothingly at her side. Raasah let her slip it off her shoulders. Her hand also had been soiled.

"Go get cleaned up," the young instructor snapped impatiently, "and bring back some cleaning rags."

Flustered, Raasah gathered her robe carefully over her arm with her clean hand before slipping out into the courtyard in search of the servants' quarters for a rag and assistance to clean up. As she rounded a corner, she spied the tall Priestess Noami looking condescendingly at an angry Martha. Intrigued, Raasah backed up just out of sight and strained to hear.

Eves-dropping has become habit forming.

"You can't throw out the truths of the old curriculum for these outlandish, ... embellished...," Martha stuttered angrily.

"You should be careful with your words, Martha. They could be construed to be heretical," said Noami, smugly. She clasped her long white fingers up to her chest as if she was readying herself to supplicate to her Maker.

"It's wrong to...." Martha struggled to compose herself. "It is wrong to teach against our ancient beliefs, ...against the truths taught by our forefathers...."

"Truths according to Martha, daughter of Sam."

"Truths according to our Great Creator as passed down from our esteemed prophets. Esrom is the only one who can be inspired to give new instruction...."

"And I receive them from Esrom and pass them on to you."

"You. You! You...? Since when does Esrom speak through you?" Martha exploded. "I know the protocol, the chain of authority...."

Zillah materialized gracefully from mid garden as only she could do. "Martha, dear, what seems to be the trouble?"

"Martha cannot accept changes our Prophet Esrom has initiated to her curriculum," Noami said coolly.

"Now, Martha," Zillah laid a comforting hand on Martha's arm. Her voice was soft. "What could be so disturbing?"

"I want to speak to Esrom," Martha demanded. "No one has seen or heard from him in weeks. Who...."

"I have spoken to him," Noami wore an infuriating smile. "He cannot give an audience to everyone who gets the urge to question his authority. If you cannot see yourself obeying the orders from the prophet, then you will be replaced. You may even find yourself charged with blasphemy. Good day, Martha. Good day, Priestess Zillah."

Martha opened her mouth to speak but Zillah gently turned Martha toward her. "Now, now, Martha."

"My family and I are upstanding citizens," Martha choked, "....never had any trouble."

"That could be because you have not had to make a public stand." Zillah held her hands. She lowered her voice. "To stand for the new teachings from our ruler's priests, you will go to hell as sure as the night is dark. To stand for the ancient teachings, yea, well, we know what could come of that...."

"What am I to do...?"

"Hush. Walk with me." Zillah linked arms with Martha as she guided her down the garden path. Raasah watched until the foliage hid them from view.

Raasah drifted her attention to a pillared platform one story up. There, standing in the shadow, was her mother, posed and serene, viewing the scene. Sablon beckoned to a young servant girl who then scurried off in the direction of Zillah and Martha. Before Sablon retreated into the building's depths, Raasah was sure that she caught a glimpse of Noami by her side.

As Raasah leaned against the wall to absorb all she had seen and heard, a voice from her right startled her.

"Are you alright?" Ada said tenuously.

Raasah nodded as her heart pounding madly.

"I volunteered to get the rags," Ada explained. "Phebe, the senior, is taking her temporary position too seriously. She is acting more like a curt general than a teacher – so I volunteered to help you clean up. Better than staying in there!" She smiled endearingly.

"Did you see….?"

"Oh, Priestess Zillah and our teacher, Martha? Doesn't look like Martha will be coming back to finish the class today."

"No, doesn't look that way…" Raasah debated whether or not to ask Ada what she had heard and if she had seen her mother by the far building, but she didn't. She didn't know Ada well enough to discuss her fears and concerns. She did not know what 'stand', if any, Ada had taken. *For that matter, I don't know if I have a 'stand' never mind what that means.*

Raasah did not feel like talking at all so she encouraged Ada to chat about fitting in as a new girl and her nervousness at helping her mother host the many parties that Darius held at his palace. Raasah had forgotten that Ada lived under the same roof of the intimidating High Priest. Raasah noted, though, that Ada did not consider the Darius' home as hers even though by law she was now his daughter. It was hard for Raasah to even believe that timid little Ada was related to this powerful, daunting man, not even as a niece.

Once the rags were located, Ada took her leave to return to the classroom. An employee from the school assisted Raasah with cleaning up her hand and robe. By the time Jaona had located her, Raasah's hands showed no trace of the mishap but her robe was still blotted with the evidence. Jaona had gathered Raasah's classroom effects. Once Raasah's robe was folded and packaged for a servant to deliver home, they bustled past the empty class, past the statue-like guards, to their next class as Jaona happily gossiped away.

ɮ~

Classes couldn't have ended sooner! Raasah was impatient to finally speak to the fowler. Tara had told Terjah that Geshem's body seemed to be healing well but he was slipping in and out of consciousness. At Raasah's insistence, Terjah had agreed to arrange with Tara so she could see him. Jaona waved good-bye from the doorway, before she gaily skipped off with Isobel to the Morcum practice. As Raasah filed out with the other girls, she saw Ada approach a lovely woman by a guilded carriage. Ada turned and smiled at Raasah as the woman put an affectionate arm around her.

This must be her mother. Raasah smiled and waved back, a little envious of the tender scene.

Raasah darted through the crowds to the stairs that led to the healing rooms – her concern for Chemish's great-uncle and the incident with Martha momentarily forgotten. Tara and Terjah were waiting at the plaza level. Tara was dressed in a simple but stylish huipile and robe with fine brocade much more flattering than the healer clothing and more appropriate for an elite citizen. With her thick hair pulled loosely back, Tara's generous brown eyes were enhanced, giving her face a prettiness that Raasah had not noticed before. Once more, Tara had her hand on her brother's arm and both brother and healer apprentice were so intense in each other that they did not see Raasah until she was almost upon them. *Terjah must have noticed the prettiness as well!*

At the sight of Raasah, Tara dropped her hands and smiled shyly. Draping his arm around Raasah's shoulder, Terjah led his sister quickly away from the stairs.

"Geshem has been moved," he said in a hushed voice.

"He is being cared for in the home of Healer Shaquah," Tara explained. "She is still attending her patients in the healing rooms here. We must hurry."

"Why was he moved?" Raasah inquired, as they hurried along.

"Shaquah believed she could better care for him if he was under her own roof," Tara said. "She is the healer in charge of Geshem. It is most bewildering why he has not responded to our efforts. He seemed to be on his way to a full recovery and then he lapsed into a delirious state, calling out names and mumbling. It is most mysterious why he hasn't recovered with the expert treatment of our best healers. I thought we were going to lose him last night."

"Tara stayed with him all night," Terjah explained. "He is alive because of her."

"I don't know about that, but he is still alive." A short silent walk later, Tara lead them through the front gate and around to the side of Shaquah's residence. She held up her hand to still brother and sister. "Let me go ahead and make sure the servants are not about the room." She looked from Terjah to Raasah. "Wait here." Tara slipped quietly toward the main entrance.

The whitewashed home of Shaquah and her family was similar to but on a smaller scale than that of the Botholuem home. Small flowering bushes lined the walk and fragrant herb filled the yard around the cluster of buildings that made up her home. Everything was tidy and organized and emulated the healer's patient, meticulous nature. Raasah mused as she spied a large macaw peek its red head through the lush green of a dwarfed pimento and then watched as he flapped heavily into the air. *Ackoutl? You look just like Geshem's pet Ackoutl.* She turned to her brother.

"Shaquah is under strict instructions not to let visitors in to see him until the fever passes," Terjah explains quietly. "We must be very careful not to be seen."

The siblings faintly heard Tara converse with one of the servants and then, between the detached rooms, Tara suddenly reappeared.

"Quickly," Tara said. "I sent the servant for an oil tincture but she is as proficient as her mistress so she won't be too long."

Tara led them through a narrow path between two smaller buildings. Pulling the doorcovering aside, they were enveloped in the heavy smell of sage and other aromic smells. A frail-looking man lay on a sterile cot. His hands were wringing together about his chest, his head lolling back and forth with hollow words forming on his lips. Geshem's wild beard had been trimmed close to his face and, at first, Raasah didn't recognize him.

"It doesn't make any sense," Tara was saying in a hushed voice. "He should be alert by now. His wounds have healed nicely but he still has fevers and only wakes in fits."

Raasah knelt beside the fretful sleeping form. "Geshem," she said timidly. "It is Raasah. Can you hear me?"

Geshem stilled then suddenly opened his eyes wide. "Look out! The blood of the people runs freely in the clearing. The face of the beast.... Hide, my child! There are too many..." His eyes closed and his head rolled to the side. Sweat beaded on his forehead. With his eyelids half open, his head turned back. "He betrayed us," he breathed heavily. Raasah leaned closer and smelt his stale medicine-y breath. Even more quietly he mumbled: "Noalas... Noalas...."

"I'm sorry. You had best go now," Tara said urgently.

"Thank you, Tara," Terjah touched her shoulder gently.

"Yea, thank you," Raasah whispered absently as she rose to her feet. "Please let us know if anything changes."

"Of course." Tara parted the doorcovering, paused, then motioned for them. Terjah and Raasah left solemnly and did not speak until they were past the gate.

"He said someone betrayed us," Raasah said thoughtfully. "'He betrayed us'…. That is what he said. Then,….. then he said 'Noalas'. Maybe he was calling for him to help."

"Noalas?" Terjah stopped and turned Raasah toward him.

"That's what he said… the last thing he said…"

"You must have heard him wrong."

"Nah, I'm sure he said that. Noalas…." Raasah was preoccupied with her disappointment. She had hoped to have learned more from Geshem but he only confirmed what they already knew – that they had been betrayed. Then something occurred to her. "Geshem said 'HE betrayed us'…."

"What?" Terjah seemed to be deep in his own thoughts.

"Geshem said 'HE', not 'THEY'." Raasah gripped Terjah's arm. "Don't you see? Geshem knows who it is – and then that person will lead us to the people responsible…. People powerful enough or wealthy enough that they could arrange an attack that could overcome disciplined skilled fighters like Noalas…."

Hope swelled in her bosom – hope for answers; hope for some form of restitution. *But what kind of restitution would make up for the deaths of so many good people, for the death of her good father?*

Terjah looked soothingly at his sister. "Noalas…, he…."

"Yea. As uncomfortable as I felt near Noalas, I was glad he and his grim-looking troop were there. The person responsible must have been powerful indeed to send THEM to their deaths." Her eyes were misty. "And Geshem knows who HE is," she choked softly.

"Noalas was at the camp during the fighting?"

"I saw him moments before. He was standing near the servants' fire. In all the confusion," she swallowed hard, "I could not say where he was when the arrows were flying."

"Now, Geshem is delirious. He may be confused...."

"Terjah," Raasah loosened the grip on her brother's arm and looked up into his drawn face. It looked like it had aged ten years. "I know you. You are bothered by his words too." Just then, Raasah was distracted by a tall wiry man that had entered the street behind Terjah. He appeared to be looking for something or someone. Raasah stared at him.

"What is it?" Terjah asked, seeing his sister's distracted look. He turned slowly to where she gazed.

"That man...." Raasah paused. As the latter's face turned her way, she declared, "Terjah, that man, the one right there.... I am sure it is a juggler that travelled with father's caravan. ...I thought Geshem and I were the only survivors."

Terjah turned sharply the rest of the way around just as this man fixed his eyes on them. For the few fleeting seconds, both brother and sister studied the stranger whose adam's apple began to bob nervously along his skinny neck; his tongue slipping back and forth across his thin lips – *like it had that night at the camp!*

"It IS him! It is!"

Realizing that he had been recognized, the juggler took a long step back while still staring wide-eyed at the siblings, and then pivoting wildly, bolted down the street, elbowing and knocking people down in his haste.

"Go straight home!" Terjah spoke sharply. "Don't talk to any-one." With that, he dashed after the fleeing juggler and vanished amid the citizens and bobbing carriages.

Concern and wonder at seeing another victim of the massacre alive, and the obvious reluctance of the 'victim' to be discovered by Raasah and her brother, brought the fearfulness from her night-mares over her like a wave. Apprehensively, she turned toward home, vying up and down the lanes for more faces that might materialize from her father's mercantile caravan. The words "be careful" swam through her head until she recognized the quarter of Ammonihah she had wandered in. Her cautious slothful steps quickened. Chemish's shop was nearby.

She remembered suddenly the conversation of the councilmen and hurried determinedly for Chemish's shop to let him know what she had overheard earlier about his great-uncle, or so she told herself. She was also wrestling with whether she should share with Chemish what Geshem had said and the sighting of the juggler despite Terjah's demand not to speak of it.

But, Chemish is not anyone – not to me anymore! He has a way of clearing my mind and helping me see things in a new light. He will help me make sense of this. Raasah had so many questions she wanted – no, needed – to explore with someone. Her steps length-ened at the thought of seeing her carpenter again.

While still a distance from the shop, Raasah detected the out-line of the carpentry plaque that hung over the road. The once sturdy sign swayed tipsy from one chain. With the sound of harsh shouts and crashing, her determined pace faltered. Warily she stud-ied the scene ahead of her and, as she did so, she spied the uni-formed soldiers. Taking a few more cautious steps, Raasah spied two strapping military men struggled to contain Chemish, one wrapping a leather-clad arm around Chemish's neck from behind. At least two more soldiers were within.

Fearfully, Raasah watched as they smashed an elegantly carved chair to the ground and benches were toppled over and cleared. She spotted Chemish's father struggling to his feet next to an ornate beam ineptly leaning against a collapsed table. A soldier raised a mallet and, with a sickening thud, it struck Adam's upturned arm. Once more, he crumpled from Raasah's view.

As Raasah hesitantly approached the shop, she noticed the glint of a short steel blade twisting in front of Chemish's face. She halted, rooted to the spot, just as Chemish turned his head toward her. He stopped struggling. Blood matted his hair over one eye. He mouthed "Go" to her before he addressed his jeering tormenters.

Raasah searched the other shops with a sweep of her head as sounds of destruction continued to thump and clammer from Adam's shop. All the occupants had deserted or retreated into the back recesses of the abodes. None of the neighbours came to their assistance. Fright enveloped her as she receded into an alley partially obscuring her behind a store display of fishing gear.

She crouched closer, hearing the cruel laughter of the tormenters and more crashing and smashing. Peering through the hanging nets, she realized the knife-wielding offender was Zeniff, once more impersonating a soldier. Zeniff's shabby little beard glistened with fresh blood from his sneering spitting mouth – a wound she hoped he had received at Chemish's hand. Zeniff leaned in close to Chemish's ear, though his voice was loud and clear.

"You think a daughter of Sablon would be interested in you!" he taunted, still brandishing the sharp lethal weapon in front of

Chemish and then lowered the knife to his throat. "You arrogant, dumb toad. I could gut you right here...." Warmth flooded into Raasah's face; her world started to spin. *Am I the reason for all this?* A mixture of anger and guilt flooded over her.

The thundering of approaching feet instinctively caused her to back further out of view. She stumbled into an old loom that entangled her sleeve, sending it crashing down next to her. Terrified, Raasah tore her sleeve loose and ran down the lane like the devil was at her feet. A tear of shame trickled down her cheek.

---

17   *Morcum Games: These were the official celebrated games in Ancient Central America and the ballcourts could be found in all the substantial cities unearthed. The name 'Morcum' is used here for lack of historical reference to what the people then really call it. The rules are only assumed from documentation discovered and elaborated on for the sake of the story.*

Chapter 10

Adam's Attackers

The sun had sunk behind the distant mountains by the time the hooded group ventured along the shadows to the heavy carved door. Having a solid door, never mind a decorative one, was a luxury most citizens could ever wish for, but being skilled in woodworking had its advantages. After another persistent but muffled knock on the door, the visitors could hear the shuffling of footsteps approaching within.

Words were exchanged at the door and the dark forms were ushered in. Once inside, Terjah lowered his hood. His face was etched in dark contrasts from the single light of the oil lamp held by a round-faced woman. Marian & Raasah lowered their shawls unto their shoulders. They had worn the coarse gardening robes of their servants over their loose shifts. Marian's insistence to disguise their departure to the Adam home added to Raasah's alarm over the things that she had rehearsed to them. Hearing the soft scuffling of feet above, she looked up the narrow staircase beyond their hostess.

Wrapped tightly in a serape, a battered-looking Adam gingerly stepped into the light assisted by a tall young lady. Adam had his right arm in a brace supported in a sling. His head was bound and his right eye was partially swollen shut. The older woman turned.

"My husband, you should be resting."

"Ethel, I am not dying yet." Adam limped slightly as he

approached and took his wife's hand. "With visitors coming this late, it must be important and I am still head of this family. I must greet our guests."

"Adam, we heard," Marian said simply, stepping forward, gingerly stroking his hurt face. "It's good to see you well, Marylee," she added as she patted the arm of Adam's assistant.

"Who did this to you?" Terjah said through clutched teeth. After having a quick look, he had returned from the shambles of the shop adjacent to the home. Now seeing a just man like Adam hurt and broken, it caused a fury that shot through him like a poison. Raasah shuffled back. The guilt that she felt for the attack surged hot through her veins even though her grandmother had graciously assured her there were other factors that had initiated the attack.

Raasah's gaze flittered from face to face until it rested on the slender lady by Adam's side. Slowly Marylee skirted the room and lit the lamps set about it. She was attractive and had her father's square face and curly hair that was tied loosely back in a wide ribbon. Raasah could see the resemblance between Chemish and his sister as well. Marylee had married last year to her childhood sweetheart. Raasah watched as she put a protective hand over the small swell of her belly. Three months ago, Marylee had announced to her family that she would be giving her parents their first grandchild. Chemish was bursting with pride at the thought of being an uncle.

And, where was Chemish? As if in answer to her unasked question, Ethel explained, "Chemish has gone to purchase some lumber so he can salvaged some of the damaged items. He thought it best to travel this evening to avoid attention in the city."

"Then Chemish is not hurt!" Marian breathed with relief.

"Nothing that the Good Lord can't heal with a little help from my ointments." Ethel forced a smile but her eyes glistened wet and Marian put an arm around her shoulders as a tear released down her pale cheeks.

"We are here to help now too," Marian said soothingly. "First, I think we all need a hot drink." Marian coaxed Ethel toward the small courtyard where they could rekindle a small fire under the griddle. Terjah took the hint and beckoned to Raasah and Adam to sit on the floor mat and cushions in the main room. Marylee fetched her father an extra cushion to make him more comfortable.

"Raasah overheard something today." Terjah began. "She was coming to tell you when she saw the soldiers attacking you."

"They weren't soldiers," Adam said gravely.

"Nah, one was a friend of Zoric," Raasah agreed. "His name is Zeniff. He was only dressed as a soldier. He has done this before – dressed as a soldier, I mean – when the prisoners were brought into the square…"

Suddenly they all went silent as they heard a muffled knock on the door. Marylee, still standing, started hesitantly for the door but Terjah motioned to her to stay and approached the door himself.

Terjah spoke briefly into the minute opening of the door and then opened it halfway to let the slender form of Tara into the light. She was followed by a solid man, not fat, with rosy plump cheeks that were generously engulfed by thick silver hair. Raasah heart lightened as she looked into her great-uncle's kind face and she jumped up to greet him, letting herself be enveloped into his thick arms.

"Uncle Normad, I'm so glad you are here."

"Now, child, it will be alright," Normad said, looking down at her solicitously.

Tara strode directly to Adam on the mat. "How are you?" she asked as she examined the sling and touched his forehead with the back of her hand. Adam enveloped her hand in his and lowered it from his head.

"I am fine, Tara," he said. "I appreciate your concern but between my daughter and my wife I have more than enough bothering about." He smiled kindly and winked at Marylee.

Normad led Raasah back to the cushioned seating area where Terjah joined them after securing the door.

"Raasah, tell us what you heard," Terjah prompted.

Raasah recounted the conversation of the council in the square. They all listened without interruption. When she mentioned Gormonaluk, she remembered suddenly that this was Tara's uncle. Nervously, she glanced at Tara but she did not seemed disturbed at the mention of his name.

Once Raasah had finished, Adam said thoughtfully, "This is a critical matter."

"I'm sorry," Raasah looked anxiously at Adam and Marylee. "I came to warn you so you would know about the meeting in time but when I came…. He was holding a knife on Chemish….. I saw them beat you down with a hammer…. I was so scared. I heard more people coming….."

"Those that came were part of the council." Adam's eyes were distant momentarily. He looked at Terjah and then off into the distance again. Raasah wondered if he was alright. "It was puzzling," he finally continued, "but I believe they saved our lives….. Though, for how long, I don't know. Absalom was there. He ordered his son to lower the knife and let Chemish go. Jashorum was there too with his son Zoric trailing behind. Zoric looked so smug. If ever I saw evil, I saw it in him today. The way he set his eyes on the knife at Chemish's neck...., it was as if he was willing it to...."

"I'm sorry. It's all my fault!" Raasah blundered. "I never meant...."

Adam's eyes came to rest on Raasah. "Of course it's not your fault. Evil has been in that boy from the day he was born. Both Zoric AND his brother...." Adam's voice trailed off.

"Oh, hon. These are dangerous times and the likes of Zoric and his family are the epitome of malevolence." Ethel had suddenly appeared behind Raasah, gently stroking her hair. "The devil uses people like them and people like Zeezrom and Issachar feed off of them like jackals."

"Issachar?" Raasah whispered. "Yea," she said aloud. "I believe Issachar was one of the councilmen I heard."

"But I don't understand," Terjah said slowly.

"What do you mean the council saved your lives?" Tara articulated Terjah's question.

Adam answered: "The nearest I can recall..... Absalom chastised Zeniff. He said 'This is not the time'.... but that my family would be made an example of.... He said 'We don't want Adam's family getting the sympathy of the people from this incident' ...or something like that. He said that this would be taken care of...."

"We must let the others know. They are getting too strong and brazen. We must come to a decision." Normad was speaking. Marian was standing behind him and he patted her hand that had come to rest on his shoulder. Then, quickly slipping her hand away, Marian gestured to Raasah.

"Come, granddaughter. You need something warm in your stomach…"

"We must contact Reuben…" Terjah addressed those sitting.

With voices lowered, the drone of conversation resumed after Raasah was led away. She glanced over her shoulder at the grave faces deep in hushed discussion.

◌

That night, Raasah dreamed her terrible dream. She saw the bodies fall around her. In the distant she saw Geshem. He was shouting "Noalas! Noalas!" His gaunt face with black empty eyes looked directly at her. He gestured toward the trees but, before she could look, the masked faces obscured her vision. Garish ear spools of gold, turquoise, and quartz exposed themselves as one of the assailants leaned over her; cruel laughter stung her very soul.

"Yon daughter of Sablon," a voice, she should have recognized, sneered.

The white palms of gold ringed hands reached for her face. She fought to push them away. She needed to see Geshem. She needed to see who he was pointing at. Her heart was thundering in her ears. She lashed out wildly at her oppressors.

"Raasah…"

Sobbing, Raasah wrestled franticly to free her pinned arms.

"Child…."

"Nah, nah!!" Raasah screamed.

"Raasah, hon…. Is's a'righ'….!"

"I must see….!" Raasah's face was damp. As her eyes flashed open, she gasped upright, momentarily unaware of the concerned face of her dear grandmother or of Hannah who was gently attempting to calm Raasah's flaying limbs. Exhausted, Raasah dropped her trembling arms and folded into Marian's arms weeping abandonly.

Chapter 11

Tara

It was not unlike Gormonaluk to make last minute travel arrangements for her brother, but it infuriated Raasah that Terjah would oblige him to leave her floundering in uncertainty. Three days had passed since Raasah and her brother had spoken so briefly to Geshem and, to make things worse, Terjah had not been able to catch up with the juggler. Terjah had told her he had to go to a neighbouring town early the next day.

Though she had promised Terjah not to discuss Geshem or the juggler with anyone, without him here, she felt she did need to speak of things to someone before she burst. And she was concerned for Chemish and his family. But Raasah had gone by Chemish's shop everyday without seeing anyone about, causing her even more concern until her grandmother assured her that the family was just staying with friends until Adam felt stronger.

Today she woke up cross and frustrated. Raasah fingered a small official-looking parchment lying loosely on her lap. She smoothed it out and re-read the contents, though she had read it more times than she could count since it arrived yesterday by a prim temple courier. He had not waited for her to read its message. Upon breaking the official red and blue seal, the message she read was brief but eloquently written in thin artistic swirls:

Addressed to Raasah of the Botholuem Household

Sablon, the Holy High Priestess of Kukulkan, regrets that she is unable to entertain your request for an audience at this time. A messenger will be sent when an appropriate time can be set.

That was all it said. Raasah brushed her forefinger along the edge of the parchment, dislodging some of the blue wax from the signet seal that had held the parchment tightly rolled. She gently picked up the small lump of wax and rolled in between thumb and finger to resemble a blue-coloured pea. *It was not right – a blue pea – so unnatural.* She looked, without seeing, once more at the message. An angry tear threatened to spill down her hot cheeks. Her mother had not taken enough interest in her to send even a short personal note, but only a generic reply through a temple scribe... *like I had been a stranger instead of a flesh-and-blood daughter. ... just like the blue pea – it was not right!*

And the eminent way her mother had been referred to in the message – this was disturbing. No one had ever before included the name of the Creator in their title. Raasah brushed the back of her forefinger against the corner of her eye to dislodge the tear before could smear her freshly-applied makeup, making it obvious how much she was hurt. Tensely she rolled the parchment up once more and laid it next to the blue pea, resisting the urge to crush the scroll with a fist and throw it across the room.

Hannah straightened out the collar of her tunic and Raasah mellowed at her tender touch. Humming a gay melody, Hannah contently busied herself with hair combs and ribbons for the finishing touches of Raasah's hair. Raasah glanced up at Hannah's intent face still sporting a discoloration below her eye, the remnants of a blacken eye Raasah's flaying arms had given her after her nightmare. Raasah had apologized over and over but Hannah kindly insisted it looked worse than it felt.

By the time Raasah headed toward the upper city, she was clear in what she wanted to do. She was tired of feeling apologetic; she was tired of her nightmares; she was tired of feeling out of control; and she was tired of people keeping information from her and treating her like a silly child. She was determined to find someone who could help her find answers.

With a singleness of purpose, reluctantly with her Amos-shadow in tow, Raasah had completely forgotten to gather charitable food items and, upon seeing the old widow and her grandson, she contritely fumbled for a few coins from her purse. Raasah bit her lower lip. She was apologizing again.

Though it was early, the streets were filling quickly with eager assemblies of friends and families filing toward the Morcum ballcourt in hopes of getting good seats. The boisterous team from David had challenged the Ammonihahites to what would prove to be an aggressive action-filled game. The bets were high and the hype higher. Sprinkled into the growing crowd were the rowdy revelators already into the spirited drinks that appeared to have given permission for them to be obnoxious and asinine.

She hurried past a group of foul-mouthed youth who had playfully surrounded a licentious young woman. She, in turn, was taunting, teasing, and enjoying their vulgar advances. Raasah pulled her veil tightly over her head. The distracted Amos lagged behind, enjoying the lustful display and barely conscience of his charge. Turning down the lane towards Shaquah's home, a relieved Raasah impatiently called out Amos' name, sending him hobble-skipping to catch up. From here on, to Amos' disappointment, there was only the occasional family group meandering past them toward the southeast section for the games.

This was a quiet out-of-the-way neighbourhood that was well suited to the healer's liking and beneficial for the fowler as he recovered. Raasah looked around for a familiar face. It was just a possibility but she hoped Terjah would be here if he had returned from his trip. She earnestly scanned the area in and around Shaquah's home until she saw a movement just the other side of Geshem's structure. As she strained to make out who it was, one of the figures rounded the corner. It wasn't Terjah, but the wild-haired figure of Tara; a second figure disappeared across the inner courtyard. Before Raasah could turn away, Tara caught her eye and quickened her pace toward her.

Tara was not much older than Raasah but… *much more mature in the ways of the world and certainly more in control of her life.* Tara beckoned Raasah to a bench in the healer's fragrant garden. Though the growing crowds could be heard in the background, it was peaceful and calming here. Raasah dismissed a thankful Amos who then hurried off to seek out a more boisterous atmosphere.

"Geshem is still sleeping," Tara explained, as she attempted to pile her wild curls onto her head with a decorative comb.

"Here let me do that," Raasah offered as wisps of hair escaped and one side seemed to fight back. Tara abandoned her attempts to Raasah's more experience hands.

"Geshem had a rough night," Tara said. "He seemed to be reliving the attack."

"I know how that feels," Raasah said quietly. She wound Tara's hair into long ringlets.

"Of course, you do. I'm sorry."

Raasah locked Tara's hair into a swirl of a bun with the ruby comb, still leaving a crusade of curls falling onto her shoulders. "Please don't apologize. There is too much apologizing…." Raasah adjusted the comb a little to the left. "There. That should do it."

Patting her hair ever so gently, Tara smiled broadly. "Thank you. You have gifted hands to be able to do anything with this undisciplined hair!"

"No problem," Raasah said, pleased with her accomplishment. The style was befitting an elite but not sumptuous and it suited Tara's oval face very well. Then looking more serious, she said, "I would like very much to talk with Geshem again…. if it is alright… actually, I heard Terjah was to return today…. I mean, I know he comes around here ….. You and he…."

Tara blushed. The hair was forgotten.

"It's not like…"

"Oh, I didn't mean…. I mean, not that it isn't ok. Oh, I am making this very awkward, aren't I?" Raasah looked sheepishly at Tara who laughed warmly.

Raasah relaxed.

"Tara," Raasah said slowly, "There are things I needed to ask Terjah but, when he was unexpectedly sent away by your uncle…."

"Nah, Raasah. My uncle didn't send him. Terjah took some personal time…."

Raasah's mouth opened slightly then closed. She studied Tara's face. She felt impressed to confide in this slim girl. With a deep sigh, she began:

"I am so weary of my brother shielding me from things that I should know. And he is not the only one keeping things from me.

It is just so frustrating! I can handle the truth much better than all this uncertainty."

Tara laid a hand gently on Raasah's arm. "If people are keeping things from you, it's most likely because they don't want to alarm you."

"I know they mean well, but the not knowing is causing me more concern than good now. How can I deal with what is going on around me if I don't understand why it is happening? I have bits and pieces and I can only come to disturbing conclusions without the missing parts. Why can't they understand this?"

Tara looked intensely at Raasah. "You are stronger than they know.... or want to believe. I will see what I can do."

Grateful for the vote of confidence, Raasah smiled and then, lowering her eyes, she said softly, "Terjah does like you, you know."

Tara's cheeks darkened again. "Raasah, I don't think it is like that...."

"Who is that?" Raasah interrupted looking past her to a man loitering near Geshem's room. He had abrasions on his left arm and a reddened scrap across his cheek. *It's the same man that was pacing at the healing rooms with the injuries received from the fat man.* She was certain she knew him from somewhere else as well but he quickly strolled off again before Raasah could study him.

"Him? Oh, that's Festus. He has taken an interest in one of Shaquah's servants. Chloe, that's her name. She is a despondent unpleasant girl and I am not sure what Festus sees in her," Tara paused, "but it certainly has brought a livelier step into the girl. She can be such a maladroit at times."

"Chloe helps look after the patients?"

"Shaquah only has Chloe do menial chores around the villa.

The girl is simple and manages to muddle up the easiest instructions. But, then, Shaquah can be very hard on her, especially lately. Since Shaquah's young daughter went to visit relatives, Shaquah is very short-tempered. I don't know why she let her go if it upsets her so." Tara frowned. "Sometimes I feel so sorry for Chloe. Maybe Festus is what she needs to feel good about herself.

"Let me see if Geshem is awake yet," Tara continued and hurried back to the building. Raasah spied Festus again as he exited the back of Shaquah's property. He gazed back at her and their eyes met. There was definitely something else she should remember about the man. Tara startled her as she reappeared beside her.

"He's awakening," Tara said, "But, Raasah, you must bear in mind – though Geshem has no fever now, he is still very weak." Then she added, "I want you to hear what he has to say."

Once Raasah's eyes adjusted to the darkened room, she sat quietly next to Geshem's bedroll. The concentration of aromatic oils was very strong. The oils included a purifier as well as a deterrent against harmful insects and pests, a necessity that the healer would demand for her patients – for Shaquah was zealous in all her profession's responsibilities.

Tara had lit two of the lamps on the walls. As Raasah's vision adjusted to the additional light, Raasah suddenly gasped at the sight of a slouched form with wide frightened eyes in the far corner.

"Chloe, what are you doing in here?" Tara snapped.

With downcast eyes, Chloe mumbled and then pointed limply to clean linen next to the bed. "I tot he could …."

"I'll take care of it, Chloe. You must go!"

"I'm sorry. Don't tell Mistress Shaquah I did wrong….Please…."

The girl scuttled out into the sunshine.

"So…. that is Chloe," Raasah mused. "She really does fear the healer!"

"And for good reason," Tara said with concern. "She should never have been in here."

Fingers brushed Raasah's arm. "Raasah, you ok…. Your poor father!" Geshem's eyes darted around the room. "We're not safe…."

"You ARE safe now," Raasah said soothingly, gently placing her hand on his. "You just need to rest and get well."

"They wore masks but…" Geshem squeezed her arm feebly. "Must talk to Reuben."

"You can talk to him when you are stronger." Shaquah darkened the doorway. All eyes turned her way at the stern sound of her voice. Her stance at the entrance and her no nonsense tone reminded Raasah of Teacher Deborah, and it momentarily unnerved her.

Geshem gripped Raasah's arm, looking from Shaquah to Raasah. "Raasah, you need to know…. Noalasss …"

"Now this is just enough," Shaquah reprimanded. "You have caused him considerable stress. The patient needs to rest," Shaquah removed Geshem's hand from Raasah and reached across her for a cup of dark liquid. Raasah shifted out of the way. Once Shaquah had monopolized the area next to Geshem, she added a few drops into the cup from a vial and lifted the bitter-smelling contents to the parched lips of the patient. "We mustn't get him agitated."

Raasah turned to go but Geshem grabbed her veil that was draped loosely around her shoulders. It slid airily to the floor, except for a corner that Geshem still clung to. As Raasah knelt forward, catching hold of it, the fowler pulled the material toward his face and reached his head closer to her.

"Must warn you," he said sluggishly. "He was the one. He

was with them. You must warn Reuben. It was Noalas.... He be-traaayed ...ussssssss...." Geshem's hand opened slowly; his eyelids fluttered and closed.

"I had to give him something to sleep," Shaquah said and, then, stingingly addressed Raasah. "So, YOU are Sablon's daughter. It's a miracle you survived that massacre with, what...? ... a bump on your head...? Now, how did you manage to avoid harm's way?" Shaquah turned as if to dismiss her. Obviously, the healer did not want an answer. Raasah hugged her veil to her as she rose to full height.

"Tara," Shaquah continued, "we will talk about this.... unau-thorized visit."

"But, Mistress Shaquah, you said when the fever was gone he could...."

"We will speak later." Shaquah snapped & retrieved the cup and wash basin. "I will send Nahuatl in to watch him." She briskly walked away.

Raasah was bristling with emotions. *What was the Healer try-ing to insinuate? And what was Geshem trying to tell me? If only Shaquah had just given me more time.* Geshem did have answers for her but now she was being ushered from the room into the bright daylight.

Tara steered Raasah to the gate. She assured her that the fowler was slowly recovering and there would be plenty of time to talk with him.

"He said that Noalas was the one.... the one that betrayed us...." Raasah looked questioningly at Tara. "But Noalas couldn't have done it.... I mean I didn't really like him – he gave me the chills just looking at him... But he and his men died...."

"Nah," Tara was shaking her head. "Raasah, Noalas is very much alive…. Terjah has visited him in his home and spoken to him."

"But there were no other survivors… I was told…. But I've seen the juggler and now you tell me Noalas…?" Raasah was shaking her head. "I don't understand."

"Look, there's someone we should talk to."

"Who?"

"Priest Onihah. He is very wise and, if he doesn't know an answer, he knows how to find out."

ཆ

Tara and Raasah quickened their steps toward another of the terraced buildings next to Palenia.

"This is where all the important records are kept," Tara explained. "Onihah is not only the high priest and first counselor to the Prophet Esrom, he is also a scribe and the chief record keeper. Here below Esrom's office are the archives of records where Onihah spends a great deal of time… going over their contents with Esrom, transcribing as dictated by the prophet,… or counseling with Esrom regarding the welfare of the people." When Onihah was not with the prophet, Tara was saying, his favourite place to be was amid the rows upon rows of ancient scrolls and codices. Today, though, the Hall of Records was locked and no one answered Tara's pounding on the heavy metal-plated door.

Discouraged, Raasah joined Tara once again in the bright sunlight. Temporarily blinded, she practically ran into Little Brother with the matron of the orphanage in tow.

Shading her eyes, Raasah stuttered, "Little Brother!" Quickly regaining her composure, she added playfully, "that is most unbecoming of a gallant young man to drag a lady across the square."

The boy released the matron's hand with a mischievous grin.

Stepping forward, Tara kissed the matron on the cheek. "Wa-ie, Mistress Eliz!"

The slender ruby-faced woman, slightly out of breath, squinted at the girls under shielded eyes. Her thick wavy hair was unsuccessful pulled back giving her head a frizzy look in the bright sunlight.

"Wa-ie, Raasah. And Tara, how are you? Staying out of trouble?" Her strained frown crept quickly into a grin.

"I am always trying to," Tara grinned back.

"Little Brother wants you both to come to the Morcum Games," Eliz said. "All the children are heading there now...."

"Of course we will be there," Tara answered for both of them. "We have a few things to do first but we promise we will come."

"You will find us at the west end." Mistress Eliz wrapped her dowdy cotton scarf protectively around her head. "We will look for you, both of you."

With one of Little Brother's signature big smiles and a nod of the matron's head, he and Eliz disappeared into the growing flow of people heading for the ball court. The girls casually weaved their way against the crowd.

"The matron seems to know you well," Raasah commented curiously.

"I spent some time at the orphanage when my parents died," Tara explained. "Eliz was so kind and patient. Back then, I had a tendency to push the rules. Oh, madders, I still try the rules! That's what gets my adoptive family so frustrated with me, I'm sure. I imagine they would prefer I had no opinion at all and did as I was told without question….like a trained monkey – at least then they might find some pleasure in me…," she said ruefully, then looked up with a mischievous smile.

Tara continued: "I didn't realize how great I had things at the orphanage until my aunt and uncle came to claim me. After just a few unbearable days in my new home, I ran away. Eliz found me. I begged her to let me stay at the orphanage. I told her I would teach the others to read and do all the chores. But during the night, my aunt came to get me. I heard her voice and snuck up to hear what she was saying. She sounded like she really wanted me – she sounded so sincere. I went home with her that night.

"But my aunt and uncle…. I don't understand why they came for me. There is no love between us. And their son, cousin Tutoris, is so resentful of my being there. I ran away again one night and returned to the orphanage. I overheard Eliz talking with another, saying how she was unable to raise enough support to feed the children and how worried she was for them. I realized how much of a burden I would be if I were to stay. At least with Uncle Gormonaluk, I have had food and shelter and was not taking it from a child that had no choices.

"I do go back regularly and teach the children reading as I offered. I know Eliz would never have sent me away if she had known I was there that night. After what I heard at the orphanage, I snuck back to my uncle and aunt's but Tutoris had seen me leave and I had a lashing when I got back and, for a month, I was confined to the villa. From that day forth, Tutoris has made it his personal duty to catch me even thinking of doing something forbidden so that Aunt Zipporah could have the pleasure of applying some punishment.

It is wonderful that Tutoris has now found other interests besides making my life miserable."

Tara paused again, realizing she had strayed once more from her subject. "Eliz really does love the children – there are never too many. It is amazing how she can make them all feel so special. But it is a struggle for her to give them all what she feels they should have."

"She certainly is a special person for all she does for those children."

"Do you see that man by the pillar?" Tara said, looking straight ahead.

"Yea. My father called him the 'Great Soldier'. He said he fought and was injured many years ago."

The beggar man sat straight-backed in a simple neat tunic and soiled wraps about his feet. He sat on his cloak of browns and orange, his cup set in front of him.

Raasah continued: "My father and I used to visit him regularly...."

"Then you know Ali."

"I... I never knew his name.... I never thought to ask him his name."

"Did you know a large portion of all he collects, he shares with the orphanage," Tara asked. "I don't know of a more generous man in all of Ammonihah."

"I didn't know," Raasah stared numbly at the man named Ali.

"He had his eyes burned while a prisoner of the Amulites," Tara said. "He had fought many battles and was considered a hero till he was disabled. Now, the same society that sung praises to him as he entered the streets and awarded him with rank and honour, shun him like lepers of old. Despite this, though, he does what he can for society by caring for the children." The last few steps they did in silence and, once standing in front of Ali, Tara squatted and laid her palm on his calloused hand. "Master Ali, how are you today?"

"Oh, my .... Tara," he said brightly. "You surprised me, and you know how rare that is for me. You .... I actually thought you were someone else."

"You mean like Raasah, daughter of Botholuem."

"Why, yea, Miss Tara, daughter of Amarihah." Ali raised his free hand toward Raasah. "The kind young Raasah is here, ...aren't you?"

"How did you know?" Raasah asked inquisitively. He wrapped his broad weathered hand around her extended one. As she squatted down next to Tara, Ali released her with a gentle squeeze.

"I know every day when you come," Ali explained to Raasah. "Once you lose your sight, the Creator gives you other gifts. My other senses have become more attune. Smells are richer, sounds more distinct, and, oh, the taste – food is much more glorious blind!" He smiled, displaying gaps in his yellowing teeth but the smile was endearing just the same.

"You've known it was me each morning.... How?"

"Oh, my honourable Miss. You have the scent of a fragrant mountain meadow.... But mostly, because of the happy tinkling of your small bracelets, always the same. They must mean a lot to you."

Raasah fumbled her precious bracelets.

"Oh, and I thought you were a magician in disguise!" Tara joked. Ali was struggling to his feet, steadying himself on Tara's arm. "Will you be going to the Morcum Games? We will be heading there soon."

Raasah scooped up his cup and bundle enclosing his meager donations of food and coins.

"You beautiful young ladies don't need to be burdened down with a grouchy old man. Besides, I've got important official business I need to attend to...."

"More important than escorting two fine young ladies?" Tara teased as she handed him his gnarled cane.

Before Raasah could deliver Ali's bundle to him, though, she noticed Ali's face tightened and all humour vanish. The cause of his grave demeanor became evident as she turned to discover the approach of Zoric and his muscle-bound devotees. Ali's keen hearing had picked some telltale sound of trouble approaching.

"Gentle Raasah. Let me unburden you of this retched creature's filth." Zoric's repugnancy oozed from him as he snatched up Ali's bundle. He flipped it over to Tola who shook its contents aggressively. Raasah made an attempt to retrieve it but a heckling Tola, much taller than her, just held it above his head. In her distraction, Zoric wrapped his arm around her in a hug of feigned affection. With his face snuggling up to hers, Raasah recoiled from the smell of his repugnant drunken state.

"Give that back, you poor excuse for a man...." Tara exclaimed angrily to Tola.

"And what do you know of a real man?" Zeniff taunted. He grabbed at her arm but she retaliated immediately with a knee to his groin. In slow motion, he doubled onto the ground, a high pitched whimper omitting from his clutched teeth. Ali, meanwhile, far from being the defenseless victim, whipped his cane against the back of Tola's knees, crashing him to the ground next to Zeniff. Tara caught the bundle as it flew from Tola's open hand.

Zoric was oblivious to the defeat of his comrades, shamelessly slobbering his tongue across Raasah's ear and down her smooth long neck. He had her so close, she was unable to get a good elbow jab in and how she ached to slap the conceit right off his face!

"Why do you fight what you know you want?" he breathed in her ear. "One must be careful or one might think you would prefer the filthy useless beggars to the bright upcoming prodigy that you are so privileged to be betrothed to."

"I won't marry you. Get your drunken hands off me!" she gagged. Inspired by the brave interception of Tara and Ali, Raasah swung her head back hard, connecting with a crunch onto the bridge of his nose. He sputtered but, angrily, strengthened his hold on her.

"And you will remove your hands right this minute!" A deep voice boomed.

Immediately, Zoric released his grip on Raasah. A tall priest in the older traditional robes, looked inquisitively over Zoric's shoulder. He had white gray hair, neatly bobbed below his ears and a trim beard, but most striking were his deeply wrinkled eyes that sparkled with life. The old, but more-than-capable priest had Zoric by the left ear and right arm pinned behind his back. Ali had his cane pinning Tola to the ground and Zeniff was still groaning, doubled over, rolling back and forth in the dust. Tara stomped on Zeniff's prim fur-trimmed hat for good measure before she scooped it and shucked it at its owner. Zoric, still restrained and bloody-nosed (to Raasah's great satisfaction), was stunned as he scrutinized the scene.

The old priest spoke. "You thought you would take advantage of a defensive blind man and two gentle ladies.... That seems to have been a mistake," he said. "As for Ali, he is of far greater stature than you could ever hope to have. I think it best that you collect your friends and.... with what little dignity you have left... be on your way." He released Zoric with a sudden fling of his hand.

Zoric stumbled and joined his buddies on the ground. Ali withdrew the cane from Tola's belly. Cursing, Zoric staggered off rubbing his arm as Tola gathered a whimpering Zeniff and limped with the hunched-over retch after the retreating Zoric.

In disgust, using her soft veil, Raasah scrubbed at her neck to rid herself of the 'Zoric' smell and slobber. "Vile! Uggh! Ouuu!" Raasah couldn't come up with a real word to describe how she felt except "Vile!" which she repeated several more times. A shiver convulsed her and, in a final gesture of defiance, she threw the tainted veil to the wind. In a shuffle of feet, unbeknown to her, a disheveled little girl snatched up the prize and hurried off down the street.

Observing the retreating would-be-tormenters, Tara announced in an official voice: "I believe that's 3 points for Ali's team and 0 for the Snooties!" Raasah looked up in surprise and then couldn't contain her laughter. Ali muffled his mirth quite successfully until their newly acquired ally patted him on the back. Then together they all laughed heartily.

Finally – "Uncle Onihah. Good of you to happen by," Tara said very formally with a little curtsy.

"Oh, I'm sure you could have handled it without me," Onihah raised his bushy eyebrows comically, "but I had my own score to settle with that hoodlum Zoric."

"And, Master Ali, the cane-fighting champion – undefeated!" Tara swept an arm graciously towards him.

Ali made a low bow. "At your service, my fair ladies," he said elegantly. Then they all laughed some more. Raasah could not re-member ever feeling so spirited and self-assured, despite the dull pain on the back of her head.

Raasah had to marvel at what their unlikely alliance had ac-complished. She also marveled at the new respect she had for the 'Great Soldier'. As she admired the two men, Raasah recognized Onihah was one of six men that she had seen her brother intensely debating with in the smith plaza several weeks prior. So much had been happening that she had totally forgotten about this incident. The congregated men had been very concerned about something and believed their safety could have been at risk. Last week's attack on Adam's family was proof of that.

"Actually, Uncle, we were wanting to speak to you, if we could," Tara said more seriously.

"Raasah, how is your sweet grandmother?" asked Onihah kindly.

"She is well, thank you, Sir," Raasah replied, straightening out her clothes to look more respectable. It had been a number of years, but Raasah now remembered Priest Onihah with her Uncle Normad on at least one occasion.

"Good, good, good," he said. Then, in answer to Tara, "It would be good to talk, my young Tara, but I was just heading out on an-other matter. Could you come by after the Morcum game?" The girls looked at each other. Not waiting for an answer, Onihah con-tinued. "Well, then. Meet me in the Hall of Records. Now stay out of trouble till we meet again.

"Ali, will you join me?" Onihah tucked Ali's bundle under his arm. The two men dismissed themselves and melted into the crowd.

Raasah stood staring after them, unaware that she was gingerly touching the tender spot at the base of her skull.

"That certainly was good fortune that Uncle Onihah happened upon us."

Raasah stammered, "Onihah is your uncle? …. My stars! If you have an uncle like him, why are you living with…? Oh, I'm sorry."

"You're sorry???" Tara laughed. "Anyone would be better to live with then Uncle Gormonaluk and Aunt Zipporah! No, Onihah is really my cousin Tutoris's great-uncle…." Tara lowered her chin and then smirked. "But he likes me more than Tutoris!" The two girls laughed heartily and most unladylike. It felt very good.

Chapter 12

The Morcum Games

An integral feature of city planning, Morcum ballcourts were constructed throughout the realm and often on a grand scale. These courts, found in all but the smallest of cities, were shaped like a capital "I" and enclosed on three sides by tall walls. Atop of the walls were stepped ramps to seat the elite spectators and honoured guests. Above them were the spacious ceremonial platforms used by the priests and royal family. Most importantly, extending from the top of the side court panels opposite each other and decorated with snake-like serpents, were the six scoring rings essential to the game.

The game itself took great skill and agility. For a team to score, their players, strategically padded, had to keep a firm rubber ball moving and pass it through the openings of the scoring rings without the use of their hands or feet. Points were scored for getting the ball through the ring, but lost for allowing the ball to hit the ground.

Fast-paced, the game was highly competitive and it was not unusual for participants to receive injuries ranging from a fractured nose with contact with an elbow to broken ribs by being slammed by several oppositional players. There was also much extreme betting among the spectators that, in the case of financially-challenged losers, could result in as much physical contact off the court as in. As in all major cities, deaths in drunken rages were not uncommon, during or after the game, but this did not deter the attendance by young and old to the celebrated sport.

Little Brother was among the energetic youngsters playing a stick game at the end of the court while they awaited the start of the games. There were no seats here, only an open grassy park at the bottom of the "I" where the citizens settled with blankets and picnic supplies. Vendors were set up nearby to take advantage of the festive atmosphere.

On route, Raasah had purchased a simple scarf for her head. She reasoned that it protect her from the harsh rays of the sun but, to be honest with herself, she was more concerned with blending in so others of her station would not discover her familiarity with the common people. With her back to the stands, she fidgeted with the scarf as Tara confidently greeted and conversed with those around her. Their friendly faces, young and old, sparkled with life and laughter. Tara reflected it back as she hugged and caressed hands in greeting. In an atmosphere such as this, one could forget all their worries (*if one could shed the stuffiness of station*). Raasah waved discretely to Little Brother but then was relieved to see the long bearded face of Normad approach, his curly locks blown back in the welcome breeze.

Normad, a long-time widower, was an important extended member of the Botholuem family. His love for their household was transparent and all the children especially cherished his visits, his story-telling, and his buoyant presence. When Raasah's paternal grandfather, Normad's brother, had died eight years ago, he was a continuous comfort in the home. Over the years, it was hard not to notice that Normad had grown a special fondness for his sister-in-law and Marian was very fond of him. Oh, how Raasah wished she could have seen even a small degree of this affection between her parents.

Normad, in traditional priest's robe and cloak, held the tall staff of his office that he often used as a prop in addition to other untypical functions other dignitaries may not think very priestly of him for. But Normad did what he felt prompted to do for the sake of those under his charge and he did it without hesitation. He truly was there for the good of the people and wasn't afraid to get his hands dirty with good honest work. The appreciation was evident in the respect that was shown him as he picked his way through the gathered citizens towards Raasah. She glanced over to Tara and, thinking of the fondness Tara had for Onihah, Raasah was so grateful she had a REAL uncle that she was proud of.

About 30 paces from Raasah, Normad stopped. He stooped to converse with a group of women sitting in a circle. After a few moments, one of them rose to continue an animated conversation with him. The gestures of the woman were familiar, though more dynamic, and, once Raasah caught a glimpse of the face, she confirmed it was indeed her grandmother. Both Marian and Normad were proof one could 'shed the stuffiness of station' among the populace – but, despite the festive atmosphere of the assembly, both were rather disconcerted and, what was most surprising, was it was with each other!

As Raasah approached tentatively, Normad was the first to notice. He laid his large hand calmingly on Marian's arm and she turned to follow his gaze.

"How is my beautiful young niece?" he asked with forced cheerfulness.

Marian rearranged her expression hastily into an unconvincing smile. "Why, Raasah, dear, you aren't here alone are you?"

"Is everything ok?" Raasah asked anxiously.

"Everything is going well," Marian replied too quickly.

"Marian, please." Normad looked plaintively at Marian.

"Now, Normad. Everything IS going well," Marian repeated assertively, giving Normad a darting look.

"Mei-wa-na, what is it?"

"Normad! See what you've done!" Marian turned to her grand-daughter, speaking more softly and measured. "There is nothing to be concerned about. Your uncle is over-reacting."

"This is not over-reacting," The natural redness in his face was growing redder. "You cannot speak to such a woman of such things without some serious repercussion."

"Mei-wa-na, what is Uncle talking about?"

"Someone had to say something to that... that..... WOMAN! It is shameful the way she treats the young lads at the temple!" Marian whispered heatedly to Normad, now seemingly oblivious to her granddaughter's presence.

"Nora is associated with those... people. To reprimand her in front of those 'beneath' her..... You know she will not let this go. She is spiteful and...." Normad seemed to be at a loss for just the right word.

"Nora – Isobel's mother?" Raasah asked apprehensively.

Raasah remembered Jaona's description of Nora's tyranny when Sablon was appointed over her. If her grandmother had seen half of what Jaona had described, she could see why her grandmother could not have kept quiet.

"Yea, but I cannot stand by and have her ill treat those tender souls...."

Raasah trembled. "It is rumoured that Nora got a man imprisoned just for slighting her in public." Raasah shot a look at her uncle. This incident with her grandmother sounded much more serious than 'slighting'. Normad looked quickly from niece to sister-in-law.

"There are other ways of handling these things." Normad slowly scanned the crowds before continuing more quietly. "We must tread cautiously until we..."

"This brotherhood of ours moves too slowly," Marian said in a strained hushed voice. "People are being harmed, being..."

"Marian, please.... Raasah, please convince your grandmother to stay away from the temple for now and, for now... conform to her station...." Normad said the latter like the words might get stuck in his throat. Likewise, these same words alarmed Raasah as if someone had called "fire!" Of all the people to have uttered them, Uncle Normad was the last she would have suspected.

"Please, Marian," Normad pleaded. "Please sit in the stands. It is safer there... both you and Raasah. This is not the time to ruffle feathers or stand out."

"This is unnecessary," Marian said.

Turning to Raasah, Normad implored, "Raasah, please help me convince your grandmother."

Uncertain what to do, Raasah looked from great-uncle to grandmother. Marian was turning to face Normad again when a voice clear and musical spoke:

"Marian, my dear, it would be my great pleasure if you would accompany me to the upper stands." Zillah, tall and elegant in all her refinery, had enigmatically appeared at Raasah's side. "Besides,

I understand Little Brother has not had the privilege of viewing the games from our advantageous seating." She had an affectionate arm around the beaming boy. "What do you think, Raasah? Won't you and your grandmother join us?"

Zillah had offered a dignified way of conceding. Hesitating, Marian glanced around her and then sighed, smiling submissively. Little Brother slipped his small hand into Marian's.

"We will continue this later," she said to Normad in a flat tone – her eyes looked so very sad. "Come along, Raasah."

"Oh, Mei-wa-na, I must let Tara know where I will be. I will meet you all there."

"Please tell Tara she is most welcome to join us," Zillah said.

Raasah watched for a moment as this stately priestess, her care-worn grandmother, and bouncing Little Brother strode off. Zillah quickly engaged her two companions in pleasant conversation and was pointing things out to the excited boy. Following close behind were Zillah's colourful escorts chatting gaily as they shielded their mistress and guests from the hot rays of the sun.

Normad rested his tanned hand gently on Raasah's shoulder. "She can be such a stubborn woman."

"Do you really think Grandmother's in danger?" Raasah asked timidly.

"Nora has usurped her political power for her own benefit too often. Now, with her husband's appointment to the council, she has more power to misuse than ever. Being in the right does not protect one from harm these days." Normad looked worried and tired. "We will talk more after the games. Onihah has told me of your meeting."

"You will be there, too?" Raasah peered into his dark brown eyes shaded under, what appeared to be, one long bushy eyebrow.

"Yea, it is time to talk. I will see you there."

A thunder of a cheer went up as the heralded competitors entered the court. Normad gave Raasah's shoulder a squeeze, nodded, and tread carefully through the populace back the way he had come.

*

Tara had declined the offer to sit up with Priestess Zillah. She told Raasah she still had someone she needed to talk to.

"I am really not interested in attending these games but..." Raasah looked down. *...but I feel I should "conform" as my great-uncle had requested* – this is what she was going to say – but she wasn't sure Tara would understand.

"Nah, you go on. I will meet you at the Hall of Records later."

The uproar of the spectators was deafening, so Raasah simply nodded and headed for the stands.

It was a spectacular view from the upper stands. The players were like small moving dolls massing in various groups that ricocheted from side to side, down the court, and back again. A tall solid fellow from the David team, flaunting dark distinguishing tattoos, pranced about the court between plays, enjoying the response from the stands. This, no doubt, was Josian, the renowned Morcum captain that Jaona was so anxious to watch.

It was hard to tell who had the ball at times because of the buoyant colourful headgear that distinguished each team from the other – the headgear also all but obliterated other distinguishing features and dealings of the players from the spectators above. At times the players fighting over the ball were just flashy coloured blobs and flailing arms until the dark red ball broke free and a torrent of cheers would vibrate through the court.

It was easy to get caught up in the excitement and Raasah's little party was no exception. There was another uproarious cheer as people sprang to their feet. Down in the court, a lone Ammonihahite player bounced triumphantly atop the shoulders of his team members. Relishing his heroic moment, he raised his thick padded arms and elated face skyward. It was Baruck, their star player. He was a ruggedly handsome young man, openly admired by frivolous young ladies, unattached and otherwise, and highly esteemed by up-and-coming zealous athletes of their city. Baruck sunk in amongst his comrades as abruptly as he had been hoisted up and the blue-red headdresses of the Ammonihahites dispersed to their defensive positions for the next set. Unfortunately, moments into the next play, there was an illegal body check by one of their own players and groans and jeers rumbled through the stands.

Before the horns could blast to announce the pending penalty, the offended David player retaliated with a blow to an opponent's face and players from both sides charged forward to defend their teammates. Referees dashed in as the horns finally sounded. Captured in the excitement and exhilaration of the crowd, Little Brother, himself, was quite a spectacle with his arms wrestling with themselves in imitation of the players fighting it out below. As much as Raasah did not like the violence associated with the game, this new little brother of hers did make her smile.

The occupants around them were in various degrees of cheering, chanting, and inanely calling out recommendations and brutal suggestions to those in the playing field. Though they were the apex of society, their finery of manners had been peeled away and soon their words were lost in the literal vibration of voices that actually hurt her ears. Raasah scanned the spectators below her.

The jewel-embellished Gormonaluk & his wife, Zipporah, were grandly positioned a few rows below them on cushioned seats. They were flanked behind by their servants and baskets bulging with food, drink, and other items of comfort. Gormonaluk was screaming, frantically waving his fist – pastry oozing slowly, blood-like, through his clutched fingers. Zipporah, on the other hand, prim and poised, tipped her perfectly groomed head toward their beefy son who listened intently as his mother spoke, a sinister grin growing on his pimply face. With a swift flick of his wrist, he sharply rapped his chalice on the shin of one of the young servant girls who had paused from her fanning to search out the excitement below. With a pained expression, she returned abruptly to her task – Tutoris and his mother both looking wickedly gratified. Raasah, who had never cared for Zipporah, now felt an intense dislike for both mother and son. Raasah lamented for Tara at the thought of her having to live under their very roof.

As the crowd started to settle, Gormonaluk rose ceremoniously. A servant dutifully slipped a basin under his hands and rung water from a drenched cloth over his viscous fingers. Once the servant had dutifully wiped him clean, he was dismissed with a wave and Gormonaluk strolled tall and deliberate further along the stands, other spectators straining to see around him as he went, until he stood where Isobel and her parents were settled. Gormonaluk leaned in close to speak to Issachar amid the noise. Issachar, the top of his braided head barely reaching Gormonaluk's chin, had to stretch to return his remarks to Gormonaluk's tilted ear.

Issachar – a jackal feeding off evil – wasn't that how Chemish's mother referred to him? And if Issachar was the personified jackal, was Gormonaluk the 'evil' or another one of the jackals?

Her mind, preoccupied with recalling the overheard talk of the councilmen, Raasah omitted seeing Issachar's daughter, Isobel, or Jaona who was standing next to her, until she felt Jaona's eyes burning into her.

Isobel and Jaona! Raasah had totally forgotten she had told them she might join them. Raasah smiled awkwardly back at her but Jaona's usual pleasant face just stared back blankly and then wagged slowly back and forth. Just then, Isobel turned with that detested down-her-nose look. Raasah tried to look apologetic but Isobel, followed by Jaona, turned reproachfully away.

Raasah was not surprised that Isobel would judge her harshly but it really hurt that Jaona had not attempted to understand. After all, circumstances do change and they certainly had in her case. Isobel leaned in close to her mother. There was a brief exchange between them that was followed by a duet of mother & daughter down-the-nose-dagger-looks thrown in Raasah's direction.

Isobel's mother, Nora ....Grandmother and Nora at the temple! Raasah felt so stupid. *Of course, the incident at the temple would have an effect on Isobel ...and sadly would influence Jaona against Grandmother as well... and me by association.* Raasah's chest tightened with hurt and anger at Jaona for being so willing to emulate any and all Isobel's actions without any convictions of her own. *Why can't Jaona see I am the one that is truly her friend?*

Suddenly the distinguished sound of the trumpet resonated

from the head of the court, signaling the late arrival of the royal governor's family. The cheering and heckling subsided, the game paused, and all stood respectfully still. Little Brother tugged lightly on her sleeve, redirecting her attention to the ceremonial platform just above them. The Royal Family and their entourage were assembling in all their pomp and glitter; pungent perfumes and body powders permeated the air. To one side of the sizeable ruler strolled his regally posed wife, Ranzel, and a good-looking, wiry boy with Ranzel's eyes and nose who held himself tall and official by his mother's side. Also, to Raasah's un-surprise, on the other side of Antionah was the strikingly beautiful new High Priestess Sablon. Raasah stood staring detachedly at her estranged mother.

The royal family chatted happily as they settled upon their exclusive platform of silky cushions and gold plated benches and stools. Admirably, the future heir, despite his tender age, sat with all the flair of regality denoted for his position, no doubt trained soberly by his stately mother, who also never forgot her place, unlike her husband who slouched slovenly in his grand chaise, reaching apelike at a bunch of grapes.

Like a breath of fresh air, joining the royal group was Reuben, affectionately dubbed Prince Reuben, who seemed to be enjoying the company of a young shy servant girl with cinnamon hair and blushing cheeks. He was dressed handsomely in a crisp kilt, tunic, and cap. His shoulder length hair curled round his face but, best of all, Raasah liked the way his eyes laughed. She liked eyes that laughed. *Chemish had eyes that laughed....*

Raasah was drawn back to her mother in her airy pastel gown, showing just enough cleavage to make men drool. She was pleasantly addressing the jovial ruler – a larger man than Raasah had remembered – definitely not in height, though it was difficult to tell how short from his sitting position, but large in girth, and he had grown another chin.

As Raasah stared, a feast was being set before them and the royal servants in their brilliant white gowns and kilts knelt and waited solemnly on Antionah and his assemblage. Wine and strong drink were liberally poured. Sablon helped herself delicately to bite-sized items as Antionah spoke, spittle spraying freely from his royal mouth bulging with questionable contents. Despite this unpleasantry, though, Sablon remained perfectly poised and alluring.

An uproarious cheer from the crowd pulled Raasah back to the game. She had been so preoccupied that she had not even been aware the game had re-commenced. Through the bobbing heads, she saw Gormonaluk and Issachar also stealing a look at the royal assembly. As these two men resumed their conversation, Raasah glanced back once more at the stranger who was her mother.

Chapter 13

Botholuem's Brotherhood

Upon entering the door to the archives, Raasah was perplexed as she and her grandmother joined a curious group of eleven people gathered around a long wooden ornate table. After the dramatic winning toss of the Ammonihah team and while the applauding roar and celebrating still vibrated in the air, they had slipped away unnoticed with Zillah unaccompanied by her usual entourage.

Onihah ushered Raasah and Marian to vacant seats at the end of the table and then eased himself into a seat next to them at the head. Raasah was relieved to find Terjah and Tara smiling across from her. Ali the Great Soldier, and Abinahah the forger were seated further down and so were Uncle Normad, the royal nephew Reuben, and, to Raasah's great surprise, Zillah seated herself next to Martha, her history teacher. There were two other young men at the table that Raasah did not recognize.

"Raasah, I think you know most of the people here," said Onihah as if reading her mind, "except maybe Azariah at the end there. This is Adam's son-in-law…."

Azariah nodded at Raasah. He had a stern oval face framed by shoulder-length hair and a close-cut beard. Onihah then gestured to the right of Azariah.

"….and, our scholar among us, Aaron, the astronomer."

A tall tanned black-haired man, youthfulness sparkling from

his clean shaven face, rose and had all the airs of a distinguished man of the world. Aaron bowed respectfully to Raasah. "It is an honour to meet you, Raasah, daughter of Botholuem."

"Many of our numbers are missing," Onihah said, as Aaron resumed his seat. "It was very short notice. For those of you who don't know, Caleb will not be joining us today. He is mourning his brother's death."

"Zeniff was killed yesterday while being arrested," Aaron explained.

"Zeniff?" Azariah sputtered.

"Yea. He was found out to be their older brother's killer...." Abinahah said in his thick raspy speech. "Wanted his brother's birthright, he did."

"Zeniff dead...." Raasah muttered absently, warmth draining from her body. She vividly recalled Zeniff beating the helpless slave in front of the justice building and, more recently, how he had held a knife at Chemish's throat.

"The good people of Ammonihah will be better off without him," Azariah said decisively as if he had just completed an in-depth analysis of the situation.

"Azariah," Onihah said sternly, "I don't believe...."

"I am sorry. I do not mean to sound so callous but he was such a cruel, hateful young man," Azariah added.

With a slight quiver, Raasah silently had to agree but even the killing of a killer did not sit well with her.

"Now, we shouldn't speak ill of the dead." Martha said softly.

"I only speak the truth." Azariah replied flatly.

"Unfortunately, he was just one of many hapless, weak-minded youth being courted into the evil web of Nehorism." Normad said, laying heavy arms onto the table.

"Oh, my! As much as I do not care for Absalom, to lose two sons in such a short time…. So tragic!" Marian said.

"Despite the wrong Zeniff did, Caleb still needs the time to grieve for him with his family." Onihah looked around the table. "Please be mindful of them. It will be a difficult time for all of them."

"And, what of Cainahah? He and his sweet wife?" Ali said. "Has anyone heard from them?"

"It is not like him to take a trip without speaking to his friends," Zillah said.

"I say Darius has something to do with this." Reuben shifted in his seat. "I know Cainahah had an audience with Antionah. My uncle had shown Cainahah favour lately in court. I'm sure Darius saw him as a threat to his own influence with my uncle."

"Anyone seen as a threat either turns up dead or just vanishes," Aaron said angrily. "One must almost sleep with an eye open." Raasah looked anxiously to Tara and her brother. Tara lifted a hand slightly from the table surface as she mouthed "later".

"We need to guard our words – we have a 'guest' present," Azariah articulated coldly and distinctly.

Raasah felt the reassuring grip of Marian's hand. Raasah had not realized how tense she had become. She had not prepared herself for accusations nor of the implied grave incidents being spoken of regarding their citizens.

"Yea, this is too much for my sister," Terjah declared. "Raasah is too young to get involved in this awful affair! She shouldn't….."

"Nah, Brother." Raasah had composed herself. "I want to hear. I need to know," she pleaded.

"I am only a year older than her," Tara interceded, looking from Terjah to the others. "She will make her own inquiries if we do not include her. In fact, she HAS been making her own inquiries. Such independent uninformed action can prove more dangerous for her than embracing her in her father's affairs."

Murmurings went around the table. Raasah retrieved her hand from her grandmother and spoke up.

"I am not an unlearned imbecile that I cannot see that things are not right in Ammonihah. I was there as my father and friends were slaughtered; I've seen the unrest in the city; I've witnessed the cruelty and intolerance of those who take authority into their own hands. I know my father was opposed to the evil practices worming their way into the government." She looked directly at her brother. "Is this what got him killed?"

The assembled adults looked from one to another, speaking low and hushed. Tara nodded solemnly.

"….and she has come to us with information," Onihah announced calmly.

"….but the circumstances of her family….." Azariah blurted.

"Terjah has been…," Aaron began.

"Now my fellow members of this honourable brotherhood," Ali said. "It was Botholuem's dream for a better Ammonihah – a safe, God-fearing land for all. Amid increasing corruption in our government, Botholuem made gallant efforts to stay strong and valiant in his influential position as Antionah's advisor. Now, without our dear 'Pochtecatl of the Iguana' here to sway our *illustrious* governor to accept wise counsel, Ammonihah has fallen into malevolent hands."

"Being the daughter of Botholuem does not qualify her to be privy to discussions of such magnitude," Abinahah boomed in his gravelly voice, forming a gnarled fist. "She does not understand…."

"We still have concerns…. We still have questions…." Azariah said coolly.

"Yea," Onihah said. "Why was Raasah spared – only a bump on the head? She is involved in all this whether she wants to be or not. She needs answers just as much as the rest of us."

Tara must have pleaded her case to Onihah before the meeting.

"She is too young…" Terjah interjected but the commitment was not in his voice anymore.

"You cannot protect me by keeping me in the dark, dear brother. I will continue to search out answers and keep up my father's legacy of decency and right. I only ask this great brotherhood that they listen to what I have to say and then they can decide if I am worthy enough to be counted among them."

"Well spoken, daughter of Botholuem," Onihah said with a heavy hand landing on the table.

With that, Onihah brought the meeting to order. Raasah rehearsed what she heard from the city council members. Reuben stiffened slightly at the mention of his own name but remained silent. Raasah also expounded what she knew about the attack on Adam's family. Terjah described the destruction in the shop and concluded by letting the attentive group know how Adam feared more violence from those connected with the Nehor affiliation.

Raasah racked her memory at the mention of 'Nehor' and

'Nehorism'. She could not recall what she had heard about it. She made a mental note to ask Tara more about this "later" as well.

"As you know, we now suspect the Nehor members to be responsible for the attack on Botholuem's caravan," Onihah continued.

"It wasn't a slave revolt...." Raasah whispered more to herself as she thought of Abul. Marian patted her hand.

"The caravan had been left quite vulnerable with an essential part of their fighters missing," Onihah said. "It was believed that Noalas was not there during the attack – he was reluctant to leave but that Raasah's father had insisted he attend his sick wife. They were so close to home – Botholuem could see no harm coming of it."

"Nah, that's not true!" Raasah's voice was louder than she had intended. "I saw Noalas only moments before the arrows flew." In her agitation, Raasah had risen off her seat. "He spoke to a guard by the servants' fire. It was dark but he was facing the fire." She slowed her speech as she viewed her captive audience. "I saw the cruel white scar that parts his hair. He looked right at me.... I remember!"

Onihah gave her a knowing nod. "Yea, it has recently come to our attention that Geshem has accused Noalas as the one that betrayed the company. Terjah has done some investigating into this." Raasah stared at her brother as he stood tall by his chair. *Why had I not been aware of this?*

"When I first was told that Noalas and several of the other men had left early, I was angry that the camp had been left so defenseless," Terjah recounted. "So I journeyed immediately to his home near the Western Mountains. He let me know that Father had insisted he attend his sick wife and how appreciative he was. But he had been too late. His wife was pale with death by the time he got there. I left him in peace to grieve." Terjah paused, gesturing toward his sister. "Then, four days ago, Raasah and I visited Geshem and, after Geshem mentioned Noalas and learning that Noalas may have been present during the raid, Chemish and I returned to Noalas' to learn more."

Chemish – so this was why I could not find him the last few days!

"We discreetly spoke to the servants on his estate. Less than a year earlier, Noalas had wed his reluctant wife, now deceased – she was part payment of a family debt. Two separate servants told us how Noalas beat her near death on their wedding night. He had no compassion or love for the young woman. She was only property to him. In fact," Terjah lowered his voice, "it is common belief among the villagers…. that he killed his wife with his own two hands – no doubt, to give himself an alibi."

Martha gasped. Marian momentarily tightened her hand on Raasah. Meanwhile, Raasah's mind repeated Chemish's name with echoes of '(Noalas) killed his wife with his own two hands'.

"If this is true," Ali said, "if he felt he needed an alibi, than we must believe that Noalas played some major part in the attack. But the men he left behind were killed as well in the attack. He could not have done this on his own. He had to have had a large troop of fighters at his disposal. We know of no such group that could have been involved."

"Yea," Terjah related, "We also learned that Noalas has connections with the Amulonites."

"Yea, the descendants and followers of Amulon and the wicked Noah priests," Ali said thoughtfully. "These people now fashion themselves after the Nehor priestcraft and usurp much power and influence over the Lamanites of their lands."

Murmurs erupted from the group.

"I hear that the Amulonites are more wicked than the Lamanites…." Azariah added.

"It is true that the Lamanites follow the wicked traditions of their fathers through ignorance," Zillah said. "The Amulonites and their fellow Amalekites brethren – they had once been enlightened by the Spirit of the one true God and have had great knowledge of things pertaining to righteousness, but these same peoples have fallen away and embraced the anciently forbidden combinations and priestcraft."

"Sadly this is true and they have become more hardened than the Lamanites," Normad explained, "Thus their state has become worse than though they had never known these things. The devil himself has become their companion."

"It is believed," Terjah continued, "their influence is getting stronger and stronger each day. It has been learned that additional Nehor supporters infest the crags and dales of the mountains now where they cannot be overpowered and they rob and murder at their whim. I am truly convinced that Noalas has been enlisting the Amulonites and their supporters on behalf of the Nehor priests of our city for their wicked purposes. Darius and his Nehor affiliates would not dare get blood on their delicately scented hands!"

"One must not casually accuse one of association with Amulonites or the Amalekites," Aaron rebuked.

"We were very cautious and discrete how we approached the citizens of the valley," Terjah's even voice did not disguise his distress. "They are deathly afraid of him. They have witnessed swarms of ruffians advancing on Noalas' estate from the high country by darkness of night. Amlicite deserters and Lamanites were among them. They are easily distinguished by the red mark tattooed into their foreheads. Some of the villagers have heard and seen unthinkable things done by them. The villagers have also felt the sting of their wickedness as these evil men have run amok in their streets and terrorized their families. And, it is not uncommon to discover that, on a morning after, one or more of their fair daughters have vanished."

"This is still a serious accusation to…" Abinahah warned as gently as his scratchy voice would allow.

"This sounds more like a scary children's story told by darkness of night," Azariah retorted.

"I have been to his estate," Terjah stood, flexing his hands. "This time my eyes were open. You can tell it once was a grand property of a respected nobleman, but Noalas acquired it under questionable circumstances and the land has gone unattended these many years. While the land is returning to a wilderness state, his home, on the other hand, is being guilded in gold and growing more sumptuous with every passing year. Labourers work day in and day out on a massive wall that will surround the whole estate…. to hide what??? Or will it be used to fortify his estate from future wars and dissention? But, importantly, how has he accomplished this? The amount of work he attains as a mercenary would not be enough to sustain such a lavish lifestyle and his massive household. And I, myself, have seen the loathsome godlessness of those he associates with."

"But still…" Abinahah said mellifluously.

Onihah raised his hand for quiet. Tara drew Terjah back to his seat. Then slowly she stood herself. Her voice was barely audible at first.

"I have other disturbing news. Geshem is not responding to our treatments. In fact, in the last few hours, he has become unresponsive. I can't explain it. I am afraid we may lose him."

"Raasah, dear," Normad paused. "We have been guarding Geshem while awaiting his recovery to learn more about the attackers and gain evidence against those responsible. We have our suspicious, and it is imperative that we bring these people down but, without an eye witness or other evidence, it would be literal suicide to approach the courts."

"Normad," Marian exclaimed, "you're not asking....? You realized what a dangerous position that would put Raasah in even if she did remember something. And she is plagued enough by her nightmares...."

"Mei-wa-na, I am more than willing to share anything I remember about the attack." Raasah looked around the room at all the faces. "I don't know how much help I will be. My memory is so fragmented."

"Honey," Marian wrapped both hands around Raasah's one but Raasah slipped it away and sat up tall and determined.

"Raasah," Onihah said softly, "your father was the founder of this brotherhood gathered here." His eyes washed over those assembled. "He saw a need to band together honest law-abiding citizens in a quest to expose the evil practices of a growing powerful group – believed now to be the Nehor sect – that were destroying the very fabric of Ammonihah that made it the great center of knowledge and commerce it is. Botholuem accepted his appointment as Chief Attendant, with a little prodding on our part, because of the corruption and injustices he had witnessed from his other positions in government. Antionah admired your father's frankness and honesty in his reports of neighbouring lands as head pochtecatl and respected your father's wisdom. So, in addition to overseeing the courts, your father advanced promptly to the position of chief advisor. Soon Antionah relied solely on Botholuem to guide him in important decisions."

"We of this brotherhood became your father's ears," Ali added, "and reported to Botholuem any corrupt practices or lawlessness being planned or bragged about as we heard of them during our daily routines." Raasah's eyes studied the sightless man, her mouth slightly ajar in surprise. "People somehow associate lack of sight with lack of intelligence and tend to speak quite freely in front of me," he said smiling, as if in answer to her thoughts. "They forget my ears are as sharp or better than ever."

"The new breed of wrong doers in our city are cunning and often prominent members of our society," Terjah continued, "and without concrete proof of their wrong doing, Father could not accuse them openly by name...."

"That's correct – one had to have discretion on how to handle this," Onihah said, "and your father did this beautifully. By careful skillful maneuvering in his smooth bureaucratic flare, Botholuem was pivotal in encouraging Antionah, unknowingly, to take measures to foul any ill being planned or to help bring culprits to justice. The city was slowly becoming a safe just place to live once again.

"Eventually we knew those whose corrupt efforts were being squashed could begin to suspect Botholuem as their...." Reuben hesitated as he struggled for the right word.

"Nemesis?" Aaron suggested.

"Yea, nemesis and spoiler of all their power-usurping plans."

"But Botholuem refused to back down," Abinihah said gruffly. "He became all the more determine, he did, wanting to expose these wicked men for what they be."

"There was a group of people who opposed Botholuem's

appointment," Onihah explained. "Botholuem discovered they had their own agenda and plans that did not include the welfare of our fine citizens. Your father felt he knew who their leader was and we were cautioned to be wary of him and those he associated with. We suspect he may have been somehow responsible for your father's demise but we have not been able to connect him with any evidence of wrong doing. And now, without Botholuem there to influence our ruler, Antionah is easily misled by those left to replace him. Fearful, many of our numbers have bowed out of Botholuem's brotherhood since his death and others, well,....

"They have just gone missing," Tara finished.

"Another that has gone missing is Cainahah, the pochtecatl," Onihah continued, "who would have been expected to replace your father as reporter of foreign affairs. In his absence, Darius now feeds Antionah information of rivalry and conspiracy from our neighbouring counties, persuading Antionah to increase the size of our army and allowing the army and council more power and liberties as Antionah preoccupies himself with the security of himself and his household. You can see now why we have been watching Geshem so carefully and awaiting his recovery. But now...."

"I will do whatever it takes to bring justice to those murdered," Raasah said assertively. "Where do you want me to start?"

Raasah described as best she could where the company members were seated at Lamonhah Ridge and where the mercenary guards were posted. She told how many of the servants and slaves seemed to have melted into the darkness just before the attack. She fought back tears as she described the scene of the arrows flying, and people calling out and screaming. Then the details became sketchy.

"I was pulled back and I hit my head. I may have blacked out....
I don't know for how long. I opened my eyes. Everything was spin-
ning and double. I believe I was on my back. I looked above me and
I thought I saw Abul."

"Who is this Abul?" Aaron asked.

"He is my... our slave...." Raasah almost said 'my friend'. "I
remember reaching for him... but then he was gone and men in
grotesque masks appeared. I remember flickering light reflecting
off their large ear-plugs and gold rings on their hands..... They were
talking... they were laughing...." A tear rolled down her face.

"All right! That's enough!" Marian demanded.

"Nah, there was one more thing." Raasah briskly wiped her wet
eyes on the back of her hand. "They knew me. One of them said,
'Yon daughter of Sablon.' And at the time I remember thinking....
I know that voice!"

"Who did it sound like?" Azariah demanded.

"It is hard to explain. I was so disoriented. I couldn't make sense
of anything then and I knew the voice but then I didn't..." Raasah
stuttered.

"What good is all this?" Azariah said impatiently. "She remem-
bers but she doesn't remember. This is not getting us anywhere."

"Azariah," Onihah said, diplomatically, "you must look beyond
the words and see the small details...."

Many of the members started speaking at once. In the confusion and contention that followed, Raasah shrunk in her seat. She
was grateful to hear her brother defend her and for the comfort of
her grandmother's hand again as it laid gently across hers. *Have I
really been any help?* Tara smiled encouragingly from across the
table.

Chapter 14

The Order of Nehor

Once outside, Tara took Raasah aside and slowed their pace.

"You were great in there," she said when they were out of earshot of the others.

"Some were not happy about me being there...." Raasah said dismally.

"Oh, Azariah. He is overly cautious – that's just his nature. And Abinihah, well, he had a good friend murdered – his whole family, in fact. Abinihah discovered them himself. The brotherhood believes they were killed because his friend provided information leading to the arrest of several Nehor followers. The brutality of the murders and finding the bodies of his wife and two little children, well..., Abinihah has never been the same since and he now suspects that anyone can be capable of similar atrocities unless they can prove themselves otherwise. Azariah and Abinihah are both good men just looking out for the Brotherhood. I could tell they were coming around to accepting you."

"Azariah makes two people now who have made mention of my escape from harm from the attackers – accusing me of... of... having some part in the attack...?"

"Raasah, you must understand that every member of your father's caravan was attacked fatally except a baby, who could not be a threat to them; Geshem, who had all appearances of being dead, and you with…."

"…only a bump on the head," Raasah finished.

"Yea, there were evidences of deliberate actions by the attackers to make sure all the victims had fatal wounds. But you, well, it is a puzzle. By your own account of what happened, that two of the attackers actually checked on you and didn't attempt to harm you in any way, well…."

"It is a puzzle," Raasah finished again.

They were walking slowly towards the astronomy building. Onihah, Terjah, and Grandmother Marian were many paces ahead of them.

"Tara, you don't think I had anything to do with…?" Raasah suddenly asked.

"Nah, of course not," Tara replied quickly, "but why did they leave you unharmed? And how were the attackers able to catch everyone so off guard, including experienced mercenaries? It does make sense that Noalas led or arranged the attack but, then, who hired him and why was he told to spare you? The main motive was not theft because many items of value were left untouched."

"I thought I was being paranoid but I often felt Noalas was watching me. It was such an eerie feeling – so unnerving!"

"The answer will make itself apparent in due time but we need to be prepared for what is to come. We can't wait passively."

"And Darius' sect, are they the Nehors?"

"It is believed they are part of the Order of Nehor."

"Tara, please tell me more about this Order. I just can't recall what I've heard about it."

The two girls stopped in the long shadow of a stela. "Members of this sect are cruel people," Tara explained, "indulging in sorceries and idolatry and capable of deceiving even the most learned men. They will do whatever they can to gain power and wealth. Remember just 3 years ago, the war against the Amlicites and the battle by the River Sidon?" Raasah nodded slowly. "Well, Amlici was their leader and self-appointed king after the Order of Nehor."

"I remember now," Raasah said. "It seemed all they were interested in were robbing, oppressing, and destroying all the god-fearing Nephite people."

"Yea, and they did horrific things to their prisoners. Ali was one of those prisoners. He was blessed to survive, though some would not believe it such a blessing. Amlici was killed in this last battle near the river gorge and the Amlicites were finally defeated. The loss of life on both sides was great but, for the enemy, it was so great that Alma ordered their bodies to be thrown in the river so that his soldiers might have room to cross and contend with the rest of their foes on the other side."

"Alma? The same Alma that preaches now in our city?"

"Yea, it is the same. Alma also was governor and chief judge of all the land at that time but he gave this all up to fulfill his calling as prophet of the people."

"He is a man of much authority. I had no idea."

"Alma could see how the Order of Nehor had corrupted the people and still influenced them and he felt the need to correct the teachings and bring them back to their true Creator."

"Though the Amlicites were defeated, the Order of Nehor survived?" Raasah asked.

"The leaders of Nehorism were killed and that uprising defeated, but the survivors further perverted the original teachings of

Nehor for their own gain. Now, if this new Order has joined forces with the Amulonites and their followers, as Terjah has suggested, it's so frightening to think what they could be capable of. We are sure the Order has infiltrated our government and are laying traps for those who may discover them. We believe this is what may have happened with your father. Many of our Brotherhood members were also among the caravan. It is hard to know who to trust anymore. The draw for wealth and power has coerced so many to join the wretched Order. They are from all walks of life. They may be a neighbour or a brother, and we suspect many of our priests, lawyers, and judges have also joined the Order of Nehor."

"Tara, this is so unbelievable, or I would have thought so only months before, but how could you know all this to be true…?"

"As you heard, we have many ears throughout the city catching conversations, hearing information, and influencing arrests. But, now, without your father in the royal court, it is difficult to pursue those who would bring harm to the good people."

"I had no idea how noble a role my father was playing but I am much more aware of the callousness around me since my return. I thought at first I was just looking at the city differently but… the city is different. The evil IS growing…, isn't it?"

"Yea, the Order of Nehor is slowly taking hold of Ammonihah. You can see now why Azariah is so suspicious. We believe they are controlling the affairs of our ruler and may plan to replace him when they have no more need for him. The same day your father left on his last trip, they wasted no time persuading Antionah to increase taxes and make new appointments to office. One of our council members was murdered that very afternoon you all left – Ether was found stabbed to death just outside his home. Another council member just disappeared, leaving his wife with no means of support. That is when Reuben became one of the council members. He reasoned that he could be a greater asset to the brotherhood if he was part of those who make decisions for the city. It wasn't hard for him to sway his Uncle Antionah into thinking it was his own idea to have Reuben on the council..."

"...and the present council members wouldn't dare oppose a candidate suggested by their ruler," Raasah said thoughtfully.

"That's right!" Tara said.

When the girls reached the wide terrace of the astronomy building, they approached Onihah, Marian, and Terjah who were seated on the edge of the tranquil pond among the flowers in the Celestial Gardens. Marian was speaking:

"Gehazi of Naaman has been trying to find an honest lawyer to take his case to the governor but...."

"But what honest lawyers are left are too scared to take this on," Terjah interjected heatedly.

"Anyone with any sense is scared to confront them," Onihah said sadly. Noticing the girls, he said, "Well, well, there you are. Raasah, I hope you don't mind, but I'd like to borrow your brother and grandmother this afternoon. Would you mind if my assistant walked you home? And Tara, don't tell me how you don't need an escort. You must think of Raasah's safety too."

Raasah shot a look at Tara who looked poised to speak but, instead, nodded obediently.

"I'll see you at the villa," Marian said to Raasah. As the three walked leisurely off, a crisp-looking scribe appeared at the girls' side and nodded stiffly at them.

Raasah and Tara walked in silence, subconscious of an outside ear. They skirted around a few rowdy crowds, drunk and still exhilarated over the Morcum game. Raasah was going over in her mind all she had learned today. Somehow she hadn't been surprised to learn that Terjah and Tara were involved in this Brotherhood but she was taken aback to realize her grandmother was. *I wonder who the other members were that had not been present today. Who else have died in their efforts to make things right in the city?* She searched the faces of those they passed wondering if they, too, were part of Botholuem's Brotherhood *or... are they possibly secret conspirators and murderers of the Nehor affiliation?*

In a small textile market enroute, Raasah paused to observe a curious gathering that was attentively listening to a lone man standing on a platform. Tara followed Raasah's gaze. Motioning to the scribe to stay, she encouraged Raasah to follow her as she gravitated over to the congregated group.

Once joining the small crowd, they could hear the speaker addressing another beside him who then replaced him on the platform. They were both older men, well dressed but not sumptuously. Raasah recognized Amulek as he took the stand. Amulek spoke of Esrom's reward awaiting him in the spiritual world in which he would be warmly welcomed. He spoke of the reward for each of them if they lived a life of charity and integrity. He spoke of the Creator's sorrow of the Ammonihah people. "...that with hearts waxed hard and ears dull of hearing and eyes that cannot see afar off, many of our leaders now seek their own counsels in the dark and evil places".

These words lay heavy on Raasah's mind as she thought of all Tara had rehearsed to her of the city's corruption. She studied the face of this passionate fellow Ammonihahite as he spoke and that of his audience. She had not thought of Amulek as a spiritual man before but she was very impressed with the impact of his words.

"Now, my fellow citizens, I would that you should hear and know that what Alma, our Creator's servant, has said to you is in truth. I pray that his words might awaken you to a sense of your duty to your God, that you may walk blameless before Him. And now I ask that you be humble; submissive and gentle; full of patience and long-suffering; being temperate in all things; being diligent in keeping the commandments of our God at all times; asking for whatsoever things you stand in need, both spiritual and temporal; and always returning thanks unto our Creator for whatsoever things you do receive.

"Now I tell you not to be concerned or worried for the future. The God of your fathers will be with you. He will bless you as you keep His commandments, that you may at last be brought to sit down with Joseph and Lehi and all the other prophets, who have been ever since the world began, to live in the Paradisiacal Kingdom. Now return to your homes, prepare yourselves for presentation to the Temple on the morrow, and may peace be with you and your families."

Amulek stepped down out of view as the small crowd slowly dispersed until Raasah saw, in addition to the two preachers, Chemish in a clean embroidered tunic, who was just releasing his Uncle Amulek from a firm embrace.

"Wa-ie, good sirs," Tara said formally as they approached.

"Pleasant greetings to you, dear Tara," Amulek said cheerily.

"And could this be Botholuem's beautiful daughter, Miss Raasah, all grown up?"

"Wa-ie, Amulek, sir," Raasah replied nervously. "Wa-ie, Chemish."

Chemish smiled liberally back. "So, you know Uncle Amulek. Have you met the Auspicious Alma, the Talk-of-Ammonihah?" Raasah wasn't so sure the word 'auspicious' was such a good choice as Alma's future didn't look that promising with so many out to silence him.

"Nah, we have not had the pleasure," Alma said, taking the lead and bowing to her. "I am very pleased to meet Botholuem's cherished daughter. I hope you are well, Raasah."

Flustered, Raasah looked up and briefly studied Alma. She could tell, as a younger man, Alma had a full head of dark hair though it was now streaked in grey; his eyes had creases branching outward that told her he laughed a lot; and, in addition, his large shoulders and powerful arms spoke loudly that he was obviously used to hard work. So, from this momentary scrutiny, she decided to give Alma a vote of approval and offered him a warm smile in reply.

"I am afraid we must take our leave," Amulek said. "It was our great pleasure seeing you, Tara, Raasah. Maybe we will see you both at our meeting place later this week."

With a nod of his head, Alma and he were on their way, leaving the young women with Chemish in a near empty plaza.

"Raasah, I need to check on Geshem. I've been away too long," Tara said, "so I will go ahead and let you visit. It is good to see you, Chemish, healthy and sound. I know you will get Raasah home safely." She winked at Raasah and, without waiting for a reply, she returned to the waiting scribe and they retreated down the lane.

"Chemish…." Raasah began.

"Raasah, you…."

"Chemish, I am so sorry about what happened – for causing you and your family all that trouble."

"Hush," Chemish put a finger gently to her lips. "The attack on my family was not your fault. It is difficult times and it was wise of you to have remained quiet and hidden. Furniture can be fixed or replaced. But if harm should have come to you… I could not fix or replace you."

Raasah blushed, but recovered quickly. "You and others have spoken so often of difficult times, dangerous times…." Raasah said. "Today I am beginning to understand." Looking around to make sure they were alone, she continued softly, "I was just at a meeting with a number of my father's Brotherhood."

Solemn-faced, Chemish visually search the plaza as well and drew her next to an empty shop.

Raasah continued. "Yea, I have learned so much today. I learned of the Order of Nehor who is possibly infiltrating our government and sanctuaries and how people who oppose them can end up dead or, worse… just missing. With my father gone, there does not seem to be anyone strong enough or in position to advise the governor to do the right thing." This all came out in a rush of words and with great relief that she could finally confide in him again.

A cool breeze slithered its way around them and a thick cloud was threatening the sun. Unconsciously, Raasah rubbed goose bumps forming on her arms before adding, "Oh, Chemish, I did not know to what extent Father had in keeping our city safe. I know

I don't know everything but I feel the difference since I came back. I feel the fear in the city, and, thanks to Tara, I know and understand many things better."

"I am so sorry for not opening up to you before," Chemish said quietly, releasing the serape around his waist and, opening it up, laying it over her shivering shoulders. "You had been through so much. I didn't want to worry you."

"I am not a silly fragile child!" Raasah felt a sudden surge of anger. "Why didn't you trust me with the truth? I thought we were being honest and forthright with each other but... but you were being guarded with me, holding back information from me. Are you one of them that think I had something to do with the attack at Lamonhah Ridge?"

"Raasah, I just didn't...."

"I loved my father. Many people I cared about died that night. Don't you think I would have wanted to know about Father's fight to make Ammonihah a better place? Did you ever think I might have wanted to be part of it?" Raasah's eyes were moist. "I could be of value to the people if I were just given a chance. Why didn't you give me a chance?"

Chemish lightly brushed her cheek as a tear welled over her lower lid. "I am so very sorry. I am a dope." He wiped away another tear as it followed the previous one.

Raasah stepped back away from his protective hands. Blinking, she wiped away the last of her tears. "I deserve the truth, every bit of the truth."

Looking intently at her, he said, "Come with me," and he extended his hand.

Chemish and Raasah sat in the back of a bakery shop in front of a low table of fresh pastry and wine. The owner was a family friend of Chemish and, after an exchange of words, the rather round owner had escorted them to this small but private room where they could talk. The first of many raindrops pitter-pattered on the pavestones outside.

Hands clasped in front of him, Chemish leaned forward. "What would you like to know?"

"There is talk that your family speaks evil of the priesthood and practices some heathen religion. Why do they say this?"

Chemish hesitated briefly before attempting to explain: "My father had watched as the practices of our ancients were slowly being corrupted and replaced. Normad and Onihah are only a couple of so few priests who hold to the old teachings and honour the writings of prophets past. My family are devoted followers of the omnipotent God of our ancestors. We have tried to honour Great Kukulkan humbly in our home and in all our dealings. It has been hard for my father to see our people's beliefs being absorbed by teachings of power-hungry men, watching our temples become places of business instead of worship."

"Those are horrific accusations," Raasah spouted. "I am not ignorant of our religious practices. I am a priestess apprentice, have you forgotten? I study the history of our teachings, the ritual applications, the protocol for the special occasions of worship...."

"Raasah, I know of your studies, not so much of its contents, I admit, but I am aware of some of the teachers of the priesthood classes. Not all the teachers teach the practices of our fathers. You learn what they want you to learn."

"Chemish, are you implying that I am ignorant to being taught lies?"

"I am not saying these things to slight you in any way, but even you have questioned some of the teachings. There are some teachers still there that are trying to hold to the old ways but they are being pressured to slowly introduce new teachings and omitting others that are felt to be too 'controversial'. Many who have refused to conform have been replaced."

"Martha...."

"What was that?"

Raasah slowly recounted: "At the beginning of the week, I overheard her arguing with Noami over a curriculum change. Noami did threaten her with dismissal if she didn't teach the new material."

"So, you see how it starts."

"I saw them," Raasah said defensively, "but I don't know whether our sacred truths were being changed."

"They work subtly. First they just muddy the truths and then they clarify them with the untruths that hand over power to those who just want to line their pockets or advance in position."

"This is so implausible. We are talking about people holding positions of such religious importance that they have taken oaths to pass down the sacred knowledge and uphold the directives given by the Creator. They would bring down the wrath of the gods if they broke this oath."

"The lust of money ... it has the power to create delusions and cloud those oaths, to make those lured to it to embrace new directives of a fanciful god of their own making – one self-serving and unmerciful."

"For sake of argument," Raasah said slowly, "are these people you are referring to supposedly of the Order of Nehor?"

"You must be careful who may hear you speak of this cult." Chemish spoke more hushed. "The name Nehor brings fear to some, anger to others, and, to those of this order, they could bring evil upon your head or the heads of those you love. You must speak its name only to those you truly trust."

"I don't know what to believe. I find this all so much…."

"Before your father formed the Brotherhood, we only suspected the Order of Nehor had infected our city. Once your father became Antionah's advisor and trusted confidant, he realized the need for an organized affiliation to effectively fight the corruption and injustice in our city. That was almost 2 years ago. The first members totaled 15 trusted friends but as others were heard struggling to hold onto the pure truths and practices of our people, the numbers grew. We were strong and effective. We had people in advantageous positions to effectively withstand the ungodly, hurtful influences of these ruthless people. We gathered and shared information we heard and worked together to secure our traditions and beliefs and assure a safe promising future."

Chemish paused. "My father says maybe we got too cocky. Jesse, son of Nephihah, was the first to receive the wrath of Nehor followers. Jesse happened upon a ceremonial rite that included a drug-induced child that had gone missing days before. Painted women were dancing in a frenzy as masked preachers summoned demonic spirits and prepared this innocent child for sacrifice. Jesse rushed to waken the chief judge who ordered the arrest of those involved. But somehow the participants were forewarned and most escaped. It was too late for the little child but the young dancers were left behind in a heavy drug-induced state in which they either died shortly thereafter or were reduced to babbling fools. The masked leaders were never identified, but Jesse and his family were murdered for his trouble."

"That is so terrible! Is this Jesse – a friend of Abinahah?"

"Yea," Chemish looked surprised.

"But, again, why do people label your family as blasphemers and cult worshippers?"

"That is how evil men work. They lie, they cheat, they twist the truth to their benefit. They flatter and they bribe people to do their dirty work. They laid a trap for my father and he walked naively right into it."

"I'm sorry, Chemish, but I still don't understand."

"I don't know if you remember, but there was a stranger that came to our city preaching just before you left with your father on your trip."

"I think I do remember. An angry mob cast him out of the city."

"Yea, that was the man."

"There was talk of stoning him. My father rebuked this talk and other good men restrained the would-be attackers and the stranger went on his way. My father spoke of this. He was very angry with the harsh way this man was treated."

"That same man came back. That was Alma of Zarahemla."

"Alma? This Alma? He came back after the people talked of taking his life?"

"When Alma left, he had no intention of coming back, he tells us. He believed a demonic darkness had taken hold of the hearts of the Ammonihahite people and, therefore, they could not hear his words. But an angelic spirit appeared to him to command him to return. He was to save the elect from those who would destroy their liberty. So he returned to the land of Ammonihah and entered by the way which is on the south side of the city. There Uncle Amulek was waiting for him. He, too, had seen a spirit in a vision. He was told to welcome Alma into his home and to learn from him.

"Well, word got out that he had taken in this preacher from Zarahemla. The anger and resentment of many of the people grew menacingly against him and his household. My father and many friends and associates tried to persuade Uncle Amulek to send Alma away, but he insisted that Alma was a Holy Prophet that would free the elect people from the evil darkness enveloping the city. The more my father spoke to his uncle and Alma, the more my father began to believe their words.

"Amuluk's father, on the other hand, though at first he had welcomed the words of the Prophet Alma, was growing bitter. His business was suffering because of their association with Alma. Finally, when he could not convince Amulek to send Alma from his home, he publicly spit upon Amuluk and denounced him as his son."

"Oh, Chemish. I am so sorry."

"My father tried to reason with Great-grandfather but he would not concede. In his effort to reconcile the two, my father got to know Alma and grew to love him and his messages. Soon we, as a family, came to know him and embrace his messages. We were the only one of Amulek's kindred who did not desert him.

"Now," Chemish continued, "my great-uncle is a man of no small reputation and has many friends. He had acquired great riches by the hand of his industry. Until this time, he had had little tolerance for religion even though he had seen much of Kukulkan's mysteries and His marvelous power. His friends could not understand why he would put his prominent lifestyle at risk to embrace this foreigner. Still, his friends and associates respected him, for he is a man of wisdom and learning and he had assisted so many on their own way to prosperity. This is why the Order of Nehor is so concerned about Amulek and want him silenced. People tend to listen to Amulek and accept his counsel. He is winning over the good people of Ammonihah to accept the truths spoken by Alma. If many more people turn away from the teachings introduced by the disguised Nehor priests and elders, their deceit and manipulation of the people will be discovered and imprisonment or worse will be waiting for them."

"The Order of Nehor..." Raasah said timidly, "you are saying that they are now some of the leaders in our temples, sanctuaries, and government. So... priesthood holders like Darius and Noami... and councilmen like Jashorum, Gormonaluk, ...and Absalom... and... Zeezrom...?"

"Yea," Chemish was visibly impressed. "We believe they could all be of the Order of Nehor and we used to believe Darius was their leader but now we suspect there is someone else that they all answer to – someone very cunning and ruthless who binds them all together, making them dangerous indeed. This enigmatic leader has evaded us and is causing us great concern."

"So, you have spoken about Amulek, Alma, and the Order of Nehor but..."

"Yea, why my family is spoken of as enemies of the church: After Alma joined my great-uncle's household, my young cousin, grand-daughter of Amulek, was attacked by ruffians, raped and shamefully ridiculed. My father was the one who rescued her. Jashorum's young son, Lemahah, appeared to be the instigator. The boy has no conscience or brains. Zoric tried to quiet his brother but he proudly took credit for the gross indignities that were done to my sweet cousin.

"Father could not contain himself. He confronted Jashorum in front of the council and judges of raising the devil himself and, when his demands for justice were met with indifference, he denounced the justice system and declared the priesthood a travesty. They had finally bated my father to say the words to get himself excommunicated. Many kindred and associates from that time forward have turned their backs on him for fear of excommunication as well."

"It is all so horrible! I had no idea!"

"In just the last few months, the callous deeds of the wicked have become more open and have grown more serious and disgusting. If perpetrators know the 'right' people, they know there will be no retaliation for their wrong-doing. Cries against injustices are quickly crushed and those good citizens insisting on restitution are often met with violence or attacks on their homes and families..." Chemish looked down at his clutched hands. "...or they 'disappear'. This is why we, Botholuem's Brotherhood, must remain united and be so cautious. Individually, we are so vulnerable but together we can be strong."

"But, Amulek.... He is putting himself and his family in such danger getting mixed up with Alma. You say Alma has come to save the good people from the evil in society and yet Amulek's grand-daughter was inflicted by a terrible wrong because of Alma.

He is cajoling the common people to rebel and put themselves at risk."

"You mean he has cajoled common people like me….?" Chemish asked soothingly.

"You are twisting my words."

"Only using your own words so you can see that it is fear making you say these things – fear I only hoped to keep from you."

"But I hear Alma has threatened to destroy our grand city…. This has caused all kinds of anger from the people. I am just worried about you. It's important to keep the right company. The wrong company, company like Alma, will cause all kinds of problems. Look what has happened to your family." Raasah realized suddenly that she was beginning to sound like Jaona.

"You must hear Alma speak." Chemish enveloped both of Raasah's hands in his. "Then you will understand. We meet just outside the city in a secret grove. Tara knows where it is." Raasah stared longingly into his soft brown eyes, wanting to trust he spoke the whole truth, but, at the same time, fearing that if it all was true, her world would be turned upside-down.

The rain steadily splish-splashed against the wall of their building like the beat of her pulse.

Chapter 15

Murder

Raasah strolled down the wide lane hemmed by vine-covered walls that concealed the ample houses and private gardens of its residents. With a pleasant expression, but her mind far from her task, she handed out alms to the less fortunate that frequented this neighbourhood. It had been a week since she had met with Chemish behind the bakery, but Raasah avoided the carpentry shop. She did not want anymore trouble to come to his family and she had a lot of information to analyze.

Amos doddled a few feet behind, gawking shamelessly at every girl who would look his way. He was so clueless of his responsibility as Raasah's escort that she had to wait for him regularly so he could keep up with her. She scoffed, not without some trepidation, that she could very well be abducted kicking and screaming and Amos would not even notice while he lusted after a pretty face. But in his own ignorant way, he came in handy if she just needed a body present when she got that feeling that someone was watching – a feeling that still haunted her from time to time when she was out about the city. Because he was so un-attentive, though, she could also feel the freedom to visit with whoever she wanted without him hovering.

Raasah greeted a frail, misshapened woman with an empty wrinkled smile, handing her the last small loaf of bread still warm to the touch. But, no sooner had the gnarled hands received the bread when it was snatched away from the woman's grasp. Her tongue wagged liberally through her toothless mouth as she bellowed and scratched the air wildly at the loaf just out of her reach. Angry, but not overly surprised, Raasah turned to confront Zoric and his sidekicks.

Stepping back, Raasah snapped: "Sir, I see you are still pursuing your pastime of tormenting the defenseless?" A grinning Tola held the small fragrant loaf even higher from the boney fingers of the new howling owner. Raasah backed away another step from the advancing Zoric.

"We're just relieving this pathetic wretch of coveted gluttony, most unbecoming of the saintly poor," Zoric said smugly. The tiny crooked woman brandished her walking stick, as bent and twisted as she, as Tola and their new recruit playfully ducked its blows and flipped the loaf between them.

"Most ignoble merciless sirs! You, of course, are masters of coveted gluttony and callous lasciviousness." Raasah looked reproachfully at the bullish scene. "But, to win the heart of a lady, generosity and compassion can warm her soul much more effectively. But what would such base animals, such as yourselves, know of such virtues." Raasah was astounding herself with her own brashness.

Zoric snatched the bread from mid-air, which was then snatched back by their victim in one swoop. "Your words sting me, sweet Raasah, but I think compassion is over-rated." The beggar woman hobbled in surprising speed off into the shadows, hunched closely over her prize.

Zoric closed the distance to Raasah. Raasah nimbly dodged his first reach and wildly looked for her dim-witted escort. As she had predicted, Amos was totally unaware of her predicament.

"It warms MY soul that you speak to me of winning your heart," Zoric beamed as his fellow accosters snickered and laughed. Zoric grabbed her hand and landed a wet kiss on its backside. As Raasah tugged at her hand in vain, he wrapped a sweaty arm around her, his body reeking of sour perfume... and garlic. Briskly, she rubbed the slobber off on the front of his tunic.

Good citizens of Ammonihah skirted around them without offering help. She hopelessly looked again for Amos. Two large strapping men, bearing the tell-tale armbands of the David team, heckled drunkenly at the scene as they stumbled by. She was on her own. Zoric stroked her face long and firm until he was holding her chin sternly with his thumb. Obviously, he was conscience of what the force of her head could have against his own.

Suddenly Zoric yelped in pain, followed by a clattering at his feet. A clamor by the alley distracted Zoric just long enough for Raasah to escape his clutches. Massaging the back of his arm, he looked around at the populace and kicked at a lone brick-sized rock. "Who throw that?" he demanded. People gave him a wider berth and continued on their way. From the alley, Raasah spied a dark form melt into the shadows, the bulk bigger than one man but which moved as one.

"Tola, Boaz! Find out who threw that!" he demanded of his companions, who looked stupefied at each other before they rushed aimlessly about looking for an unknown attacker. The large form retreated farther into the alley as, thankfully, she saw Isobel and Jaona fashionably stroll into view. Tola also was distracted by their presence. Zoric recovered quickly and grabbed Raasah's hand painfully.

"Wa-ie, Ladies," Tola said with a slight bow. Jaona giggled

sweetly before she bubbled over in pleasantries with the heartless young man of a few moments ago. Isobel continued without hesitation toward Zoric and Raasah.

"Well, Raasah, it is nice to see you escorted by someone of distinction for once," she said airily. She lazily watched as Boaz continued to probe behind fruit stands and benches for the illusive someone. "Did you lose something, Zoric?"

"Nah, Miss Isobel. Just a little trouble we had to look after." He threw out his chest and smiled charmingly. His hand loosened his hold on Raasah.

Isobel smiled charmingly at Zoric. "Come along, Jaona. We mustn't be late for our classes. Wa-ie, Master Zoric."

Finally, a bewildered Amos became cognizant of the activity around Raasah and he sauntered over to her side.

"Ah, Amos," Raasah said in mock cheeriness, abruptly whipping her hand free of her persistent pursuer. "Good of you to join us. We had best be on our way."

Throwing her shoulders back, she followed Isobel and Jaona toward the Hall of Instruction without a sideways glance, though she had braced herself for the possibility of a hand gripping her shoulders and was strategizing how she would shrug free of it and confront its owner. With a sigh of relief, she made it to the archway of the school's gate where she finally gave herself permission to glance back. Zoric and his sidekicks were nowhere to be seen.

Once she had gathered her satchel from Amos, she smiled absently at the sentinels, dutifully at attention – as they should be. She was sure the guard closest to her was new. He stared straight ahead without twitching – that, in itself, was new.

As Amos meandered off in his loopy way, Raasah was

exceedingly pleased to see Onihah standing next to one of the columns talking with a slightly taller priest – a sharp breeze lifted the hood away from the latter's face. *Mathonihah! But you look so much older than I remember. Your hair and beard more bushy and wild, your robes unkempt.* What struck her most, though, were his eyes – they looked like they had seen a hundred sad lifetimes.

This was Botholuem's long-time friend and Ammonihah's celebrated Patriarch, who had not only been a regular at the Botholuem home but one of Raasah's first teachers – a beloved, awing-inspiring icon, a man of great faith gifted in futurist insights and sacred understandings. In the classroom, Raasah had been entranced by his presence and the glow of his countenance as he spoke of their premortal home and glorious spiritual truths of the Omnipotent's plan on this earth. He had stood formidably tall and regal in those days, nobly attired in impeccable robes, emitting always a welcoming warmth about him.

The year that Raasah was in his class was also the year Mathonihah had bestowed upon her her patriarchal blessing. She remembered it like it was yesterday. He had spoken to her of her gifts of beauty and virtue, of her marrying for now and eternally in the holy temple, of blessings as she strove to obey the Lord's commandments, but, foremost in her memory, she remembered him foretelling that she would be the savior to others, bringing them to safety in this world and in the next. Her mind had churned this personal prophesy over and over – *me, a savior?* – *an ordinary girl who looked to others to protect her! It was so implausible, so outlandish,* but it had been Mathonihah who had spoken these words, this man she looked up to with such trust. Thus she had no choice but to accept this as truth, her destiny in some distant future, because she believed in this Icon of Faith, in all he stood for. After these many years, these inspired words that had inevitably faded into the recesses of her mind, as memories do, now rose hot to the surface.

Raasah gazed at this reverse morphing of a grand Man of God. She thought back to the last time she had seen him – he had been with her father and they were arguing fiercely. The wondrous glow was gone from his face, as it was today; his appearance was dark and frightening, and she remembered cringing at the sight of him. She tried to remember the man she had admired. Her memories ebbed once more back to the night of the argument. *If only they had known that was to be the last time they would see each other, maybe they would have acted differently – more tenderly.*

Mathonihah no longer taught; people no longer clamored to hear his counsel or inquired of his blessings; and he no longer visited their home. In fact, rumours had it that he spent more time in the taverns than in the temple these days. She couldn't even recall if he had come to Botholuem's burial ceremony.

Mathonihah raised his voice angrily, filling Raasah with that same apprehension she had felt the night before that fated trip. As she stared his way, he turned slightly. Their eyes met ever so briefly before he tore his away, said some final words to Onihah, and then strode off in a bellowing of gowns.

Onihah turned and exchanged his netted brow for a friendly smile. Raasah wandered over to his side.

"Are you all right?" he asked kindly looking beyond her.

"Oh, that?" she looked back the way she had come. "I am fine."

"You know if you need anything, you can come to me?"

"Thank you, sir," she said gratefully. "Wasn't that Priest Mathonihah?"

"Yea. We were just going over some business."

"He seemed upset."

"Yea, he has some problems he has been trying to work out. Priesthood concerns," Onihah said as if to himself while his gaze drifted after Mathonihah.

"Sir, do you know how Geshem is doing?"

Onihah returned his attention on Raasah. "I have been told that he was not able to speak yet, but Tara is working her magic on him. Reuben will be going by to see him today. Will you be able to come by the Hall of Records after classes? I can get Terjah to come for you. He would make a much better escort then that ... forlorn lad," Onihah tilted his head after the retreating Amos.

"I would be pleased to come by," Raasah replied. "I'll look for Terjah after class."

"Who can tell me the most important role of the priestess?" Prisca, the music and dance teacher, surveyed the class. She was a tall graying woman with long limbs and a tall slender neck – and the students feared her. Her gimlet-eyes, when focused on a whisperer or giggler, could turn the stoutest knees to water. Prisca took her role as instructor most seriously and expected perfection and professionalism from all her students. She did not have much use for the inept.

Ruth was waving her hand enthusiastically above her head as the rest of the class fidgeted quietly, distracted by the young musicians busily setting up their various drums, maracas[18], and wind instruments at the far end of the studio.

Ruth stood. "The most important role of the priestess is to signify the Mother Deity and assist in the rituals to honour and pay homage to the deities." Pleased with herself, she sat back down.

"Very good, Ruth," Prisca said. "Someone has been doing their homework. And what are the symbols for the deities?"

Ruth's hand was waving once more in the air. Jaona, on the other hand, was fluttering her eyelashes at a trim musician with a small goatee as he adjusted the mouthpiece on a decorative flute[19].

"Jaona."

Jaona whipped her head. "Honourable Teacher?"

"Jaona, you will reserve your shameful flirtations to outside my classroom!"

Embarrassed, Jaona gave a fleeting look at the goateed musician who, in turn, stole a humorous look back. Jaona lowered her eyes sheepishly.

Ruth was still waving her hand. "Ruth, do you know the symbols for the deities."

Ruth stood proudly again. "The sun symbolizes the Creator of our world and the moon symbolizes the glorious Goddess Mother," she said portentously and added, "The Acropolis of the Moon looks across the Great Plaza at the Temple of the Sun but at a slightly lower elevation – not to insinuate that the Creator is more important than our Glorious Female Deity but because He holds the Mother-of-all Spirits in such high homage that He wishes to protect and shelter Her. In fact, He upholds Her so sacred, that He has never revealed Her name to mankind but instead revealed that the Goddess should be denoted as the Moon to tangibly enable the people to show respect and reverence for Her. Because of this, the creation wall was built high above the city upon the Palenia Palace to depict the Sun and Moon ruling the Earth together."

"That is very good, Ruth." Looking around at the other students, Prisca said, "Now, if you could all be such outstanding students."

Ruth smiled broadly as she returned to her plot of floor with the other girls. As Ada looked past Ruth to Raasah, Raasah rolled her eyes, causing Ada and her neighbours to have to conceal their giggles. Even Riphlia joined in. Ruth looked suspiciously about her. She still hadn't recovered fully from the 'Sucking Leech' title, therefore blaming Raasah for any negative connotations that she perceived around her, but she stayed clear of Raasah and that suited Raasah just fine. Prisca, never letting anything get by her, bore down a stern stare that encompassed the entire class. The girls composed themselves immediately and focused on their teacher.

They had been learning a new dance for the Founders Festival. This was a week-long celebration of the founding of Ammonihah City, when they gave honour to the many heroes and dignitaries that made the city great. There would be actors, story-tellers, entertainers of all kinds, and, of course, the dancers and singers from traditional and folklore to those of religious connotations.

The girls were dressed in the soft pastel gowns of the dance. Ada had been added to Raasah's small group and Raasah had enjoyed getting to know this shy but intelligent girl as they danced with the tambourines and streamers. Their steps were a series of long jumps, and twirls, and portrayed the dedicated citizens building the great temples of Ammonihah. Isobel's and Jaona's group, now donning elaborate head-dressings, portrayed the gods and their pleasure of the Ammonihahite people; Ruth's group proudly portrayed the elegant robed priestesses honoring the gods. Weeks of work had gone into the dance and, with only days to go, Prisca was quick to find fault.

"Riphlia, a little more graceful with the hand and, Zaraphath, dear, smile. Ruth, that was excellent. ...Ada, ...what are you doing, girl?" All eyes turned her way.

"It's s-stuck..." Ada stuttered. She had twisted back to try to unhook the tambourine from its hold on her skirt while ineffectively keeping up with the dance. In the confusion, one of the other girls danced into her, and they landed in a heap on the floor. The haunting melody came to a staggered halt.

"Clumsy, girl!" Prisca snapped. "Go, get yourself organized. As for the rest of you, from the top!"

There were groans from the class and Ada, disheartened, walked to the side of the room amid accusing looks. Raasah shot her a warm smile and shrug. Ada worked hard on her dance but dancing was not high on her talents. In all fairness, though, this could be due to the fact that she had joined the class late in the year. Raasah felt bad for her.

Sweaty and tired, the class finally came to an end. It had gone a little longer than usual with constant fine tuning by Prisca. Raasah shuffled wearily toward Ada. Ada had resigned herself to sitting the rest of the class out, with what little confidence she had seemingly washed away.

"That was so embarrassing!" Ada said gloomily.

"Oh, it could have happened to anyone," Raasah said reassuringly, laying her tambourine next to the slightly bent one, a piece of material clinging to its rattles. She wiped her moist brow with her arm.

Isobel stormed over with Jaona not far behind. "You clumsy boar!" she said in a hushed hiss. "If it wasn't for your idiotic blunder we would have been done ages ago."

Ada got to her feet to face her accuser.

"Yea, why don't you go back where you came from!" added Zaraphath, knocking Ada's shoulder against the wall.

"Isobel, Zaraphath, it was an accident," Raasah exclaimed, straining to speak quietly.

"She is an accident!" Isobel retorted a little less quietly.

"What is wrong with you, Isobel?"

"How can you defend such a sad-sack humiliating imposture? She belongs in a dung shack among the other filthy commoners. She pollutes our sacred buildings and she is a shameful irritant to our Supreme High Priest."

"Isobel!"

"Raasah, it's all right," Ada said resignedly.

"Nah, it is not all right! Isobel, you are a hurtful, callous, self-absorbed ...."

"Girls!" the teacher's voice rang out from across the room, though her attention never strayed from the costumes she was examining on the bench. "Is there a problem?"

Even when her back was to the class, Prisca knew who was fidgeting behind her, who was thinking of talking to another student, and who was trying to be excused from class who really only wanted to escape to the market for a refreshing grava drink. But these thoughts were only a squiggle flashing across her mind. Raasah and Isobel were staring fiercely at each other.

"No problem," Zaraphath announced loud and crisp, without looking back.

"I am glad to hear that," Prisca called back. She never altered her focus from the costumes. Though Raasah was sure the teacher knew what was going on, she either did not care OR – *which sadly is the most probably reason* – *Teacher Prisca approved of the persecution of Ada!* For whatever reason, Prisca had been vexed with Ada from the first day she stepped across her threshold. Nevertheless, at this point, Raasah was glad the teacher had left it just between them. She wanted to see this through.

Zaraphath gave Ada a second shove and brushed past Raasah in a huff. Isobel continued to stare.

"You had better rethink your questionable associations, Daughter of Sablon, if you know what's good for you."

"I know a citizen of integrity when I see one and she is not standing in front of me!"

Colour rose in Isobel's perfect cheeks. Her moist lips parted for a long moment before she said slowly in a strained even tone: "You have entangled yourself with the wrong person!" With that, Isobel threw her head in the air and marched off. Jaona, a stunned, concerned look on her face, peered hard at Raasah before hastening after Isobel. Raasah sadly watched them go.

"Oh, Raasah. You shouldn't have provoked her!" Ada said remorsefully. In the heat of the moment, Raasah had actually forgotten Ada was there.

"Someone needed to tell her like it is!"

"I never meant to come between you and your friend…."

"We've gone down different roads. She USED to be my friend…."

๒

Onihah and Raasah, joined by Terjah, Tara, and Reuben, sat around the flickering light of the single oil lamp. The faces were grim. Terjah leaned heavily back from the thick claw-foot table. Raasah's eyes came to rest on Tara.

"Geshem – dead," she repeated for the second time to let it sink in, adding, "and you think it was murder?"

"Yea, when I entered the room to attend Geshem, it was dark, and I was knocked against the wall by someone rushing out," Tara explained. "I lit a lamp and went to Geshem. He was dead. He had an odd odor to his mouth and a yellow residue on his lips. He appeared to be poisoned."

"I arrived right after," Reuben said. "I didn't see anyone leave."

"The man – what can you tell us about the man?" Terjah asked.

"He was a tall man," Tara said, "His hand was clammy; it touched mine. A funny thing: I remember, as he pushed by me, I touched something hard with a smooth symmetrical design in his hand – possibly a cut stone on top of a scepter or staff? I can't think what else it could be."

"Tara," Onihah prompted. "Go on...."

"I went to see Shaquah, but she wasn't with Esrom at Porahah. Esrom was lying frail and pale on the bed. His breathing was shallow and laboured. Next to the bed was a desk. Carved in its top, as clear as day, was the eye of the snake. Onihah, you had shown me this sign before."

"Yea," Onihah said. "It is the sign of the occult, the ancient priestcraft of the devil himself."

Tara was visibly shaken. "Then Esrom's hand gripped my arm

and he weakly said my name. I had to put my ear near his mouth to hear what followed but what he said didn't make any sense. Then he just mumbled and mouthed air. Shaquah came into the room. She was angry. I told her I had come looking for her to tell her of Geshem's death. She became distraught. She said over and over: 'He couldn't have died.' She didn't blame me. She told me to go and not to speak of this visit to anyone."

"Shaquah did not ask details about Geshem's death?" Reuben asked.

"Nah, not one question but she wanted me to go right away."

"That is strange, isn't it? Wouldn't a healer want to know the immediate cause of death of one of her patients?" Reuben asked.

"You're right! Shaquah always thoroughly questions the cause of death but this time she seemed more interested in having me leave. When I hesitated, she ordered me out. So I left, but I stopped just outside the door. I saw Shaquah kneel down beside Esrom. She asked, nah, she begged Esrom to hear her, to plead to Kukulkan on her behalf to give her the strength to do what is right. Then she called out to the Creator to forgive her and to protect her family." Tara looked at Onihah, "I couldn't find you, Uncle, so, when I returned to my home, I gave Terjah the message to get hold of you."

"Shaquah is not herself. Something's wrong." Reuben said.

"Wrong indeed!" Onihah repeated thoughtfully. "Two months earlier, Esrom summoned me to his chamber. He looked peeked and tired. He insisted on giving me a special blessing of protection saying 'difficult times were coming.' That was the last time he summoned me. The prophet has been acting like a stranger ever since and now Shaquah acting peculiar...."

"...and evil people reappearing..." Raasah whispered darkly.

"…and good people disappearing," Tara whispered back.

"...or being charged with bogus things," Terjah added absently.

Onihah suddenly looked up at Tara. "Wasn't there a guard at Esrom's door? Darius had arranged a guard to be posted there, who even I have had difficulty getting past."

"Nah, I didn't see the guard today. Even I thought this strange, but no one was there. But I did hear someone approaching after I left the room so I slipped away before anyone saw me, as Shaquah insisted. It could have been the guard returning."

"What was it that Esrom whispered to you?" Raasah asked.

"I don't know if I heard it right. It didn't make any sense. He said – I'm sure he said, 'A kiss. Must heed.'"

There was silence.

"On another note…," Onihah said quietly. "…after seeing this second incident with Zoric, I am very concerned about Raasah."

Terjah leaned forward, his handsome brow furrowed. "What has Zoric done now?"

"He is just being obnoxious as usual." Raasah tried to sound off-handed.

"Dealings with the Jashorum Household are not to be taken lightly, Miss Raasah," Reuben said kindly.

"It's almost like Zoric feels he has some right to her," Onihah said. "I am afraid for the prophet's safety and, after what I saw today, I now am worried about your safety as well, young Raasah."

---

18 *Drums and Maracas: Percussion instruments of ancient Central America included mainly drums and maracas, made mostly of wood, gourds, and occasionally tortoise shell. Archaeological evidence from Pacbitun, which*

dates back to about the time of this story, also prove that sophisticated forms of maracas along with the small balls inside them were actually crafted in fired ceramic materials.

19 *Clay Flute: Ancient flutes were made in different materials, wood, bamboo, and clay, sometimes shaped to represent the gods, prominent people, or local animals.*

Chapter 16

The Juggler

It was the first day of the Founders Festival. Performers, surrounded by their appreciative audiences, dotted the gaily decorated square on provisional platforms. Little Brother, with a broad smile on his face, was transfixed on an animated puppet show. Hands clapped with delight as the hand-held characters performed their light-hearted antics. But Raasah's thoughts were far from the festivities. She was reflecting on her history teacher's last dramatic lesson:

'History has a habit of repeating itself,' Martha had thundered. 'Ancient records teach of past civilizations. Take heed from the lessons written by Ether.' She fervently raised the ancient scroll above her head. 'These records are here to teach us, to warn us. Take heed, young students. History will repeat itself if we are not careful!' Silence gripped the room. Then a sudden slow steady clapping by the entry turned startled heads in that direction.

Head priestess Noami smiled coldly. 'Most theatrical, Teacher Martha! I don't recall this being part of the curriculum though.'

Martha returned to her desk, her continence pale and downcast as the formidable priestess strode up to the front of the class. Ruth had sat a little taller as her mother addressed the class. 'Students of Priestess Studies, I am here on behalf of our revered Prophet of our Omnipotent Kukulkan.'

As Noami proceeded to inform the students that there was a

new curriculum, there had been a terrible sadness about Martha. With no delay, the new tablets had been handed out.

"Raasah!" Twisting around, she saw Tara weaving her way toward her through the assembled people. Raasah whispered to Hannah and rose to meet her friend. The girls wandered over to the fountain near the center of the square.

"Have you seen Teacher Martha?"

"Nah," Tara replied.

"She was most upset in class yesterday. Noami came in with new material to teach. She told the students we were to be taught word for word from these tablets. I couldn't concentrate on the contents – Zoric's mother makes me so nervous – and the animosity between her and Teacher Martha was thick enough to cut!"

"What did Martha do?"

"Nothing. Noami had herself posted at the entrance. After a long pause, Martha told us to read our lessons – said that her input was not needed anymore. I can still see her sitting at the head of the class in icy silence. Noami, on the other hand, looked very smug. Martha left without a word after class."

There was a round of laughter from the puppet show audience as a ruby-lipped mop of a doll screeched comically from its box theater.

"Chemish warned me this would happen," Raasah whispered. "He told me that we were slowly being taught false doctrines. He said that if the teachers didn't agree to teach them, they were dismissed."

"Maybe she beat them to it and quit!" Tara suggested. Raasah did not like the sound of that much better.

Two men stepped next to the same fountain. The older one was angry. As the girls ceased speaking, they couldn't help but overhear.

"That is crazy talk! Who does he think he is that he can tell us what we should do! Ammonihah has its own prophet with heavenly visions and visionaries with prophetic dreams. If I wanted to hear heavenly messages, I know who I can go to!"

"But, Father!"

"And what makes Amulek so special? If our great God will talk to an entrepreneur, he will speak to an esteemed scribe just as well."

"What the scribe does not understand," a deep voice whispered next to them, "is that God doesn't speak to men who will not listen." The girls looked up into the bearded face.

"Onihah!" Raasah was very pleased to see him again.

"If only....," Onihah continued wistfully but quietly: "The scribe would study the words of our Creator, kneel in prayer… and then he must listen so he will know the truth when he hears it. It is so sad."

Raasah glanced over to the stout sturdy man with thinning hair while his son pleaded with him.

"Alma performed a miracle," he claimed. "He prayed to our Creator for the power to heal me and my hand was healed…." The young man flexed both hands freely in front of him.

"The account of Amulek's call to preach has incensed the scribe," Onihah said, as he led the girls away. "Though he used to be good friends with Amulek, not a day goes by now that he doesn't think of him without resentment. His pride has obscured his reasoning."

"The father is the chief scribe for the governor. His son worked closely with him learning the trade," Tara clarified.

"Wasn't it a falling wall that crushed his hand?" Raasah whispered, straining to remember the stories.

"Yea," Tara replied softly. "The small bones and nerves could not all be repaired, no matter what the scribe paid the healers."

Onihah explained quietly: "He was an engraver of stone, the apple of his father's eye, reduced to busy tasks – no longer able to do the meticulous detail needed to record important events or engrave dedications…at least until now."

Once more, the father rebuked his son loudly. "You will not have anything more to do with those heretics! You will not bring disgrace on our family.…" The rest of his words faded as Onihah directed the girls next to a closed shop.

"Raasah was just telling me about the curriculum being changed in Martha's class," Tara said.

"Yea, I did hear about that," Onihah said.

The crowd was dispersing. The curtain had closed on the puppet show.

"I must get ready for the dance performance in the Grand Plaza," Raasah said. "You will come and watch, won't you?"

"Of course, we will," Onihah smiled.

Little Brother bounded toward them.

Behind the colossal raised stage, Raasah lifted the hem of her silky sky-blue gown to assure that the wide bands of rattles were securely fastened to her ankles. A fretful Ada was repeatedly tapping the repaired tambourine against her hip as she counted the beats aloud.

"Ada, you will be fine. You have been through it a thousand times!"

"Mother and Darius will be here. I can't make any mistakes."

As if on cue, Darius in his full ceremonial dress, accompanied by his striking gold-laden wife, stepped forward on the platform. Their mere presence sent a hush over the assemblage. Darius raised his arms to the people as his beautiful wife stood dutiful and serene at his side.

"Our Creator goes by many names," Darius boomed. "He is Kukulkan and Hurricane; he is Heart-of-Sky and Modeler. But in the beginning, there was no one to speak his names; no one to praise his glory; no one to nurture his greatness. And so Kukulkan thinks, 'Who is there to speak my name? Who is there to give me praise?'[20]

"Kukulkan only has to think the word, and there it is. 'Earth,' he thinks, and the earth rises like a mist from the sea. But it does not speak his name. 'Mountains', he thinks, and great mountains thrust their peaks to the sky. But they do not praise him. He makes the birds, the deer, the jaguars and snakes and each is given his home. 'You, the birds, your nests are in the trees. You, the deer, lie down by the rivers. Now multiply and fill the Earth.

"Then Kukulkan says to the animals, 'Speak and pray to me.' But the creatures can only squawk and howl. They cannot speak; they cannot pray. So Kukulkan summons Our Grandfather and Our Grandmother Spirits who are most wise.

"'Determine how we can make man that will speak my names, praise me, and pray to me,' commands Kukulkan. They run their hands over the kernels of corn. They run their hands over the husks and the stems.

"'We will make man that will speak and pray,' our Grandfather says. 'We will make man that will nurture and provide,' our Grandmother says. They give their answer to Kukulkan, 'It is good to make your people with the dough of the corn. They will speak your name. They will be givers of respect; givers of praise."

"And, so it was, man was born and he placed them with honor upon the earth. Kukulkan gave them music to link them to the Heavens above and man gave Kukulkan respect, they gave him praise. And man grew in intelligence and multiplied and filled the Earth. But there was one man whom Kukulkan loved more than all the others. His praises and music swelled the bosom of Kukulkan and his dance and song created a sacred space, closing the gap between here and the otherworld, releasing the noble dead from the grasp of the Dreaded Void.

"This man was Ammonihah. Kukulkan blessed Ammonihah. Kukulkan empowered the noble beings with him to build our great city. We, the descendants of Ammonihah, and those he has graciously adopted in, we have become heirs to Kukulkan's blessings and his great city. Through our music we celebrate life and express our gratitude to our Creator. This music, from where our soul expresses itself, enables us to feel the responsibility to continue with the traditions left by our ancestors."

Drums softly pulsed like the sound of soothing ocean waves. Darius continued dramatically: "We are the chosen people! We are the true children of our Creator! Today we give praise, and song, and dance[21] in honour of Kukulkan. My dear Ammonihahites! Through our music we celebrate life and express our gratitude to our Creator for our great city of Ammonihah."

Darius' voice was growing in volume along with the drums. A low haunting chant was growing in the background. "It is my duty now to introduce the pride of our city, the future Priestesses of the Gods! Here are the Dancers of the Moon, our mediators, our Givers of Respect, our own Givers of Praise to our Creator! Oh, praise to Kukulkan!"

The singers broke into song, mixing with the pulsing drums and bewitching chants. The musical bows[22], rattles, and flutes followed as Darius and his wife faded to the side and the dancers for the gods gracefully leapt onto the spacious stage. Raasah felt the music coursed through her veins as the first set of dancers sensually twirled and dipped and swayed. It was elating, it was stirring; it made her feel like she could fly. As she waited excitedly for their debut on the stage, she flashed a broad smile at Ada, who now looked a shade paler. Raasah gripped the frightened girl firmly and yelled, over the band, "Let the music take you!"

On stage, Raasah allowed the melody to enwrap her, gliding her through the story of her dance. The haunting sounds of the flute, the enchanting beat of the drums, took on a life of their own and possessed her, leading her through her joyous steps. Raasah had become one with the music, and the magic of the dance transcended her on a journey back to the time of their ancestors, feeling their awe for and love of the Creator. It was invigorating as her small group intertwined with the other dancers before the citizens below. Intense drum rhythms, mixed with high pitched flutes, climaxed and fell and the beauty of the dance mesmerized the audience.

Their portion of the dance completed, Raasah and Ada, chests heaving with adrenalin, looked on from the edge of the stage, exhilarated as the remaining students finished the interpretive dance. Even Ada now looked elated at the wonder of the dance. The sound of flutes and drums still vibrated through their spirits. As the dance approached the end, Ada suddenly hugged Raasah.

"We did it! I feel so renewed, so free! Oh, I couldn't have done it without you. You are such a good friend!"

Speechless, Raasah grinned brightly at the excited girl, but the elated feeling faded abruptly. Incredibly, she once more spied the intimidating juggler from Lamonhah Ridge who now was arguing with Darius by the side of the stage. With a flip of his robes, Darius was replaced by a large scowling soldier who knocked the wiry man against the back corner of the stage and out of sight. The soldier followed briskly behind the curtains in one long stride. Raasah couldn't let the juggler get away again. As the other dancers boisterously bounded off the stage, she shoved her tambourine into Ada's hand.

"Hold this! I'll be right back."

Raasah sprinted around the corner where the two men had disappeared and, then, stopped dead. The sneering soldier, only some 20 paces ahead, was standing over the sprawled juggler now sporting a bloody lip. Darius was nowhere to be seen. Raasah retreated just around the corner. The soldier glanced shamelessly to the side without seeing her and then, with a rumbling belly laugh and a swift kick at the cowering man at his feet, he marched off toward Porahah, leaving the wretched entertainer curled in a fetal position upon the ground.

Raasah stepped boldly into view. The juggler's stunned face transformed into anxiety as he recognized Raasah staring fixedly at him. Gracelessly rising to his feet, never taking his eyes off of her, he shuffled back. With each step he took, Raasah took one forward. The faster he backed up, the more Raasah took courage and kept pace. Slowly, though, realization sunk in that she had no plan whatsoever if she 'caught him'. As she became cognitive of this fact, it didn't take much to get distracted. Someone called her name. As Raasah twisted slightly to locate the voice's owner, the juggler took the opportunity to turn and run. Tara had caught up to Raasah.

"It's him! It's the juggler!" Raasah cried as she grabbed Tara's arm to pursue her quarry.

Little Brother saw the girls running and joined the race. "The juggler! It's the juggler!" she repeated to the boy pointing to the tall figure now straining a quick look behind him as he thrust himself into the throng of people. The girls and young boy shouldered their way through the same crowd. Raasah jumped up regularly to keep track of the top of his head, thankful that his height usually exceeded those around him. Despite this advantage, though, the elusive juggler once more seemed to evaporate into a thick mass of people. Little Brother bolted into a seemingly impenetrable crowd and vanished too. Abruptly, Raasah halted, with Tara, thankfully, following suit.

"Ok," said Tara, taking deep breaths. "Who are we following?"

Raasah blurted out in frustration who the juggler was as she proceeded once more to vigorously push through the milling bodies, searching madly for signs of him. Tara kept up doing her fair share of pushing and squeezing through the crowds.

"I've got to find him. He has answers," Raasah breathed heavily. "He knows…." She jumped up and down again trying to spot him. She squinted through doorways and behind vendor stalls and, then, as the hairs on her neck prickled, she looked suspiciously behind her. She had that odd feeling again.

"Someone is watching me…," she declared.

"Raasah," Tara said, looking around confused, "we are

surrounded by hundreds of people glaring at us! We just rudely barged our way through them...."

"There!" Raasah shouted, pointed over the crowd. "He has a dark hood. He is staring at us...."

Raasah could not make out the face and it was turning around as Tara twirled in that direction.

Raasah hoped Tara saw him, if only for a brief second, but, after a moment all hope was dashed as Tara said slowly, "Are you sure you saw someone. He would have had to be a giant for you to have seen him in this crowd!"

Tara made a deliberate survey of the crowd once more to satisfy her companion.

"I guess you're right...," Raasah said regretfully. She realized how silly she must have sounded, how immature....

Raasah heard the scream first.

Down a narrow lane, people were gathering to gape. Little Brother materialized out of the assembly and motioned to the girls. Taking Raasah by the hand, he led her calmly around and through the people to the scene in question. There, slumped against a dilapidated wall, the un-dead juggler was now dead – his chest oozing with blood, his empty eyes staring where his assailant had been.

Raasah gasped. Tara shimmied up beside her.

"Nah, nah, nah," Raasah was repeating dismally. She turned to Tara. "He could have told us so much. Just when I think we are close to answers...." Raasah turned with disbelief back to the juggler but her thoughts were back in the clearing that last night with her father.

"Someone is keeping one step ahead of us," Tara mumbled disquietly. "We'd better get out of here."

Raasah slowly turned to address Tara but instead was drawn into the crowd beyond. "There he is again!"

Tara turned sharply as Raasah pointed. A black hooded figure towered over the crowd for less time than it took for her to blink and he was gone. Raasah lunged forward but was grabbed abruptly by Tara.

"What are you doing?" Raasah said near hysterics. "He was following us. He must be the one who did this."

"Think, Raasah," Tara implored. "What would you do if you caught up to him? He's bigger than all three of us together. And, Raasah, you don't know he did it. You can't just assume it was him just because, because… he is big!"

Confused, Raasah stared at Tara and then at the crowd that now took on a sinister air. Questioning eyes turned their way and the whispers took on an ominous tone. She hugged the boy to her unaware that Tara was urging her back into the crowd.

Raasah never did make it back to Ada or the other dancers by the stage. She was led passively back to the villa. Tears of frustration stung her eyes.

---

20   Story of the Creation: This account of the creation was inspired by the Popol Vuh translations. All editions of Popol Vuh came from the records of the Dominican priest Francisco Ximénez who lived in the 1700s in Central America. It is generally believed that Ximénez borrowed a phonetic manuscript from a parishioner for his source, though, such a manuscript is said to have never been found. His manuscript has no organizational divisions and does not exhibit consistent punctuation or capitalization. For all of these reasons, editing the manuscript was a challenge and a great deal of judgment by editors was used in preparing print editions.

21   *Dance: There was thought that there was little information about dancing left behind by the ancient Central American people beyond a few paintings on murals and vases. But, in the spring of 1990, Nikolai Grube deciphered the glyph for "dance" (pronounced ak'ot) in Maya hieroglyphics. After this decipherment, it seemed clear that dance was a central component of social, religious, and political endeavors for the ancient Maya. It is now believed the entire community danced, including kings, nobles, and common people, much like the ancient Hebrews.*

22   *Musical Bow: is a huge gourd with the top and bottom cut out. Around the top rim is an armrest to hold a long bow. When played, the string makes two very unusual tones enhanced by the gourd.*

Chapter 17

The Dark Stranger

Raasah had her nightmare again but, this time, as the juggler stumbled into her, she saw the distinct form of someone in the trees. It grew hideous – three fiercely grinning heads loomed on its shoulders – people were screaming; the juggler ran past her, looking back white with fear. Bolting awake, Raasah sat wide-eyed and shaken in the dark, her legs drawn rigidly up to her chin.

She stared into the black starless sky beyond her narrow window. The misty moon shone its eerie light across her bed. To calm her thumping heart, she began to hum, haltingly at first, her grandmother' song that spoke of a gay country garden and a chorus of flowers nodding in the breeze. She struggled against the distortions trying to invade her thoughts, threatening to transform her mind's image of delicate flowers into disturbing sneering masks with empty eyes. Despite her efforts, her humming choked off. The sound of rustling leaves took on the embodiment of malevolence serpents bent on binding her soul. She daren't leave her bed or cause a sound for fear that grasping fingers would whip out and capture a shivering limb. Her mouth was dry parchment, her throat constricted.

She didn't know how long she huddled like that, wretchedly terrorized by table shadows and gentle breezes. Mercifully, her heavy eyelids did close eventually, and she dozed, tossing restlessly to the high-pitched buzz and drone of the night-winged creatures until the sky displayed tinges of golden light. Then, once again, she startled herself awake, now instinctively aware someone was watching her.

"Wake up, Sleepy Head," Terjah said amusingly. "We have to get off to the Hall of Records. We can't keep Onihah waiting." He paused. "By the way, you look terrible."

"You are no pretty sight either," she snapped back.

Brother and sister met Tara just outside the heavy door safeguarding the vital records of their people.

"I hope you haven't been waiting long," Terjah greeted her. "Someone slept in." He shot a comical glance at Raasah.

Raasah glared back, just to be irritated even more by the brightness of the morning rays that momentarily blinded her. Restraining her urge to retaliate, she slugged her brother in an attempt to look playful but the force of the fist told him otherwise.

"Nah, I was early," Tara stated distantly.

"That's not like you, Tara of Amarihah," Terjah said, rubbing his arm while giving Raasah a curious 'what's wrong with you' look.

"My uncle and aunt were arguing and I just wanted to get out of there," Tara said, unaware of the brother-sister undercurrent. "Aunt Zipporah always gets into such a foul mood when this guest comes. Even Uncle Gormonaluk seems upset when he arrives but he still entertains him. Luckily he doesn't come often."

Footsteps were echoing down the corridor toward them.

"Young ladies and gentleman," Onihah said cheerily as he neared the group. "Good to see you all here. Come in, come in."

He released a series of latches and they entered the massive library. Inside, they were greeted by several of the Brotherhood: Priestess Zillah, Uncle Normad, 'Prince' Reuben, and Ali. Talking around the table were Aaron, the astrologer (whom Raasah now recognized as one of Terjah's peers); Azariah, Chemish's brother-in-law (whom Raasah learned was a gem-cutter); and, to Raasah's delight, Chemish himself and his father, Adam (still sporting a simple sling). In addition, Raasah was introduced to Caleb, Absalom's middle son, who arrived as they were entering the hall.

Raasah was pleased to observe that Caleb was nothing like his brother, Zeniff, in looks or demeanor. He held himself straight and had a pleasant square face with a trim dark beard. He wore fine handsome clothing typical of the wealthy but was modestly adorned with one fine-looking pendent and matching ear spools. Raasah liked him right away despite his blood connection to the sadistic Zeniff. In fact, she felt a pang of sympathy for this friendly man who had to associate daily with family that comprised of Zeniff and his father. Her own foul mood started to lift.

"I am so sorry for your family tragedies," Terjah chose his words carefully as he addressed Caleb. There was an awkward silence followed by murmurs of agreement and quiet words of condolences.

"I appreciate your thoughts but I am fine," Caleb said simply. To everyone's relief, he changed the subject: "Now, where is Martha? I expected to see her here today."

"Martha and her family have had to take a sudden departure. They are journeying to Gideon at this very moment," Onihah explained. "She was fearful for the safety of her family."

"Martha and her brother went searching for her son last night when he didn't arrive in a timely manner," Zillah stated. "They found him in an alley near their home."

"Oh, nah, nah! He isn't...," Raasah stammered.

"By the grace of God, he was rescued by the most unlikely allies," Onihah continued, "– some drunken heavy-weights that had a grudge against one of the assailants."

Concerned murmurs circulated the room. "How is the boy?" Azariah asked.

"Her son suffered cuts and bruises and some possible broken ribs, but, it could have been much worse," Onihah said. "Of course, poor Martha is terrified of what could happen next."

"Does this have something to do with the new curriculum?" Tara asked.

"I'm afraid so," Onihah replied. "It happened later that evening after she refused to teach the new curriculum at the Hall of Instruction."

"She is smart to be fearful," Aaron said.

"Yea, Abel son of Dan, he was found beaten to death outside a tavern shortly after he refused to teach the young priests a newly required text," Adam said. "They said he was drunk and got in a fight. Though the witnesses were of questionable character and their stories were conflicting, nothing was done to find the culprits. Yea, Martha has good reason to be fearful for herself and family."

"Abinahah sped up the delivery of some farm tools to a neighbouring community," Onihah continued, "Before daybreak, he smuggled Martha and her small family out of the city with his load. She will be going to stay with her father's kin. Abinahah should be back later today once he secures the last portion of her travel arrangements."

"She has done what she needed to do," Reuben said. "A widow on her own.... She stayed strong and did her part. We wish this brave lady all the best."

"Before the scavengers get wind she is gone, I'll see what I can discretely salvage from her home to forward to her," Normad offered. Other simultaneous offers of help were relayed to the old priest.

"Now to the immediate matters at hand," Onihah took charge. "I wanted to let you to know I have tried several times to see Esrom and I have been blocked or forbidden: 'He is in a meeting', 'He is resting', 'He is not well'-- all contrived excuses. This morning, I saw him being led away supported by two guards. Before I could approach him, Darius's arrogance intervened once more. He said the Prophet had an important meeting and he gets too tired to give an audience to everyone who wants one. Darius was then joined by two more guards who blocked any hope of me getting by him."

"Darius stands between us and all our answers," Ali said. "He is too smart to be caught doing anything wrong and yet we find his presence whenever things of concern come up."

"I have spoken with a visionary," Onihah said, "And I assure you that this visionary indeed has the gift. This person has had a dream – a vision – of our Prophet Esrom. In the dream Esrom reached out and in his hand he held a small vial. He looked pale with black lifeless eyes. He pointed to the bedding and it lifted. Shaquah, our healer, tried to push it back down and Darius laughed."

"Who is this visionary?" Chemish asked. Tara turned to Chemish and then looked intently at Onihah.

"The visionary has good reason not to want to be named," Onihah said patiently, aware of murmurings among the group.

"Everyone wants to be a visionary," Azariah asserted in his suspicious tone. "What makes this person more believable?"

"I have witnessed the fulfillment of this visionary's interpretations," Onihah said, "but the talent is still in its adolescent stage and the meanings are not always clear."

"Are you saying the visionary thinks Shaquah is hiding something," Chemish asked, "… knows something about Esrom's illness that she has not told us about?"

"Now Shaquah has dedicated herself to the prophet's health," Caleb said defensively. "No one loves Esrom more than she!"

"I am saying the interpretation is vague and means no reflection on Shaquah. In any case, I returned to Esrom's quarters once I believed it would be vacated and, finding it empty, lifted the Prophet's bedding. Indeed, there was the vial!" Onihah held up a tiny vial with a milky liquid inside.

There was an intense silence before Azariah said, "This visionary could have planted it there himself. This so-called visionary could be the cause of the Prophet's sickness."

"Believe me this is not the case but someone is causing Prophet Esrom harm. We have suspected it for some time, but I thought with Shaquah as his personal healer, she would protect him or ask for our assistance if she needed it. I have always believed Shaquah to be a woman of integrity…. Tara, I will give this to you to analyze."

Tara accepted the sealed container and gingerly put it in her pouch.

"What can we do to protect him?" Zillah asked. "Darius has practically announced Esrom's approaching death."

"If there is indeed a conspiracy to harm Esrom, I have no doubt Darius is forefront in this," Adam said. "He isolates our Prophet from his friends; he controls all that he does...."

"Darius is, indeed, a powerful man," Normad said. "We need someone who can get close to him to find out what he is doing."

"Let us contact all our brothers and sisters. We must come to some consensus of what we are to do." Ali offered.

"With the juggler now gone," Azariah said. "We have lost even another source for information regarding the demise of the Botholuem Company and the leader of the attackers."

"Someone is working overtime to wrap up all the loose ends," Normad said thoughtfully. "As thankful as we are, it is still most mysterious that you, Raasah, have not become, or in the first place, didn't become, among the deceased."

"They are taking a big gamble that Raasah cannot relay information to condemn them," Zillah commented.

"And, why are they willing to take that risk?" Caleb asked almost to himself.

"No insult intended, but why is it so important to them to keep Raasah safe?" Adam asked.

"I have been giving much thought to looking beyond the words to see the small details," Azariah said quietly, recalling Onihah's subtle admonishment at the previous meeting. "Onihah has great insight. When Raasah relayed what she could remember of the attack, she did bring up some interesting details that need noting."

Addressing Raasah, he continued: "You said one of them called you 'Daughter of Sablon'. Don't you think that strange? One is usually referred to as the child of the father – especially since you were in your father's company at the time. Why would an attacker refer to your mother? It must have been someone very familiar to your mother, more so than your father."

"This would mean they were probably an Ammonihahite," Terjah commented.

"Yea. Earplugs of precious stones and large medallions," Azariah continued, looking at Raasah. "The fact that they were lavishly adorned means they were of the elite society. The elite can be so vain. Even the sons of ill-gotten wealth know better than to flaunt their jewels when committing a crime!"

"So, because the attackers had expensive extravagant jewelry...." Chemish summarizes. "That eliminates the slaves and servants and common ruffians."

There was a pause, eyes downcast at the thought of the senseless beating and death of the captured slaves.

"I never told you, Raasah, but it was I that found you," Terjah said. "You gave me quite a fright. You were at the edge of the trees, separate from the rest of the company and a good space from Father. But, you said you were next to him when the attack happened."

"I believe, now, that Abul pulled me from the carnage," Raasah explained and then she sat up sharply. "How could I have forgotten this, but... I overheard Zoric talking about the attack with some of his companions. This was shortly after the slave prisoners were mobbed," Raasah looked about the room, embarrassed with what she was about to share.

"He said because of Abul I was saved. I'm sorry I didn't put the facts together before now," she said dejectedly. "But how could Zoric have known Abul was protecting me by the trees? I realize now that was what he was doing. I had blamed Abul for the attack but, now that I can look back objectively, I realized that he was encouraging me to wake, holding me when the masked murderers came across me."

"Now, memories can play tricks on you. Maybe this is what you want to believe," Terjah said gently.

"NAH!" Raasah was adamant. "Zoric told his thugs that Abul had saved his prize! That I was his prize! ...I'm sorry I didn't say anything before. I was so insulted, so humiliated. And so much has happened. Zoric called me a...," Raasah lowered her voice, "a strumpet...."

"...a what?" Azariah questioned.

"He said I was a strumpet," Raasah said louder and abruptly before she changed her mind. She diverted her eyes from those around her. "...said he was going to make me into his courtesan, begging...." She choked; warm tears cascaded down her cheek. She looked down as she wiped her face.

Tara put her arm around her. Raasah was so thankful that her grandmother was not there but she couldn't face Chemish.

Slowly Raasah composed herself and, fixing her gaze on the compassionate face of Onihah, said, "There is one more thing. I don't know if it is important, but Zeniff," she looked cautiously over to Caleb, "Zeniff was also there in the alley with Zoric. Zeniff was also there at the mobbing of the slaves. He was dressed like a soldier that time." Raasah hesitated again, then boldly looked up, "Zeniff assaulted the slave woman. It was Zoric, Tola, and Zeniff that encouraged the mob to kill the slaves."

"Now, Raasah, it was chaotic and emotional when the slaves were brought in...." Azariah said prudently.

"Nah, nah. Raasah is right," Terjah announced. "Tola was inciting the crowd into a frenzy. And there was a prisoner that ran to Raasah. I think he was trying to say something to her but Zoric personally ran a spear through him."

"The slave spoke to you?" Azariah asked surprised.

"Yea, just a few words. He said…." Raasah hesitated. "He said …"

"You're badgering her," Chemish said protectively. "How can she possibly remember…?"

"Nah, I can never forget that scene, the words, his pleading eyes," Raasah whispered harshly. "It's been chiseled permanently into my memory… but I just didn't want to think about it." She wiped her moist eyes. Her makeup smeared across her face. "He said we were being deceived. …said we were living among murderers!"

There was a moment of quiet as the thoughtful group took in the new information. "So, again," Chemish said slowly, "more witnesses were silenced before we could find out the truth."

"One might not be silenced," Raasah announced ardently. "Zeniff said Abul was alive and he was 'going to tame him'. It must be our Abul, Terjah. Oh, why didn't I say anything earlier? How could I have dismissed it? I was so angry and hurt. Oh, I pray Abul is still alive," Raasah said miserably.

"Do you have any idea where he might be?" Caleb asked.

"Zeniff had him under guard somewhere. Abul could be at the quarry." She looked pleadingly at Caleb.

"I'll see what I can do. You will have to give me a description of him," Caleb said.

ֆ

By the time Tara had helped Raasah clean her face, most of the brotherhood had parted but Chemish was still waiting for her. Raasah avoided his eyes.

Chemish walked casually toward her until Raasah was looking directly at his broad chest. He was wearing a smart tunic with simple but beautiful brocade along the front. The details started to blur as a tear filled each eye. Chemish lifted her chin with the crook of his finger.

"You are a very brave young lady," he affirmed softly.

"It is so humiliating... what Zoric said. I didn't want you to hear.... I am so ashamed!"

"You have nothing to be ashamed of. Zoric should be the one to apologize for living!" Chemish said angrily. Then, after a brief pause, he tenderly added, "I've missed you."

"So much is happening. And I didn't want any more trouble for your family so I've tried to stay away...." Raasah said in a rush and then looked up into Chemish's gentle eyes. "And I missed you too," she smiled timidly.

Terjah cleared his throat to get their attention. "We need to get going, Raasah. I don't want to leave you unescorted. Grandmother would skin me alive!"

Raasah looked indecisively at her brother standing next to Tara and then back at Chemish.

"Normally I'd be more than willing to leave you in Chemish's capable hands," Terjah explained sympathetically while Raasah continued to stare into the handsome face before her, "but, at this moment, being seen with Chemish would only cause a whole new set of problems."

Chemish crooked his finger under her chin once more. "Terjah is right." Chemish looked so inviting as he drew her to him with his eyes. "Being seen with me would only get tongues wagging and make trouble. We will see each other soon. Just keep safe."

Slowly he slipped his finger away and stepped back. He held her hand briefly before he turned sharply to exit the heavy door with his father. Raasah longingly gazed after him.

Terjah shuffled uncomfortably as he gave his sister a moment to collect herself. "Let's get going," he said quickly as she looked toward him. "Tara needs to pick up something at her house, so we will go by there first."

$$\text{\emph{\c{e}}}$$

"You really think Abul might be at the quarry?" Tara asked as they walked thoughtfully toward her villa.

"I don't know why I was so stupid not to understand," Raasah said wretchedly. "Zoric referred to him as the new stone-cutter. Why didn't I remember before now?"

"You are being too hard on yourself," Tara said comfortingly. "After everything that has happened…."

"I didn't know that Zoric had come with the families to meet father's caravan," Raasah said.

"He didn't," Terjah replied.

"He must have come across Abul when his party was hunting down the slaves that they captured," Raasah said. "Zoric and his thugs must have kept some of them to sell or secure as quarry workers."

"Now that is possible," Tara said thoughtfully.

"It's hard to know what to do and what to think – so much is happening," Terjah emphasized. "Martha running for her life, the priesthood being deceived with corrupt teachings, Amulonites and Nehor members aligning themselves with our corrupt leaders, and then this foreign priest, Alma, stirring the people up and angering the judges and lawyers against the good people…."

"Terjah!" Tara exclaimed, twirling around to face him. "You can't lump Alma in that list as a problem. He is just pointing out the truth."

"…the truth is that things ARE very wrong, Brother!" Raasah agreed. "There was contention and corruption here long before this Alma came to our city. Father just minimized the effects while he was alive."

Terjah was taken aback as he looked from one determined look to the other. "Am I being ganged up on?"

"Alma may be upsetting some people," Tara said seriously, "but that is because he is openly pointing out the wrong doings of those in power. He is saying what the good people of Ammonihah are afraid to say and offering them the truth and a better way to live."

"Well, those people Alma is upsetting are powerful and have many friends in low places," Terjah said impatiently. "This is a recipe for disaster."

"And, if we keep quiet and let it go on, it will get better?" Tara retorted.

"You know that is not true, but it just must be done subtly and cautiously."

"You mean the way the Nehor priests do it!" Tara said sharply.

"Now, children!" Raasah said maternally. "Play nice."

There was an awkward silence.

"I'm sorry, Terjah," Tara replied more pleasantly. "I just meant

Alma is only trying to bring those who are good people to know the truth. He is not trying to cause the people trouble."

"You really think highly of him, don't you?" Terjah said quietly.

"You haven't heard him yet, Terjah. You have to hear what he has to say."

They rounded the corner to the Gormonaluk home. Tara stopped walking and let out an exasperated sigh. "He's still here." Her tone was tinged with anger. Noticing Raasah's puzzled look, she added, "See the massive chariot by the gate."

"That chariot is big enough for ten people! The weight of that must be horrific to bear!" Raasah exclaimed. A number of muscular young men idly paced or sat nearby in the shade of a large flowering tree.

"That chariot looks familiar," Terjah said, thoughtfully. "Who did you say was here?"

"I told you about him. It's the stranger from another village. Very wealthy, from all I can gather, but crude and rude. He always seems to wear dark clothing, a leering sneer, and looks quite unkempt. And he has a wicked scar…."

"…that parts his hair." To Tara's surprise, Terjah accurately finished the description. Then the realization of what was being said sunk in not a moment too soon. Out of the door stepped Noalas, the mercenary. Terjah pulled the girls back against the neighbour's stone wall.

"Do you think he saw us?" Raasah asked anxiously.

"You know him?" Tara questioned.

"That's Noalas – he was the one who was supposed to be protecting my father's caravan," Raasah whispered harshly.

"He is a lying, immoral son of the devil," Terjah growled under his breath.

"Let me go ahead," Tara whispered anxiously. "He DID look this way and it will look suspicious if no one walks out." Terjah continued to hold her arm. "I will be all right."

Reluctantly, Terjah released her. Tara bent down, rubbing a discarded rotting papaya upon her skirt before venturing out toward the villa and the foreboding Noalas who was now accompanied by a very unhappy Gormonaluk.

Raasah waited breathlessly as she listened to Tara's receding footsteps. The siblings could hear Tara greeting the men: "Wa-ie, sir. Wa-ie, Uncle." Raasah wrapped an arm around her fluttering stomach. She watched Terjah's face tense and she grabbed him as he made a gesture to step out.

"Nah, Brother. She can do this." Raasah held her breath as she willed herself to believe her own words.

"And this young lady is...?" Noalas inquired sharply as Tara approached.

"This is my niece, Tara. I'm sure you have met her before."

Tara wiped at her skirt. "Would you believe it?" she said. "This obnoxious rascal tried to steal my satchel. And, of all things, I fell on something disgusting. Please excuse me. I must go in and change." Noalas did not move aside.

"A fine young lady in the streets without an escort? But I thought I saw a young man with you."

"If you saw who it was that knocked me down, sir, I would be grateful if you would track him down so I can charge him before the judge. But I am sure he is far gone now, a desperate filthy youth like that."

Tara stared at the large dark stranger. Noala's deep narrow eyes returned the stare. Thankfully, her uncle broke the stalemate.

"Girl, get inside and clean up. You are a sight."

Tara stepped around the large bulk of the visitor but his ring-studded hand caught her arm in a powerful grip. Tara shuffled her satchel into the crook of her free arm.

"You best be more careful, Tara, niece of Gormonaluk. A pretty young thing, like yourself, should not walk the streets alone."

"I will keep that in mind, sir. Wa-ie, sir, and have a safe trip home." She stared pointedly at him, waiting for him to loosen his hold. As she felt the grip slacken, she jerked her arm free and retreated into the inner courtyard.

The men remained on the step by the entrance. "I was sure I saw her with someone." Noalas said presently. "A young man...."

"Our fair city does possess its share of hoodlums these days...." Gormonaluk said absently.

"He didn't strike me as a filthy hoodlum," Noalas said slowly. "Your niece...."

"Tara?"

"Yea, Tara. She is an attractive young woman of marrying age. Does she keep company with a special young man?"

"She does speak often to my scribe," Gormonaluk said, puzzled at the question. "Too familiar with him, I say. We have tried to train her in the social graces but...."

"What is this young man's name?" Noalas demanded.

"Terjah. His name is Terjah," Gormonaluk replied. "But he is not due here until this afternoon."

"The same Terjah, son of Botholuem?" Noalas barked.

Raasah cringed against the wall staring nervously at her brother.

The voices became indistinguishable as they heard the two men walk off into the walled garden, the sounds now mingling with the wind that was growing in intensity.

"We better go," Terjah said. "Noalas may send for his henchmen to check out Tara's story." They hastened off toward a busy nearby square.

Chapter 18

A Rural Refuge

It was fourth day of the week – the day each week that Grandmother Marian routinely scheduled to spend at the orphanage. Though the items were assembled the night before, normally Raasah was at school when the carriage was loaded the next morning but, because of Founders Week, school was closed and Raasah, mind far from her task, was in the midst of the activity folding and passing up donations of blankets and clothing that had been collected by the servants for the parent-less children. There were even a couple of cute pairs of leather sandals.

Marian and Tamar were busy boxing up baked goods, fresh fruit, and vegetables. Enoch and Vashti, Tamar's young children, were playfully gathering small bundles while Little Brother scampered up among the loaded items in the carriage and was adeptly organizing everything with all indications that he had done it many times before. Meanwhile, Elihu and Mosia hoisted up a large wrapped carcass of venison, depositing it on the narrow platform on the back of the carriage. As they roped it snugly down, Raasah found herself drifting through her memories of her father loading a carriage for one of his many journeys abroad, in particular of him securing a load on the same platform, with a twinkle in his eyes, singing a child's nonsense verse....

'Four carefree little frogs hopping through a puddle.

Four silly little frogs swimming past a log.

Four foolish little frogs jumping Master Snake.

Gulp, Yum, Happy Snake!

Three frightened frogs hiding in the mud.'

"Done!" Elihu said loudly with great satisfaction, transporting Raasah briskly back to the present.

The thick curtain of the carriage was tied back, displaying the treasures piled high inside. The only vacant area left was a small section of the seat that was quickly filled by Tamar's squirming giggling children – their arms full of more small bundles.

"Are you sure you do not want me to come?" Raasah asked in a monotone that displayed no enthusiasm.

"Nah, dear granddaughter," Marian said kindly. "You go meet your friends and enjoy the festivities. Amos is here to assure your safety. Besides, the orphanage can only take so many guests."

There, in a far corner of the garden, her 'protector', pucker-lipped and huddled over on an upturned bucket, flipped a struggling black beetle over and over again with a stubby stick. Raasah raised an eyebrow and grimaced. She had no intention on counting on Amos to assure her safety!

As she leaned on the low wall on the foremost upper terrace, Raasah watched her tiny family caravan head out the villa gate toward the south quarter. Grandmother walked beside the bearer-held carriage next to Tamar and Elihu. Little Brother scampered furtively around, repeatedly popping up between the bare-chested bearers to surprise and delight the curious small passengers inside.

Music and gay crowds could be heard in the distant streets while pods of people were jostling and strolling down their road toward Ammonihah's center for more Founders festivities. She was not in a festive mood but her eyes forlornly followed two boisterous youth feigning blows at each other as they turned into a bakery. Stunned, she recognized a figure in the doorway as they passed. Chemish – he had his familiar leathers on but it was his handsome face warm and inviting that held her eyes. She thought she saw a smile and then, as if it had been a mirage, he was gone. An empty vacuum sucked at her heart. Gazing once more at the empty doorway, she wondered if she had really seen him *or was it just wishful thinking?* She pushed him forcibly from her thoughts.

She sighed as her mind went over the conversations from yesterday's meeting and the images they had conjured up for her. She recalled the reprehensible way Zoric spoke of her that day in the alley with his friends; she thought of poor Teacher Martha having to steal away to protect her family; she could picture the shackled slave clutching the bloody point of the spear; ...and she thought of Abul – ashamed how she had blamed him and, now, longed to find him safe and well, praying it was not too late. She was despondent, tired, and longed only to curl up in a quiet corner and wish the world away.

Raasah sighed again, looking out across the city without seeing.

"Why so glum, little sister?"

Raasah spun around, pressing herself against the pony wall. "Terjah, you scared me!" she hissed.

"Grandmother said you were looking a little upset. I thought I would check on you."

"How did you know I would be here?"

"Now, Raasah. Since you were old enough to climb, you have come up here whenever you were sad or troubled. I remember a time you had the entire household looking for you – you must have been about five – and I found you curled up with your floppy, bobble-head doll on that striped blanket of yours – next to this very wall, I believe."

"Paksie Praddle…."

"What?"

"The doll – his name was Paksie Praddle."

"Yea. Bobble-headed Paksie Praddle."

Raasah had to smile at the thought of the silly old doll with the floppy head that had meant so much to her. Then her smile vanished.

"I think I remember that night. That was when I overheard one of Mother's and Father's terrible arguments. I hated it when they fought."

Terjah joined Raasah and looked thoughtfully across at the mid-branches of the massive oak. Raasah joined his gaze and spied the glossy yellow breasts of two blue macaws stretching their thick wings before nestling into each other affectionately.

"Terjah, do you think Mother and Father ever really loved each other?"

The more dominate macaw gave a gentle wavery squawk and nuzzled his hooked black peak into its partner's downy neck. A long moment passed.

"I'm sure they did," Terjah answered slowly. "Mother just could not understand why Father could turn down positions of power to be a travelling merchant. She could not see the wonder of exploring other cultures and experiencing other lifestyles."

"Maybe Mother just wanted to secure our standing in society. Maybe Father didn't try hard enough to understand her concerns," Raasah said, trying to justify. "I prayed we could all be a happy family. Nights when they would fight, I would sneak up here and search the stars for Kukulkan, begging Him to make them stop – to love each other." Her voice croaked. "But it never happened."

"Kukulkan will not force people to feel what he wants them to feel," Terjah said simply.

"...Father was persuaded to accept the appointment of Antionah's Chief Attendant. I thought Mother would have been very pleased he would be part of the royal court but, instead, she seemed even more upset with Father," Raasah recalled. "It is all very confusing. They just seemed to drift down different roads. In fact, Terjah... in fact, Mother seemed to have drifted away from the entire family, ...from us. I thought if I could be a better daughter, she would come back...."

"But she has accepted another life separate from us," Terjah summarized.

"I believe we've lost both parents," Raasah said remorsely. Another long moment passed.

"Enough of this!" Terjah declared. "You need a change of scenery!"

"Terjah," Raasah replied, startled. "I don't want to.... Don't you have to go back to work?"

"Not today! Gormonaluk gave me the day off. After all, it is the week to celebrate our great city. Come," Terjah took her limp hand. "Come," he repeated when she didn't respond. "There's a special place I want to show you."

Raasah didn't have the energy to protest. She let herself be led back down through their living quarters out into the garden. There, deposited like a shrine outside the gate, sat the polished personal carriage of Terjah's employer. The gold embroidered curtains were tied back with thick golden tassels. Crocs and colourful frogs were painted in busy scenes around the outer shell and the interior was padded in silky cushions and soft thick furs. As Raasah tentatively approached, eight bearers displaying the Gormonaluk golden crest on their tunics, stood abruptly at attention.

Astounded, Raasah gazed at her brother.

"My boss lent me his carriage for the day," he said, pleased at the effect the sight had had on his sister.

"But, why…? It's his…." She looked up at the gapping jaws of one of two life-sized ceramic crocodiles extending over the roof of the carriage; its large bejeweled eyes fiercely peering down. Each front clawed foot, effectively placed over the edge to intimidate and impress, bore the embossed scaly swirl that encased Gormonaluk's glyphed crest.

"Enough questions. Come," he repeated for the third time, drawing her eyes away from the claws.

A bearer produced a padded stepping stool next to the carriage and extended his arm. She looked up at her brother to protest again, but, seeing the sincerity in his eyes, she dissolved and stepped up into the plush interior. Terjah followed her inside. With an "Ei-uh!", the bearers lifted the carriage in a smooth swoop.

Silently, past the carriage curtains, Raasah stared out at the busy city, barely registering the flame throwers' flashy dance in a small square, or the blue-painted contortionists twisting themselves into awkward shapes, or any of the other performers expertly executing their skills along the way; she was barely conscience of the beautiful renditions of familiar tunes in instrument and song that resounded from the many small plazas and squares they passed, or the decreasing volume of the crowds as they skirted the Grand Plaza and headed off toward the south.

Instead, she was searching her memories for details she had forgotten about Lamonhah Ridge. She pictured her father carefully fashioning his toy chariot on the wobbly disks; she remembered the growing fire in the clearing, flames leaping high as the grease dripped from the carcass; she recalled the unexpected touching remark of Abul saying "You are a good person, Raasah".

Raasah remembered feeling perplexed by Abul's latter remark that night – not so much about the compliment, but the way Abul said it. *And he had used my given name!* Abul always used his pet name for her when they were alone. Raasah remembered thinking at the time that Abul wanted to tell her something more. *Was there something else I was supposed to remember?*

Terjah tapped his foot against hers and grinned. Raasah glanced at her brother with no expression and then back to the scenes around them, relieved they were not heading for the hub of the festivities. Terjah leaned low out the side of the carriage to give directions to one of the bearers.

Some drunken laughter boomed out of a noisy tavern down a brick-lined lane; brown speckled hens clucked chattily as they meandered by on spindly legs; and gleeful children skipped in circles around their parents as they passed by. Further on, Raasah studied the one-story homes about them and slowly began to recognize them as those that she had passed with Little Brother the day she had first met him. They looked a little different when she was viewing them upon the shoulders of men. They were heading to the southeastern quarter of the city. This was the middle-class section of Ammonihah. The homes were modest but, on the whole, roomy and well-kept. Neat picturesque gardens skirted many of the homes and pretty paths squeezed between the buildings.

Ahead, she heard gay music and excited voices. They were approaching a busy plaza where a tame but joyous crowd filled with children had assembled in front of a good-sized amphitheater. As their carriage slowed to a stop, hands applauded. Several comically attired actors entered center stage. One sad-looking character in over-sized clothes exaggerated a trip, flipping over several times to the delight of his audience.

Baffled at Terjah's choice of destination, Raasah hesitantly accepted brother's extended hand to exit the carriage. As Terjah slipped his satchel over his shoulder, he spoke to the head bearer. Then, with an "Ei-uh!", the bearers hoisted the carriage back onto their shoulders.

"Terjah?" Raasah called, watching them march away.

"It's all right," he smiled, extending his hand. "Come this way, little sister."

The delicious smells of cornbreads, chili dumplings, and tortillas filled their nostrils, awakening Raasah's appetite and reminding her that she had not yet eaten today. After some smooth bartering by the charismatic brother, the two siblings were soon seated under a tall shade tree to the rear of the other patrons munching on steaming dumplings and spiced beans.

"You had that poor girl swooning with your shameless flattery, dear brother."

"Just trying to brighten a young girl's day," Terjah replied airily.

"You had her melting in your hand, as if you didn't notice! If I had allowed you to continue, she would not only have offered you the dumplings for free, she would have given you her first born as well!"

"Now, sister, I would never have thwarted her efforts from obtaining what was her fair return!" he teased as he scooped up tender beans with a rolled tortilla. "I would only have insisted on her second born!"

And so they sat as they enjoyed the comic relief of the light-hearted performance on stage and talked – mostly talked. Raasah's dark disposition had paled. She even found herself laughing as they reminisced of their childhood days, often speaking of fun antics they participated in with their father. As the conversations advanced, Raasah was poignantly aware, in the back of her mind, how their mother was absent from their fond recollections.

"Do you remember old Mandula's wife, Bettelina?" Raasah asked, in sudden recollection.

Terjah tipped his head with interest. "She's the round, stern woman that has her servants quaking at their knees...."

"Yea, that's her," she laughed. "Father saved her from much embarrassment at one of our camps."

"Oh, she tends to take herself far too seriously," Terjah smirked.

"But, this would have been most unfortunate for her if Father had not intervened when he had." Raasah smiled broadly, catching Terjah's interest. "Stepping out of her carriage that evening, our grand Bettelina slipped literally head over toes into a shallow sink hole. Father happened to be in a position to scoop his arms under those plump shoulders of hers just before she hit the ground." Raasah was laughing in spurts as she described the scene. "Oh, Terjah, it was so funny! Her robes had flung up and over both their heads – they had to fight their way out of all the cloth! Father rose red-faced with his effort and Bettelina – well, the look of horror on her face was one I'll never forget!"

Terjah's face shone with delight at the mental picture.

"Oh, and the bearers – they were at a loss at what to do! I thought Bettelina was going to take a strip out of them but Father… oh, he has such a gift…." Raasah stuttered with sudden emotion and then looked blankly past her brother, the humour now gone out of her voice. "He always knew how to make it easier for others to laugh at themselves and he could do it without them losing their dignity, no matter how awkward." Her voice broke but, recovering, she continued: "He righted the situation before the rest of the caravan had time to know what happened – saving her such embarrassment," Raasah paused again, swallowing hard. "…and Father had her laughing at herself in no time." Her voice was flat. "He saved the bearers from a good whipping."

Raasah stared off into the distance. "Old Mandula and Bettelina died that night…." Raasah sat stone-faced. Terjah solemnly put an arm around his sister. "I miss him," Raasah said simply.

"I, as well," Terjah replied softly, cognizant that they were both speaking of their father. They sat for a moment in silence – still, expressionless, within a rapturous crowd. Then Terjah abruptly stood.

"Now it's time to go to the special place." He extended his hand to her.

"You mean, this is not…."

"Nah! First we had to ditch Gormonaluk's servants. Can't have that lot finding out about it," he said slyly.

Raasah stared long at her brother's laughing eyes before gingerly taking the outstretched hand.

They skirted a few stragglers behind the crowd and slipped through a thick hedge behind the amphitheater. Here, under a small grove of old trees, through the unkempt bushes and saplings beneath them, Raasah followed her brother. They did not go in far before they came upon the high vine-covered city wall. Bewildered, Raasah slowed and watched with fascination as Terjah's pace never slackened. He headed straight into the wall and disappeared. A moment later he was back, another big grin on his face.

"You're going to like this. Come on," he beckoned.

Tentatively, she approached and parted the vines against the wall. A ragged opening revealed itself. Stepping over the remains of the wall base, Raasah entered a small dark alcove like a shallow cave. Terjah laid his hand on a protruding rock high on the inner wall and lifted it easily. A narrow door swung in slowly.

"Terjah, what is this place?" Raasah asked with awe.

"This isn't the place – just the means of getting there. Step inside, my lady."

Terjah entered first and lit one of two lamps on a makeshift ledge just inside the door. Raasah stepped in cautiously. With a slight pull on the door, it clanked securely behind them. Raasah felt a wash of claustrophobia and scratched at the darkness to lay hold of her brother's arm.

As her eyes adjusted to the dim light, her urge to hyperventilate gradually subsided. She spied a set of steep rough stairs directly ahead of them, a mixture of stone and wood, descending into a murky black. The air was damp, cool, and old. Gingerly, Raasah started her descent behind her brother, her hand now grasping his shoulder in case she should fall.

"That's quite the grip you have there," Terjah commented as he pretended to shrug her off. "Leave some circulation in there, if you don't mind."

"If I am going to be swallowed up in these murky depths," she replied firmly, "I vow I am not going alone!"

"Where's your faith?" Terjah laughed.

Almost immediately, she heard the sound of moving water. Obediently, she finished her descent to stand spell-bound beside her brother on a smooth rock bank of a wondrous underground river that sparkled by their small flickering lights. Raasah could smell damp mineral rock, similar to that she had smelt at a hotspring not so long ago, but of a cool nature, not unpleasant.

Lifting her lamp high, she surveyed her surroundings. They were standing on a wide shelf of shiny rock, only about 4 cubits in length, which disappeared under more massive rock on either side of them. Even more rock towered above them, eerie shadows wavering stealthily amid the deep crannies and shimmers of light that reflected off the mounds of smooth wall. In its vast emptiness, Raasah felt like an insignificant micro-creature before the creation of time.

"Good, it's still here," Terjah announced.

Before she could question her brother, his voice echoed ever-so softly back at him – twice – and Raasah closed her mouth on her unspoken words so as not to interrupt the intimate cave-to-brother interlude. Instead, she just followed his gaze to make out, tied to the bank, a crudely carved boat that could seat three to four people if they didn't mind being cozy.

The river flowed ever so slowly against them. Terjah dipped the paddle carefully through the water as he maneuvered around jagged cone-shaped deposits that were dotted like little islands on the shallow river bottom. Sitting low in the boat, Raasah clung white-fisted to the sides, gazing apprehensively up at the obscure multi-leveled ceiling above them.

Their little boat bumped up lightly against one 'island' that was barely gracing the surface. Raasah overestimated her corrective weight shift and feared them both plunging into some inexplicable quandary that had no foundation of possibility. She sucked in a cry trying unsuccessfully to look brave and then, to her horror, struck their sole source of light with a foot, distinguishing the flame and any valor left in her.

"Raasah..." – the voice was calm in the blackness. Terjah had laid a comforting hand on her knee. Somehow he had quickly settled in next to her as the darkness folded in upon them.

"Just watch. It is most beautiful," he continued gently.

Stunned, Raasah gazed into the blackness and, incredibly, she started differentiating little glows of yellowish-green light until they intensified into distinct eerie flickering dots that cast a subtle mystical haze. The majestic subterranean beauty took her breath away. Not only that, she was awed with the extensiveness of the limestone channels, rooms, and caverns that nature had so patiently carved and illuminated in sparkling mica-studded stalactites and stalagmites that had formed throughout the centuries just, or so it seemed, to enchant this wonder-struck child at this time, on this day.

"All the riches of the kingdom could not outdo this stunning beauty," Raasah muttered. She looked once more upon her smug brother but, this time, she only felt appreciation. "It is remarkable."

They glided on. Speechless, Raasah marveled as small bats screeched loquaciously and dipped from the sparkling dancing lights; a pair of playful ferrets tumbled with each other along a narrow sloping ledge; and a sleek striped snake slithered smoothly along the river's surface.

It was like a bit of heaven – underground heaven– where the imprint of the creators hand had not been smudged by man's incisive need to modify and reinvent perfection. The absence of engineered palaces and pompous adornment was overwhelmingly refreshing. At that moment, Raasah would have forsaken all that she owned to have been able to hold on to this blissful sensation of wellness and rightness. The world as she had known it had been washed gently from her skin and she felt light and free. Sadly, though, all too quickly, daylight reached its fingers into their private sanction and snubbed out the intriguing mica-glow.

A spooky vapor began to form and linger in the dimness just over the shimmering water before it enveloped the two passengers. Through the wisps of mist, Raasah could just make out shadowy evidence of the inevitable human encroachment along the water's edge. At first it was just decorative earthen jars, unremarkable pottery, and large deposits of ashes that peered out from the mist along the ledges and outcrops. Further along were dark recesses that seemed to glitter of ornamental objects carefully organized in small pods. In the growing light, through swirls of white, Raasah eventually glimpsed decorator combs, necklaces, and other items of personal nature laid out as if they were on display. Though they were ordinary household items, in the numinous atmosphere, they seemed to have taken on a sacred aura.

Terjah knelt tall in the boat in front of her just as the brilliance of the light soaked through the haze illuminating him like a glorious shining being. Then, as suddenly as it began, it was over. They broke through the mystical fog and out into the blinding sunlight. With one smooth stroke and the crunch of stones, the belly of their little craft grounded to a halt.

Squinting in the light, Raasah scrambled out of the boat to follow her brother onto a clearly defined path through dense trees and brush. As he helped her over a moss-encrusted log, Raasah finally verbalized her gratitude. "That was indeed a special place, but, where are we going now?"

"There is still more," he said. This time his smug smile gave her a tinge of annoyance but she bit her lip. As she continued her walk, she tried desperately to hold onto the awe of the sparkly caves and her feelings of contentment she had found there. But as the path twisted sharply, the spell broke with the sound of a desperate shout, a scream, and a struggle in the water. Terjah disappeared in a rustle of leaves.

Heart pounding, Raasah cautiously immerged from the shadows of the trees next to her brother. Raasah stood stunned at the unexpected scene before her. Amid cascading waterfalls and blue-green water, scantily dressed children splashed and tumbled with screams of delight. A lanky boy in a droopy loin cloth swung recklessly from a thick shaggy vine. With a wild war whoop, all legs and arms, he landed with a stupendous splash to the laughter of dark bobbing heads around him.

Terjah draped an arm around his sister. She looked questioningly up and followed his gaze. On the sandy shore directly ahead of them lay a budding young woman in a light water-soaked shift leisurely leaning back on an elbow. As this woman mopped her wet hair with a towel, she turned. Though her hair hung in tight ringlets and her whole appearance was of dishevel, Raasah knew without a doubt who it was.

"Tara!"

Chapter 19

The Lehiha Family

"Sounds like you got the deluxe cave tour," Tara said sleepily as she lay back on her arms to enjoy the warmth of the sun. Her bare slender fingers raked through the fine sand lining the massive rock basin that formed the swimming hole.

"It really was something to see, but so is this." Raasah marveled at the frolicking youth crawling like limber ants over the misty wet crags to then propel down the smooth worn rocks like wiggling spiders caught in a sudden gush of water from a rainstorm.

"I came upon this place shortly after I arrived in Ammonihah," Tara smiled, her eyes fluttered closed. "Of course, the children of Lehiha laid claim to it far before my time, but they generously permitted me into their clan." Tara opened her eyes slowly and nodded her head towards the laughing, sputtering child rising out the water on the shoulders of a long-limbed youth. Unceremoniously, the young man tossed the wiggly screeching boy back into the shimmering water. "The tall one – that's Shem. Most of that brood out there are his siblings."

Most did, indeed, have the same thin frame and heads of jet-black hair in many degrees of curls, some of which fell into ringlets when soaking wet. From her right, Raasah was drawn to a broad shouldered exception to the latter – her own brother who was now wading out to join the Lehiha shenanigans, wearing only a loincloth wrapped tightly into his belt. His thick brown hair was pulled snugly back and he dove smoothly into the blue water. Raasah was not surprised to see Tara's gaze also shifted in his direction. Terjah did make a handsome sight with his muscular browned chest and tight abdomen that flexed slightly as he rose from the water.

"Sometimes, I would come out here in the quiet of the morning," Tara said absently as she slowly closed her eyes once more, "so I could collect my thoughts. That's when I discovered the limestone caves."

"You discovered them!" Raasah said, returning her attention to Tara.

"Well, not exactly," Tara turned sheepishly to face Raasah. "The locals have always known about them but many of the farm folk out here hold to old superstitions. They believe that the caves mark the dark underworld kingdom of Xibalba that harbour the spirits of the deities. They do not venture deep inside. They say they are filled with death and decay, but also – it's confusing – they say the caves have a connection with life and is the gateway to blessings of the gods. Since the Ammonihah priests started turning the native and rural folk away from the temples, these caves have come to serve many of them as 'the' place to commune with the spirits. They come to the mouth of the cave to learn the correct time to plant corn and to burn the milpas[23] and often to offer sacrifices." Raasah could understand the draw for the local people to look for a hallowed place to worship. And she could think of no better substitute for a temple then this mystic mist-enshrouded cave.

Raasah turned to stare out across the pooled water to the trees beyond as her mind envisioned the ceremoniously dressed priests, splendid serpent staffs in hand, shamelessly waving the humble rural people away with bejeweled arms. Her mind raced with all the negative implications that she had heard lately of the priests and the priesthood that she had been taught to esteem all her life. Her trepidation and self-doubt regarding her own commitment to the priesthood order washed mercilessly over her. Forcing these thoughts from her head, she probed, "You have explored deeper into the cave?"

"You just saw an introduction to the extensive cave system that runs under this land!" Tara's mischievous grin mirrored that of Terjah's annoying one. "It's a world of its own," Tara continued in a haunting whisper. "There is a literal maze down there[24]. One could get lost for days – weeks – if they didn't know what they were doing. The aquifer that supplies water to the city is fed from the many underground rivers and streams that carved out this cave system. There is even one cavern with its own waterfall that spills into this amazing mineral pool. The water there is deliciously warm. We'll have to take you there someday."

Raasah looked around, distracted by a rustle of bushes further up toward the cliffs and the sound of distant giggles. "Where has everyone gone – the boys?" Raasah asked, searching the vacant water.

"Oh, we've got to go too!" Tara said mysteriously, rising abruptly to her feet. "It is quite the experience. First we will have to get you a change of clothes…!"

Sometime later, Raasah stood nervous and self-conscious high above the glittering pool and sandy beach they had previously occupied. She was donned in a bulky shift that had been pulled awkwardly up between her legs and fitted into a belt at her waist. Her venomous protests of dressing in this frumpy ill-fitting gown fell on deaf ears as her hostess light-heartedly insisted it would all be worth it. Still breathing heavily from her climb, feeling outlandish and embarrassed, she turned her attention to her surroundings.

The view was amazing and almost made her forget how unsightly she must look! At her feet, lay the entire valley, the forefront thick with forest and, beyond, the patchwork fields of the farm folk that melted into the distant rugged hills and darkness of the wilderness on the western horizon. To the northwest, over the canopy of the trees, she could just make out the tops of the highest more prominent buildings of Ammonihah in their blues and reds. And from behind her, on this precarious jut of rock, babbling streams escaped beneath the thick undergrowth of the pine forest. In turn, these streams funneled steadily into several narrowing grooves in the rock, increasing momentum as they flowed toward the very cliff Raasah now found herself perched upon – like a timid bird afraid to take her first flight.

The gushing water almost knocked Shem off his feet as he stepped into its path on its way over the cliff. Bracing himself against the pounding water, he squatted before nestling a squirming black-topped child on his lap, a little leg wrapped firmly onto his own. Suddenly, with exaggerated flare, the older boy released his grip on a tall imbedded pole to his side and succumbed to the pull of the rapid water. With his war-like 'Whoop!', Shem and his passenger disappeared over the bubbling edge. After a long moment, to Raasah's great relief, she heard a distant victorious yelp and laughter, signaling their safe arrival in the pool below. She released her breath that she had unknowingly held. Timorously she stretched her neck over the periphery to spy, way below, two bobbles of black in the glittering pool. Satisfied, she stepped back quickly as she felt a wooziness overcoming her.

"Now just wrap the back hem securely in your belt." Tara was explaining, seemingly oblivious to Raasah's consternation. Tara tugged at the cloth at her own waist exposing her long golden legs below her bunched up shift. "It could be quite embarrassing if it should come loose," she smiled. Grabbing hold of the same imbedded pole, Tara lowered herself into the pounding wash of the water.

"And then prepare yourself for the ride of a life-time!" she shouted over the strain of the churning water. Tara released her grasp on the pole and, holding both hands over her head, she walloped her own war-cry and shot out of sight in a rush of water just as her peers had done before her. Not yet recovered from the last quick departure, Raasah gazed anxiously at empty space where flesh-and-blood bodies used to be.

"Tara calls that the 'stretch-out-and-glide'."

Raasah shot a dazed look at her brother now standing beside her, his loin cloth sagging bizarrely against his muscular thighs and his hair splattered recklessly about his head.

"It does look daunting the first time. You just have to remember to keep your body low to the water," Terjah further explained. "Come. Let me help you."

Unbelievably, Raasah stared at his offered hand. She was shocked that he would even suggest that she partake in this insane activity.

"Come." Terjah said again like he had said so many times this day already. *Each time, though, things had turned out fine – nah, more than fine – things had turned out wonderful – so far....* At a loss for words, she tentatively took his hand and allowed herself to be lowered in the cool pummeling water, reassured by Terjah's strong grip. The water was welcoming after their long sweaty climb.

"Now, just remember to lean back into the water. You might want to cross your hands on your chest the first time," Terjah explained patiently. "It's not as steep as you think and the water has worn down the rocks into a marvelous smooth slide."

Raasah tightened her hold on Terjah's hand at the mention of the 'slide'. She looked imploringly at her brother but, just then, Terjah whipped his hand from hers. Raasah's heart skipped a beat as she felt herself sucked forward with the foaming water. Gathering all her courage, she forced a peek at the distant horizon just in time to feel herself lift slightly with the increased decline and then propel like an arrow down the curved rolling crest of the rock – trees, sky and rock just a blur beside her.

After what seemed like a frozen moment in time, when she thought it could not get anymore death-defying or foreign, she suddenly flew through the air, like a disoriented bird that had finally found its wings. Before she could wrap her mind around how she was going to make her appearance to her Maker, gratefully, alive and well, she landed in a cushion of consolingly tame water but the force of the landing had her sliding feet-first across the smooth rock bottom. Coughing, sputtering, heart racing, Raasah was hauled up by the strong grasp of the gangly Shem to find herself back in the pool of water where they had started. With shiny eyes, Shem beamed down at her. Remarkably, Raasah realized her terror had evolved into an elation that energized and thrilled her very being.

"Not bad for a first time," Shem said with a toothy grin. Water was steadily dripping off his nose and his glistening black hair stood straight up above his forehead where he had rubbed it off his face. Raasah rubbed her own wet strands away from her eyes and realized, as ridiculous she thought Shem looked, she was sure she looked just as unsightly. She beamed wordlessly back at him. Then, hearing a victorious hoot and a splash behind her, she whirled in time to glimpse Terjah shooting across the same shallow bottom toward her. She easily stepped aside. In a rupture of water, Terjah theatrically sprang to the surface. Defensively, Raasah raised her hands against the wild spray.

"You look like a beached dolphin, dear sister!" he said as he shook.

Recalling a brief sighting of the graceful sleek creatures on their seaside trip, she decided to take the latter as a compliment. "But you, brother, look like a drowned rat!"

The rest of the morning was carefree and rejuvenating. Raasah braved a couple more slides, played water games with the children, and waffled down a simple feast supplied by the Lehiha family. She learned the Lehiha's had a maize farm not far from the swimming hole. Shem's two slightly younger sisters, Suzanne and Morsiline, born on the same day, were identical in looks and energy and seemed constantly engaged in 'annoying pranks' (as further eluci-dated by Shem and confirmed by Tara). A couple of Shem's cousins had joined them this day too.

Impressed, Raasah realized she knew, or knew of, Shem's older brothers – Aaron, the scholar of the Botholuem Brotherhood, and the oldest brother, Baruck, the Morcum champion of Ammonihah who also was enlisted as a full-time soldier for the local regiment when not training or playing the national game. These latter broth-ers were not enjoying the pleasures of the waterfalls but were back home helping their father finish the seeding for the season.

"This season is very important to the farming community for, as you know," Tara explained, "the yield from the last couple of crops have been miserable – almost a waste of energy to harvest."

"Yea," Shem confirmed, "with the lack of rain and then the descend of the black-winged menace...."

"In the last two years, those small beetles have devastated the crops in our valley," Tara said. "It is amazing how such a tiny pest can have such an overwhelming effect on a people."

"Our neighbours and friends have fasted and prayed for many days for a good season this year," Shem continued. "Priest Normad has blessed our fields and supplicated the Great God on our behalf. With our first meager crop out, my family now plants the seeds that will bless us with an abundant next harvest."

"Tonight we will celebrate what will be a year of plenty," David said proudly. He was the youngest Lehiha brother, who had to be just a little older than her own Little Brother. "Mother says that our crops' harvest will make our lives easier – that I will be able to get my very own kilt like brother Baruck."

One of his sisters ruffled his shaggy head. "Master David," she mocked, "for lack of a waist, with what shall you hold up a proper kilt?"

"Don't worry, brother," said sister number two, "in order to save your honour, I shall have to appoint myself 'Holder of the Kilt'!"

"Yea, little brother," said the first sister, "we will never abandon you."

David stuck out a flat pink tongue at his sisters and hobbled next to his big brother so as to solidify his masculine allegiance and rights that, no doubt, a girl could not understand.

"Master David," the girls chimed together as they gave a little bow, "forever at your service…," they added cheerily before they danced off into the trees.

Raasah looked affectionately on the young boy who was now chatting happily with his fellow male companions. She eyed his light frame and then gazed at where his left leg should have been. Little David had been badly injured a couple of years earlier, she had been told, at the time of the first draught, and now sported a short stump where one of his legs used to be. Raasah couldn't help but be drawn to this bubbly youngster, not in pity, but in admiration, for this tragedy never seemed to slow him down and he was so at ease with his disability that Raasah had not even notice the missing limb until he crawled out of the water on his own after her first slide.

In the water, David was a natural and, on land, he was either 'rump' walking or swinging from his unique crutch, actively participating in all the childish antics. Furthermore, it appeared, he was often enlisted in the implementation of sister-related exploits: his innocent facade an effective ruse to entice victims. The infrequent times David was in need of a helping hand, it was usually Shem that stepped in, and Raasah marveled how Shem, despite his thin frame, had the remarkable stamina to repeatedly climb with his brother high upon his shoulders to the top of the falls.

As the damaging rays of the afternoon sun began to bear down, the children retreated to the protective shade of the canopy trees. Donned once more in her own street clothes, Raasah joined the girls under the tall breadnut tree. High in the thick branches weighed down with the pale orange orbs, David was shimming stealthily along its weedy limbs almost hidden by the density of the bunched leaves.

"He'll be all right up there?" Raasah questioned one of the twins.

"Oh, he's always been at home in the trees and is now best suited for the task," the impish girl replied. "He doesn't have that extra leg that can so easily get hooked up in all the thin branches and twigs. He slithers like a snake up there!" Just then she dodged a rather large breadnut that grazed her shoulder. Momentarily stunned by the off-handed remark, Raasah nearly got clobbered herself by a large clump, saved only by the merry warning from the tree-slitherer above.

With a contagious laugh, David began to vigorously shake loose the breadnuts to the waiting girls below. Forming a circle and holding out their cloth aprons, the girls gleefully swooped up the falling fruit, shrieking excitedly as they were bombarded by stray fruit. In gleeful abandonment, Raasah joined the fun.

First to return for the next round of plunging fruit, Raasah squinted up into the branches for the young boy.

"Here, catch!" she heard called before she had located the body above. He was shaking the branch directly overhead. Cringing at the prospect of being killed by raining fruit, Raasah jumped back with her borrowed apron held out as far as her arms could stretch. The other girls were quick to join her. With eyes squeezed shut, as if the lack of sight would protect her somehow, fruit plopped into her apron while leaves and twigs caught in her hair. David's distant melodic laugh filled the air.

The boys, suddenly appearing, taunted the mischievous David to rain upon the girls once more. Raasah, peeled of any elite narcissism, immersed herself in the pure joy of the moment and felt the unconstrained awed child awake within her. Her other life of worry and fear seemed far removed from this here-now reality.

It was late-afternoon when the light-hearted band finally began their trek down the well-defined trail toward the Lehiha farm. The huge trees on either side of them rose up to form a vast, cavernous canopy. Frazzled hanging vines brushed by them as they balanced their bundles of breadnuts amongst them. David was the only exception, leading the way like a bounding mascot, making so much happy noise, no harm would dare intrude upon them. Terjah, Shem, and the cousins were each stooped over with their generous load of fruit secured to their backs. The twins had hoisted an entire branch of breadnuts between them on their shoulders – one that David had managed to snap off backing down from his perch. And Raasah and Tara, trailing just behind, were let off lightly with only a whickered bin between them.

The boys called friendly insults to each other, as boys do, and knocked each other playfully as they trudged heavily forward. The twins, on the other hand, were deep in hushed discussion when, with a mischievous grin between them, they quickened tip-toed footsteps to within a stone's throw of their cousins. Suddenly, both sisters release a deep squeal so convincing of a charging taper that Cousin Lehi twirled frantically, almost knocking himself over with his shifting load tilting to the ground!

Expressing obvious not-so-sincere apologies, the girls lowered their own load and, with unsuppressed amusement, helped to gather the escaped fruit to return to their cousin's pack. Wordlessly, Lehi heavily re-shouldered his load. Initially throwing a stern look at the sisters, he then trotted up to join his brother who was now chortling hysterically at his brother's mishap.

"Quiet, Joshua," Lehi warned, "or I will remind everyone how Suzanne suckered you...."

"Oh, now, now, now," Joshua said soothingly. "There's no need to bring that up," he said more solemnly. They walked briskly on, bantering inaudibly, making great strides to distance themselves from the girls.

"Morsiline, I guess that wasn't very cousin-y of us," Suzanne said, almost sounding sincere until she broke out into a titter! Raasah took note of a small reddened scratch across the back of one hand. Finally Raasah had a distinguishing mark to tell the two girls apart.

Morsiline couldn't resist imitating the satisfying grunt of a foraging peca as the two girls hoisted up the branch of beechnuts back onto their shoulders. Consequently, a startled Lehi strained a look behind him and, though it was only for a blink of a moment, the look of distain was unmistakable.

"We must make amends, sister," Suzanne said in mocked kindness. Snickering, they padded quickly to catch up with their cousins who had trotted around the massive trunk of a mahogany tree beyond their view.

"What was Lehi talking about?" Raasah whispered curiously. "What did Suzanne do?"

"What hasn't she done?" Tara started, poorly containing a wide grin. "Suzanne is the worst of the practical jokers – or best, depending on how you look at it! Knowing Joshua's weakness for cantaloupe, one day Suzanne left one conspicuously on the table where Joshua was preparing to eat his lunch. The cantaloupe had already been cut in half but was still fitted together like a whole. Joshua couldn't resist. He lifted the top portion off but, trapped inside was a large tarantula eager to make its escape." Tara lowered her voice, leaning in toward Raasah. "Well, Joshua hates spiders with a passion! He screamed like a stuck pig! The tarantula, probably just as frightened as he, raised its front hairy legs and lunged at him! No one had ever seen anyone run so fast!" Tara laughed. "Lehi has never let Joshua live it down…. And I don't think Joshua has ever quite forgiven Suzanne – AND the poor spider was probably traumatized for life!"

As Raasah and Tara laughed gaily and chatted like life-long friends. Suddenly they were startled by a high-pitched yelp! This was followed by cursing, retreating feet, and then more feet in a fast pursuit. The twins were at it again! As Raasah and Tara rushed over the wide root of another mahogany tree, they spotted the tipped over bough of breadnuts abandoned on the ground amid other rolling fruit. Off to the side of the path, an annoyed adolescent anaconda, the width of a man's forearm, was laboriously slithering its silvery body under the thick ferns along the path. Smiling, Raasah could imagine what had just happened. A distant male voice could be heard yelling: "Suzanne, you better run if you value your life!" Other deep laughs and good-natured hoots cut through the awaken forest.

Raasah shaded her watering eyes as she immerged from the sun-blocking canopy of trees. She saw a corral of scraggly grey goats with swollen bellies congregating under a wide open shelter, looking like they were going to burst with their new little bundles. Nearing the shelters, at the far side of the grassy yard, Raasah spied the cousins being chastised by a rather short plumb woman, hair tied back under an airy scarf. The twins, in turn, were being lectured by a slim no-nonsense woman with sternly knotted hair that looked vaguely familiar. With their wayward expressions wiped solemnly from their culpable faces, the two girls, now outfitted with a large basket between them, retraced their route into the forest with shuffling steps.

Turning, their mother exclaimed in exasperation, "And don't come back without each and everyone of those breadnuts!" That was when she took notice of Tara and Raasah.

"Oh, Tara," she said pleasantly, still sporting an irritated glare that she shot like a dagger at the retreating twins. Her face softening, she added, "And this must be Raasah. Very nice to meet you at last."

Raasah gazed around her, suddenly recognizing where she was. Raasah swept the horizon for confirmation: the maize field had been plowed under and was now newly cultivated but she recognized the path heading toward a distant steady incline behind the row of buildings and she could just make out the ridge of Guarumo trees on the narrow plateau where the cairn of stones had been laboriously arranged – Little Brother's special place. Returning her gaze once more to the woman in front of her, Raasah knew when she had seen her before.

"Raasah?" Tara said, puzzled, and then, as if to try to clear up some confusion, she said, "This is Anna, wife of Lehiha…."

"And mother to those two delinquent daughters," Anna said, the annoying tone returning momentarily as she stared in the direction that the twins had taken. "My stars, my manners!" the woman said with a sigh. "It is so good of you to join us, Raasah, and finally be formally introduced. We have a mutual friend."

"Little Brother…." Raasah murmured, ill at ease as she remembered how she had held back suspiciously among the tall dry stalks the day she first saw Anna, trying lamely to hide herself. "I came here with Little Brother the day I first met him," Raasah explained to Tara quietly.

"You are even prettier close up," Anna said kindly. "You have such a warm, loving face. I can see why 'Little Brother' is so taken with you."

"It was generous of you to provide the bread and fruit for our… hike," Raasah stammered.

"Oh, it's always nice to share our bounty with friends," Anna said warmly. "Now, the others are under the lean-to by the main house. Hurry out of the hot sun before it's your undoing."

The humble farm of Lehiha was an assembly of shelters with neat curtains hung over the doorways of the windowless buildings. A stone pit with a small fire held a steaming pot on a spit and several roasting fowl on a separate spit– the delicious smell of spicy stew and sizzling meat arousing the appetite of all that approached. Once depositing their fruit, the girls entered the wash hut to freshen up.

Glistening with sweat, the men were trudging in from the fields. Unlike his son, Shem, Lehiha was a solidly built man with a thick neck and close-clinging, curly black hair. His arms and hands were massive and Raasah learned he was a part-time soldier in addition to being a full-time farmer. Like most farmers of the area, he wore a simple colourless kilt but, after cleaning up at the large outdoor tub by the house, he had slipped on a tailored orange robe provided lovingly by his attending wife.

Tara introduced Raasah.

"Raasah of Botholuem. It is an honour to meet you, my dear," Lehiha said most sincerely. "Please consider our humble home an extension of yours." He bowed politely.

Before excusing himself to attend the fire with Shem and David, Raasah couldn't help notice the thick jagged scar on his dark whiskered face and more rugged scars on his chest and arm that disappeared into his airy robe. No doubt these were the reminders of the horrors of war. She pulled her eyes away from the old wounds and, looking into his sparkling deep-set eyes, she cordially returned a friendly greeting.

Baruck, once cleaned up, donned his own robe. He was joined by Terjah who guided him over to the girls.

"Baruck, this is my little sister. Raasah, I'd like you to meet Baruck, Morcum champion of Ammonihah and soon to be champion of the entire civilized world!"

"Raasah, your brother is a delirious optimist, but we shall put up with him, shan't we?" Baruck said bowing slightly. "It is a great pleasure to meet another off-spring of the wise visionary Botholuem. And such an enchanting creature she is," Baruck had turned to address Terjah. "I can see why you have been so protective of her."

Raasah blushed. Baruck oozed with charm like his father. She could see the physical resemblance in father and son in his high cheek bones and dark eyes. Baruck also had his father's bulk, void of the scars. It appeared, as the lean Lehiha boys mature, they fill out quite nicely. She was glad she had had time to clean up and tidy her hair before the men had returned from the fields.

"Not bad looking, is he?" Tara teased in a hushed voice as Raasah watched him cross the court and settle beside little David.

"I wasn't...," Raasah said, blushing redder. Looking up, Tara was smiling broadly. "Oh, you're awful," Raasah guffawed as she gently elbowed her in the ribs.

Two other weary men returned from the fields. They both had broad chests and large arms baked deep brown by the sun. Once cleaned up, Anna offered each a simple but colourful tunic that slipped easily over their heads. The introductions were short and formal. They instinctively bowed, in recognition of her rank in society, despite her less-than regal appearance. Now, in the company of her new friends, this time-honoured custom seemed so unnatural and unnecessary, but, she, in turn, habitually responded with her off-handed nod followed by an immediate sensation of embarrassment.

Raasah learned Aaron had to leave earlier for a meeting in Ammonihah but more guests were arriving. Lehiha slapped a burly man on the back as he entered the compound with a heaping basket of dark berries. "Jacob!" Lehiha scoffed. "You're a sight for sore eyes!"

"Good to see you too, Old Man," he mused. Looking to the sky, he added, "A good day to celebrate our successful year of seeding."

"That early onset of rain really had him worried," a female voice said behind him. "He was just about ready to give up on getting the lower fields seeded." A pleasant-looking woman in a decorative huipile patted his belly as she retrieved the basket from him. Anna greeted her with kiss.

"I never did," Jacob replied in a playful pout. "I knew Kukulkan would look after us."

Ignoring the retort, both woman continued as if the men were not there. "Let our husbands talk weather and crops," Anna said, "while we catch up on more interesting topics – like how's that granddaughter of yours, Sister?" Raasah now saw the resemblance in the eyes and nose.

"Oh, growing sweeter with each season," the woman answered with pride, as they wandered toward a make-shift table in the shade where the other women were preparing to set out the food.

Jacob, prompted by a tug on his tunic, stooped and gathered David in his arms, swinging him high in the air. "By the stars above, I declare, you grow a full measure every time I see you," he teased the boy. Lowering him carefully, he stepped back and grinned at Lehiha. "Old Man, whatever you are feeding this young lad, I could have sure used on my last dreary crops!"

"David, get this thieving beast out from under my feet," Anna yelled from across the court as she whipped a towel in the direction of a loaf-sized animal scampering off under the table, "or I will roast it up for dinner!"

David swung his crutch around and bounded toward it. "Nephi-boy," he said soothingly as he folded down on his one knee, "it's alright. Mother didn't mean it...."

"I meant every word of it," his mother replied sternly, but David had disappeared under the tablecloth, only the base of his crutch tell-taling where he had been.

Ignoring the mother-son retaliatory, Lehiha merrily slapped his brother-in-law on the back before steering him in the direction of the gathering men. "Let us old men go join the other ancients," Lehiha said good-heartedly.

As several other families arrived, each dutifully pitched in, laying out the rich variety of fare for the consumption of all. The noise grew proportionately to the glee of the growing number children romping and playing around the fire and enthusiastic greetings of the adults. Meanwhile, the twins, looking rather flushed, had stumbled back onto the compound in the thick of the activity with their heaping bin of beechnuts. They quickly cleaned up and joined the festive atmosphere.

With all the generous contributions from family and friends, the humble meal evolved into a fabulous feast. After giving thanks to the Creator for all their good fortune and promise of a bounteous harvest, all enthusiastically gathered around the food, chatting happily and filling their plates with all the assortment of tastes. So began the celebration in honour of the 'Successful Seeding of the Milpas'.

---

23 *milpas: fields*

24 *subterranean cave system: Hundreds of millions of years ago, the beginning stages of limestone formation occurred, creating the extensive cave system that became the backbone of Belize and surrounding areas. Over a million years of wind, rain, and faulting created underground rivers that etched through the soft bedrock and outcrops. Deep in the ground, the region is riddled with channels, rooms, and caverns often adorned with stunning stalactites and stalagmites and studded with sparkling mica. These caves reveal intriguing stories about the ancient inhabitants through the pottery, personal items, and human remains that have been found within.*

Chapter 20

The Secret Visits

Feeling deliciously full and content, Raasah leisurely helped clear away the left-overs as the men finished off their second and third helpings. As she wrapped up the last of the rice, she couldn't help but overhear bits of conversations. She settled on a bench to the side of the men as several of the wives gravitated toward their husbands.

"You know the scribe's son?"

Raasah recognized this speaker as an old farmer that worked a small piece of land near the orphanage. He was a round elfin-looking man with a hooked nose and a head as bare as a dried out desert. Deep brown eyes were set below a wrinkle-layered forehead and above more sagging wrinkles that reminded her of an old alligator. He continued to speak.

"His wrist is now straight and flexible. Best of all, his hands can bear the brunt of the hammer hitting the chisel." As he swung an invisible hammer sharply in the air, he scanned his growing audience. "He can once again deftly form the glyphs that tell the stories of the past. He feels not a single shot of pain, nothing that gives any hint he'd spent the better part of a year as a useless cripple without any hope of supporting a wife and family."

"Joseph, this could be the work of a demon or it could all be just a great sham," said a tall peevish-looking man. He had narrow hooded eyes, downturned mouth, and a mustache over his upper lip that resembled the whiskers of a rat.

"Galif, dear boy, for what purpose would this be a sham?" Joseph reasoned. "Besides, I was there and saw the bloody pulp of a hand when they pulled him out. As for this being of a demon, no good comes from the devil. The lad -- his heart sings with joy."

"Alma cured him as sure as there is night and day," Jacob confirmed, "but takes no credit for himself. He claims his power comes from our great God."

"If this stranger Alma possesses such great power," Galif persisted, "and comes doing the work of Kukulkan, then why does he hide and meet in secret? Why do the priests of Ammonihah seek his silence?"

"Oh, do not get me started on the corruption infiltrating our glorious priesthood!" Joseph declared. "There are few honest priests left in our great city and those that exist fear their own safety from those whom they should deem their brothers."

"Shush, my father!" A plump but handsome woman whispered harshly, looking sternly past him into the fields. "Ears are in the wind if they are not in the trees. They will hear and it will not go well." This was the woman reproving Lehi and Joshua as they arrived from the falls.

"Daughter, we are among friends here," the man retorted. "If we cannot speak our minds in this circle, where shall we relieve our fears and debate our cause?"

"Be comforted, woman," Galif said passively. "We talk because we worry and we seek understanding."

He turned to Lehiha and inquired, 'What do you think? Is it

wise to follow the ruler's priests and elders or this new preacher and his following?"

Lehiha smiled broadly, "On the advice of a fine priestess, I have decided not to take a stand."

"You know that is not what she meant," one of the twins chastised him. "In the end, you know we will have to choose."

"Well, Suzanne, we mustn't rush that decision, shall we? I have another crop I need to get in and don't need any trouble."

"In my opinion, Priestess Zillah has become too bold with her own opinions," Baruck commented solemnly. "She will one day turn a tide that will roll over her and drag her under. It would not hurt her to do a little fearing for her own safety."

"It's only the love of the good citizens that keeps her safe," Lehiha agreed.

A rather round sour little man broke his silence in the back. "Oh, the priests are too preoccupied with this Alma and Amulek right now. But I'll bet you my farm that you will see this new preacher in the palace dungeons before the harvest ripens."

"You will do no such thing!" the miniature woman declared beside him. "And may the heavens forbid that any harm come to these good men."

"Good citizens are afraid to trust their neighbours. Too many unexplained deaths," Terjah remarked. "And what of our useless grand Antionah! He has handed the affairs of our city to hoodlums and thieves. And our temple workers are more interested in our tithes than our welfare."

"You can't lump all our priests with the unscrupulous dealings of a few," Tara spoke up firmly, taking many of the men by surprise.

"Tara, Onihah is a great man, and so is Normad, but you know they rare exceptions...." Terjah stumbled.

"Enough of this serious talk," Anna ordered from behind, causing Raasah to jump. "This is our celebration of the crops. So let's get the festivities started. Let's see if you can work as well as you can talk. Joseph and Galif, you can get the platform set up. Lehiha, I need your help over here."

"The boss has spoken," Lehiha said compliantly, standing heavily to his feet.

Laughing, and making a big show of it, other men quickly joined Joseph and Galif to briskly disassemble the large makeshift dining table, reducing it to planks that were set side by side on the ground to form a raised wooden floor in its place. The women good-naturedly gathered children and organized the seating with blankets and cushions.

Off to the side, however, Anna was far from jubilant. She had a hard expression on her face as she expounded to her husband in short phrases, waved her hands. Interest perked, Raasah shamelessly concentrated on their lips to try to make out what was being said however Terjah suddenly appeared. He offered her his arm.

"They will be needing your bench. I'll escort you to a much better vantage place."

The twins had disappeared but were now returning from the house with an old bow and a large hollowed-out gourd they placed in front of their father. Lehiha adeptly slipped the bow in strategically placed grooves in the gourd and, with some final adjustments, he made several practice plunks on the make-shift instrument. David lopped his way over to Shem, handing him an ancient wooden flute as he chatted warmly with his big brother. In the center of the gathering, the cooking pit had been transformed into a heightened fire now heaped with extra fuel. Settling next to her brother and Tara under the expanding shade, Raasah waited expectantly for what was to follow.

Lehiha strummed the taut sinew of the bow. All talk trailed off. As primitive as his instrument was, when Lehiha played its cord, the homemade musical bow was just as resonant and soul-touching as any bow Raasah had ever heard. Baruck cushioned a tall log drum between his knees. He lightly thumped its firm leather surface with the padded sticks to produce a beat complimenting his father's bow. Shem joined in with the eerily haunting sound of the flute as the older women chanted softly to the tune. The simple family rendition was beautiful and soothing.

As the shadows lengthened, the air became filled with the wonderful home-spun sound of the drum, flute, rainstick, and rattle. As the music became livelier, the children could not contain themselves. They bounced and swayed to the beat bringing laughter and amusement of all. It wasn't long before Raasah felt compelled to join the other guests with happy feet stomping, knee-slapping, tongue-clucking, and all-round fun-enhancing body mediums, joyously elated with the impromptu musical sounds. And, to everyone's delight, Baruck even gave a hilarious performance of rude sounds using his hands and arm pits to play the uniquely adapted tune of the popular melody of the courts.

After one more energetic round of heart-pounding melodies, Lehi and Joshua mounted the plank-laid stage to perform their own version of a stomping stick dance to the hoots and ruckus approval of their peers. The twins then joined in with a graceful twirling dance of their own. Clapping in tune, they weaved around their accompanying cousins who were still tapping and bounding out the beat in perfect unison.

Once the boys then melted into the background, Tara joined Morseline and Susanne in a polished and charming 'Dance of Gratitude' for the newly sown crops with their own heart-felt comportment. The soft shuffling of their wrist-bound rattles[25], though of simple cocoon husks, were soothing and rhythmical and Raasah felt herself totally absorbed into the improvisation.

As the fire rose high and the shadows more deep, the animated tunes became more subdued and visiting became more prevalent. Terjah and Tara had begun to hold hands at some point and Raasah pretended not to notice. She glanced around at the cheerful warm people around her as she chatted uninhibitedly with the twins. Raasah was pleasantly taken aback at how at home she felt at this humble abode.

After a short pause from the sudden end of one more rowdy musical number, Shem quietly and skillfully breathed out a meditative tune on his ancient wooden flute that washed the audience with a cover of serenity. The music with its innate power to guide the emotions of the soul had sleepy children curling upon their parents' laps and older children quieting and poking dreamlike at the fire. David, the previous one-legged jumping bean, cuddled against the broad chest of brother Baruck as he, himself, snuggled a snoozing rodent-type pet in his own. The older women paused in their exchange of domestic tales and delightful stories as they poured jugs of wine out for the guests.

While staring at the fire, Raasah was transported, without warning, back to Lamonhah Ridge, her mind on the edge of remembering some tidbit of information.

What is it, Raasah, you need to remember? she berated herself, the present tranquil setting obscured from her vision.

Then the realization came. Just before the arrows flew, she realized that Noala's men were not standing guard when she looked around. And just before she passed out, she had heard someone speak, "Mo...., nah, she smu pr..., smu pr...!" Raasah strained to hold onto the memory, to remember the words. That voice....... Raasah's head was hurting. An exploding cinder startled her.

"But I dreamt she was in eminent danger!" Tara was whispering urgently. Dreams – in an ironic way it was comforting to Raasah to know others feared their dreams as well. She looked off at the activities in an effort not to eavesdrop – but it was becoming a natural thing to do!

"Zillah knows the risks. She is a wise woman," Terjah replied, but he added, "I assure you I will look into it when I get back. Now let's just enjoy the evening."

Terjah pulled Tara close to him, whispering a few more words to her before he slipped away to join the men. One of the twins, returning from the main building, immediately plopped herself back down in his place as Tara rose to retrieve a log to throw on the fire.

Looking for someway to start a conversation, Raasah said, "Your brother does play remarkably well," referring to Shem's newest musical rendition. Raasah had wanted to call the twin by the name of Morsiline, but she was still not confident enough yet to be sure without seeing the hand for the scratch.

"Even though he is my brother, I must agree he plays mighty nice!" she whispered back as if it was a desperate secret.

"What a wonderful day this has been!" Raasah declared. "You have a wonderful family!"

"Yea, Morsiline, you do have a special family," Tara agreed as she joined into the conversation. "And I am so glad I could be here for the celebration. I had planned to stay longer at the orphanage but the matron had taken most of the older children to watch the folk dancing in the Grand Plaza."

Surprised, Raasah asked, "Tara, you were at the orphanage this morning as well?"

"Yea, I go regularly mid-week. I thought I told you. This is the day I teach the orphans to read and write."

"Then you must see my grandmother each week," Raasah inquired conversationally. "This is also the day she goes there."

"Yea, occasionally I see her as she drops Tamar and children off to help out. Of course, Marian doesn't stay as she usually wants an early start to…." Tara trailed off as confusion crossed Raasah's face. "…she likes to…."

"We sometimes go with Grandmother Marian when she delivers the packages to Barba," Morsiline vivacious added. "We love to find out who he has added to his collection of animals. It has grown so. He had a baby tapir there last time we were up – a snorty, smelly fellow but Big Barba was cuddling it like it was a sweet little rabbit. …Oh, and Caggy has become massive. Just his paws are …." Morsiline also trailed off as she gazed past Raasah where Tara was frantically gesturing with her hands the cutting of her own throat. Raasah continued her stunned look at Morsiline before she turned and shared it with Tara.

"She doesn't know," Morsiline concluded, looking pained toward Tara as if Raasah was deaf. Then she turned awkwardly back to Raasah. "I'm sorry." Suzanne was approaching from beyond the fire. Relief in her voice, Morsiline said quickly, "My duplicate beckons. I've got to go," and she rushed off before either girl could reply.

Raasah's stare bore down at Tara for a long moment before she spoke. "Who is this Barba that Grandmother is seeing?" she asked slowly.

"Barba…" Tara, searching for words to explain, paused. "His full name is Barbabos. He is just a poor misunderstood soul exiled from the city. Simple that he is, though, he has a wonderful gift – he looks after injured animals – and they trust him."

Terjah sauntered over to the girls, unaware of the sticky situation that Tara was trying to dissolve.

"Did you know of the man Grandmother was secretly seeing, Brother?" Raasah asked abruptly. Terjah looked quickly from Raasah to Tara and slowly back to Raasah.

"Barbabos?" Terjah enunciated the name distinctly. He looked again at Tara who, apprehensively, just stared back. "Raasah, you know Grandmother's charitable heart. Barbabos, well, he's slow; he's different. Society frowns on people like him and it would not look good on the Botholuem family if it became common knowledge that Grandmother visited with him regularly on Onthar Hill."

Raasah stammered, rising to her feet. "…on Onthar Hill? The bravest men of Ammonihah avoid going up Onthar Hill and you… and you knew about this? You let her go up there to see a wretched outcast who lives with the animals, collects dangerous animals…?"

"Raasah, you don't understand," Terjah reached out for her but she backed away. "Grandmother doesn't go alone," he continued. "When I am not able to go with her, Elihu is always there. And Barbabos would never let harm come to our Grandmother.

Barbabos knows the animals.... They say he can talk with the animals."

"Nah, this is just plain crazy talk," Raasah said shaking her head. "A Wildman that speaks to the animals, living in the treacherous Onthar jungle, furtively meeting with Grandmother – our grandmother who is sneaking around in the name of charity! Is this what you're trying to tell me?" Anger had grown in her voice to the point that her last words were almost spit out.

Tara looked helplessly on as Terjah tried to explain further. Raasah's outburst had drawn the attention of others, but she was beyond caring. From the direction of the twins, Anna was striding toward them. Raasah backed another step away from her brother.

"Raasah, Grandmother was trying to protect you," Terjah said. "What you don't know, you don't have to be accountable for or keep secret. It has been very difficult for her all these many years keeping this quiet."

"Many years?" Raasah exclaimed. "My grandmother has been lying to me for many years?"

"Raasah, dear," Anna said consolingly. "What is the matter?" She reached tentatively out to her but Raasah swung about, staring defiantly.

"Do you know too?" Raasah shouted at Anna. "Did you know my grandmother sneaks off to Onthar Hill to visit a degenerate man among beasts?

"Barbabos is the kindest, gentlest..." Anna said patiently, but was cut short.

"Terjah, I want to go home," Raasah said through clutched teeth.

"Raasah!" Terjah snapped. "Be civil!"

Raasah straightened defensively, bracing herself for more opposition. "Am I the only one ignorant to what is going on in my own family?" Raasah looked from concerned face to perplexed face to others just plain staring. "Take me home, Brother," she said, straining to keep her voice steady.

"Raasah, you mustn't tell anyone about Barbabos," Tara implored.

"What's to tell? I don't know anything," Raasah said fiercely.

Her chest was tight; her head was swimming. A tear fought its way out as she tried to regain control of her emotions. "I want to go home," she repeated to Terjah. The feeling of betrayal rose like a lump in her throat and all her feelings of despondency and confusion from the morning – which she had believed had been dissolved away – once more engulfed her.

"Please," she looked piteously at her brother, "I want to go home."

---

25   *cocoon rattles: gave a soft soothing sound. It is believed many natural items were utilized by the innovative common people to use as instruments, including cocoon rattles, the pounding and banging of sticks, drums of wood or hollow logs, and pots and other household items that would be played at gatherings such as celebrations or burials as well as get-togethers socially and politically.*

Chapter 21

Barbabos

Raasah woke from a restless night to an anxious shouting of a feminine voice.

"Terjah! Terjah!"

Raasah bounded from her bed, seizing a blanket to wrap around her cool shoulders. Distant steps padded on cold stone in answer to the urgent call. Raasah shuddered as she gingerly stepped toward the doorway; a cool breeze sweeping back her long loose hair.

As the morning sun strained to pierce the clouds, she gazed down on the shadowy courtyard from the second-story terrace. A lone pacing figure below was quickly joined by Tamar wiping her hands on an apron. Despite the dim light, Raasah could still make out the frantic-looking visitor – it was Tara.

"Tamar, has Terjah left yet?" Tara asked breathlessly. "Has he left with the caravan?"

Hannah and Marian also rushed over; Marian was wrestling on her night wrap.

"What is it?" Marian asked.

"I had a dream," Tara uttered anxiously.

"Terjah left early," Tamar said. "He was concerned about the weather."

"Uncle Gormonaluk…. He…."

Marian put an arm around Tara's stiff shoulders.

"But there is more!" she blundered. Marian hushed her as she led her into one of Botholuem's old meeting rooms. Hannah and Tamar both turned and gazed up at Raasah and, after a few words between them, Hannah ascended the stairs to join her young mistress.

Raasah lounged solemnly as Hannah did her usual fussing to get her ready for the day. Raasah had not spoken a word. As if in a trance, she kept reliving the details of her trip from the Lehiha farm yesterday with her brother, realizing now that he had started to tell her that he had to go away. She also recalled, with growing shame, the concerned effort he had extended to clarify why she had not been made aware of the man who lived with animals. 'Raasah, you were too young at the time to understand Grandmother's need for secrecy. She made a promise to his mother, before she died, to look out for him.' Terjah's voice had been sympathetic. 'When he was exiled, she refused to relinquish her responsibility but she did not want to ruin the family's reputation or standing in the community. Mother would have been appalled to have heard Grandmother was still keeping contact with him. …she would have stopped it.'

Raasah had wanted to ask questions – such as, why was Barbabos exiled, how did Grandmother know him, and if she was the only one in their household (besides her mother, obviously) that did not know about the visits – but she had been angry and willfully obstinate, not wanting Terjah to know she was even listening to him.

'I wanted to share with you a happy part of my life today before I had to go to…,' Terjah then paused. 'This is not a conspiracy against you…,' he had blurted unexpectedly. 'You were inconsiderate and rude to my friends. Sometimes you can be so egotistical!'

Raasah had shot her brother a loathsome look and then abruptly turned away again.

'…so much like Mother,' he mumbled under his breath. 'Or are you just being childish?' he said louder, like it was an epitome. Then, still stripped of his usual flare for diplomacy, he said, 'It was your immaturity that prevented Grandmother from telling you about Barbabos. I can see that that has not changed!'

As soon as Terjah said these words, she could see he regretted them but, though he tried to take them back, Raasah refused to acknowledge him; her face hot with hurt and anger. Finally, in frustration, Terjah resigned himself to a silent trip home. His last words were more like a plea. 'Please, you mustn't mention Barbabos to Mother.'

Once arriving home, Raasah stormed to her room without a word to anyone.

Raasah's face was hot once more, but now with regret. Possibly, just possibly, she may have acted childishly, possibly even hostile, upon hearing about her Grandmother's secret. She also felt some embarrassment thinking back at the ungrateful way she had left the Lehiha home. But, still, a part of her remained angry for being treated like a silly girl who could not be trusted with, what seemed to be, an important on-going deception.

Raasah sat back as Hannah, humming absently, scrutinized the beaded obsidian jewelry box for just the right accessory to Raasah's outfit. Raasah stared past her as she reflected on her mother. She had never thought of her mother as egotistical but, within this extended silence, as she dwelt on the description, the more she believed it did indeed fit. She could picture her mother, in all her pomp and finery, standing aloof amid admiring crowds. Yea, her mother – constantly surrounding herself with arrogant and influential people, too busy to acknowledge insignificant common labourers… who, Raasah was suddenly clearly aware, were the essential backbone of this wonderful country.

Am I guilty of behaving egotistically – like my mother? Raasah pondered the question. Before the ill-fated journey with her father, those struggling or in need were all but invisible to her. She had idolized her mother and worked hard to be more like her. She had 'practiced' walking aloof and had strove to do so in the 'right' circles. Yea, she 'had' – she HAD yearned her mother's approval and wanted to make her proud BEFORE this trip with her father.

It was different now. She was different. Raasah now saw the suffering of the less fortunate and her heart went out to them. The few times she had found herself in her mother's presence, she had found herself scrutinizing her as if Sablon was a perplexing stranger. Their life's paths had separated. *Would the old Raasah have opposed her Grandmother's dedicated visits of an outcast simpleton? Or, would she, in fact, have sold out her Grandmother for fear of her own station in life being compromised?*

With new conviction, Raasah numbly scanned her comfortable surroundings, all the luxuries she possessed, and the loyal servant who cared after her so efficiently. In one mind sweep, she revisited the simple joy that she had felt warm her heart as she gave to the less fortunate and partook in the homemade pleasures of the humble farm folk.

"I'm not that same person anymore," she muttered determinedly.

Hannah, startled by the first utterance from her charge, dropped a jade hair comb with a soft clatter onto the polished granite floor.

Raasah sat tall as Hannah recovered. Returning her thoughts to Tara's harried morning inquiry, she asked Hannah sheepishly, "Where was Terjah headed?"

"He'd had ta delive' a message ta Milan for Go'monaluk. He'd be gone fo' 'bout tree days."

"Tara seemed pretty upset," Raasah said.

"Yea." Hannah, usually full of comments, did not elaborate at all as she clasped a large ornate necklace around Raasah neck. The room was eerily quiet. Raasah brushed her fingers over the large ruby dominating the gold pendant.

'Sometimes you can be so egotistical ....'

"Nah, Hannah," she said self-consciously. "This necklace is over-stating. Please choose something more... reserved."

ڡ

Raasah found her grandmother in her room seated at a stone-slab table where she lingered over a yellowish parchment, the rugged edges showing its years of repeated handling. Raasah recognized this scroll as a copy of scriptures that Marian often searched out, especially when feeling down.

"Good morning, Granddaughter," Marian said without looking up.

"Is everything all right?" Raasah asked quietly.

Grandmother rolled up the parchment and set it aside. She set her hand next to her on the cushioned bench. "Come sit."

"Tara seemed concerned about something. Is Terjah in some

danger?" Why Raasah had come to this conclusion, she wasn't sure. She lowered herself slowly beside her grandmother.

"Terjah has made this trip several times now for Gormonaluk. All preparations had been made to ensure it will be a safe trip." Marian replied softly, reaching for Raasah's hand. "Kukulkan will protect him."

"Terjah told me about your conversation last night," she added, her kind eyes searching out Raasah's.

"Barbabos," Raasah said. She was surprised that she had remembered his name.

"You were very upset."

"I was surprised," Raasah replied, choosing her words carefully. "I was hurt that you felt you had to keep these visits secret from me."

"We all have secrets, some bad, some good...."

With a flash of coveted memory, Raasah thought of her secret friendship with Abul.

"...and some necessary," Grandmother finished. Her wise eyes scanned Raasah's face.

The repentant young woman looked down at her grandmother's wrinkled hands, hands that had done so much good, now lovingly embracing hers.

"I behaved terribly last night," Raasah said, eyes downcast.

Marian brushed a hand gently along her granddaughter's chin until her gentle brown eyes drew Raasah's whose tears threatened to spill over. "I'm sure it is nothing that cannot be repaired."

Marian withdrew her hands. Raasah followed her grandmother's gaze to a stray ray of sunshine that had broken through the clouds, resting just outside the door, dispelling the dismal heaviness.

"Barbabos' mother and I had been friends most of our adult life," Marian began. "She was never a well woman. Barbabos was so very welcomed in their family when he arrived but, as the years went by, it became more apparent that he was …special. Believing there was no future for him and fearing shame on the family, Barbabos' father arranged care for him in the country away from prying eyes. As more time went by, he grew big and strong but, in every other way, he remained a precious child. My friend – his mother – never stopped loving him. As her health further declined, I accompanied her on her visits to him. I grew to love him as well.

"Before she died, I promised to look after Barbabos and keep him safe. Barba didn't take the news of her death well. He snuck into the city scared and confused one night seeking solace and understanding but his family only gave him rejection. I tried to intervene but his father called him a… a freakish mistake and ordered the guards to take him away. Barbabos fought them off and, sadly, one got hurt. Then he ran off. It took your father two weeks to find him high up on Onthar Hill." Marian paused. "Fact is: that night Barbabos saved Botholuem's life."

Botholuem – her father. Raasah realized that she had not heard her Grandmother speak of him since the day of his burial. She studied her grandmother's pale drawn face. Her heart went out to her but words escaped her. After another long pause, Marian continued.

"Yea, Onthar could be a dangerous place – if you don't know the animals," Marian said, as if she knew what Raasah's next comment would be. "And it is best that our fellow Ammonihahites continue to think of Onthar as dangerous because this is where Barbabos makes his home and there are so many narrow-minded citizens that would want to do him harm just because he is different. But

Onthar is less dangerous to Barbabos then walking down... down Lahotite Lane would be to your father."

Lahotite Lane.... calm during the day – the lair of undesirables at night where, much too often, the frequent fights resulted in serious injuries and death. She looked questioningly at her grandmother still gazing at the brightening sun-filled doorway.

"Barbabos has a miraculous gift," Marian continued to explain. "He can communicate with the animals and has befriended some of the most feared beasts of the forests. That day, when Botholuem wandered toward the top of Onthar Hill, a puma suddenly sprang out from a bough above him. Your father...," Marian clasped her hands together, "also agile and fast, managed to sidestep it just in time but not before its sharp claws ripped across his shoulder."

"The scars on father's shoulder," Raasah recalled aloud. "I remember, as a child, asking him about them and he laughed them off. 'A reminder of gifts of God', was all he said!"

"Yea, those are the scars that were left. The puma must have been over four cubits long, so the story goes," her grandmother said. 'Knocked to the ground, your father thought his demise was at hand, when a jaguar just as suddenly leapt out between him and the puma. The young jaguar couldn't have been half the size of the puma, but it bravely confronted it, ever pacing to ensure it remained between the other cat and your father. That's when Barbabos arrived. He yelled and snarled at the puma, waving a large stick. To your father's surprise, the puma backed off and disappeared into the forest. We will always be grateful to Barbabos and Caggy for their bravery that day."

"Caggy. Yea, Caggy," Raasah repeated. "I hear he has become quite big."

Marian smiled and the lines softened on her face. "All this happened when you were very young. To associate with an exile can be considered treason against the city's leaders. We could not bring that condemnation on you. Years went by and ....when does one know when it is the right time to pass on certain knowledge? The secret had been suppressed for so long and your life, well, I did not see how this knowledge could have done you any favours." Marian turned and faced her granddaughter. "But I do now. I would like you to meet Barbabos... and Caggy... if you would like to."

"Yea, I would like to," Raasah said softly.

Grandmother and granddaughter stepped out into the warming sun. The threatening clouds had shifted to the east. Little Brother sat expectantly on the steps.

"Eavesdropping, were you, young man?" Marian smiled warmly at the boy. "Go find out from Tamar what she has for us to take to Barba." Little Brother sprang to his feet and skipped down the remaining steps toward the large clay oven emitting smoky whiffs from its long chimney.

"Even Little Brother knows about Barbabos?" Raasah asked in disbelief.

"That Little Brother of yours is very light on his feet. He followed me up there one day. Barba took to him right away. It was not planned but Little Brother has become a great help to me when I go for my visits. After all, I am not as young as I used to be." Grandmother Marian looked fondly down at her granddaughter.

"And there is little chance he would let slip your secret," Raasah mused as she turned to watch the boy expressively gesture with his arms and hands and then point back in their direction. Tamar nodded knowingly at him, having learned to decipher much of this primitive communication, and retreated into the food storage room with the boy trailing behind.

Little Brother ran ahead and led them down a gully through a thick stand of trees. Raasah was not to see Barbabos' cavern home. Little Brother had scrambled up in advance and returned to indicate they were to go in another direction.

"Barbabos often leaves a sign by the cave to let us know where he is." Marian explained.

She squeezed Raasah's hand before following after the beckoning boy. Enoch and Vashti slipped by her to catch up with Little Brother, startling a couple of bobwhites in a blur of brown wings. Raasah studied her wise grandmother, as she trudged ahead with some effort over the rocky sloped path. Raasah hadn't noticed the slight hunch in Marian's shoulders before. Tamar had relieved her of her bundle earlier and now carried it under her arm, her own balanced expertly on her tightly bunned head. Elihu brought up the rear, armed with bow and dagger ever ready for trouble, though Raasah was told there was nothing to worry about.

They had all laughed at her look of astonishment and disquiet when she had been assured, matter-of-factly, that Barbabos' animals would protect them. Tamar called out to Raasah and directed her gaze off into the trees. Raasah thought she spied the gleam of two eyes stare back at her and then they were gone.

"That is Fab, a very attentive ocelot Barbabos rescued some time ago. He has been following us since we arrived on Onthar Hill," Tamar explained.

"Look up there," Elihu pointed into the broad cool canopy. A golden ball of fur with a white hairless face swung slowly back and forth. Clucking loudly, the small monkey swung its lithe body onto a bare branch, its beady eyes ever focused down on the group. "That's Noddy. A very curious creature. There is Nappy, his mate…"

Raasah was now aware of another lush fiery-red primate further up into the tree; a miniature version of her clinging to her breast. All three sets of shiny eyes bore down on the travelers below. "I don't know if the little one has a name yet," Tamar said.

"Come on, doddlers," Marian called. "I think I hear them just up ahead."

Raasah hurried forward to join her grandmother, not so sure how comfortable she was by the revealed presence of their animal escorts.

As the brightness of the clearing ahead beckoned them forward, Raasah did indeed hear several familiar voices and the babbling of water. Stepping out into the sunshine, a small cluster of individuals were revealed leaning over a small fire on the stone banks of a stream. As this group parted to greet the newcomers, Raasah could see that they were braising small gray fish on crude wooden skewers.

The twins waved them a warm welcome with soiled greasy hands; little David jumped up with mouth bulging, swinging his crutch in greeting. Then, rising slowly from a couched position, a bulky black-bearded man stood up on legs like the trunks of towering ash casting a murky shadow over the youngsters. He wore a navy cotton tunic and kilt, large enough to house the twins and their brother 3 times over. With three heavy strides, he was looming above them, a toothy yellow smile in the middle of a chubby tan face. Under a head of bushy unruly hair and thick eyebrows that didn't seem to stop or start anywhere, shone out intense pewter eyes set wide over a large bulb nose.

"Aun' Marian!" the big man boomed, startling Raasah in spite of herself. "T'ese here girls, T'ey say you migh' surprise me taday."

"Not much of a surprise then, is it?" Marian laughed. Barbabos swept her up in his arms. Raasah gasped. Her grandmother, looking very small and doll-like, hung toe-dangling off the ground in the man's barrel arms.

"Gets some getting used to seeing those bone-crushing arms whip people into the air," Elihu mused slowly. Raasah nodded absently in agreement, transfixed on the scene.

Placing Marian gently on the ground, Barbabos titled his chin down to consider who had accompanied her. "Raasah, daughta of Bot'oluem! You have come ta visit me."

"You know me?" Raasah said incredulously.

"I see you sometimes when I come by the house. You were so sad afta Bot'oluem die'. She wouldn' let me stay bu' I saw you. You fat'er, he was my goo' f'iend. I wan'ed to say goo'-bye."

Raasah recalled a disturbance when her father's parade of mourning had paused – a towering hooded man gripping an old gray robe about him – the crowd had fearfully parted for him as he neared the burial litter. Her mother, though, flanked on each side by burly guards, had barred his path. Even these muscle-bound guards were dwarfed by the confrontation of this large being but they stood steadfast as duty required, hand on the hilt of their swords.

Raasah had thought at the time he was a drunken trouble maker, possibly an unemployed mercenary. On this 'the day the city mourned', in her foggy recollection, she had thought she had heard a gurgled sob from the faceless intruder that she had dismissed then but, now, watching the watering eyes of this massive man -- it was as clear as if it had happened yesterday -- that Barbabos had been that uninvited guest that had been turned heartlessly away. In a wide sweep, he wiped his wet eyes with the large slab of his palms. His quivering nostrils sucked in with deep gurgling sounds.

Shuffling half a step closer, he laid the other huge hand carefully on her shoulder, totally enfolding it. He was almost six cubits tall casting a dark shadow over her like her own private canopy.

"You mus' be careful, Raasah, daughta of Bot'oluem," he said, eyes narrowing. Head back, she studied his kind round face, his mouth almost undetectable under his thick facial hair. "T'ose boys are bad. Barba not like it when t'a' Jas'orum boy touch you."

Raasah's eyes widened. "You were there in the alley! You threw that rock at Zoric. You helped me get away from him." Raasah touched his hand, still lying heavily on her shoulder. "Thank you, Barbabos."

"Have you been sneaking into the city again, Barba?"

Barbabos looked sheepishly at Marian.

"Oni'ah been worried 'bout Raasah...."

"I will be talking to Onihah," Marian said sternly.

"Oni'ah, he di'n' tell me ta go. I di' it fo' Bot'oluem ...and Raasah is ma fam'ly too."

"All right, Barba. We'll talk more later."

Raasah looked warmly at her grandmother. It was so typical of her to make this rejected son feel part of their family.

Tamar and Elihu had joined the children at the fire. "Well, you'll be needing some bread and other goodies to go with that fish," Tamar announced, drawing the children around her. Laughing and talking excitedly, they opened the packages she offered them, sharing and passing the food around. A tiny timid monkey darted about their feet.

Enoch slipped away from the friendly frenzy harboring a small sweet roll. He saddled up to Barbabos and pulled at his tunic.

"Where's Caggy today?" he asked, before tearing off a morsel.

"He ne'er is fa' away," Barbabos said looking left than right. "I shew 'im away. He be scaring the fis' with all his sp'as'ing and smas'ing in the water."

"Oh, Caggy is just sulking upstream," one of the twins called as she picked away at the black seeds of a papaya.

"Suzanne, I think he was doing more than sulking," the other twin said, pointing up stream. A large magnificent orange and black jaguar padded regally across the water; a fat rainbow bass laying limp from its curled jaws.

"Show-off!" Suzanne shouted at the cat as she adjusted her own tiny skewered fish on the makeshift grill.

Caggy sauntered around the occupied fire. The cat must have been four cubits from snout to haunches, with a thick, switching tail that added another three cubits to its overall length. About ten paces away, the spotted feline paused.

Raasah could smell the sweet scent of its fur and hear the soft steady breathing. The cat and girl, eyes transfixed on each other (Raasah's frightfully wide), stared a long moment. Caggy's ears flutter back and forth, as if it was deciding whether she was friend or foe and the hairs on the back of Raasah's neck rose. Raasah recalled hunter-talk to never show fear and she tried to slacken her tense shoulders, though her heart beat furiously. Caggy's ears stilled and flattened out against its wedge-shaped skull.

After a long moment, the cat lowered its eyes and, somehow, Raasah knew she must have passed some kind of Caggy test. Stepping forward, it dropped its glistening catch at its master's large leather-bound feet, voicing a low whining, mewing sound. Barbabos reached a large gnarled hand down and rubbed the big cat gruffly behind those expressive ears as it sat heavily down on its hunches.

"Oh, Caggy," Barbabos said, "you needn't have b'ought me a gif'. You know I nev'a 'eally mad a' you."

Raasah stood rooted like a shaky leaf on a branch. Caggy, now purring deep like a rhythmatic corn grinder, looked intently at her again with its big yellow eyes. These eyes never left her as it rubbed its smooth head against Barbabos' shins.

"Now make Raasah feel welcome, Caggy. S'e's fam'ly, fam'ly like Bot'oluem." Caggy continued to stare as its mouth seemed to turn into a smile. Raasah noted an arrangement of spots on its forehead that formed the outline of a butterfly. Black ring-like spots arranged in rosettes decorated its softly rising and falling sides. It – he – was a beautiful animal, almost cuddly, *if it wasn't for the fact that he could tear me limb from limb if he got the whim.*

The big cat rose and took two heavy steps up to Raasah; his head came just under her chest. She could feel his hot breath on her belly and her insides cringed. Shakily, she willed her stiff fingers to lay atop of the robust tawny head and timorously stroked the soft warm fur. In response, the purr that erupted deep within vibrated through her finger tips and tingled through her very bones. Timidly she withdrew her trembling hand.

"Look at t'a'! 'e sure is taken by you!" Barbabos grinned.

The smile was so corny, so wholesome – Raasah began to thaw.

Raasah re-evaluated the cat. He had a noble look about him; his long whiskers tickled her arm. Astonishingly, she looked now with admiration at the giant pet.

"He is a most beautiful animal," she said.

"Oh, ya should 'ave seen 'im when 'e was jus' a wee baby," Barbabos replied proudly. "'e was the sweetest t'ing. 'is mother was capture' by royal 'unters an' 'e was lef' all alone."

"Oh, that's terrible! But you found him and you looked after him."

"I was alone an' 'e was alone bu' t'en, toget'er, we were nev'a lonely ag'in. We look af'er each ot'er."

Caggy brushed his wet black nose against Raasah's hand forgotten in mid-air. Raasah felt warmth now in his hypnotic gaze. Gingerly she rubbed the fur between his ears and felt the erupting purr beneath her hand once again.

"Come, ol' boy," Barbabos said, giving the jaguar a quick solid shoulder scratch. "Bring you' catch to da fire and we'd cook it a bi'."

Caggy swung his head toward his big friend and fluidly turned from Raasah. First nosing the limp silvery fish, he swatted it playfully and then grabbed it once more in its teeth. Quickly he padded over to join Barbabos at the fire where everyone was gathering. Raasah regarded the graceful sway of the animal's body – the rosette of spots seemed to roll across its muscular back, its long ringed tail swinging wide behind. She thought how much more lovely the jaguar's skin was on the jaguar than off.

"Raasah," Vashti said, taking her hand. "You have to meet Pabla, too. He's the cutest!" Raasah pulled her eyes away from the spectacular cat. A reddish squirrel monkey had wound his toy-like body around Vashti's arm and its tiny hand was stroking Vashti's neck in gentle sweeps as if it were searching for a hidden jewel. As Vashti tickled the monkey under its soft chin, a high pitched clicky purr erupted from its throat. Looking cautiously at Raasah, its round eyes appeared to shine out of its little white face. Vashti made the introduction: "Pabla, this is Raasah."

"Hi, there, Pabla," Raasah said, reaching to touch its clinging hand. In response, though, it clucked shrilly and slipped down Vashti's back, bounding across the clearing over to David, perching high upon his head. Without removing him or even looking towards him, David slipped a small piece of negrito fruit into the miniature tan fingers. Pabla munched in quick darting bites, repeatedly shooting Raasah guarded looks.

"It was orphaned," Vashti explained. "Barba needs to find a home for it. Isn't he cute? Come," Vashti added, and taking Raasah's hand, they approached the circle of friends and pets.

ɞ

The boys were returning noisily from washing up on the banks. Caggy was splayed out on his back as the twins encouraged Raasah to give the cat a vigorous tummy rub. She could feel the rumble in his chest as he arched his back to gain the most pleasure from all the fussing. She couldn't believe how natural it now felt to play with this huge cat when she had just met this terrifying creature only hours before. On the other side of the fire, Barbabos was saying something to Vashti to which she gave a glorious whoop!

"For me? Really?" she cried. "Mei-wa-ni, Pei-wa-ni, can I really? Pabla can come home with me?"

"Yea, dear child, if you promise to look after it," Tamar replied. Elihu slipped his arm around his wife's shoulders, smiling.

"Oh, yea. I will, I will. I promise I will love him and care for him as long as the stars shine in the sky."

"And you keep it out of trouble and don't cause Grandmother Marian any concern."

"Oh, I will train him in all the social graces and he will be obedient and…."

"Now, don't get carried away," Elihu smiled. "Just keep him out of trouble."

"Oh, yea, Pei-wa-ni, I will."

Tamar laughed. "Then, Barbabos, I guess Pabla has a new home."

"Thank you, thank you!" Vashti cried.

She gave her mother and then her father a big hug before returning to the little monkey now resting on Barbabos' arm.

"Now, Vas'ti," Barbabos said in a deep but kind voice, "jus' 'emembe' what I tol' you – and don' feed 'im too many of dose b'ue be'wie'. 'e can become quite piggish an' t'en he don' feel so goo'."

"Oh, I won't. I'll remember," Vashti said as the monkey wrapped its tail around her arm and nimbly transferred itself over to her shoulder. Slipping her finger into the gasping hairy hand, she said motherly, "You are going to be so loved, my Pabla. I love you so much already."

"Mei-wa-na Marian," Enoch said, already settled beside his mother. "Tell us a story."

"Yea, yea, Marian," said David, "one with mystery and magic."

"Mystery and magic?" she said slowly. "I'll have to give it some thought."

"Oh, please. Aun' Marian. A sto'y, a sto'y," repeated Barbabos. His large juvenile face beamed with excitement. *If it wasn't for the menacing size, the wild hair, and deep growly voice, Barbabos could have passed for a sweet inquisitive child!* He settled submissively on the ground at Marian's feet. Caggy flopped over onto his big paws to join him, collapsing heavily against Barbabos' side. The jaguar rooted under his arm until Barbabos' hand began to stroke him affectionately along his side. It was such a unique imitation of a domestic scene!

"Marian, let us tell the story," one of the twins said. "Morsiline, you know the one."

"The other story with the Great-grandfather and -grandmother spirits?" Morsiline asked with a big grin.

"Tell us, tell us," Vashti said, big eyes pleading as Pabla drew his fingers contently through her hair.

Marian nodded pleasantly. With David nestled on one side of her and Little Brother on the other, she contently settled in to enjoy the story with the others.

Suzanne began. "Our Great-grandfather and our Great-grandmother are most wise spirits but, as with all of us, they too had to learn from their mistakes. When Kukulkan first asked them about making humans to praise him, they counseled him to make this new creation of humans out of mud and earth. They caused the animals to be humbled so the humans could have dominance over them. But the mud and earth people did not look very good. They kept crumbing and softening and looked lopsided and twisted."

"And they only spoke nonsense," Morsiline added quickly.

"Jibber jabber! Jabber, jigger!" Suzanne mimicked in a silly voice.

"And they cannot multiply."

"That means they can't have babies," Suzanne whispered to the children – nervous giggling erupted amongst them.

"So," Morsiline said, with an annoyed look at her sister, "Kukulkan let them dissolve away and he inquired again of Great-grandfather and Great-grandmother. 'Determine if we should carve people from wood,' commanded Kukulkan.

"Great-grandfather and Great-grandmother Spirits went off to consider this and then they came back and gave their answer, 'It is good to make the humans with wood. They will speak your name. They will walk about and multiply.' 'So it shall be,' replied Kukulkan.

"As the words were spoken, it was done," Suzanne continued. "The new humans were made with bodies and faces carved from wood." She began to walk stiffly around with straight arms and legs.

"But they had no blood," Morsiline said.

"They had no sweat," Suzanne said, lifting her arms to air out her armpits.

Morsiline plugged her nose. The children giggled again.

"They have nothing in their minds," Suzanne said, tapping on her temple.

Morsiline let her face go blank, her mouth dropped open comically. The children snickered.

"They have no respect for Kukulkan," Suzanne said sadly. "They just walked about but they accomplish nothing."

Morsiline boosted Vashti to her feet, Pabla bounding across her parents and onto the top of Enoch's head, while Vashti mimicked the stiff walk of the twins with a similar puckered face.

Suzanne continued again, "'This is not what I had in mind,' said

Kukulkan. And so it was decided to destroy these wooden people. Kukulkan caused a great rain."

Morsiline held her hands to the sky with a horrified upturned face. Vashti slipped next to her mother, Pabla returning to its perch on her shoulder.

"It rained all day and rained all night," Suzanne said. "There was a terrible flood and the earth was blackened. The creatures of the forest came into the homes of the wooden people."

Morsiline held her hands out like she was warding off some evil.

"The animals growled, 'You have chased us from our homes so now we will take yours.' And their pigs and turkeys cried out, 'You have abused us so now we shall eat you!'"

The children cuddled closer to their maternal grown-ups.

"Even their pots and grinding stones spoke," Suzanne said in a deep haunting voice. "'We will burn you and pound on you just as you have done to us!' they said. The wooden people scattered into the forest. They ran and ran. It became dark and they ran some more. They could not see. They ran into trees, and rocks, and fell down cliffs."

Morsiline wildly feigned a fall, flaying her arms to ward off invisible objects.

"When the morning light came back," Morsiline said, "the wooden people had changed. Their bodies had become soft and their faces were crushed."

The girls gingerly touched their bodies and faces.

"They were different," Suzanne forced a whisper. "They were now fuzzy. They were covered in thick fur."

"They had been turned into… MONKEYS!" Morsiline screeched as she started dancing around in monkey-type leaps, arms flaying high over her head. Little Brother joined her suddenly, his imitation much more convincing. Barbabos looked on with open mouth and wild eyes. Vashti stroked a nervous chattering Pabla pulling abruptly at her collar.

"And this is why monkeys look like humans," Suzanne concluded, looking intently at each child (and Barbabos) and whispering hoarsely: "They are what was left of what came before -- an experiment in human design."[26]

There was a large pause.

"Is that true??" quietly asked the inquisitive girl at Tamar's side. Vashti hugged her twitching monkey to her.

Little Brother and the twins laughed and leapt away, shrieking like a band of howler monkeys. Pabla whipped itself onto Vashti's back and, with its tail around her neck, it chattered nervously.

"My little Vashti," Tamar said soothingly, pulling her to her. "It's just a story. The monkeys and forest creatures are all wonderful designs planned by a perfect creator."

"Yea, yea," Barbabos echoed tentatively. "Jus' a sto'y." He definitely was trying to convince himself more than to confirm Tamar's statement. Pabla scampered over him and pulled at his cloak.

"Jus' a sto'y," he repeated again as he reached over to calm the monkey, his eyes darting from face to face.

"Just a story," Raasah repeated, hoping to relieve his doubts while trying hard not to laugh. "Who would like some cake?"

---

26 *Story of the pre-humans: This adaption was inspired by an account of the creation in the Popol Vuh translations.*

Chapter 22

Esrom

A grave Botholuem Brotherhood met that next morning. Aaron and Lehiha had just arrived, releasing the clasps of their wet cloaks, shaking them just outside the door before entering. The threatening rain had finally come in a flurry. The deep rumble of thunder permeated the room before the heavy door was once more latched closed.

Raasah hesitantly approached the two men. "Lehiha, sir, I wish to apologize for my inexcusable behavior the other day at your home. I had no right...."

"No need to apologize," Lehiha interrupted gently. "We all have days that upset us. I hope you have come to some satisfactory resolution."

"Oh, yea, sir. Everything has worked out very well, thank you." She looked at this man of little means that she was addressing with such respect. All her lessons on class distinction and protocol were thrown to the wind. *The people of this brotherhood were much classier than most elite that I know!*

"I do not see Marian," Aaron said, peering past her. "How is she?"

"She said she was feeling a little tired. I am to report to her all I hear today."

Actually Marian had looked VERY tired and her hands were

shaky though she had tried to hide this from Raasah. Upon seeing this but saying nothing to her, Raasah did not leave until she knew Tamar would be keeping a close eye on her. Normad had come by the villa under the pretense of sharing their morning meal and he kept Marian company until Raasah was ready to go. Raasah sensed a tender intimacy between them. *Was there another secret Grandmother is keeping from me – one regarding Uncle Normad?* This time Raasah hoped there was.

Knowing Amos was not to be her escort this morning was as if she had been relieved from a tiring weight. He was like a disobedient pet that constantly had to be kept in check, hindering her from where she needed to go. Today she would have more control over her little part of the world, or so she thought.

It was the last day of Founders Week and remnants of revelry had been evident along the streets. There were discarded jugs of strong drink lying about along with many of their intoxicated recipients who were still sleeping it off in the archways and doorways of public establishments that her uncle and Raasah spurnfully avoided.

Just as the rain began to fall again, they slipped into a shop of a textile merchant near the Grand Plaza. Here they exchanged their robes for heavy hooded cloaks and climbed into a covered carriage at the back of the shop that circumvented them around the Grand Plaza to the side entrance of Onihah's archives.

The rain had been falling in sheets when they arrived which formed the perfect cover for their secret meeting. The carriage paused only a moment to allow the two passengers to quickly disembark and rush into the cavernous ziggurat base. Raasah was finding all the sneaking around and disguises exhilarating and unnerving at the same time.

Looking around her now, she saw that several members had already seated themselves at the over-sized table. There was an empty chair where Martha usually sat that her peers reverently skirted around like it was a monument erected on her behalf. With deep regret, Raasah discovered that Chemish was absent as well but she couldn't dwell on the latter when there were important matters at hand that needed discussing.

Excluding herself, she counted ten members – a noble group of dedicated citizens that Raasah no longer looked at in the sense of social standing. Adam, Aaron, Lehiha, Onihah, Tara, Normad, Caleb, Abinihah, Azarish, and Zillah – they were all brave intelligent individuals who strove for the good and noble. She felt insignificant in their presence and hoped she would earn their respect. She realized Reuben was also missing. She felt a fondness for this dignified young man, in kind of a sisterly way. She hoped everything was well with him. Once more, the juggler's fate was being discussed.

"It is now believed that a royal guard delivered the fatal blow to Raasah's juggler," Onihah announced. "He was seen following the juggler into the alley and then left in rather a hurry."

"This would confirm corrupt elite in the royal courts," Adam said, followed by murmurs of agreement all around him.

"This has all the signs of involving Darius and the Nehors." Azariah bounded the table.

"If there was just some way we could bring him down.... But each day he seems to become more powerful instead," said Lehiha uneasily.

"Terjah spoke of his mother," Aaron said. "… I got the impression that it had something to do with Darius. When Terjah returns from Milan, he wishes to present these thoughts to the brotherhood …and he had some concern over his mother's appointment to High Priestess."

"Is she in some kind of danger?" Raasah asked hastily.

"I didn't get that impression. I am sure that, with the extent of the security around her, no harm could come to her. It was most curious, though …Terjah said he believed she knew information about the juggler. He did not want to jump to false conclusions and was going to check into a couple of more things before he discussed it with us. It is most inopportune that he should have to travel at this time but he did not want to raise any suspicions by insisting on delaying."

Raasah looked to Tara at the mention of this trip. She sat motionless, staring down.

"Reuben had some information about Shinar, as well," Aaron continued, "that may tie some very influential people to the Nehor Order. He will hopefully join us shortly."

"Yea, as you all know, Shinar now fills the shoes of our great friend, Botholuem," said Caleb.

"No one can ever fill our friend's shoes, of course," Zillah said kindly. She looked over to Raasah and explained, "Shinar was appointed by Darius. He is now in charge of diplomatic relations and sits as court advisor."

"And dis Shinar," Abinihah said with irritation, "despite de imbecile he is, has become quite a thorn in our side."

"Yea," agreed Azarish, "we had thought Darius appointing this conceited buffoon to the court to be his undoing, but we were so very wrong. Clueless Shinar has become a dangerous puppet, lavishing in the flattery of the scheming councilman and corrupt priests who pull his strings. Shinar could care less what they ask him to do as long as it does not interfere with him lining his pockets and revengefully strutting his status over those who used to shun him."

"He believes he is untouchable," Lehiha said, "as he throws his weight around and inflicts harm at a whim – he is relishing in this feeling of power."

"– but it will not last," Aaron finished. "When the Nehor Order has no more need for him, he will be disposed of like last year's sheaves. Meanwhile, we must figure out how we are to deal with this."

"Antionah is just as clueless," Azarish snapped. "Botholuem had kept him grounded and, at least, going through the motions of being a ruler. Now Antionah has distanced himself from affairs of the people, leaving it wide open to ambitious individuals such as Darius. This is a perfect platform for whatever devious plans Darius and the Order of Nehor have set in motion."

"Reuben is attempting to bridge the gap left by Botholuem," said Normad. "He is young and inexperienced but he has already proved to be a valuable asset. He was to meet with his uncle in his royal chambers this morning, away from outside influences –Darius and his kind. We will be looking forward to his report."

"Of course, our biggest concern," Onihah said as he got everyone's attention, "has been our prophet's health. Shaquah has taken over from Cyrus as our prophet's exclusive healer…"

Raasah remembered Cyrus, a small nervous man by the healing rooms, seeming to be looking for someone. *Could it have been the*

pacing young man that had just left, the one that got clipped by the
fat man on the stairs? Haven't I seen that young man somewhere else
since then?

"...but Shaquah has been behaving particularly peculiar lately,"
Onihah was saying. "Just yesterday evening, I caught up with her
in the hall leading to Esrom's room. She tried to dismiss me, then
insisted I leave. At the sound of footsteps at the far end of the hall,
she earnestly begged me to go -- said Esau must not see me. There
was so much fear in her voice. It was so unexpected. I did as she requested of me but she slipped away later before I could speak to her
privately. I have not seen her since. I am not sure what to make of it."

"There has been suspicion about Esau belonging to the Nehor
Order for some time," Normad said.

"Yea, I have heard talk at different times of Esau meeting in the
night with Darius and others we suspect of this sect," Onihah said.

"I was relieved to hear Cyrus was no longer attending Esrom,"
Zillah said softly. "He seems too eager to please Esau these days."

"But now we worry about Shaquah," Azarish added.

"Tara had some concerns about Shaquah as well," Adam said.
He no longer sported a sling but his hand repeatedly was drawn
to massaging the hurt arm. "Tara, tell the Brotherhood what you
told me."

Tara remained sitting ridged looking down.

"Tara?" Adam prompted. Startled, Tara stared at all the faces
staring back.

"Tara, tell us what you told me about Shaquah," he repeated.

"I, uh, Shaquah...," Tara said slowly. Adam nodded his
encouragement.

"Something is very wrong," she said. "I have never seen her so short with her staff and so angry. At first, I thought it might have had something to do with her daughter being away. She has been gone a long time."

"Orphah?" Aaron asked.

"Yea," Tara said. "Shaquah said Orphah had gone to visit a relative."

"That is so unlike Shaquah to be separated from her daughter for any length of time," Zillah remarked.

"Since her husband died," Tara continued, back to sounding more herself. "Shaquah does dote on her – such a bright child for her nine years. I thought, at first, Shaquah's short temper was due to loneliness for her daughter. But Shaquah is too professional to let her personal life interfere with her obligations."

"How long has Orphah been away?" Abinahah asked thoughtfully.

"It's been well over a month," Tara replied.

"I di'na know she had any relatives living," Abinahah said. "I rememba her telling me how de Lamonites attacked de small village of Lomah. All her family lived dare. Everyone was killed."

"I am quite sure she said a relative," Tara replied. "Or maybe I just assumed it was."

"Shaquah is our means of keeping tabs on Esrom but she has offered no useful information lately. She could also be our ears to Darius but she seems to have distanced herself from the Brotherhood." Azarish said, adding slowly, "Can we really trust her anymore? Our very existence as a brotherhood could be in jeopardy if she has turned on us."

"Not Shaquah!" Normad snapped. "She would never! I stake my life on that!"

"You may be staking all our lives on that," Azarish said flatly.

"Now, Azarish, we know…." Adam said.

"Shaquah's integrity…." continued Zillah.

"There is more," Tara said softly. This was the same phrase she used the morning she rushed into the Botholuem villa. All eyes turned back on her. "The vial that was taken from Esrom's room, the one I was to analyze – it was…." Tara hesitated. "…it was knocked over. Shaquah came to see me yesterday morning at my uncle's. She rarely has visited me in my home -- I was caught unawares. She snapped at me when I asked about Esrom and then she noticed the vial on my side table. The look on her face – she knew where it had come from!"

Tara paused to look around the room.

"Her hand shook as she picked up the vial. She picked up the other vials that I was using for testing. I was waiting for her to start interrogating me about my home lab work, to chastise me for using equipment that should never be in my private possession – but, she just stared at the vials for a long moment and then there was a noise outside. She laid the vials down quickly and as she turned she knocked them to the floor. All the contents spilled. She mumbled an apology and left in a hurry. It was as if she was trying to avoid someone," Tara said with concern. "Shaquah looked so frightened."

"She has good reason to be frightened if she is poisoning the prophet!" Azarish thundered.

"No one said he was being poisoned," Onihah said soothingly. "We mustn't jump to conclusions." Despite this caution, the shocked expression on each member's face seemed to shout either concern for the prophet or condemnation for the healer.

"My testing was not conclusive but I did find traces of a

hallucinogen." Then Tara added quickly, "… and there is no evidence that Shaquah was administering it to Esrom. She did seem to recognize it, though. But why would she hide a full vial of mind-altering drugs under his mattress?"

"But you said she became anxious when she saw the vial," Aaron recapped.

"There must be a reason for her behavior," Tara stammered.

"Guilt is her reason!" Abinihah barked. His aggressive gravelly voice and his mere bulk made Raasah cringe. She would not want to be on his list of enemies.

"Now, Abinihah," Zillah said gently. "We must speak with Shaquah. We must…."

"Onihah has tried to speak with her," Azarish said, as if he was examining the situation in great detail. "She prevents us from seeing the prophet. She meets with Esau regularly and, for all we know, Darius as well. Her strange behavior…."

"Not Shaquah," Lehiha said with conviction. "She wouldn't be part of this evil Order."

"Maybe it's about money," Abinihah suggested angrily.

"There has to be another explanation," Normad said sadly but unconvincingly.

"No more theorizing," Azarish stated adamantly. "We have to find a way to protect Esrom before it is too late and we know we cannot depend on Shaquah."

Just then there was a clatter and then blundering at the door. The room became silent as a tomb. Onihah motioned for everyone to stay seated as he rose casually and walked steadily toward the door. "I'll be right with you," he called in his most authoritive voice.

"Onihah, it's me, Reuben," a muffled voice called back.

"Reuben?" Onihah quickened his pace to the heavy door in a flap of robes. Chairs shifted around the table as he lifted the heavy iron latch and, with creaking groaning hinges, Onihah swung the door open just enough to let in an anxious gesturing man. He spoke in raspy whispers to the old priest. All eyes were resting on the young man and then on Onihah who turned back to the group with a distraught look on his face. A long moment passed.

In a voice that broke with emotion, Onihah announced, "Prophet Esrom is dead."

It was already too late!

The meeting with Botholuem's Brotherhood had come to a weighty close as the members came to grips with Prophet Esrom's death. There were voices of anger but mostly sadness and shock. Before they took their leave, Onihah cautioned them not to take matters in their own hands. Zillah floated graciously toward Raasah and Normad as they retrieved their borrowed cloaks.

"There is always so much worry and contention among the people once a prophet dies but there will be so much more so without him formally announcing his successor. This no doubt was part of the plan."

"Just the situation those devilish Nehors would induce," Normad clarified dismally. "Chaos and confusion – the instruments of the devil."

Tara broke away from the questioning members and hustled over to the three by the door. "I must locate Shaquah," she said

urgently. "There will be much to do to prepare Esrom's body and….
I must confront her regarding the vial."

"You mustn't do this alone. I should come…." Zillah offered.

"Nah," Tara said decisively. "It would be expected that I assist
with Esrom and it gives me the perfect opportunity to work and
talk closely with Shaquah. Onihah will arrive shortly. If others arrive right now, it would be suspect. I will see if Shaquah will meet
with the Brotherhood after the burial. There will be too much to
do tonight. I had best go now," Tara flung her cape around her
shoulders and was gone.

The rest of the Brotherhood were slowly dispersing singly and
in pairs through the thick door of the massive library.

"Please excuse me for a moment, Uncle," Raasah said as she
spied Caleb donning a cape. She hurried over to him.

"Caleb, sir…."

Caleb turned toward her voice. "Raasah! Aw, I know you must
be wondering about my inquiries regarding your Abul."

"Yea, were you able to find him?" Raasah couldn't contain her
excitement but it was crushed as she explored the look on Caleb's
face.

"I believe indeed that he had been detained at the quarry but
he overpowered a guard about five days ago and escaped. I learned
this only after much inquiring – some workers finally came forward
who remembered a rather large Lamonite man who Zenith and
his friends were especially cruel to. It was the demeaning name
that Zeniff gave Abul that helped me learn about him. Earlier in
the day… the day Zenith was to be arrested, he made a visit with
two other thugs, I understand, to torment the boy once more. The
workers remembered the special… attention that Zeniff gave him.

They said Abul heard Zeniff talking about a caravan of merchants and something he said made him very angry. He struck out so unexpectantly, the guards had no time to react. Abul said he had to get somewhere before it was too late. He seems to be quite a powerful young man, your Abul."

"So he IS alive!" Raasah smiled. This fact was the happiest news she had heard in a long, long time. She felt a new hope rise in her chest.

"I am sorry I couldn't bring him back to you. But I hope it is some comfort that I took disciplinary measures against the guards that were excessively harsh with him."

"Yea, Caleb, sir. I so appreciate your diligence," Raasah said sincerely.

"I was going to speak of this but the meeting was cut short."

"I understand," Raasah said. "Thank you, again."

Caleb reached for a hand that she had cupped in front of her. "Don't worry. I am sure your Lamonite friend got safely away."

Caleb smiled warmly down at Raasah. She knew he had read her well. She knew he knew the closeness that had grown between Abul and herself and that he accepted and respected her feelings. She looked into his kind eyes, and, as she nodded to him, he knew she knew. Nothing needed to be said.

Chapter 23

The Ring

As Raasah emerged with Normad into the drizzling rain, they heard mournful cries and excited talk coming from the Grand Plaza. A multiple of royal scribes had appeared, with official tubed scrolls tucked under their arms, and were fanning out with their monumental news.

A growing crowd was milling about in the plaza below where an announcement had been posted on a pillar by the Palenia palace. As the relentless rain continued to shower down on them, the hunched crowd listened intently as an individual by the official poster read out its official decree:

"On this month of Juniper Rising, Our glorious Creator has chosen to take our great Prophet Esrom home...."

...and no doubt it will continue along these flowery lines. The citizens will not read about his decaying health, or his inflicted sickness, or how he lay deliriously on his bed, or the suspicion of the cause of death. But they will be anxious about who will replace him, who will become the Deity's spokesman and spiritual leader of their city. But, in reality, the citizens of Ammonihah had not had a spiritual leader for some time now.

A loud assembly of revelators entered the plaza and the proclamation was drowned out. The drunken multitude surely did not know about the prophet's death... *or they did not care.* Though

Normad was close by her side, she felt very alone in hostile territory. How she wished her brother was here.

Normad and Raasah mirrored concern as they looked toward Porahah Palace where the temporary suite of Esrom had been vigilantly occupied these last few months – *or was it more of a detainment during his slow death? Shaquah could answer many of the questions but will she?* Raasah had much to discuss with her grandmother. With their hooded disguises in place once again, the young girl and her great-uncle hugged the walls of the buildings toward the textile shop, careful to avoid the small streams cascading off the step platforms of the ziggurat.

Once entering the rear of the textile shop, the owner motioned to them to stay quiet. At the front of the shop, Raasah could hear the uneducated voice of a youngish man with a stutter. Curious, she peered around a rack of clothes. It took a moment of close scrutiny for Raasah to realize it was Festus, Chloe's boyfriend she had seen at Shaquah's villa. What had confused her was his crisp, groomed appearance. It was his extra-long nose and nervous hands that had given him away. But despite the several times she had come across him, she had never heard him speak before.

She looked again at Festus' hand. On the inside finger was the largest rock she had ever seen on a ring. Though no doubt a precious gem, it was gaudy and ridiculously pompous on his finger.

She gazed again at his face and, suddenly, she knew he was also the pacing man outside the healing rooms. The cut he had received across his upper cheek that day had never healed well and now portrayed itself as a pinkish scar below his eye giving the impression of blushing at first glance. He strutted before this tailor in his richly coloured silk tunic and sparkly jewels, but the expensive clothes did not hide the awkward uncouth man he was as he swayed hunched with strong drink and bragged unashamedly how 'f-f-favours done f-for da elite bring gr-gr-great re-rewards'. The merchant was handing him a buoyant plumed hat that matched his new red and gold kilt. With his long bony legs, he looked like a child's stick puppet.

Normad gently pulled her back out-of-sight.

"What a f-fine sight I am!" Festus expressed delightfully. "Here, my g-good man."

"There is no need…" the tailor protested.

"Dare's m-m-more where dat came f-from! It's y-yours."

"Most gracious of you, kind sir," the recipient answered politely. "Be careful on that step…"

There was a bit of a clatter, some mumbled profanity and then the unsteady footsteps grew more distant. Only then did the merchant reappear. He smiled and directed them down a short aisle of cloth rolls slotted in cubbies on either side of them. At the end of the row, a second tailor was working doggedly on a gold stitch on fine silk.

"Uncle," Raasah whispered, "I know that man – that man that just left. He is courting a servant of Shaquah's."

"Oh," Normad said simply.

"But he has always been dressed as a poor commoner, never in such grand clothes…"

"Is that right?" Normad remarked off-handedly.

"And the ring," Raasah continued, remembering Tara's account of the brush she had with the fowler's possible murderer, "he could be Geshem's killer. The ring could have been the.…"

"Umm, yea, many are under suspicion," Normad said calmly. "Now we must see about getting out of these wet clothes."

Put out by Normad's lack of interest, Raasah resigned herself to wait and ask Tara more about the young man when they next met. They peeled off the borrowed robes and laid them dripping on a hook against the far wall.

Normad turned toward their approaching host. "Isaiah, we do not want to put you anymore at risk."

"It's all looked after," the man named Isaiah remarked cheerfully. His grey eyes, hooded under lazy drooping lids, belied a quick mind, as Raasah was to find out. He motioned out the front door and, on cue, a sweet-faced amenable boy revealed himself in Raasah's own wet cape.

"This is my son, Noah. He has been a diversion since you were gone. If you had been watched, they will believe you were either here or shopping nearby the whole time!" the merchant grinned. Scrutinizing the boy, Raasah realized, with his height and build, and wrapped in her own cloak in this rain, one could not help but think she and he were one and the same. If they had been followed, this semblance would have surely fooled them.

"Noah, don your own robes and fetch the bearers from their villa to carry them home."

"Yea, Pei-wa-ni."

"And see if you can bring back a dry robe for young Raasah," Isaiah called.

"I will, Pei-wa-ni," Noah replied. He transformed into a tailor's boy and hurried off into the wet street.

"Thank you, good friend," Normad said.

"We all must do our part," the merchant said graciously. Then he handed Raasah a large bundle. "Now you mustn't leave empty-handed after all the time you have spent here," he smiled.

"Of course," she replied, as she received the bound cloth package.

She admired all the foresight and adroit planning of both Normad and Isaiah. This was obviously not the first time they have had to resort to sly deception to ward off potential enemies. She felt a tingle of danger run its fingers up her spine. She was beginning to understand more clearly why her grandmother and brother had kept certain secrets from her. '...and some (secrets are) necessary,' Grandmother had said.

Foremost, Raasah was flushed with happiness to learn of Abul's escape after all he had been through. She couldn't wait to share with Terjah the good news. At a time of so much fear and uncertainty, she clung to this knowledge – her childhood friend was alive!

Terjah should be back tomorrow. Meanwhile, she must show her grandmother she did not make a mistake disclosing her secret parts of her life. She hugged the bogus package to her chest and straightened her shoulders. She would not let her down.

That night, feeling far from strong, Raasah had her nightmare again but this time, as she lay trembling, she forced herself to remember what she had seen. As the steady patter of water dripped past her window, she willed herself to recall the frightful screams again more clearly than she would have liked and the blurry chaos of bodies falling and that hand reaching for her and a voice saying, whispering something:

"...My pr... My presh-sh...."

"Oh, why can't I remember!" she cried softly, her face flushed with the effort.

There was a ring, though – she remembered a ring. This was not like the one Festus displayed, but one of some significance and fashionably set. Raasah closed her eyes tightly, trying to conjure it up again in her mind. But, instead, her mind conjured the indistinct mask of one of the assailant and a large adorned earplug that dangled…. She could almost smell his perfumed sweaty body and she resisted the impulse to push the image away beyond her closed lids.

Eyes still squeezed shut, she sucked in a deep breath and concentrated on slowing her pounding heart to the steady patter of dripping water. As she did so, a flash of the hand with the ring surfaced once more on the back of her eyelids – a large band with a crest and stones on the third finger. The image faded as quickly as it appeared and she gratefully blinked her eyes open, relieved to be safely back home in the villa. She rubbed her hand across her beating chest.

Questions bombarded her, threatening to drive her mad. *Why were we attacked? Why didn't they kill me? Who were behind the masks? Who murdered Geshem and the juggler? And the ring! Where had I seen it before?* She whipped the blankets off and lit a stout candle by her bed. Then she snatched up a sheet of parchment, vial of ink, and a pen and began to sketch the ring before the details faded completely from her memory. Bathed in the flickering blue-grey light, she sketched like she was possessed, until her jaw hurt from gritting her teeth. When her hand slowed, she sat back and stared.

She studied her crude drawing, turning the parchment slightly to the right and then the left. The image before her seemed familiar. She stared some more, searching her memory, events in her life, and people she had met in passing, for some connection.

She stared for a long time, but a mind has a way of protecting itself from bombardments of thoughts that threaten its sanity. Her mind wandered, slipping off to remember a happier time, one with her father, relishing in his warm smile. She remembered how tense and tired he looked when he was on the judgment seat – but, as the 'Pochtecatl of the Iguana', she had never known him happier. She remembered again their final campsite and Old Mandula's wife who was still unsettled from her embarrassing fall. *'Madam Bettelina, take my seat.' Pei-wa-ni had said. Bettelina had blushed and regarded him guardedly. But Pei-wa-ni was cheerful and complimented her. Pei-wa-ni was always a gentleman.*

Of course, Botholuem could afford to be. He was at the pinnacle of his profession, respected by his peers, and esteemed by the royal court. He seemed to own the world he moved in and made enormous money for those he associated with but still he was generous and down-to-earth caring in the way he treated others. Raasah pictured the scene once more. Bettelina had appeared to wrestle with her reaction to Botholuem's remark. Finally, looking sheepish, Bettelina wagged her finger at Botholuem before accepting his offer. She knew the details of her 'incident' were safe with him. Joining Bettelina directly had been grey-haired Mandula who sat heavily at his wife's side. He clasped her hands in his and snuggled in close.

Raasah attempted to envision her parents, cuddled together exchanging tender looks. She strained to see the possibility but it would not come. She search her memory for a period in their lives when her parents mutually showed caring and affection for each other but, instead, the flashes of memory were of her mother's tirades and of her father's heavily retreating footsteps through the door.

Persistent, she continued to search the farthest reaches in her mind for domestic bliss between her parents until her chin came to rest on her chest, and, despite all her efforts and yearning, she would only be awarded with waking up several hours later with a sharp creak in her neck and a perplexing image of a ring that may or may not exist.

Chapter 24

The Proclamation

The streets abounded with anxious, but subdued, citizens meandering toward the Temple Square for the Sabbath worship – such a contrast to the last week when these same citizens, rowdy and disorderly, had headed for the festivities of Founders Week. Prestigious carriages bobbed conspicuously above the crowd ahead of them. Their own carriage lay idle in the back garden. Her grandmother had always preferred walking amongst the people than to being burdened on the shoulders of bearers and Raasah, herself, had avoided the carriage as often as she could since she had returned that fated night because of the memories that lingered with it. It had not occurred to any of them this day to enlist the aid of any bearers to transport them through the masses even on this monumental occasion.

Normad had joined the silent Botholuem household. The smaller city temples would be deserted today as all the citizens of Ammonihah wished to be present at the Palania's Temple of the Sun where they hoped to hear the proclamation regarding Ammonihah's new Prophet and Seer.

Many, a few contentiously, were speculating who may have been chosen and others walked solemnly, whispering apprehensively – almost fearfully – amongst themselves. As they walked, Marian flexed her hands tensely over the whickered handle of her basket from which she had been determined to hand out food to those in need following the burial ritual.

"Oh, my stars! I didn't...!" Marian had suddenly stopped and Vashti, preoccupied with soothing her 'fretting doll', ambled right into the back of her legs.

"What is it, Marian?" Tamar asked as she steadied Vashti and drew her son close to her, for the mass of people seemed to be engulfing them as they stood at a standstill in its midst.

"I left the corn bread by the door," Marian replied agitatedly. "... and my headcovering...."

"Mei-wa-na," Raasah said quickly, looking into the frightened faces of children as the crowds pressed upon them. "I will go back for them. We haven't gone that far. I can catch up." This was not a selfless gesture. She welcomed the distraction to relieve some of her own tension. Little Brother tugged on her sleeve and looked imploringly at her.

"I don't think...," Marian protested.

"Little Brother will go with me," Raasah countered quickly with Little Brother smiling in agreement. She shuffled forward as she was elbowed sharply from behind by an elderly man being herded along by the mere movement of his fellow pedestrians.

Marian looked up at Normad who nodded slowly in response.

"We will meet you just in front of the Temple Square," Raasah said quickly before her grandmother could protest. With that, Raasah and the boy turned and wormed their way against the crowd back to the villa. Mosia, attentive as always, immediately opened the gate for them and they located the two items easily. In the little time it took before they merged once more into the street, though, it had become a solid sea of people center-bound.

Little Brother and Raasah held tight to each other as they slipped into the mass of people. One burly man brashly pushed his way past, who should have knocked her over but the bodies pressing about them forbid it. Panic slowly rose thick and warm from the pit of her stomach as she felt the heat of the bodies and seeing no end to the parade of humanity surging and converging upon her. Little Brother's small grip tightened.

Gradually, she felt the flow of people interrupted. A deep commanding voice became more distinct as it snapped orders to clear the way. Following the other turning heads, Raasah spotted the bobbing spectacle of a carriage being born high above the crowd. Welcoming the relief from the unyielding flow of the crowd, she shielded her eyes from a sudden break of the sun to make out the family signet adorning the top of the carriages.

People parted quickly as the large gruff attendant pushed a path through the human deluge for his carriage-bound master. With the morning glare blocked, her relief was replaced with dismay. She spied the distinctive mark of the red and blue viper family signet. The crowd made way for the gold-leafed carriages of Jashorum & his entourage.

In vain, Raasah attempted to melt into the crowd out of its path. The commanding voice belonged to a muscle-bound man branded excessively with tattoos. He wore simply a wide leather belt imprinted with the viper about his pleated kilt and gold bands upon his upper arms. What caught her eye, though, was the sneer on his pierced plated lips and the way he set his eyes on her that reminded Raasah of an eagle sizing up its prey. Before she could react, his talons grasped her arm painfully and planted her alongside of the first carriage.

A painted bejeweled hand parted the sheer curtain enclosing the single occupant. Jashorum smiled broadly as he motioned to the towering jackal to lower the carriage, who, in turn, barked out the command.

"Cainihah, where are your manners? Assist the young lady to ascend above this human riffraff." Immediately, her arm was drawn forward in that same powerful grasp and another hand on her elbow directed her to a cushioned bench across from Jashorum. Jashorum's expression of superior satisfaction, though, abruptly changed to stunned disbelief as Little Brother scrambled to seat himself next to Raasah, his hand still clasped tightly to hers. Jashorum recovered quickly and, without acknowledging the boy, he smiled.

"It is not safe for a pretty young lady of distinction to be wandering the streets alone. Did you get separated from your Household?"

Raasah rubbed her arm tenderly where she was sure the imprints of Cainihah's fingers lay imbedded. "I was not alone and we were just on our way to join them."

With a scowl, Jashorum inspected Raasah's boy-escort. Little Brother, to Raasah's delight, stared back unflinchingly.

Jashorum returned this attention to Raasah. "You must be a proud young woman. Your mother has earned the appointment of the highest honour the priesthood can offer. She now shares the position as spokesman for the gods."

"It was a momentous proclamation," Raasah said simply, looking out at the tops of heads as their carriage sailed smoothly and calmly toward the city centre.

"Yea, it was a great day when Sablon was called to officiate over our glorious city. With your mother's divine guidance, Ammonihah will once again shine and agitators will be eradicated from our streets," Jashorum declared proudly, then added slowly, "You have heard of Amulek's folly of associating with that troublemaker from Zarahemla?"

"I know only that Amulek is a wise, influential man. What he sees in this stranger of Zarahemla MUST be worth his trouble." Raasah surprised herself with her boldness of answer. As she returned her gaze to his, she asked, "Why do YOU think Amulek is so entrenched with this Alma? Why does he risk his reputation and family?"

"It is said," he replied slowly, "that this Alma uses sorceries of the most powerful magic to frenzy the mind and Amulek no doubt has fallen under his spells. Amulek has indeed been a valued member of our society," he added. "His father has consulted doctors and priests and all will be done to undo the curse binding him to this disastrous path. We must do all we can to bring good people such as he back to their right mind."

"That is most noble of you to be concerned about Amulek." Then, remembering the recount of the cowardly attack by Zoric's brother, she chose her words carefully, as disgust welled inside her. "I do understand that his grand-daughter was seriously molested by some sadistic brutes. I pray that as much concern will also be extended toward her well-being."

Jashorum's lips twitched as he struggled to retain a sincere face. "The welfare of all our elite is always of my greatest concern," he said.

"This Alma," Raasah said quickly. "What evidence do you have that he is a sorcerer? Has he broken any laws?"

Jashorum looked fiercely at her. "You speak as if you are defending him."

"I do not defend him, Sir. I have no opinion of the man, having never had a conversation with him. There is so much talk of him that I feel I should become more informed and believe, with your boundless source of knowledge and intelligence, that you would be a most enlightened person to educate me."

Jashorum sat a little straighter, his chest puffed slightly. "I heard that you were an inquisitive young woman," he said. "There is much more depth to you than eyes alone can behold. Your mother is a wise woman of depth, not so unlike yourself when she was your age. I knew your mother back then, you know. But, of course, blessed with the sacred role she now holds, she has inherited the divine wisdom of the gods. You would do well to take her counsel, pretty Raasah. She knows for a certainty of the danger in associating with the likes of Alma or any that support those kind. They preach foolish prophesies and incite the people to go against the authorities."

"Is that right?" Her voice was steady and strong and she took courage from it. Feigning shock, she continued, "This is terrible! You know? I believe I did hear rumors that the preacher Alma has accused the leaders of our great city of conspiracy of some kind. If this is true, the council must be most distressed. How will the council handle such accusations?"

"At this moment they are contemplating his arrest for treason but he now hides like a frightened ferret in the forests."

"It is so.... so scandalous that in such a short time, one man, an outsider of no reputation, has had such a powerful influence over the people of Ammonihah. Why have not our learned men and priests been able to confound this preacher? Surely the power of our priesthood is superior to squash the babblings of a single sorcerer."

Jashorum searched Raasah's face, his confident smile momentarily vanished as she stubbornly kept his gaze despite the trembling deep inside. Then his mouth suddenly puckered and he heckled uproariously. "You are a surprising young lady. These are noteworthy questions. It is good to see that Zoric has sense to choose a bride with a bright thinking mind."

Ignoring his last comment, Raasah continued, "I will be most interested in hearing Alma's defense at the upcoming trial. Will it be held in the high court?"

Jashorum's eyes narrowed and for a long moment Raasah thought those eyes would burn a hole right through her. Her brief wave of courage began to ebb away. "Daughter of Sablon," he began, all pleasantness gone from his voice, "a tender child of your status should not be concerned in such… such dreary business."

As he leaned forward, she shifted her gaze from his face to the dangling medallion and chains upon his chest. He continued, "I'd be careful about listening to any outside preachers or their sympathizers. In fact, it would be wisdom on your part not to be concerned about them at all. This Alma should have stayed in the south where he belonged. He will not last long in this city – or those who support him."

The pace of the carriage was slowing and, looking past him, Raasah was relieved to see that they were approaching the temple square. "My grandmother waits by the temple gate. She will be looking for me."

"Yea, that brings me to the important matter that I wished to talk to you about. It was good that I spied you from within the crowd. I will be inviting your family to my home for the celebration of my son's appointment of Elder. Zoric is a gifted young man – will go far – as you are a gifted beautiful lady. It will be held eight days hence at our palace of Nathor. Of course, Zoric will be most pleased to see your presence alongside that of the great Priestess Sablon."

"I don't know… I didn't…."

The carriage was being lowered to the ground. Cainihah extended his hand to assist her from her seat but this time he waited like a statue, palm up, ready to receive her. She realized that one of his feet was placed on the back of a bearer who was to be used as a step. Raasah, like her father, abhorred this practice of using a human being as a degrading stool. Reluctantly, Raasah placed her small hand into the sweaty palm of Cainihah as she could see no alternative to relieve herself from Jashorum's presence. Little Brother daftly scooped the items retrieved from the villa and scrambled ahead of her unassisted from the gilded carriage.

"No need to thank me," Jashorum said as Raasah rose to leave. "We look forward to seeing you then."

Raasah wiped her hand on the folds of her shift in an effort to decontaminate herself on the entire encounter. Then she heard a familiar voice. Gracefully skipping, as only Jaona could do, she cheerily approached with her attendant bustling directly behind struggling with the feathered sunshade.

"Oh, Raasah," Jaona exclaimed. "That was Jashorum! That was JASHORUM! To ride with Zoric's father. Oh, Raasah. Look at the eyes upon you!"

Sure enough, there was a hush about the crowd and eyes were indeed upon her as the carriage was born away. Jaona continued to chatter on as she linked her arm in Raasah's.

"What a magnificent carriage! What a spectacular way to enter the plaza!" Jaona rambled, going on even more about jewels, gold and prestige and then said breathlessly, "You are so amazingly fortunate to be embraced into the House of Nathor. What things does Master Jashorum speak to you about? What things do you say to him?"

"Oh, um," Raasah debated what would be most appropriate to share with her friend and then said, "He told me Zoric will be appointed Elder next week."

"Oh, Raasah. Of course you will be going! What a wonderful opportunity to be with so many influential people! And their home…. Nowhere is there a more spectacular home than that of Jashorum of Nathor! Except maybe Governor Antionah …. But his taste borders on gaudy. My mother says he decorates like he wears jewelry – too much, no sense of beauty or style. Oh, Raasah!" Jaona exclaimed again. "What will you wear? It must be something exquisite, something to turn heads. I know a tailor…"

"I don't think I will be going."

Jaona stopped abruptly, looking dumb-founded. Then she stuttered, "Not going? Are you mad? Decline an invitation from the Jashorum Household! That would be outrageous, insulting, …unheard of!"

"Well, they will hear of it now. I am not going!" Raasah said irately. "I will not be dragged to an overly gluttonous feast to watch a… a… an unscrupulous arrogant bully receive the undeserved title of Elder."

"Raasah, how could you say such things?" Jaona lowered her voice. "If people heard you speak so, only ill could come of it. The Jashorum family have position, power, and resources to make your life so very comfortable or, if they choose, unbearable. To keep one's own position and security, we must prize our social relations with powerful families and accommodate, no indulge, in their celebrations and associations."

"Jaona," Raasah took Jaona's hands in hers and stared longingly at her. "You are my good friend. I love you like a sister. I appreciate your concern and am touched. But don't you see the treachery in choosing your friends by the wealth and influence they possess?"

Jaona pulled her hands from Raasah. "It is with some risk that I speak to you today after the ill that your grandmother has done to Issachar's Household. Yea, you are my friend but what your grandmother did to Isobel's mother, and, now you, speaking against powerful people …as if you had the gods' protective shield about you. …But, then again, you do, don't you? …with your mother's new appointment in the Temple and Royal Court!"

"I know you are my friend because you are here now with me. But now, because you are afraid of what Isobel will think, must I become your secret friend only to be shunned when in Isobel's presence? Is this the way you want to live the rest of your life – keeping company with people you fear reprisal from and avoiding those that you really want to be with? Is this how it's going to be?"

Jaona looked down at her gold embroidered sandals as her assistant tensely shifted the sunshade behind her. Jaona said quietly, "Isobel's family, they mix with the right people, there is opportunity with them…."

"Right people? Don't you see," Raasah reached for her friend again, "to associate with those who abuse their positions for gain and prestige, to let yourself be drawn into their deceit and unsaintly practices, may bring you the praises of the world and material things, but to what end for your soul!"

Jaona backed away from Raasah, knocking the assistant off balance. "This is easy for you to say. My family is not protected by a mother in a sacred position. My parents have made many sacrifices. All efforts must be made to appease those in power, to keep our status."

Raasah stepped forward in an effort to keep their conversation private. "For what reward, Jaona? So you can have fancy clothes and go to sumptuous parties! To spend your days trying to please those you associate with and being what they want you to be – without doing what you know in your heart is right. It hurt when you turned your back on me at the game last week. Did you mean to hurt me, or were you just trying to appease Isobel?"

Jaona looked down again. "I did not want to hurt you," she said softly. "Your grandmother.... That was Isobel's mother that she insulted...."

"Deservedly!" Raasah said adamantly.

"One cannot anger...." Jaona trailed off.

"Jaona, you have been my friend since our seventh year. I know your views are not Isobel's. Isobel, well, she has chosen a different road to walk, one that is cold and aloof. You are a warm, caring person, capable of such love and goodness. Would you throw that all away for unfeeling wealth and title?"

"Easy for you to say," Jaona snapped. "You, with all your wealth, all your opportunity! Would you throw all that away for mere love and goodness?" She continued without waiting for an answer. "I will not wallow in poverty and hopelessness for your ideals! I like my nice clothes; I like the way people look at me; I like the attention of young promising men. Look at your fine clothes. You do not shun them either."

"Jaona, I do not wish you a bleak future, but one of true honour and happiness. I ask you only to be true to yourself. To think about what you know to be right, and not what Isobel expects you to think."

Jaona screwed up her face. "How dare you!" she cried. "I am not a dizzy little girl who can't think for herself."

"Then stop acting like one!" Raasah shouted before she could stop herself. The hurt on Jaona's face was more than she could stand. "Oh, Jaona, I didn't mean …I only want what is best for…."

Before Raasah could finish, Jaona had turned, misty-eyed, into the crowd.

The sun buried itself behind a growing blanket of gray.

Onihah was conspicuously absent on the alter platform. Traditionally, the prophet's advisor was the officiator at his passing. History has proven also that the keys of the prophets were often passed down to such a man in a formal ceremony performed by the chief priests. But, today, Darius officiated. Sablon sat erect and nobly in the seat of honour that should have been Onihah's. If it wasn't for the occasional flutter of her long dark lashes, one would have thought her to be a stunningly adornment upon the base of the Most High Temple. In contrast with the dull, overcast morning, Sablon appeared illuminant above the crowd. Raasah gazed longingly.

The Sabbath ceremony progressed without deviation and, at the conclusion of the blood-letting, the city of Ammonihah was hauntingly silent as Darius raised his arms theatrically in all his splendored dress. As he did so, out of the cavernous black of Palenia emerged the High Priests in their flowing ceremonial robes, holding high the gold-laden staffs of their revered status to stand on either side of Darius. Raasah searched the faces under the lofty headdresses. Onihah was not among these priests either.

"There are only ten priests present," Marian whispered uneasily.

"Only ten need to be present to proclaim the next prophet," Normad reminded Marian.

A tall priest walked ceremoniously to the front. His ringlet beard lay fanned out upon his jeweled chest. With a lump in her throat, she stared numbly as the man she used to know rapped his staff three times on the platform.

"I, Mathonihah, as appointed by the twelve High Priests of the Sun Temple, do solemnly stand before you to officiate in the handing of the keys to the successor of our brother priest and prophet, the beloved Esrom. Esrom, Prophet of the Great White God of the Skies, has now ascended to be in his Omnipotent's presence. Because of his untimely illness and death, unfortunately, Esrom was unable to pass on the keys of his office in this life and we have humbly been left with the mammoth responsibility of appointing the new prophet of Ammonihah in his absence." He paused as murmurings rippled through the crowd. He held his staff high in the air, hushing the stirring populace. "My dear citizens of Ammonihah, our great God of the eternal skies has not left us alone." At this point, Mathonihah's voice changed, softening as he finished the last words. His voice was choked and somehow hollow as he added, "he will never leave us alone." He paused briefly again. This time Raasah thought she saw a tear glisten out the corner of one eye. Nevertheless, his voice reverted strong and forcible the next instance, causing Raasah to question whether she had really heard the intermittent of emotion. "Through much deliberation, fasting, and fervent prayers, the Creator has revealed to us who the new prophet will be." Hushed murmuring once more sounded all around her. Raasah caught her breath, her hand pressed against her breast. She searched the platform for Onihah once more.

A fellow priest came forward with a silver and gold-etched tray brightly reflecting the late morning sun that had forced its way out of the clouds. Mathonihah exchanged his staff for the tray and held it high, chanting, chorused by the young priests and priestess on the lower terrace. As if in a trance, Mathonihah lowered the tray ever so slowly and held it out to the congregation.

"The Creator has selected us a new Prophet and Seer, one that will be not only over our grand city of Ammonihah, but over-all the land of our fathers. We have heard the voice of our Great Kukulkan – it filled our Temple, it filled our whole being!" His voice grew in volume. "It has been divinely appointed! I present to you, your Holy Prophet and Seer! I present to you the honourable descendant of our great prophet Lehi of old -- our own Darius, son of Able!"

There was a deafening cry of exhilaration from the crowd followed by the excited hum of voices as Darius ceremoniously stepped to the front. As the priest to the left of him retrieved the tray, Mathonihah lifted the large bejeweled medallion from it and clasped its chain around Darius'neck. With his palm under the melon-sized medallion, Mathonihah lifted it glittering to the heavens. The crowd hushed.

"To the Father of all Gods, to the Father of all spirits, we thank you for a prophet. Amen."

The square thundered with the response. In contrast to the masses, though, Marian remained quiet, shaking her head slowly, colour fading from her face. Normad drew her stiff body close. Raasah could not make out the words he spoke to her but his tone was soothing and she wished he could whisper reassuring, soothing words to her as well. *Darius, Prophet and Seer for the people? This could not be! Onihah should have been the successor.* A shudder overcame her.

"Good people. Hear your Prophet and write his words on your heart." With these short words, spoken like they were taken from a well-rehearsed script, Mathonihah melted back into the line of High Priests as they filed to the edge of the platform. Sablon was once more visible as a picture of beauty, enhancing Darius, now the solitary most important man of the civilized north lands.

Darius raised his arms, his stance demanding silence. His audience was swift to respond. "I, Darius, soon-to-be your ordained Prophet, seer, and spokesman for our Omnipotent Creator, I greet the good citizens of Ammonihah. This city was built in honour of a celebrated man, a fierce soldier, commander of thousands, and defender of what's noble and great. Ammonihah was the son of Elias who was a descendant of Lehi, who is father of this glorious land, from sea to sea, from the Wilderness and beyond. It is upon the traits of this lineage that our grand city of Ammonihah was established. Kukulkan has blessed our efforts and has favoured us as his treasured children.

"He has many blessings waiting for us. He has shown them to me in a dream. In this dream, I was lifted up, high above the earth, and looked down, like the gods, upon our city and our lands. Many things I saw, wondrous sights, many of which I was cautioned not to speak of to you but to hold in my heart until commanded to reveal them. I saw things not of this earth, so marvelous, that there are no words to describe. I also saw things of this earth that brought shame and sorrow to my soul. I saw great tears fall to the earth from our Creator because of the corruption of this blessed people by words of strangers and sorcerers that have sought to fill the minds of our great people. As the privileged spokesman of our omnipotent Kukulkan, I have been commanded," Darius boomed, " to tell you – we must continue to raise ourselves above those others who try to degrade our way of life, to hold strong to the traditions of our fathers and stay true to the standards and truths that built our grand city!"

Cries of acknowledgement and excitement rose from within and without the Temple Square. Stone-faced, Darius raised his arms for silence once more. As the din subsided, he surveyed the congregation. Acquiescently, he said, "I am humbled by this massive responsibility and honoured …"

"Humbled, like a jaguar in heat," Marian mumbled suddenly. Normad hugged her, cautioning her to be still.

Darius continued. "…but not surprised, as it was foreseen in my dream. With our All-Knowing Creator as my guide…."

"He is speaking heresy. This is abominable. I have had enough…" Marian stammered, struggling to brush away Normad's grip.

Normad sternly held her arm. "For your sake, and the sake of your household, you WILL sit through this, as blasphemous as it is."

Marian looked first into his face and then into the alarmed face of her granddaughter and, reluctantly, settled back down. "I am sorry. My pride got the best of me. We will 'conform' at this time and make it through this."

She took Raasah's hand softly and sat expressionlessly through the ensuing speech as Darius expounded his general promises of a better life for all, blessings, and the assurance that prayers on behalf of the people would be heard and granted. He had the elegant gift of speech and, all around them, their neighbours seemed mesmerized by his words. As an inimical cloud obscured the glowing face of the heightening sun, though the heat of the day was still tangible on her bare skin, another shiver rippled up Raasah's spine. It was a difficult task 'conforming'.

At the conclusion of his flowery dialogue, the professional wailers and singers circled the platform. The lavish funeral litter with the anointed body of the gentle, dearly loved Esrom was lifted high upon the shoulders of the High priests. As the wailers and singers raised their voices, the people rose in honour of the great prophet that had gone onto the hereafter, a righteous man that would leave a tattered hole in the fragile fabric of their Ammonihah City.

Light sprinkles of rain delicately brushed her arm. Listlessly, Raasah gazed up at the darkening sky. The growing dreariness of the morning resonated with the cold wash of sorrow and bleakness that was now constricting in her bosom. And, gazing again at the newly appointed prophet, she feared dearly for her people.

Chapter 25

Shaquah's Agreement

Citizens were literally vibrating as they dispersed from the Temple Square. Normad slipped away to have quick words with a harried man with thick cowlicked hair. But, by the end of their discourse, the man was smiling, transforming his long austere face into a rather pleasant one as Normad slapped his back firmly to send him on his way. Normad quickly rejoined the silent Botholuem clan.

"Ela had her baby – a strong healthy boy. And mother is doing well."

Raasah felt a small ray of sunshine. *Little Lydia will be so happy to have her new brother.*

"It is good to hear such delightful tidings on such a day as this," Marian smiled weakly. "Of course, you will be going there to perform the ritual for his birth."

"Not before I safely escort you all home," Normad said grandly.

Marian submissively took his outstretched arm. Though Little Brother had typically vanished in the crowd, the other children and servants kept in pace without speaking. Raasah had been looking around for Jaona but, instead, spied the stern-faced Isobel on the Palace terrace, returning a look that bordered on contempt, before she flipped back her head and stepped off the platform. With a heavy heart, Raasah watched Isobel's departing form until two temple guards, in their flowing capes, barred her view as they approached.

"Marian, daughter of Omar, your granddaughter, Raasah of Botholuem, has been summoned to the Palace of Palenia by the Most High Priestess."

"Summoned, like in commanded?" Marian said irritably. "If she wishes to visit with her daughter, why does she not do so at the family home or invite her politely to break bread? – but to send temple guards like she was a rebel or...."

"Now, Marian," Normad cautioned once more.

"Mei-wa-na, it is all right. I would like to see my mother."

Marian looked lovingly – or was it sympathetically? – at her granddaughter. More subdued, she said, "I guess we should be pleased that your esteemed mother has taken the time to speak with you at all. We will wait for you by the Celestial Gardens."

"There will be no need," the second guard informed. "The High Priestess has arranged for a temple carriage to carry her home."

Marian parted her lips to speak, but, anticipating her retaliatory remark, Normad said quickly, "Let her go, Marian. All will be well."

Clenching her teeth, she nodded slowly. With a quick embrace and a tender look that words could never speak – they parted.

§

The bowels of the Palenia Palace were pleasantly cool and dry after the growing mugginess outside. The winding corridors were lit by narrow endless troughs of flickering flames along the walls. Branching off into other decorative corridors were the personal suites of the temple elite. Raasah walked dutifully, single file, between the guards listening to their echoing steps that kept them company and, finally, descended down the steep steps to the Offices of the High Priestesses.

Raasah would have expected to meet with her mother at the Oluffa Gardens, and she was intrigued to have been summoned to this secured section of Palenia, reserved for only the high ranking priests, priestesses, and their attendants. As their pace slackened, Raasah examined the frescos on either side of her and brushed her hand delicately over the embossed images of their ancestors. Then, hearing the sound of water ahead, she strained to peer through a distant archway that, curiously, seemed to emit the light of the noon day, despite the depth.

At the threshold, the foremost guard turned and offered his hand as Raasah hesitantly stepped into the cavernous chamber. It abounded in plush furniture and articles of the most exquisite detail sitting upon luscious fur rugs. Miniature gardens of ornamental trees and flowers miraculously stretched toward the high ceilings that sported potholes of daylight somehow funneled in to fill and enhance the elegance of all the treasures and give the life-giving essence to the plants below. A large pool and fountain dominated a far corner under sweet blossoming trees.

Lounging elegantly in a simpler yet exquisite gown, her mother motioned to them with a graceful sweep of her arm. At her feet, purring rhythmically like a bellowed fire, crouched a fierce-looking jaguar in a jade-studded collar. With its tail twitching tensely, its shiny black eyes warily followed the approach of the new arrivals.

With a sudden snap of her slender fingers, the jaguar keeper tugged sharply on the cat's chain. The orange beast heaved itself to its feet and lumbered off with the keeper straining for control behind it. Simultaneously, female temple attendees entered from another part of the building with golden platters mounding with food, pitchers of drink, and a heaping basket of flowers.

Raasah, like a lost soul, stood before 'the most powerful woman in Ammonihah' as the attendants bustled around them. Nervously she searched the sculptured face of the woman in front of her, searching to establish if her mother was really in there.

Dismissing the guards, and, as they and the young attendants retreated, Sablon said pleasantly, "Please, my daughter, sit."

I am not 'Du-ba-ni' today....

Sablon gestured to a lounge across from her. On a low ebony table the gold platters were set amongst the soft hues of pastel petals. Though it was an inviting display, Raasah possessed no desire to eat.

"Mei-wa-ni," Raasah said timidly, "It is good of you to see me."

"In all my great duties for our gods and our city, my duty to you should also be of my great concern."

The words were pleasant to Raasah's ears but the sincerity seemed to be lacking somehow. "Is it your duty that calls me to these significant surroundings?"

Sablon's painted face never altered in its expression. "You are the daughter of the most formidable orator that this people will ever know. But, here, away from the world, I can contemplate and express my personal feelings and relax from my cares. My duties are very pressing and much care must be taken to know that my actions are not perceived to be anything out of character for the High Priestess of our Great Creator. As my daughter, you have duties as well. Much care must be taken on your part to make sure your actions are not perceived to be anything out of character for the daughter of the High Priestess of Kukulkan."

"Honourable Mother, have you brought me here to instruct me of my additional duties as your daughter?"

"I have brought you here to understand my daughter and so she can understand me," Sablon said coldly. "I hear Jashorum had to rescue you from the common mass of the city this morning."

"I did not need rescuing. He plucked me from the crowd like a turnip from a garden!"

Ignoring Raasah comment, Sablon extolled, "Your grandmother is a fool for not attending in the carriage. It was dangerous and beneath the standards of your title. We cannot have you portraying yourself as a 'common' people. You put yourself in harm's way, causing people who care about you great concern."

Raasah looked longingly at her mother at the reference of caring but, her hopes that her mother was referring to her concern were quickly torn asunder. "Zoric would be devastated if something should happen to his betrothed."

"Mother, as prominent as the Nathor Household is, I do not feel what I can offer Zoric is harmonious to what he expects in a wife. I...."

"Daughter, as much as your father no doubt had put whimsical thoughts in your impressionable head, you are a young lady of distinction and you must shed these wild dreams of exotic adventures and mysterious ideals. You have a duty to your Household to live the proper standards of nobility and honour and to marry in the station of society demanding that respect and power."

"It is of honour that I speak. Is it honourable for me to pretend to be what I am not? I cannot be the empty-headed submissive handmaiden that Zoric yearns for. He is the one that must shed his illusions of me filling his licentious dreams of ...."

Sablon cut Raasah off sharply. "Daughter, this is not talk suitable to a class of social superiority."

"Mother, I mean no disrespect to you or those honourable elite of Ammonihah. But I have heard and seen behaviors of Zoric and his brother that do not deserve any form of respect."

"Impertinent child, after your act of dishonouring your teacher, disappearing in the middle of the night, walking the streets with the degrading commoners, taking in dirty waifs and strays, and whatever else you have been doing that I have not been made aware of, you should be grateful, nah, on-your-knees thankful, that the Nathor Household still wants to make you part of their house."

Raasah looked away, hand to her chest as she felt her throat constrict. A long moment passed as she composed herself. Slowly she turned to address the cold insensitive individual in front of her, now delicately biting into a square of melon.

"Mother, it's been so long since we have talked. At no time did I intend disrespect to my teachers nor have I done anything to make you ashamed of me. I have studied hard, worked diligently on my domestic skills, and followed in your footsteps to the best of my ability. As a future priestess to the temple, I do not feel Zoric will support me in my calling. You know how important it is for the support of your family in temple work."

"As your husband, Zoric would have say whether you can perform your duties. As your head, he will be inspired to know what is best for you."

"And I am to follow as YOU followed Father's inspiration?" Raasah snapped in frustration, regretting it almost immediately.

"Enough!" Sablon snapped back. "You are becoming an embarrassment to me and to yourself. You will start to act like the refined lady you were trained up to be."

Raasah's cheeks grew hot as she struggled to keep calm. "I only know," she countered, "that you would not lower yourself to act in a way you did not believe. I only ask that you hear me out. To embarrass you is the furthest from my intentions."

Sablon's voice softened. "Daughter, I do not mean to be so harsh with you."

Raasah thought she spied a glimpse of her mother. "And I do not wish to be contentious with you," Raasah replied quietly and then, adding imploringly, "I have missed you." As she choked out the words, she realized how much she meant them. Swallowing hard, she looked slowly down in the silence that ensued.

Hearing the swashing of cloth, Raasah waited apprehensively for a gentle hand, or, wish-of-all-wishes, a warm embrace from this woman that gave her birth. She barely breathed as her heart filled with emotion so long denied. But no hand touched her; no arms embraced her.

With the disappointment and longing almost too much to bear, Raasah lifted her face to the figure standing before her and stared into her stone-still eyes. She might as well been looking at a statue – her mother was not there after all. A tear threatened to betray her and she lowered her face to will it gone.

Sablon held out a small silver tray on which was placed an official scroll with a red and blue seal on it. Without examining it closer, Raasah knew what it was. Still she waited until her mother spoke.

"This is an invitation to the Botholuem Family to attend the grand occasion of Zoric's appointment as Elder."

Raasah still did not respond but looked fixedly at the scroll. "Daughter of Botholuem – Nah, Daughter of the Most High Priestess!" Sablon snapped, the silver tray trembling slightly, causing the scroll to roll precariously close to the edge. "From now on, you will consider yourself Daughter of Sablon, the Supreme High Priestess! As such, you are no longer the carefree daughter of a pochtecatl, but the noble daughter of the Oracle for Kukulkan. From this day forth, you will act like the daughter of this higher calling: you will ride in the carriage of the Temple elite, you will sit tall in the seats of highest titles, you will surround yourself with the society of your stature, and act according to your station!" At this point, Sablon was flushed and pacing, the scroll rolling haphazardly back and forth on its perch. Raasah watched spellbound at this brisk, emotional imitation of her mother, as the words slowly seeped into her brain. Raasah stood suddenly and faced her approaching mother.

"Is this all, Esteemed Mother?" Raasah asked matter-of-factly. "May I go now?"

"You will go when I tell you to go!" Sablon shouted, a cruel curl to her lips. Raasah remained standing as this stranger of a woman paced and gnashed her teeth.

Briskly turning in a small circle, Sablon re-approached her daughter. With a heave of her shapely chest, her hands now steadied, Sablon dropped the tray with the scroll onto the thick furs at Raasah's feet. Then, as if the outburst had never happened, Sablon retreated, curled up on the lounge, and reached regally for a grape. Raasah continued to stand, confused as to what to do next. Time passed as Raasah stood nervously, wondering if her mother had forgotten she was there.

Finally Sablon spoke. "You are commanded to attend Zoric's celebration and you are commanded to be charming and attentive," Sablon said simply. She rose to a sitting position, gracefully sinking her bare feet into the furs. "After the rite is completed," she said slowly, "I will be discussing your betrothal to Zoric and you WILL comply." Sablon stood, slipping her feet into a pair of silky shoes. "The temple guards will take you up. A carriage has been assigned to you and you will attend in it for all your activities. Your attendants will wait for you after all your classes and your teachers will be notified. That will be all."

Rising fluidly and with a whisk of gowns, reminding her suddenly of Isobel, Sablon disappeared deeper into the bowels of the palace.

With a sickening feeling regurgitating inside her, Raasah stood rooted to the spot, staring at the empty archway that had received the 'Supreme High Priestess'; her mother's words still swirling inside her head. Every grain of decency told her that she could never live with a depraved man such as Zoric. She couldn't let this happen. She had to make this powerful priestess understand.

Raasah traced her mother's path deep inside the palace. The ensuing unkempt passage turned and sloped as it wound its way down and down until she was sure the earth itself would suck her into its fiendish merciless belly. No more inspiring murals on the walls or troughs of glowing light. Dripping candles littered the walls sprinkling wavering light into the blackness; uneven paving met her stumbling feet. As a despairing, decaying odor began to fill her senses, a wave of fear drained her of all warmth.

Cringing, she recalled childhood tales of lost souls wandering the forgotten underworld where their dried bones lay in forlorn darkness. A shudder engulfed her at the thought of boney fingers reaching for her to drag her down to a forever undeath. Silence squeezed in upon her, threatening to take her breath away. Shuffling to a stop and turning wildly, she brushed up against the damp dead walls, shrinking from them as she imagined horrors materializing from its revolting surface.

Panic smothered all logic as she quickened her step, wildly searching for something familiar, something that resembled the world above to assure herself that she had not been claimed by the damned. No longer conscience of the direction she was going, fighting the despair welling inside her, she paused under a flickering wick, straining to hear any mortal sound. Dreading what might be revealed, whether it be of the undead or of her world, at first she heard nothing. Then, there it was – unearthly, mumbled, barely audible.

Cautiously she tip-toed forward, careful not to kick a loose stone or make any sound that would alert the groping wretched underlings. It was a soft quivering sound that echoed distantly – hauntingly. Steadily she willed herself forward. The belief that her path may be leading her to unholy personages did not deter her for it appealed to her more (in a morbid fashion) than languishing in forever-darkness in constant terror of when the evil would pounce.

The sound was growing louder and she could sense more than see a dim light ahead. Her goose-bumps seemed to dance with anxiety but she continued her steps closer and closer. The sounds ever so sluggishly began to clarify themselves into echo-y voices. Her steps came faster. Relief slowly seeped into her bosom. The voice – one of the voices – belonged to *("Oh, thank you, Great Kukulkan!")* the very alive woman she had sought. She had never been so happy to hear her mother's voice.

Wrapping her arms consolingly around herself, she rounded the sloping corner and approached an old splintered door that stood an arm-width ajar, illuminated with a faint glow through its warped cracks. Drawing nearer, Raasah could hear some of the distant words of the High Priestess: "..... higher purpose... your responsibility...."

Her heart pounded. Now that she had found her mother, she did not know what she was to say to her. She tip-toed the final steps to the ancient door and pried it open a hand-width more.

Raasah could make out two people and another in a darkened far corner. Small metal cages were clustered together just inside the light, their occupants slithering sluggishly in circles two or more deep.

Snakes! A harsh shiver cascaded down her spine. *Oh, how I hate snakes!* Raasah had witnessed her mother's special gift that charmed the snakes, even pacified them, but, most disturbing, was the fact that Sablon seemed to enjoy their scaly cold bodies wrapping themselves on her body. This was a side of her mother that frightened Raasah to this very day. In the past, she had tried to come to terms with her mother's preoccupation. There was a time when she had submerged herself into the study of snakes, specifically their viper counterparts, but it had done nothing to alleviate her fears. In fact, it alarmed her all the more. She shivered again. *Yea, I hate snakes!*

Pulling her eyes away from the viper cages, Raasah surveyed the room. Small pots of light dotted the smoky walls and cast eerie shadows across the sparse furnishings and figures. Raasah recognized the figures in the light. Shaquah, the healer, was now speaking angrily as Sablon looked serenely on, with the down-the-nose look that Raasah detested. Raasah had a sudden realization that Isobel and her mother had a lot of similar qualities. *Isobel could have been a daughter that Mother would have been proud of!* A spark of jealousy washed over her.

"I will not be part of this evil web of lies," Shaquah was saying. "Sablon, I was there when Esrom passed on the Priesthood Keys. I know he is the true prophet. You cannot allow this travesty to go on. This is a mockery to our Creator."

"Are you sure you heard correctly?" Sablon said patiently, "Esrom was very sick and most delirious at the end."

"I know what I heard. And now he is dead. Oh, Great Creator, forgive me! I never meant it to come to this!" Shaquah's shoulders shuddered as she shrunk to her knees and wept into her cupped hands. She crawled over to Sablon, groveling at her feet. "I cannot be part of this deception anymore. I will not damn my soul to eternal torment."

"I am sure you have misunderstood the intentions set out for you." Sablon said unmoved. "You are a gifted healer, one worthy of great works. Sometimes the Great God of our Fathers must test his most loyal servants though their understanding may be far from them. Be assured, I will entreat the Creator on your behalf. But, as you know, we have been most concerned recently regarding your actions. You, yourself, seem racked with guilt and look upon me to relieve you of its weight. I would like very much to oblige by purging you of your misdeeds. All essentials, though, must be fulfilled to bring to pass the promises assured you."

Sablon removed a parchment from the table and motioned to a well of ink with a feathered quill projecting from it. "Sign the needed document and affix your seal, good woman, and your conscience will be unburdened."

Shaquah slowly rose tall and straight, taking a step back. "I will have nothing more to do with any of this. I have kept my end of the agreement. I will sign and declare anything you want after you let her go."

"Now, Shaquah. You know she is being held in my protective custody. You would have put her in great danger without my assistance. I would never let any harm come to her."

"I have followed all instructions given me but I will not have any more blood on my hands. I will not do this terrible thing he asks of me!"

"Calm yourself, my dear. I would not have you do anything that would not uplift you to a higher sphere. I will let them know you have fulfilled your agreement. Your obedience to what has been commanded of you will be rewarded."

"And what of Orphah?"

"Moses will take you to her." Sablon extended the roll of parchment once more to Shaquah.

With shaking hands, Shaquah slowly reached for the parchment and waited expectantly. "Moses, escort her to the child," Sablon said, smiling, "and, Shaquah, the signed document is the last of your obligations to the priesthood order. Be reassured."

A large figure in temple guard uniform marched into the light. Shaquah gripped the roll of parchment firmly as the guard gathered writing materials. Without looking back, she wordlessly followed the guard back out the far door.

From the darkened corner, not one, but two figures materialized.

"You let her go?" a hooded figure said hoarsely.

"Don't worry. All is unfolding as the wondrous vision had foreseen," Sablon said carefree. She reached for an item off the table but Raasah could not make out what it was before the third figure came into the light and blocked her view. Now in a new set of clothes, looking more like a courting bird than a socialite, was stuttering Festus. *What is the common thread drawing us to the same places?* Raasah listened intently.

"Festus, come here, boy," Sablon ordered. With her back toward Raasah, Sablon spoke to him in a quieter voice that seemed to be absorbed by the walls. Unable to make out the words, Raasah studied this tall awkward figure. As Sablon spoke, Festus shifted from foot to foot and, seeming unsure what to do with his fidgeting hands, clutched them over and over, the outlandish ring glittering in the weak light of the lit lamps. Raasah was on the verge of remembering something when he quickly scrambled off in the same direction Shaquah had exited, holding something close to his chest.

"Make sure my documents get signed," Sablon commanded after him. Festus, turned, nodded grimly, and exited the same lower door.

The hooded man turned slowly in Raasah's direction. In anticipation of his disclosed identity, she leaned forward, squinting in the dim light. But, as she did so, she heard a muffled patter behind. Whirling around, her hand slipped against the broken surface of the door, painfully embedding a sliver into her palm. Stumbling back against the cold stone wall, she stared as the door creaked forward ever so slightly.

"What was that?" the hoarse voice said beyond the door. Behind her, the muffled patter was materializing into a waverly shadow advancing around the blackened corner. Raasah looked wildly around. Unable to escape discovery, she crouched like a trapped rabbit, waiting for the ravenous enemy to pounce. The threatening figure was solidifying ominously out of the darkness.

Raasah cringed against the cold walls, her skin imitating its coldness – the hair rising off her arms. Time seemed to slow to a near stop. The features of the approaching personage smoothed sluggishly into shape. White hands reached from cavernous cloth, deep shadows punctured hollow eyes. Unable to breath, Raasah awaited her fate.

The pounding in her ears was deafening; her knees weakened from under her. Then, to her great astonishment and relief, the menacing figure threatening to devour her became the welcome personage of Tara! With a finger to her lips, Tara knelt silently next to Raasah's crumpled figure.

Sablon's silky voice purred through the door: "Holy Brother, Fearless Leader, would you have a small draft reduce you to a spooked bird?"

"Beautiful priestess, indulge my cautious whims," he purred like gravel back and then thundered, "Guard, check the passage!"

"This way!" Tara quietly commanded, tugging on Raasah's arm.

With her head still thumping, Raasah let herself be led into the darkness just inside a more narrow passage off the more travelled one. She wondered why she hadn't noticed the additional arm of the passage before.

Heavy steps approached, a dark form passed their hideaway, and then the steps faded quickly into the distant. Raasah stared in disbelief at her unexpected savior.

"Tara, what are you doing here?"

"Shush, he will be back. Come with me!" Tara drew her deeper into the blackness of this new passage. Raasah groped at the walls, but she recoiled abruptly as her hand touched something mushy and questionable. Lighting a candle that gave a wavery glow, Tara lead Raasah by the hand through the blackness along the stoned lined passage. It smelt damp and old, and sounds of scuttling and tiny scrapings, imaginary or otherwise, added a quiver to Raasah's shiver.

After the passing of much ominous time, the air became warmer and then fresher and, not too soon for Raasah, she glimpsed a dim glow ahead, tinged with the promise of life. The closer they came to the opening, the more thankful Raasah was that she decided not to drag her hands against its wall – small fungus growths spouted in the ominous cracks and dirt-caked outcroppings mixed with rodent droppings, cobwebs, and decaying matter.

Raasah's pace quickened, and Tara was, no doubt, grateful that she no longer had to haul her reluctant companion forward. The walls were now appearing to glisten and the air smelt sullied. Water dripped from the ceiling, its coolness touching her ear and then rolling down her neck. Lichens and small plants were struggling to grow out of nicks in the walls next to them and splashes of puddles marked where their feet marched on toward the light.

Once climbing a set of primitive stone stairs, a low opening in the rock completed their flight. Here the sulliness had faded; the ground was dry. Strays of light filtered in through the bush and vines at its entrance. Tara, raised her hand for silence, and, stooping, carefully parted the long vines to peer out into the sunlight. Satisfied, Tara beckoned Raasah to follow, squeezing nimbly past a large rock and into a tiny pebble-strewn plateau.

The sound of babbling water and the freshness of the lush trees met her. Squinting, Raasah soon realized she was now outside Palenia, next to the governor's grand home on the other side of the canal. The ground was damp from a heavy rain but the sun had pushed its way out to dispel any further threat of immediate deluge. The sounds of the city permeated the cleaned air, though their own presence was obscured by the thick ramble of bush, trees, and large boulders that lined the water's edge.

"This is… unbelievable. How did you know about this?" Raasah waved toward the shrouded exit of the passage where Tara positioned a prickly bough and rolled a rock in front of that.

"Many of these palaces are littered with old passages that the workers used to gain quick access to their work." Tara puffed with the exertion. "Most of them were filled in upon construction or blocked off, but a few were just neglected and forgotten. Once I discovered them, I enjoyed playing in them to fill my days away from the villa. Very few people are aware of them. Knowledge of their existence usually died with the workers."

Tara's eye was drawn to Raasah's hand that she was babying to her chest. "You hurt yourself," she said. "Let me have a look."

Raasah extended her hand to observe the jagged splinter protruding out of her reddening palm. It was large enough that she couldn't close her hand without it bringing tears to her eyes.

"We need to get that out of there," Tara said. She disappeared and reappeared moments later with a broken rimmed bowl filled with water. "I have accumulated a few things here over the years," she said simply.

Then she produced a small knife. Raasah jerked her hand away impulsively.

"It's all right. I just need to loosen the skin a little so I can make sure I can pull it all out. It can cause infection if I leave any in."

The girls sat on a large boulder already dried from the growing heat. Tara carefully widened the opening of the wound ever so slightly and gently prodded the reddened sliver out. Raasah's simulation of bravery was debunked by her sucked in whimpers. Finally, with great relief, the tiny culprit was extracted and it was proudly held up in triumph between thumb and forefinger.

"I present to you 'The Stick of Irritation'!" Tara announced.

Gratefully, Raasah submerged her aching hand into the old water-filled basin.

"It will need some ointment but I seem to have forgotten my medical bag," Tara smiled.

"Oh, it will be fine," Raasah said, just glad to have the wood removed, though a trickle of blood was mixing in the water.

"Nah, as soon as you get home…."

"Home! Oh, my! The temple guards will be looking for me. They were to escort me home in the temple carriage. If Mother discovers I am missing…."

"Quick," Tara said, handing her a strip of cotton to wrap her hand. "I know a short way to get to the carriage grounds!"

There were so many questions Raasah wanted to ask and things that she wanted to share but there was no time. As Raasah wound the simple bandage around her hand, the harried duel slipped through the trees, careful not to brush against broad rain-filled leaves that could tell-tale soak their clothes along the way. Squeezing through a break in a wall, Tara drew Raasah into a short neglected alley that opened up into a busy square. Slipping her sash from her waist, she offered it up to Raasah.

"No one must see you," Tara said. "Wrap it around your head."

Raasah was impressed with Tara's foresight. Wordlessly, she placed it on her head and then wrapped it loosely around her neck, obscuring the lower part of her face.

Satisfied, Tara said, "Come quick." Crisply, they strolled down through the bustling square to a narrow servant's bridge that extended over the dike. Following Tara's lead, Raasah slowed to a more casual walk till they came along the far side of a stout stone wall next to Palenia where the carriages were regally positioned. Once behind a pile of bulging racksacks, they ducked down. Raasah's heart beat had once more resumed a fast thud in her ears.

Temple guards were posted on the terrace along the other side of the wall and servants ran busily to and from the palace. The girls were between the wall and the bustling merchants selling their wares. Raasah crouched lower following her collaborator toward the larger of the carriages, feeling like a want-a-be thief contemplating her first unlawful stint. Tara halted so suddenly, Raasah almost fell into her.

"How can I ever get over there without causing questions?" Raasah whispered hopelessly.

"Wait until I distract them and then get yourself over this wall as close as possible to that carriage. Do your best acting. Remember: you are the daughter of the powerful High Priestess. Exercise your status." That said, Tara slid her sash back off Raasah and then stole her way toward the servants' huts before she disappeared.

Raasah waited confused, not sure what she was supposed to do and looking for some indication when she was supposed to do it. Nervously, she removed the wrapped cloth from her hand with which she brushed some caked dirt from her sandals. With some water in a small pocket of rock on the wall, she rubbed the dried blood from her hand and willed herself to look more presentable. Last of all, she drew her hand across her hair to assure it was in place.

Suddenly she heard a clatter in the distance and the guards all turned the way Tara had gone. Tara popped up from behind a barrel and motioned to Raasah. Athletic she was not, but Raasah determinedly laid both hands on the short pony wall and swung her legs over the rugged surface. Surprisingly, she landed on both feet and intact. Without a moment to revel in her accomplishment, Raasah threw her shoulders back and assumed a noble pose, trying to picture how her mother, or, better yet, Isobel, would act. Sticking her nose in the air, and before she could loose her nerve, she walked bravely up to the nearest guard who happened to have delivered her to her mother.

"Where have you been?" she demanded, submersing herself into her role.

"Miss Raasah," the guard stammered. "We have been...."

"I don't want to hear your excuses," she snapped, adding the intonations and superior rudeness of Isobel. "I am hot and tired and I wish to go home! You will be grateful to know that I will not be reporting your irresponsibility to the High Priestess. She is far too busy to be bothered by such... trivia, so this time I will let you go with a warning."

Turning with the Isobel-flair, she did her best imitation of the graceful confident Isobel-walk and headed for the nearest carriage. Without looking around to see if the guard was responding, Raasah lifted her hand expectantly, every fiber of her being tensely waiting to see if her charade had been effective. A long moment passed, her heart pounding and perspiration building, and then, wonders-of-wonders, the guard gingerly took her hand and respectfully assisted her to her seat. Poised and aloof, she nodded solemnly to the guard as he replaced the folds of the curtains. But, once the carriage was lifted and being born on its way, Raasah felt faint with relief, collapsing into the embroidered cushions and furs.

Yea, wonders-of-all-wonders, Raasah could not believe she had pulled it off! She then suddenly thought of Tara. A pang of guilt pricked her as she envisioned the mess of trouble she could have left her in. But, quickly rethinking it all, Raasah knew Tara could look after herself. With a deep breath, she revisited all that had happened in Palenia Palace. Questions, always more questions, were compiling in her head as she mulled over all she had heard and seen and was astounded when she realized she was already nearing her villa.

Confidently, Raasah composed herself into her Isobel-role once again, preparing for her final act. A smile of satisfaction crossed her lips. Shockingly, she actually was finding her role in this ruse empowering and revitalizing!

ᏝᎾ

That night, on the threshold of sleep, Raasah suddenly sat up in bed. The fidgeting hands, Festus, who could not stand without twitching, who was unnerved when Raasah saw him – he had also been the guard from the Palace of the Moon. She had so often felt his eyes upon her, but had dismissed it as her imagination.

How had he risen so quickly in status to equate the audience within the exclusive Palenia? What had he been holding as he was sent away on her mother's errand? And what was Shaquah's agreement and who was it with?

Raasah longed for her brother's return. She had anticipated him arriving that evening but there had been no word. Surely Terjah would arrive tomorrow for they had so much to discuss. Together, Raasah was sure they could come up with a plan to break the Nathor hold over her and discover the true leader of the Nehor Order. Then, joining with their father's valiant Brotherhood, they would somehow be able to restore their grand Ammonihah back to its honourable state where god-fearing citizens could walk the streets without fear.

In spite of the daunting opposition still ahead of her, in spite her inadequacies and dismal failures to rectify her world, Raasah felt her heart lighten. She had to believe, whether it took a month, a year, or a decade, that right would overcome all that was wrong in Ammonihah and all the fear and uncertainty would be replaced by joy. She had to believe....

Epilogue

Watch for Book 2 of the series:

Order of Nehor & the Pact.

Turn the page for a sneak preview....

Sharp muffled commands were heard near the Civil Building's entrance, followed by a clattering. Heads turned. Zeezrom, stripped of his status headgear and robe, stumbled forcibly into view and, as he regained his footing, was followed by two guards, laughing and shoving him again to the ground. Directly behind, other men were paraded onto the expansive platform between guards. Raasah thought she had counted 12 dejected men but she lost count as more soon followed, gruffly prodded to the front of the platform with the others. One of them she recognized right away, despite his rumpled appearance and blackened eye – it was Isaiah, the impeccable tailor. He stood silently, staring at his feet. Then there was the husband Shemna as well, who appeared to be straining a look down into the crowd below. Hastily, Raasah followed his gaze, searching among the women for his pregnant wife but, before she could be found, Raasah's attention was once more directed to the platform by the blast of a trumpet. In a grandiose appearance of quetzal feathers and layers of jade, Jashorum took center stage.

"Citizens of Ammonihah, I present to you the co-conspirators of the criminal Alma. These are they that reviled against our law and our lawyers and judges. They sought with their lies to free the blasphemous sorcerer, the infamous stranger who, given the chance, would further bring down the destructive wrath of our

Omnipotent Creator upon our glorious city. Because of our indifference to silence these blasphemers, our Most High God had instructed Oluffa to show us his fury in her fire and smoke; He had instructed Oluffa to show his rage as she shook our city's very foundation! These pathetic fools would help this Alma bring the fires of hell upon our city and destroy you fine Ammonihahites!"

Dark murmuring rippled through the masses. Jashorum strode up to Zeezrom who looked uncharacteristically meek, his noble head lowered submissively. Jashorum grabbed the back of the bound man's hair, lifting his face to the crowd.

"Gaze upon the product of Alma's sorcery. Our esteemed citizen – the Pride of Ammonihah, son of Maob, descendant of Coram the Great Warrior – Zeezrom was Ammonihah's celebrated lawyer. We tried to reason with him but he has been swallowed whole by the sorcerer's spell – now only a vessel for the devil himself ...BECAUSE OF THAT TREACHEROUS PREACHER!" Jashorum shook Zeezrom's head. "Zeezrom is lost to us now – unredeemable, caught in the clutches of the dark, treacherous realm! And these...," Jashorum spread his arm out to include the other displayed men – his voice was thunderous. "...these men are also poisoned by the Alma preacher just like our promising lawyer here ...and they have freely spread this poison to their wives and children. These are the men who would help destroy our great City one soul at a time, then one family at a time, and continue until we are doomed! Citizens of Ammonihah, we must rid our city of this cult of Alma to appease the gods, to satisfy great Oluffa, and save our grand city!"

"Yea, yea, punish them, punish them," the cry rippled through the larger mass but, closer to the platform, sobbing and soft cries filtered in. Raasah now recognized Joseph in the line of the convicted as his name was called out by a woman lost in the front. Galif also recognized the bald, elfish farmer whom he had prodded about Alma and he turned quickly away as their eyes met, fidgeting as he looked far off over the crowd.

Jashorum released Zeezrom's hair with a slap to the back of the head. Zeezrom shirked slightly with the insult and then straightened his shoulders, facing the crowd. Jashorum continued in his booming voice: "These men must be cast out from among us, never to anger the gods against us again!"

A shout of agreement rose from the square. Quieter cries of despair went up from the corralled women and children. A soldier, gripping Zeezrom's arm, dragged him to the platform side and threw him down the stairs. He staggered halfway before crumpling and rolling to a heap onto the Grand Plaza floor, only a few paces from the gasping women and children. Guards at the base of the steps jerked Zeezrom back to his feet and he walked unsteadily forward, now cut and bloody. His fellow prisoners followed close behind, pushed and shoved along, some stumbling and falling, to be pulled back to their feet and shoved along again. Galif timidly gave the men a large berth as they passed.

Then a voice resonated, "We should stone them…!"

"Nah, nah, please, have mercy!" a woman screamed. Raasah then saw her, straining to break through the guards. It was Chalon, Shemna's wife, reaching toward her husband one moment and then knocked to the ground by a cuahuitl the next. As the offending guard swung his leg to kick her, she curled protectively around her bulging belly.

"Yea, stone them!" Another cry went up and then another and

another. As the crowd pressed forward, Raasah could no longer see the assaulted woman.

"Rid the devil of his possessed vessels!" someone else hollered. "We must cleanse our city!"

"Stone them, stone them," the call went up more vigorously.

With a sinking in her stomach, Raasah watched as the tide of men that followed the doomed prisoners grew exponentially, bending and arming themselves with whatever they could collect that could do damage – and laughing! As the frenzy grew, her blood went cold. Raasah turned toward the offending instigator.

Jashorum remained posed and regal – a smile of contentment upon his cruel face. At the sight of him, Raasah felt more hate in her than she had ever felt possible – threatening to seep out every pore. But the morning spectacle was far from over… the extent of her emotions yet to be tried!

About the Author

S.J. Kootz was born in Toronto, Canada, the first daughter of 5 children. Kootz has always enjoyed studying history and its rise and fall of great civilizations, but is especially fascinated by the mysterious lives of the ancient inhabitants of Central America. *What would the people have been like prior to anno domin? What would their daily life consist of? Why were their advanced civilization and all their cities abandoned?*

Through exhausting research and the recent enlightening discoveries of the last few decades, Kootz has pieced together a scenario of how life may have been like in 82 B.C. during the time of the prosperous pyramidal cities of present-day Guatemala. By incorporating a documented story as told in the Book of Alma, the author strives to draw the reader back in time to experience the extraordinary courage and faith of an ancient people of the Nephite nation.

Order of Nehor & the Brotherhood is the first book of the Nehor trilogy. Soon to be on the shelves is Book #2, Order of Nehor & the Pact. Currently, Kootz is working on the third and final book, Order of Nehor & the Visionary, that is hoped to be on the shelves by Christmas 2018.

The author can be contacted by writing to:
Box 1264, Coaldale, Alberta, Canada, T1M 1N1

CPSIA information can be obtained
at www.ICGtesting.com
Printed in the USA
LVHW04s0842250518
578443LV00001B/1/P